"Rowley skillfully dissects the myth of having it all in this unputdownable, late coming-of-age story set in rarefied Manhattan. Her flawed and complex characters will stick with you long after *Life After Yes*'s final pages since they are all too human as they struggle with love and loss."

—Julie Buxbaum, author of *After You*

"*Life After Yes* is a hilarious and heartbreaking story that explores the halfway-there terrain between accepting the proposal and saying 'I do.' A tale of love, grief, confusion, and the quest for certainty, this brave debut explores the choices we make, and the ones we must forgo to keep moving."

—J. Courtney Sullivan, author of *Commencement*

"A must-read modern love story for any woman wondering which man, and which direction, is the right one."

—Tatiana Boncompagni author of *Hedge Fund Wives*

"A moving look at post 9/11 life, love, and loss. Aidan Donnelley Rowley writes with a deft hand. A great new talent."

—Molly Jong-Fast, author of *Normal Girl*

"Aidan Donnelley Rowley paints a tender portrait of life post 9/11 Manhattan through the eyes of a confused, grieving yuppie who should be happy and doesn't know why she's not. Quinn O'Malley's search for meaning is touching and universal."

—Kristina Riggle, author of *Real Life & Liars*

"A resounding 'yes!' to *Life After Yes*—a novel that explores, with charm and humor, life after loss. Readers will root for its endearing narrator, Quinn O'Malley, as she confronts the road not taken and navigates the conflicting and complicated intersections of head and heart."

—Mameve Medwed, author of *Of Men and Their Mothers*

JUN 2010

By Aidan Donnelley Rowley

LIFE AFTER YES

Life After Yes

Aidan Donnelley Rowley

AVON

An Imprint of HarperCollins*Publishers*

F

Grateful acknowledgment is made to the following for permission to reproduce song lyrics:

"Dear Prudence" copyright © 1968 by Sony/ATV Music Publishing LLC. All rights administered by Sony/ATV Music Publishing LLC. 8 Music Square West, Nashville, TN 37203. All rights reserved. Used by permission.

This book is a work of fiction. The characters, incidents, and dialogue are drawn from the author's imagination and are not to be construed as real. Any resemblance to actual events or persons, living or dead, is entirely coincidental.

LIFE AFTER YES. Copyright © 2010 by Aidan Donnelley Rowley. All rights reserved. Printed in the United States of America. No part of this book may be used or reproduced in any manner whatsoever without written permission except in the case of brief quotations embodied in critical articles and reviews. For information address HarperCollins Publishers, 10 East 53rd Street, New York, NY 10022.

HarperCollins books may be purchased for educational, business, or sales promotional use. For information please write: Special Markets Department HarperCollins Publishers, 10 East 53rd Street, New York, NY 10022.

FIRST AVON PAPERBACK EDITION PUBLISHED 2010.

Designed by Diahann Sturge

Library of Congress Cataloging-in-Publication Data
   Rowley, Aidan Donnelley.
      Life after yes / Aidan Donnelley Rowley.
         p. cm.—(1st Avon pbk. ed.)
      ISBN 978-0-06-189447-3 (pbk.)
      1. Young women—Fiction.   2. Women lawyers—Fiction.   3. Yuppies—
      New York (State)—New York—Fiction.   4. Life change events—Fiction.
      5. September 11 Terrorist Attacks, 2001—Influence—Fiction.   6. Manhattan
      (New York, N.Y.)—Fiction.   I. Title.
   PS3618.O884L54 2010
   813'.6—dc22   2009044957

10 11 12 13 14   OV/RRD   10 9 8 7 6 5 4 3 2 1

For Mom and Dad
Here, Gone, Forever

It is never prudent to start a novel with a dream. No, it is clichéd, a telltale sign of amateur craft.

—Everyone

Prudence is an attitude that keeps life safe, but does not often make it happy.

—Samuel Johnson

Nothing happens unless first a dream.

—Carl Sandburg

January 19, 2002

The Dream

I'm choking. I can't breathe. The air's as thick as cream and smells like peanut oil. Everything is white. I begin to see shapes: the smooth surface under my elbows, the big box in front of me with the soft glow, my own trembling hands. I'm in my office. But there are no windows or doors. Just walls. My eyes burn. My hair hurts as if someone is pulling it strand by strand. The first color I see is a blinking red dot, an angry firefly, but each time I grab for it, it disappears into the whiteness. And then flashing green—three big numbers 6–3–0. It's a digital. It's morning. The room grows brighter, but the lights are still off. I can now see a little better. There is a pile of paper. All white, but as I watch it, black dots appear, one next to the other until they fill the page. Words. Sentences. Then red scribbles. I drink liquid the color of urine and things get clearer. The words on those pages are mine.

A small beep crucifies the deep silence. A cartoon paper clip dances on a screen. "Today is your day," it says to me. My hands stop shaking. My eyes stop burning. My hair stops hurting. I look down and see it: *a bright light sparkling, shooting rainbows at me. A stone sits there, but I can't see its shape. I stare and stare, trying to see beyond its glittery rays, but then everything goes white again. Even that red dot is gone.*

Suddenly, I am standing in a new place, holding that stack of papers and a big black bag. The walls are shiny and chestnut. The ceiling is as high as the sky. A man with a snow white mustache says hi. He knows my name. He takes my bag and I let him. And then he says words that echo: "No cell phones." He places my bag on a rectangle of black rubber that moves, and in a moment's time, it disappears. I'm in the courthouse. At the metal detector. I walk through. The man with the mustache says, "Nice veil."

I wait for my bag, but it doesn't come. Three white flowers pop out instead, one after the other, rolling toward me on the black rubber. The man hands them to me.

And now I am waiting outside a big wooden door. I mumble to myself, reading from my papers. The door opens. The room is full of bodies in white. Heads swivel around on necks and stare at me. I'm wearing a dress. The top is made of fishing net, transparent as glass. The bottom bells like a trumpet. And is covered in pinstripes. My body is bare underneath.

A voice sounds announcing the judge. He walks through a hidden door, a blob of black with a kind face I can't see. His features are blurred. A band of gold sparkles from his hand as he slams down.

Music plays. Dad appears. He wears white too. His old Irish sweater. He links his arm in mine, but won't look at me. He walks slowly, dragging me forward. There is a jury in the box: I see Mom and Michael. Britney and Nietzsche.

And there is a small woman. Skinny, wearing black, blinding silver buttons. She cradles a sparkling gun in one hand and a steaming pie in the other. A vast smile.

It's your mother.

I keep walking with Dad, eyes fastened to the floor. When I look up, we are finally there. And something is very wrong. There are three faces, not one. Three bodies, not one. Three grooms. Not one. I look at Dad, but his eyes have grown hollow. I try to touch him, but my hands are now linked.

Big white handcuffs.

Now Dad is gone. I study the faces. Everything grows sharper. There are two of them. And then finally you. Your dark blond waves, your glacial blue eyes. You smile at me. You all do. Each of you holds something: a key. In unison, like robots, you all lift them and dangle as if I am to choose.

The blurry face begins to talk. "We are gathered here to witness . . ." he says, his words sharp and clean. ". . . the marriage of Prudence to . . ." and then he lists too many names, ending with yours. He asks me if I take you all to be my lawful wedded husband.

And, like a good girl, I say, "I do."

Now my handcuffs are gone and so are the keys. White petals rain from the ceiling. A thunder of applause. All three of you walk toward me, arms outstretched. And then there is a piercing sound, a scream. It comes from the jury box. From a small girl with strawberry blond curls. She drops her white wicker basket, scattering black petals that smell like smoke, blackberry smoke, then burning flesh. The flower girl. A few moments later, I realize who this little girl is.

It's me.

I feel faint and my eyes close. I fall, but I have a trinity of strong men to catch me. And you are only one of them.

The judge slams his mallet over and over. And then everything goes black.

Chapter 1

I'm already with another man. He touches me. And I let
him.

　　He moves behind me. His strong fingertips press into
the small of my back. His hold is somehow both delicate
and firm. My heart flutters wildly. Only a few minutes have
passed, but I'm already glazed with sweat, my own.

"At my wedding, there were too many grooms," I say. My
words come out gentle whispers, fragile notes muffled by the
music which is simply too loud.

"Tell me about it," he says. His voice is ocean deep, his accent an enigma, fading in and out. "But first, do me a favor
and spread your legs wide."

His name is Victor. I follow his command. Eyes are on us.
Yes, people are always watching.

"Okay, now turn your feet out and bend."

Our silences are never awkward. They are filled with errant grunts and giggles, and the persistent techno beats, deafening footsteps of the psychedelic creature in our midst.

"That's good. *Very* good. Just like that, Quinn." I like it when he says my name. It makes it all more personal. "Now repeat for twelve," he says, looking away. His indifference is delicious.

I like to be told what to do. Like a child. It's easier that way. I do what he says. I always do. I bob up and down. Twelve times. He stays behind me the whole time, hands lingering at my waist, shadowing my imperfect dips and rises. He mirrors most every move, dancing with me to the music that won't surrender.

He's the Brawny man without the mustache. Born in Cuba, he played college soccer, and desperately wants to be a photographer. His muscles are impressive, borderline over-developed. He's not too tall, but tall enough. He just turned thirty, but I know he's more worried about his abs than about finding a wife.

He's my personal trainer.

"Start from the beginning," he says, looking into my eyes. His are bottomless and black; the opposite of my pale Irish blues.

"Okay," I say.

Early morning. Monday. I returned from Paris late last night a newly minted fiancée. Sage picked me up early from work on Friday afternoon. He took me to the airport. We didn't have a trip planned. In fact, I was supposed to work all weekend; my very first trial is fast approaching. When he led me to the Air France security line, my suspicions piqued and I stared down at that finger that had been naked for twenty-seven years.

We flew to Paris. I downed champagne the whole flight to calm my fiery nerves. I've always been an anxious flier, fixated on the obvious things: the sleepy pilot, the slick runway, the antiquated engine. Nothing a few mini bottles of vodka couldn't solve. But now, I have something new about which to obsess: A plane, full of fuel and folk, can be a weapon.

For most, this grand gesture, this impromptu whisk-away, would be the portrait of romantic spontaneity, of modern, almost celebrity-caliber courtship. The type of fairy-tale fireworks you spark when you mix vast quantities of love with vast quantities of money.

But for me, this international escapade was an odd choice. Because of Dad.

It's time to stop catching babies and start catching fish, Dad, a renowned Manhattan obstetrician and avid angler, said.

Fittingly, we had this, our last conversation, over a glass (who are we kidding, a bottle) of wine. As Dad contemplated his impending exit from the professional world, he preached cryptically about my existence in that very same world. I'd started as an associate at a big law firm, Whalen Stanford, two years before. Dad told me about this young hotshot banker who'd been assigned to his accounts.

He's addicted. And we know a well-chosen addiction here and there can be a great thing, Dad said, smiling, shaking his glass of wine, *but he's addicted to a black piece of plastic.*

A BlackBerry, Dad.

What happened to eye contact and conversation? The screens and buttons have gotten in the way.

I looked at him and nodded. Under the table, my own BlackBerry was cradled in my palm, red light blinking, beckoning me, but I kept my eyes on his.

Just don't become one of them, Dad said, draining his glass.
One of them?
A Berry Baby, he said. *Life's too short.*

A few days later, on that fateful morning of September
eleventh, Dad met with that same young hotshot for a four-
star breakfast on the top floor of Tower One for a status check
on his portfolio. So Dad presumably spent his final moments
slurping caviar and talking taxes when we all know he would've
preferred eating Cheerios and talking trout any day.

So, I guess you could say this Berry Baby didn't anticipate
being forced to make any grand life decisions so soon after
everything happened. And, more than that, when that proposal did come, I expected it to be more of the Cheerio than
caviar variety.

But this isn't about Dad. At least that's what I keep telling
myself.

Sage insisted the trip was a belated birthday gift, but I
knew better. I know when his eyes are honest, when the vi-
brations of his deep voice change. I know how he scratches
his left earlobe when bluffing.

On Saturday night, he proposed. I said yes. Now I have an
impressive bauble on that finger, a fixture he insists I never
take off. In particular, I'm worried about the gym, about
knocking it around.

*Diamonds are the hardest substance. A barbell has nothing
on that ring*, Sage assured me, pinching the stubborn remnants of baby fat on my right cheek.

So, here I am thirty-six hours later at the gym, wearing a
colorless rock bigger than Mom's with my stretch pants and
ponytail.

Victor is fixated; he won't stop staring at my ring. "If that was two months' salary, I want your husband's job," he says.

"He isn't my husband."

"Yet."

"His mother picked the ring," I said.

"So?" he says. "It's a *diamond*. And it's *big*. You shouldn't care if the devil picked it."

The proposal. It was wonderful, majestic, classic, the stuff of pigtailed daydreams (I never had). But on Saturday night, after we drifted off, our naked bodies intertwined, glistening with champagne sweat under impossibly soft hotel sheets, I had a dream. The dream.

That's where this other man, my Herculean trainer-cum-therapist, comes in. Certainly, he's no Freud. He has no higher degree. But the man has ears. Right now, that's enough.

I dreamed of predictable things: an office, a computer, that blinking red dot of my BlackBerry, Diet Mountain Dew. All par for the course, really. This was pretty much my reality.

"Everything was white," I say. "I was trapped in my office. There was no way out."

"Trapped?" Victor says. "Is that really that strange? You always tell me that your office is like a prison! You sure this was a dream, counselor?"

He's right. I do complain. *A lot*. Truth is, two years into my legal career, I'm not sure whether I hate my job. Secretly, I like to think I thrive on the periodic brutality that's inflicted upon me, that I'm an existential trooper in the storms of professional inhumanity I'm forced to weather. But to be part of the associate club, I've learned to put up a good front, an impeccable façade, spending the bulk of my spare time—

and there isn't much of it—bitching about my job, lamenting my life path, whining about the hours, the loans I don't even have, the cruelty of it all.

"Time is limited. I need you to *listen*. Commentary can wait until Wednesday," I say.

I train with him three times a week. At ninety dollars a pop, it's not clear whether my six-figure salary affords me this indulgence. But like so many others in Manhattan, I keep it up anyway, driven by a fear of fat, a phobia more paralyzing for some—for me certainly—than debt.

"Yes, counselor," Victor says, and bows. He loads three slim plates of iron on the shoulder press machine. "I love it when you slip into lawyer mode. It's so hot. You can cross-examine me any day." Yes, he's flirting. But it's basically harmless banter at most and it makes that hour fly.

"So, I'm sitting there and I couldn't really breathe. It felt as if I was being asphyxiated."

"How many times have you been asphyxiated, Quinn?"

"Touché, big guy. You know what I mean. It's like saying that something tastes like dirt. Now, zip it."

An older woman, slow motion on a StairMaster, watches us, a modicum of disapproval in her cloudless brown eyes. She wears an oversized Michigan T-shirt—Dad's alma mater—knotted seventies-style over a lavender leotard hiked up high. White hair crowns her face, bleeding into her honey blond ponytail of stiff curls. The grooves on her face run deep, rivulets of an age she seems desperate to deny.

"In my dream I was alone," I say. But Victor doesn't listen. His eyes escape to a young girl with cappuccino skin bouncing on a machine in the corner. Crescents of sweat have formed under each honeydew-sized breast. Her long black braid swings like a pendulum behind her.

"I think I'd been sleeping," I continue anyway. This is as much about my hearing my own words as it is about his hearing them. "I had been up all night drafting a brief for court, but I guess you could say fatigue won the race."

"I love the athletic references, blondie. I'd like to think that is my influence on you?"

"Think whatever you want as long as you stop ogling Pocahontas Barbie for a minute and listen."

He hands me a pair of ten-pound dumbbells. "Biceps," he mutters, stealing another glance at the girl in the corner. I extend my arms in unison and bend them slowly, methodically, feeling the muscles tighten and swell each time.

"It was real. *Too* real. I was working on an assignment for this bastard partner I have told you about, Fisher." In reality, he isn't a bastard, but a corner-office superstar, a rainmaker with monogrammed rose gold cuff links. Sure, there are those alleged mistresses—there always are—but he's for the most part a decent man, and far less acrid than some of the others.

"Why are you so worried about this dream?"

"Patience is a virtue, Victor."

"Well then, I guess you could say that I'm having a hard time being virtuous this morning."

"The cartoon paper clip, you know that icon with the googly eyes—it announced that it was my wedding day," I say. "It was one of those computer reminder things."

"Okay, now we're getting somewhere," he says. I lie down flat on the rubber mat, hold tight to his ankles, and lift my legs one at a time.

"It was my wedding day and I didn't realize it. Then I was in a courthouse in this bizarre fishing net dress and a veil. And I was naked under it all."

"Veil?"

"Yes, I was wearing a veil. In a courthouse. And my brief-case turned into orchids. And then, all of a sudden, I was practicing an oral argument outside of a courtroom."

"I like oral," Victor says, and laughs. Another trainer near-by doing squats laughs with him.

"You're disgusting. Now *listen*. I walked into the court-room and everyone turned around to look at me. Everyone was wearing white. Everyone but *her*."

"Her?"

"His mother," I say. "There she was walking down the cen-ter of the courtroom in all black with silver buttons down her back, her hair bopping along. She turned around and smiled. She cradled a gun in one hand and balanced a pie in the other. Her smile was frozen."

"Ah, the benevolent bailiff," he says. "Lucky you. Hold up," he says. I stop doing my crunches. "No—five more of those. You can see through fishing net."

"Yes, genius."

"Naked underneath?"

"Uh huh."

He pauses. "Nice. Were your boobs bigger in the dream?"

I whip Victor with my towel. "Inappropriate, you sicko," I say, red-faced, a fraction of a smile.

"The judge's face was blurry like on those crime shows."

Finally, Victor seems captivated. I'd like to think Poca-hontas could do a striptease atop her Arc Trainer and he wouldn't notice. He loses track of how many sit-ups I have done for the second time.

"Then the music started. And Dad was there to take my arm," I say. And without warning, the tears come. Along with the realization that when this happens for real, when I get married, Dad won't be there.

Victor grabs my shoulders, looks me in the eye. "I'm sorry," he says. "Are you okay?"

I nod. "I'm fine," I say, because this is what you're supposed to say, what people expect you to say.

But this pity party is short-lived. He hands me a medium-sized ball, deceptively heavy, made of thick blue rubber. "It's a medicine ball," he says. "Thought to work wonders back then. Rumor is that Hippocrates used these balls to sweat fever from his patients."

And I'm thankful for this timely diversion, this history lesson du jour from my trivia buff of a trainer. And I'm pleasantly surprised that he knows marginally sophisticated words like "benevolent" and how to pronounce "Hippocrates." As if such knowledge is reserved for those of us with an Ivy degree (or two).

"A miracle worker?" I ask, twisting from side to side, holding the ball. "It can get rid of a fever, but can it banish belly fat?"

Victor smiles. "Sure thing."

So, as quickly as those tears come, I've sent them away. "I'm sorry about before," I say. "This isn't about Dad."

In my dream, Dad wouldn't look at me. As if he was already gone from my life. As if I was already gone from his.

"There was a jury in the box. I saw Mom and Michael and *Nietzsche*. And guess who Mr. Friedrich Wilhelm Nietzsche was sitting next to? Britney Spears."

"Hot couple," Victor says, and I wonder whether he even knows who Nietzsche is.

"Dad started walking me down the center of the courtroom. He walked slowly, limping from his college football injury, and I looked ahead, eager to see my future husband. But something was very wrong."

"Time's up," Victor says, pointing at the oversized clock above us. It's ten to eight. "Just kidding, keep going. This is fierce. Soap-opera silly."

"There were *three* men," I say. "Three *grooms*."

"Shit."

"I studied the faces. Everything grew sharper. Two faces and then, finally, Sage's. Phelps and then poor Sage. He was just one of the guys on our wedding day."

"Phelps? Ah, the infamous Rowboat Boy," Victor says, grinning.

"My hands were suddenly behind my back, trapped in huge white handcuffs, and each groom dangled a key," I say. "As if I were to choose."

"Handcuffs? Kinky, Quinn. And here I thought you were the square attorney type."

I shut him up with my eyes. "The music stopped and the judge slammed his mallet. He said, 'Prudence, do you take . . .' and then he named all of the guys' names, '. . . to be your lawful husband.'"

"Wait—"

"Let me finish," I say.

"Okay, but please tell me you said no," Victor mock-pleads.

"No, I said what a happy bride is supposed to say at the altar on her big day. I said 'I do.' Then my handcuffs were gone and then so were the keys. Everyone clapped. Everyone was happy. I didn't know whether I was supposed to kiss all of them, but then there was a loud noise, a piercing scream. It came from the jury box, from a little girl, my flower girl. And at first I didn't recognize her. She was *screaming*, but then I realized who she was . . ."

"Who was she?" Victor asks.

"It was *me*. As a little girl. And when I realized this, I passed out, but my husbands—yes, husband*s*, all of them— they caught me. And then everything went black."

"Gnarly dream, girl," he says. Now, our time really is up." Victor's next client, a portly CEO type, white and bald as a golf ball, hovers, scratching his crotch.

I follow Victor to the back of the gym. To the massage tables where trainers stretch their clients. I hop on one and lie down flat, like I always do.

"I have a question," he says, grabbing my leg and straightening it out.

"Hit me," I say. I'm sweaty and nervous. My pulse: rapid-fire.

"Who's Prudence?"

"That's me. My name's really Prudence."

Confusion contorts his face, rearranging his features. "That one can wait until Wednesday, Miss Witness Protection Freak. You said there were three. Three grooms. But you named only two."

"No, there were three." ·

Now he's rubbing my shoulders, getting the kinks out like he does at the end of every session. "Well, who was the last guy?" he asks.

I pause. I realize something. The music charges on. CNN terror alerts scream silently from muted televisions. Hurried souls braid in and out of each other, racing off to work with sopping hair and untied sneakers. Business as usual. The gym smells of sweat and burnt coffee.

"It was you."

Chapter 2

In the locker room, nipples face north and south. Cobalt and eggplant veins stretch like spiderwebs over winter white skin. Floppy breasts and varicose veins welcome me. Mozart floats faintly from camouflaged speakers, drowned out by the buzz of hair dryers and morning gossip. Near the entrance, a squat woman in faded black stacks warm towels that smell like marzipan. A middle-aged woman sits naked and cross-legged, raving to no one in particular about her daughter's performance in the holiday play. The room smells like burning hair and watermelon shampoo. Bodies snake by each other in various stages of undress; some are swaddled in crisp towels far too small for coverage. Some sport stringy thongs; others, sensible briefs. Many wear nothing at all.

A skeletal woman with a forest of pubic hair stands in front of the mirror, hips jutted forward, cleaning her nostrils with Q-tips. She leaves the yellowed and bloody cotton swabs on the faux granite countertop, angering the woman who stands next to her painting a freckled face with makeup many shades too orange.

I sit on the bench in the middle of the locker room, hunched over, ponytail flipped, eyes fixed on my tattered gray New Balances and the sea blue floor of tiles, wondering what's wrong with me. Victor's arrogant grin is tattooed in the front of my mind.

"Quinn!"

I turn and see Avery, my oldest friend and fellow West Sider. She bounds toward me in her matching pink sports bra and shorts, her blond ponytail dancing behind her.

"I just finished my first Buff Brides class," she says, flexing thin arms. "That instructor kicked my butt, but hopefully it'll show come wedding time."

Avery is getting married to Jonathan, a lawyer like me, in the fall.

"Maybe I'll have to join you in that class," I say.

Confusion washes over Avery's face only briefly, and then her eyes light up. She grabs my hand, lifts my ring to only inches from her face.

"Oh Quinny!" She hugs me hard. "You're getting married! We're both getting married!"

And she jumps up and down, jogging in place like a kid on Christmas morning.

"We're not little girls anymore, huh?" I say.

She shakes her head, still grinning, perfect teeth shining bright.

"The ring is stunning, Quinn."

"His mother picked it," I say. "Same setting as hers."

"That's *so* sweet," she says, smiling. "I love family traditions."

And I nod. Because maybe, just maybe, "sweet" is the appropriate word for this "family tradition"? "Maybe you're right," I say.

"You don't like it," she says, pointing to the ring.

"I do like it," I say. "What I don't like is that he's her little puppet."

"No, he's now your little puppet. Take the strings. Quinn, you should've told him what you wanted. Men need directions. They're like kids. They need to be told what to do. They *crave* instructions."

And I nod again. Because I have no doubt Avery, a kindergarten teacher, a sunny and sensible creature, is right about such things.

"But what if I don't know what I want?" I say.

And I think we both know that we're not just talking about diamond cuts and ring settings and meddling in-laws.

Avery, ever the optimist, grabs my shoulders, looks me in the eyes, and says, "You *do* know what you want. And here you are, getting it. You're a lucky girl, Quinn."

She grabs her things from her locker. And hugs me hard.

"I've got to run," she says. "I want to get home to make Jonathan breakfast."

While my friend hightails it home to fix her fiancé eggs, I decide to linger, to hide out in a public shower.

Normally, I would go home to shower there. My apartment is only a block away, and I much prefer the privacy of my own bathroom to this nudist shower scene. But I'm not ready to emerge from this haven to see Victor or Sage. A master avoider indeed.

So I grab three towels, turn toward my locker so no one can see me, and slither out of my sweat-soaked clothes. I wrap one towel around my top and another around my waist—a makeshift terry bikini—and tiptoe along the cold tiles to the showers.

The shower doors are transparent. Anonymous bodies twirl around, hands soap away. I step into an empty shower and drape the towels over the door so no one can see in. As I fiddle with the faucet, I notice the rainbow of hairs—blond, brown, gray, and black; curly and straight; long and short—slicked on the tiles. I remember Katie Couric's exposé on foot fungus and long for a pair of flip-flops.

When I said those three damning words, "It was you," Victor's dark eyes glimmered and confidence rode his butterscotch lips. In the mirror behind him, I caught the beet red of my face; I have an unfortunate problem with blushing.

"See you Wednesday," I said to him before I escaped, not sure if I meant it.

"Looking forward to it . . ." Victor said, and winked, patting me on the back I pay him to sculpt. ". . . Prudence."

Yes, my name is Prudence. I'm not in the Witness Protection Program, though that would be an infinitely more fascinating rationale for my alias. The truth: I was born Prudence Quinn O'Malley on January 12, 1975. I'm about as Irish as they come, keeping those naughty stereotypes nice and robust. Despite religious visits to an overpriced midtown salon, hints of auburn pierce through my dirty blond hair. My skin is translucent year round, alabaster sprinkled with connect-the-dot freckles.

Most importantly, I love to drink.

Especially since September.

Phelps Rafferty, a.k.a. Rowboat Boy (Boyfriend, 1987–1999). I could easily blame everything on him; my sudden and severe allergy to my given name, my fondness for cocktails, my soft spot for fishermen.

On my twelfth birthday, he called. Phelps lived in Chicago and I only saw him for a few weeks each summer when both of our families stayed at the private fishing club Bird Lake in Wisconsin. Though he's my age, to me he always seemed older, and as far as I was concerned, the boy was full of infinite wisdom.

The summer before that phone call, Phelps kissed me for the first time. On the dock of the lake. We had told our parents we were catching tadpoles, but we came back that afternoon with an empty jar and big smiles.

"Happy birthday," Phelps said, when Mom handed me the phone. Then he paused and laughed. "Remember to be prudent."

"Huh?" I said.

Maybe he had been studying extra early for the SAT, but Phelps stumbled upon the truth about my name before I did. "Your name is a word," he told me. "And not a cool one."

When we hung up, I sneaked into Dad's office and thumbed through the P's in his battered maroon leather dictionary. I learned what it meant: *exercise of sound judgment in practical affairs; wisdom in the way of caution and provision; discretion; carefulness.* I was horrified. Why would my parents give me such a name? I didn't understand why my older brother, Michael, had gotten so lucky.

I walked into the kitchen. Mom sliced big red tomatoes for my birthday dinner when I asked her the simple question that would change so much.

"My name is a word, isn't it? It has a meaning," I said.

"Prue, all names have meanings. Did you know Michael's

means 'resolute guardian'? Yours just has a meaning that people know. Like Brooke or Charity. Yours is one of those names," she answered, smiled, and went back to her chopping. As if that would be the end of it.

I became Quinn a few days later at my birthday party. It was a cold Saturday afternoon in winter; local weathermen paced in front of colorful backdrops buzzing about a looming nor'easter. Mom and Dad had rented the basketball court at the public school on the corner of our street for the evening. I divided my friends into two teams. Mom and Dad donned striped polyester and plastic whistles. Michael kept score.

The night before my party, I stayed up late with Mom and Michael spray painting numbers and names in green or red on the white Hanes T-shirts Mom bought in packs of three at the pharmacy.

When it came time, I wrote my name on the back.

My new name.

Quinn.

"What are you doing?" Mom asked, peeling plastic from a red whistle.

"I don't want to be Prudence anymore. I'm Quinn now."

Mom froze. She stopped blinking. She just stared at me. Finally, she moved, looping her long fingers through the red whistle cord, and muttered that one word: "Why?"

Sure enough, as anyone would have predicted—as my parents should've—my classmates had begun to call me Prude. We kids could be cruel. But I didn't really care. In truth, I kind of liked the attention and the swells of laughter around me even if they were at my expense. And, anyway, I wasn't a prude. At nine, my art teacher caught me kissing Bobby Sands under the metal slide on the school roof. Manhattan kids had recess on rooftops; we ran around in circles on concrete patches overlooking city streets. Bobby was king of the monkey bars and all the girls liked him, but no one admitted it. At that age, we girls weren't worried about herpes or HIV, but something just as scary and equally enigmatic: cooties. Luckily, Mom and Dad, a lawyer and a doctor, ever the pillars of parental reason, assured me cooties didn't exist. Little did they know this little lesson led to my first kiss.

The truth came too late to make a difference. My parents didn't expect more of me than they did my brother with the more mundane moniker. They didn't envision me, their baby girl, as president. They didn't pray that with such a name, I would mature into the earthly embodiment of the Christian virtue. It was nothing like that.

The truth: They were huge Beatles fans. Mom said John Lennon appeared in her dreams. And Mom was a fervent believer in the importance of dreams. Dad said Lennon was the only other man Mom could kiss given the chance because he loved him too.

Together, Mom and Dad sang one of their favorites to me, their little girl—"Dear Prudence," bodies curled like commas over my cedar crib when I was a baby and over my bed when I was a bit older.

"It was the only song I could bear to listen to at the hospital while we waited for you to come," Mom explained, tears glossing her blue eyes. "When I was five months pregnant with you, we learned that you were a girl and it was obvious what your name would be. We loved you, little Prudence, even before we saw you."

She said Dad played the song over and over on his boom box on that bitter cold day in January while they waited for my arrival.

Dear Prudence won't you come out to play?
Dear Prudence greet the brand new day
The sun is up the sky is blue
It's beautiful and so are you
Dear Prudence won't you come out to play?

Dear Prudence open up your eyes
Dear Prudence see the sunny skies
The wind is low the birds will sing
That you are part of everything
Dear Prudence won't you open up your eyes?

Look around round
Look around round round
Look around

Dear Prudence let me see you smile
Dear Prudence like a little child
The clouds will be a daisy chain
So let me see you smile again
Dear Prudence won't you let me see you smile

Dear Prudence won't you come out to play?
Dear Prudence greet the brand new day
The sun is up the sky is blue
It's beautiful and so are you
Dear Prudence won't you come out to play?

"You loved the song," Mom promised. "Each time Dad and I sang it to you, you opened your eyes and looked up at us. And every time we trailed off, you flashed that gummy smile even when you were almost asleep."

So it was not a surprise that my parents were deeply sad-
dened when I decided to shed Prudence, the name they so
carefully, so organically, chose for me their daughter. On
that night after my basketball party, I overheard Mom crying and peeked through their bedroom door. Dad mumbled
something to her in his deep crackly voice, rubbing her back
in small circles. "She will always be Prudence," he said, "if
only to us."

To cope, my parents maintained a staunch loyalty to their
decision and to my name, to their beloved lullaby, the theme
song of my young life. They refused to call me by my middle
name, Mom's maiden name, the name she herself had forsaken fifteen years before, upon exchanging vows with Dad.
I think they were confident it was all a passing phase, a fit of
rebellion or adolescent fire that would flicker out.

But it never did.

Fast-forward six years. The Quinn-Phelps anti-Prudence
movement continued. It was a balmy June night. Our parents picnicked a few miles away, oblivious to the romance
that had been brewing for years now between their eighteen-
year-old children.

Phelps and I went fishing on Bird Lake.

Dad taught me how to cast when I was very young. Out
on the grass by the lake, he'd show me his watch, the leather
band battered and brown. He'd point to the numbers, and
though I was just learning to tell time, I got it. *Ten o'clock,
two o'clock, ten o'clock, two o'clock*, he'd repeat rhythmically
as I flung the fishing line back and forth. Dad said I was a
natural. Only now do I wonder if he meant what he said,
or whether this was a prepackaged parental lie uttered to
encourage effort.

Anyway, fishing with Phelps, I started out confident,

ready to brandish my skills. But soon, my casts were robotic and awkward, more like nine o'clock, three o'clock, far from the fluid arcs I effortlessly accomplished with Dad. After ten minutes of fishing, I caught Phelps above the lip with my fly.

Thankfully, he was a good sport about the mishap. "Right body part," he said, pulling the hook out, wiping away the small trickle of blood with his sleeve. "But wrong creature. You sure you're Daddy O'Malley's little girl?"

I smiled. "Maybe that was intentional," I said, my flirtation skills in high bloom. "Maybe I'd rather snag you than a slimy old trout."

"Could be," he said, blue eyes sparkling.

We brought our own picnic—peanut butter and jelly sandwiches and lemonade, and Phelps swiped a couple of Bud Lights from his parents' summer stash.

"WASPs don't notice missing booze," he said.

He pulled out his Swiss Army knife and popped the cap. He handed me the bottle and I protested. He couldn't believe that I wasn't a big beer drinker. I told him we did things a bit differently back in Manhattan. It was true. But he was a Midwesterner through and through, already a big fan of brewski, and eager to convert me.

"I know it's not prudent to drink at such an early age out in the open for all to see, but give it a try," he said, taking a swig. He peppered as many sentences as he could with this word. Cabins surrounded the lake, lights on. "It's good practice for college. Plus, rebellion can be delicious."

I looked at him: blond hair, blue eyes, golden skin, blue-and-white plaid flannel over lemon-colored polo, khaki shorts hung low on his waist, untied Nikes; hardly the revolutionary. He would attend Williams that fall.

I copied his movements, holding the amber bottle up at the same forty-five-degree angle and taking a big swallow.

"Delicious," I said, smiling, lying a bit.

He held his beer in one hand, but with his other, he began carving something with his knife on the side of the boat. Our initials.

"The precocious vandal," I said, swallowing. The beer really wasn't so bad.

"The *snag-worthy* precocious vandal," he clarified, "who can outfish you any day."

He rowed us through the still water to one edge of the lake, a small spot hidden under a canopy of overhanging trees. He handed me his empty and pulled the line through his rod and began casting. The fly arced over us and landed softly in the water. Before long, he caught a rainbow trout and a brown trout, pulled the hooks from their mouths and released them into the water.

"They're too young to die," he said, wiping blood and water and fish slime onto that flannel shirt.

The bugs started biting and he pulled a tiny bottle of repellent from his khaki vest—his father's old vest—and handed it to me. And when I got cold, he handed me that flannel. It smelled like fish guts, but it kept me warm.

That night as the sky grew dark, Phelps stopped fishing and looked at me.

"What?" I said, uncomfortable, but unable to look away. Anchored by his glance.

He didn't answer me, but grabbed my hand and pulled me close. He peeled off that flannel and started unbuttoning my shirt.

He stopped for a moment and kissed me. His tongue tasted like beer and peanut butter.

I kissed him back.

He slipped his thumb in the waistband of my jeans and I said: "I can't."

"You don't want this?" he asked, kissing my neck.

"I didn't say that," I said.

"You're right," he said, still kissing me. "It probably wouldn't be prudent."

A girl named Prudence wouldn't do this.

But a girl named Quinn just might.

I kissed him hard and unbuckled his pants. The boat swayed beneath us, the oars slapped the water. Phelps reached for the anchor and dropped it into the water.

He had a condom in his back pocket. Apparently, the boy wasn't completely allergic to prudence.

There was only a little blood, but we flushed it out with water from the lake.

A week later, my body was still covered in the bug bites from that night. It was the night before we left Wisconsin to come back to New York. Phelps and I went out on the same rowboat, this time without rods. He brought his guitar and a cooler full of beer.

Many beers later, back at that same hidden spot, he took his guitar out and played "Dear Prudence."

Before we fell asleep on the boat, me in that same smelly flannel resting against his skinny golden chest, he pulled a daisy chain from his fishing bag and put it around my neck. Then he said those three words we hear and say so often, too often maybe, once we grow up. He said: *I love you.* And I said it back.

I woke up the next morning and felt different. I couldn't decide whether it was because I had my first hangover or my first love. I decided it was probably both.

Four years later, college under those proverbial belts of ours, Phelps left the Midwest and came to New York for medical school. I began law school. Beds replaced rowboats. Dirty martinis replaced Bud Lights. Roses replaced daisies. He worked long hours. I worked long hours. His guitar gathered dust. That flannel sat folded in the back of my bottom drawer.

I turn off the water, re-create my terry bikini, and make my way back to my locker. A woman in a black suit rushes toward me, clicking the tiles with her heels. She looks down at her BlackBerry as she hurries by me. Her elbow catches my towel and it drops to the ground. A faint "Sorry" echoes as she rushes out.

For a brief moment, I'm topless like the others. A woman peers through a mess of frizzy black hair and stares at me, at *them*. I catch her eyes, but they don't retreat.

"Nice ones. Whose are they?" she asks, stepping into a pair of chocolate brown trousers.

"Mine," I say defensively, just registering what she is asking. She thinks they are fake. Is this a compliment or no? I'm not sure.

Now Kenny G drifts from the ceiling. I put my sweaty clothes back on and slip out the back of the locker room. I slither along the back wall of the gym, ducking behind the machines. I can see Victor across the room laughing with the fat man whose belly dips below the bottom of his JPMorgan T-shirt.

I walk out the front door into the cold January air. People wait on corners, arms outstretched, gloved hands waving lethargically at taxis that don't stop. A fire truck speeds by, a blur of American flags. Two small Korean women shiver as they unlock the rolling gates to the dry cleaner's. A Heineken truck is parked in front of the corner deli. A cigarette dangles from a man's lips as he unloads cases down a rolling ramp. Dying Christmas trees recline on sidewalks, browning needles littering the damp frozen pavement, waiting to be taken away.

I run home so my leggings and hair won't freeze. I run past the playground on my corner. A father in a bright blue parka pushes his little girl in a pink pom-pom hat on the swing. They both giggle as she flies high in the sky and loses a purple mitten midair, their breath forming clouds that fade into frigid air.

Chapter 3

Manhattan's Upper West Side is the land of chubby babies and skinny mommies. Thanks to waves of panic and fertility drugs, double strollers have taken over, narrowing sidewalks and blocking grocery aisles for the rest of us single units who just want to go about our day.

Well-fed Labs and Goldens run the show, sporting collars with embroidered Nantucket whales and Scottish plaids, trotting proudly on grassless streets, lifting muscled legs to spray electric yellow, claiming patches of concrete as their own. Little dogs in sweaters and booties and bows are yanked by impatient owners with legs unfairly longer, or, more thoughtfully, toted in small bags designed just for their travel. Deliverymen snake through this mayhem, bicycling without helmets and with alarming speed, through and against the video game traffic, causing a symphony of illegal car horns, just to deliver morning bagels and late night pizzas to folks too lazy to walk a block.

I've lived in this world my whole life, and Sage and I have lived here in our apartment for almost a year. Our place is charming and cozy—NYC code for "small"—with rugged walls of exposed brick and black-and-white photographs on the walls; "very New York," as Sage's mother remarked, and "very Pottery Barn," as my mother did. Neither, I'm sure you've gathered, was a compliment.

We love it, though. We even have a working fireplace. Well, I am pretty sure it works anyway. The previous owner left a Duraflame in it, so I'm assuming it works.

Back from the gym, I climb our cracked brownstone stairs, stairs littered today with a medley of soggy delivery menus and abandoned bottle caps. This is what a million gets you in this neck of the woods. I fidget for my keys. Once inside, I hear our neighbor's Labradoodle complaining about something (perhaps about the fact that he is a combination of two breeds that shouldn't mix?). I hike the internal set of stairs that invariably turns furniture deliverymen into madmen who expect outrageous tips. I kick open the door to our apartment and slide through.

Sage prefers the blond and polish of Diane Sawyer, but I guess he figures it wasn't worth the battle. So, Katie Couric sits on the small flat-screen in our kitchen, hyperactively crossing and uncrossing her suspiciously bronzed trademark legs, batting her mascara-caked lashes, and chirping about early menopause, or something equally dreadful. For a few minutes each day, she and the others take a break from covering terrorism, a phenomenon no one really talked about before September.

I trip over Hula Popper, our small gray tabby cat. Sage is a dog man. But I argued that a kitty would be the perfect companion for two overworked young professionals. Sage stayed strong, holding out for the dog he was convinced we'd one day welcome. After a while, I gave up on the cat thing. But after Dad died, Sage brought home a kitten, a stray he adopted from our local holistic vet. Perhaps he hoped this ball of fur could numb the pain I would someday let myself feel. I told him he could choose the name. For me Prudence/Quinn, this was no small concession. So he named our little critter Hula Popper after the fishing lure perfect for catching pike and largemouth bass.

Dad would've liked the name.

Sage is here, in the kitchen, only half awake, strikingly, effortlessly, handsome even at this early hour. He putters around, picking up coins and a Popsicle wrapper from the floor by the fridge.

"Hey," I say, standing in the doorway, shivering.

"Hey, Bug," he says. I too have the fortune of a fly-fishing nickname. Apparently something in me reminds Sage of the Jitterbug, the Hula Popper's rival among classic topwater plugs. He gave me the lowdown on this breed of bait, telling me that this lure wobbles across the water's surface. Its gurglings, he explained, send out waves. Per my man, the Jitterbug's for fishing at night, in stained water, and on gray days because the steady gurgle helps bass hone in on the bait. Most anglers fish the Jitterbug slow and steady, he told me, neither pausing the bait nor adding any action with twitches or jerks. Sage said this was also a good name for me because I can't dance.

"How was the workout? Why is your hair wet?" he says, and scrubs orange Popsicle juice from his hands.

"Oh, I decided to shower at the gym."

"Ah, I see. Someone wanted to flash her new ring around overtime," he says.

"Something like that," I say, and smile. This morning his

ego must be five carats. "Workout was good, just a bit harsh after Paris. I think champagne is still pumping through my veins."

I plant a soft kiss on Sage's cheek like I always do and shimmy past him. "What have you been up to?" I ask. Admittedly, it's a stupid question. I've been gone just more than an hour, and judging from the creases on his cheeks he's been in bed until five minutes ago. But I ask it anyway, filling the morning quiet with small talk, a phenomenon I once foolishly thought reserved for acquaintances and uncomfortable strangers.

"Oh, just got up. Just trying to mitigate the damage of this week's tornado," he says, wiping a small mountain of white powder off the counter with a paper towel decked with faded Christmas bells. In our early days, he never used words like "mitigate", and I feel a momentary surge of pride. He strokes the counter with great care, as if the white mounds might be some unknown and devastating cousin of anthrax and not artificial sweetener that escaped my coffee cup some morning last week.

"I hate that you use this stuff," he says.

"I know you do. What breed of cancer am I getting from it this week? Uterine? Or brain?" I say, and smile. Sage regularly shows me articles from magazines and medical journals and I love that he wants to protect me, but still, I shrug and sprinkle away, shunning calories, courting the unknown.

"Beatrice is coming tomorrow. Don't worry about it," I say, but he keeps cleaning. Beatrice, an aspiring opera singer, deems herself a housekeeper while under our roof.

"Honey, isn't it a bit telling that I feel I have to clean before she comes?" He knows just how much I hate being called honey, so he saves it for special occasions.

Here we are: back to reality. Yes, he whisked me to another continent and slipped that ring on my finger, but that didn't change much. A diamond, however sizable and with fanfare presented, can do only so much.

There *is* one major problem with our place. It has nothing to do with a scarcity of square footage, or with a lack of sunlight, or with an acidic *New York Times*–stealing neighbor. No, the problem is not among those that plague so many of my friends and colleagues who are growing homesick for the space and serenity and sanity of suburban childhoods.

The problem: me. I am a consummate, steadfast, committed slob. My dishes crust over and pile up, forming precarious towers that threaten to tumble and crash. By Friday, my suit jackets and bras blanket our hardwood bedroom floor, creating an obstacle course for the two of us and poor Hula.

Hence, our "need" for "help." It did take a while, many months and some delicately woven arguments and bouts of self-deprecation, but finally I convinced him, or wore him down, as Sage would have it. The "consensus" (as I like to call all decisions I make that involve both of us): We needed a housekeeper once a week. My man hit me with the obvious: If I cleaned up after myself, a housekeeper would be unnecessary. This argument, however bland and bulletproof, did not stop me. Predictably, I went lawyer on him as I've been known to do, wielding arguments that weren't necessarily as sound as they were dramatic. While shyness overtakes me at the office, I fancy myself a gifted negotiator at home, and in these situations, I argue articulately and adamantly. I told him I led a stressful life at the firm and I refused to spend my "downtime" cleaning house. Certainly, it helped when I fattened my already ample lower lip. And yes, it didn't hurt when I gave him my best sad eyes and delivered some variation of my trademark apology about not being domestic enough.

Yes, he's a sucker.

My sucker.

Sometimes, he probably wishes he had fallen in love with someone a bit sweeter. Someone more like his mother.

So Beatrice comes once a week and we pay her a hefty one hundred dollars to vacuum cat hair and fold underwear. It's a luxury we can technically afford, but Sage insists we can't justify. But it's one that I, like so many of my breed, have decided—like triweekly sessions with a trainer—is absolutely essential. (Yes, I'm almost as spoiled as I am messy. At least I own it.)

"I have a question, and be honest," I say.

And, playfully, Sage rolls his eyes, presumably waiting for the latest no-win situation to materialize.

"Do my breasts look fake?"

"*What?* Where is *this* coming from?" he says.

"Nowhere. I'm just asking."

"Your breasts are beautiful," he says. Smart man. "I wouldn't marry a girl with ugly ones." Okay, not quite as smart.

"Oh, so are you going to divorce me when they stretch and sag, then? Perky isn't forever."

The coffee machine beeps and Sage pours two cups and hands me one. We sit together.

"One day, I am going to get my act together, I promise. I'm going to be so clean, it will annoy you. I'm going to be more Martha Stewart than either of our mothers."

This is a lie. At best, a weakling of a promise.

There is no way I will ever surpass his mother, a woman, perpetually primped and perfect, who practically tidies in her sleep.

And Mom, a retired law professor and odd breed of feminist, preaches that cleaning is both a mindless escape from a stressful existence and a rudimentary form of female empowerment. One time I made the grave mistake of breaking out some Betty Friedan from my college days, telling Mom that domestic life was like a "comfortable concentration camp," that I didn't want to morph into an "anonymous biological robot in a docile mass," but I should've figured that quoting a vanguard out of context would get me nowhere. *You don't have to be a Betty to be a feminist, Prue. Betty wouldn't want blind allegiance to her ideas; that's exactly the kind of thing she fought so hard against.*

Sage laughs hard, nearly spitting his coffee. "I'll believe it when I see it. Too bad I wasn't born a generation ago; I could have given that ring to the other O'Malley woman, the one who knows how to replace a vacuum bag."

"You would've had to fight Dad for her. We both know how that would've turned out," I say. Tears find me as I squeeze Sage's thin arm. I've seen pictures of Sage from college when he played shortstop at Duke, and he was definitely bigger, a brawnier version of his current self.

Dad was six-four. He was a walk-on on Michigan's football team who spent four years on the bench. Unlike Sage, Dad never lost his bulk. The first time Sage met Dad, fear overtook Sage's big blue eyes. But when Dad opened his mouth, Sage's face relaxed. Dad was a barbless critter, a "brilliant teddy bear," as Mom liked to call him. Dad was always a big fan of Phelps and thus prepared to hate Sage. But when Dad learned I had reeled in another angler, everything was okay. These two men—Dad and Sage—separated for mere moments by a generation, an estranged almost-son, and the formality of a first meeting, were in no time united, talking shop about wet and dry fishing flies, antique reels, and future fishing trips. For better or worse, and lucky for Sage, Dad had an immediate and implicit trust of a true angler.

"We should probably call Mom. Let her know we're getting hitched," I say. We had decided to keep Paris for us and call everyone when we got home.

"She knows everything. I asked them for your hand last summer in Wisconsin."

"Last *summer?*" When Dad was alive. He knew about this.

After everything happened, Mom abandoned her teaching post at the law school and packed up my childhood home, an old Manhattan brownstone. Michael and I not-so-jokingly begged her to give us the brownstone and if not, to stay here, to stay close, but she wasn't up for the grief and pity game. She moved to the private cabin where we spent summers on Bird Lake.

"It was June. I was so scared. Your parents and I sat on the big porch overlooking the lake. I think your dad could sense I was nervous or wanted to punish me for what I was about to do because he mixed me the stiffest Irish Delight. You were just back from a run, showering in the cabin. When I asked, their eyes lit up. They hugged me. Your father nearly crushed me."

"Good call asking Mom too," I say.

When Sage describes this moment, this pivotal moment in his short life and mine, I smile, fighting tears and losing. The image is striking and simple and beautiful. I have to imagine any glee in their eyes was mixed with equal parts sadness. This was the very first step in the process by which they would lose me.

"Were they sad?" I say.

"A little," he says. Maybe because it is true, or maybe because he knows this is the right answer. The kind answer. "I think they were a little sad."

"I can't believe neither of them slipped," I say. Keeping secrets does not run in my family.

Sage nods. "Unlike you, your parents can keep a secret. I thought your mom would let it out though. I'm impressed. Even Michael kept his big mouth shut."

"Michael knows too?" My older brother, Michael, is a seasoned gossip—even worse than I am. He reads Page Six like it's the Bible and speaks of celebrities as if they are close comrades, drinking buddies who just happen to grace the cover of weekly magazines.

"Well, let's call then. Mom's probably worried that you've come to your senses and are having second thoughts. It's been six months."

I call. The phone barely rings once before Mom answers. For a moment, I think I hear Dad's gravelly voice on the line too, which of course I don't because he's gone and because Dad hated the telephone and almost every other breed of technology. I tell Mom what she already knows and hear what I predicted I would hear: repetitions of that one easy word—"congratulations"—that fits most every kind of good news. While we're still on the phone, Michael calls and demands to be patched in, which I don't know how to do. He cannot fathom how I'm a big-time lawyer at a fat Manhattan firm and I don't know how to use the conference function on a phone. I tell him I've inherited the Luddite genes of our dear father and I confirm what he too already knows: He's finally getting the brother he's always wanted. He asks about the ring, and I tell him it's beautiful. I leave out the part about how my nemesis picked it since said nemesis's darling son is standing by. At the end of our short call, Mom asks to talk to the "man of the moment."

I figure she must mean Sage.

I hand him the phone.

I can't make out what they say, just voices weaving in and out of each other and periodic rumbles of potentially authentic laughter.

"I know. Thanks, Mrs. O'Malley." Mom and Dad urged Sage to lose the formality, but Sage insisted he was a Southern boy, and addressing them like that was nothing but pure instinct.

"Well, we haven't gotten that far. Bird Lake is definitely in the running, though," he says.

"Bird Lake?" I whisper.

"This summer? That seems soon, but maybe. We'll see," Sage says, fiddling with his coffee spoon.

"Well, here's your daughter again," he says, playing it safe like always. He's careful not to refer to me as Quinn because he knows how it would upset her. And he's careful not to refer to me as Prudence because he knows how this will upset me.

For whatever reason, this is not how I envisioned things. Truth is, I haven't envisioned things. These things. But this college athlete and banker with a penchant for fishing and hunting and beer and wings and all things male shouldn't be the one making the prize-winning suggestion about locale and picking our wedding date. I am the girl.

Sage mutters a quick good-bye, yet another thank-you to probably yet another congratulations, and hangs up.

Sage won't look at me. He fiddles with the milk carton, staring at the grainy face of a missing little girl on the back. Where is this girl? Is she alive? Will she grow up and find a man to pester and love? Will she too enjoy this coveted form of permanent and lovely torture?

"Last time I checked you were my fiancé and not some brown-nosing wedding planner." (My words are swords, harsher than even I intend.)

"Simmer down. Your parents mentioned it to me last summer and I just thought it was a good idea, one you would love," he says. It *is* a good idea. And one that I'm already starting to love.

"Well, I would've liked for you to run it by me first before getting the parents all hot and bothered."

"I didn't think. I'm sorry," he says. His words are soft and childlike, his apology the mea culpa of a little boy who has shattered his mother's favorite vase. "Anyway, the ideas were *theirs.*"

And, again, he's right. I have a way of doing this, twisting his words into my own self-serving pretzels. Blame it on the legal training.

Usually, our mornings are far simpler, far more charming than this. Usually, we sit side by side swallowing Starbucks, too tired for conversation. The silence is sweet; the calm before the inevitable swell of storms, delicious.

But this morning, I'm shaking. And I hope it's the coffee, but I know better. Sage is quiet. He slowly slurps the milk from his bowl of Cheerios. His steely confidence is missing, like that poor little girl on the back of the milk carton.

And suddenly I remember his face in the dream, his eyes distant and misty, brimming with salty sadness, that overwhelming sadness at being in the midst of many on the one day he's supposed to stand alone.

"No, I'm sorry. You're right. Bird Lake would be perfect. And you and your groomsmen could go a few days early and fish the streams. It could be like a bonus bachelor party," I say, and think of Phelps, our old rowboat, the sweet smell of his bug repellent, our long talks on the cabin porch swing.

"Now you're talking," he says quietly, surprise in his tired eyes, and takes my hand. It is not like me to apologize so quickly. Usually, I stew for some time, let him suffer a little, before embracing that little thing called reason.

His smile returns, wide and bright. His eyes drop once again to his newspaper. Sunlight streams through our kitchen window, and he squints to fight the brightness, and glides his index finger down a slim column of stock quotes.

Yes, ring or no ring, the world goes on. The stock market will do its thing, creeping up and down. Dishes will pile up. For a fleeting moment, everything is okay, more than okay, and I wish that I could press pause.

But I can't.

A familiar buzz kills that good moment and ends the temporary silence. Then I do it. I reach for the dreaded object which sits cradled in quiet subversion. My BlackBerry. When I first got it, I thought it was so cool. It made me feel important and adult. It was Sage, with his three years of life and wisdom on me, who helped me understand just what it was: a curiously shaped leash. It took him more than a month to convince me that I didn't need to sleep with it inches away from my ear on the bedside table. A couple years into my litigation career, that little black devil still harbors the power to panic me.

"Do you think if Dad had one of these things, things would be different? Most cellular connections were down that day, but I think BlackBerrys worked."

"He would never have carried one of those things," he says. "And no, I don't think things would be different."

I nod. And look down at the little screen, the tiny buttons. I scroll through my messages.

"Bug, don't do it," Sage pleads. But I fumble with it anyway, escaping, my fingers dancing deftly across those miniature buttons.

"What, is *this* going to cause cancer too?" I ask, waving my BlackBerry.

"Probably," he says.

"I just have to check and then I will have some coffee with you. I will deal with everything when I get to the office, but I just need to see what I missed," I say, eyes fixed on the tiny screen, knowing it's never this simple.

Thirty-seven unread messages linger in my inbox.

"Fuck," I say. "Fuck."

"My favorite word. And notice how I didn't hear it all weekend. I thought you had forgotten all about that dandy four-letter gem." Southern Sage hates profanity; I love this about him.

There's an e-mail from Fisher. Ask any associate—e-mails from partners are scary. The e-mail is short and cryptic and asks me (unapologetically of course—"This is a seven-day-a-week-job," we were told on day one) to complete a research assignment by Monday, as in *this*, afternoon. Fisher sent it on Friday afternoon about the time Sage and I were giggling like overcaffeinated teens fondling each other in the Air France security line. Fuck.

"Fuck," I say again, this time for effect. I hop up from the table, leaving a shallow pool of tepid coffee at the bottom of my cracked mug. Sage barely looks up from his newspaper.

For no good reason, I take another shower. And then bundle up in my old bathrobe. A college send-off gift from Mom, once pristine and fluffy, it's now dull and ragged.

In my bottom drawer, I reach for a pair of wool socks and pull out Phelps's flannel. Hula watches me disapprovingly as I hold it up to my face and inhale deeply, that old familiar fishy smell, and put it back where it was.

Antique heating pipes whimper and moan in valiant but failed efforts to keep us warm. Sage, a half-full kind of guy, admits he has come to crave those crackling sounds. Those, and the sirens and car alarms that break the nighttime silences. He assures me that this city symphony has replaced the soothing songs of crickets he fell asleep to as a boy. But I worry I am the reason he has abandoned the utopia of his childhood days for this wonderful and callous concrete jungle.

Sage is still there in the same chair at the small round mosaic table in our kitchen, putting off the inevitable start to another inevitable day. I return to my mug of Guatemalan or Costa Rican or Mexican coffee more cringe-worthy than Robitussin, so bitter that last Equal wasn't even worth it. Grains float on the ebony surface, mocking me. But I swallow anyway, and wait for that familiar buzz to pump through my flagging veins.

I sit across from Sage, sipping and cringing, getting new wrinkles, finally adding a third Equal to the sludgy mix.

"What am I going to do when I'm pregnant?" I ask.

"Breast implants and now a baby? What's going on with you this morning? Is there something you need to tell me?"

"It's just that I *depend* on this," I do say, pointing to my mug. "I *need* it to function. What am I going to do when I'm pregnant and some lady in a white coat who spends her days looking at vaginas tells me I can't have it anymore?"

"Isn't this a little premature?" he asks. "We'll cross that road when we come to it." Another cliché. Of course. It takes

time to wean someone off truisms. Thankfully, I have forever to do it.

"You think I am just going to get pregnant, give up the
coffee, give up the alcohol, and sit still for nine months as
your baby grows perfect, don't you? How am I going to do
my job?"

Sage looks at me like I'm crazy—which, apparently, I am.
We have been engaged for all of five minutes and I am talking
babies and boobs, spouting feminist rhetoric more warped
than Mom's.

"I didn't even *say* anything. What's wrong?"

"Nothing. I'm just stressed. I missed an e-mail from a
partner about an assignment that is due *today*."

Sage's face spells defeat. There will always be other men
in my life. Living and gone. Men with more wisdom, more
money, more power.

"Well, I guess that's my fault too. Sorry for taking you to
Europe and asking you to be my wife. I should have timed
it better," he says, and stands up. His hair is spiky and adorable, a mini morning Mohawk. He pours himself the rest of
the pot of coffee—which he would usually offer me—and
escapes to our bedroom. Little Hula picks a side and trails
behind Sage. Both are careful not to trip on my high heel
that lies in the middle of the doorway.

Shrouded in the heavy silence I have created, I watch him
go. I don't know what to say. My body twitches. I feel my
heartbeat in my fingers. I can't move. I don't go after him.

I don't know. I don't know.

What I do know is that this isn't how it's supposed to be. I
should be deliriously happy. I should be calling all my friends,
even though it's still early. I do love him. But right now, that
ring is the only thing that sparkles.

Chapter 4

I met Sage on Halloween. In 1999. It was a random encounter in a smoky bar downtown. He was dressed as a fisherman, and I wore all black and American flag–print wings.

He was surrounded by banker buddies, a herd of tall and cocky creatures sporting the same belts and button-downs and hearty laughs.

But even from a distance, I could tell he was different. Wounded. Exuding confidence shaded by struggle, by real life. Lugging a secret or two.

He stood at the bar funneling Hershey's Kisses into the pockets of his neoprene waders when I approached.

"Kiss?" he asked, smiling, offering me a candy.

"I'm not that easy," I said. "Stocking up for Y2K?"

"My mother didn't let me eat the candy on Halloween," he said, smiling, grabbing another fistful, unwrapping one and popping it into his mouth.

"Ah," I said. "Making up for lost time?"

He smiled again. Ordered me a drink.

"Well, I was allowed to eat the candy," I said. "But I never got much of it. Mom would follow me around and I'd grab as many candies as I could and she'd make me put them all back. And she'd say, 'Take just one. All you need is one.' Only then would I take the one I really wanted. Usually it was a Tootsie Pop. In case you were interested."

"I am."

Buoyed by alcohol and the confidence it divines, we bantered beautifully, washing down Kisses and conversation with wine and whiskey.

We talked about Halloween, how we both still loved the holiday. How we could be kids for one day and pretend to be someone else, something else. We talked about our all-time favorite costumes (his: Batman, homemade; mine: Strawberry Shortcake, store-bought). I told him about Halloween in the city; how kids from the neighborhood would convene on our block on the Upper West Side and go brownstone-to-brownstone en masse, collecting candy from perfect strangers. I told him how much I hated it when some wiseass would hand out toothbrushes.

We debated the virtues of open bar and came to the consensus that it was both a beautiful and a dangerous thing.

"Where is your girlfriend?" I asked, pulling a small fishing fly from the fleece drying pouch on his vest and studying it under the red lantern that hung above the bar.

"Don't have one," he said. "Where is your boyfriend?"

"Uptown," I said. "Is it wrong that I'm still fishing even though I've already snagged one?"

"Not at all," he said.

"A Parachute Adams," I said, reattaching the fly to his vest.

"An oldie but a goodie. Perhaps the most important and versatile dry fly. One of Dad's favorites."

"Not bad," he said. "Tied it myself."

Before I knew it, there we were trading vital statistics, like clichéd young drunken souls in bars do, like we were reading from the backs of baseball cards. Names. Colleges. Hometowns. Occupations.

Sage McIntyre. Played baseball at Duke. Savannah-bred. An investment banker.

Quinn O'Malley. Dartmouth. Columbia. City girl. Law student.

That night I went back to his apartment, a glorified dorm room with a fake wall.

Though the apartment smelled vaguely of beer and pizza and bad aftershave, his room was clean. On the windowsill, silver picture frames glimmered, but in the dim light, I couldn't make out the faces. His bed was made, and while he was in the bathroom I lifted his comforter and saw something at once amazing and alarming: meticulous hospital corners.

"So let's talk about this fishing business," he said, reappearing.

"What do you want to know? I'm an odd species. A fly-fishing New Yorker. Never done much spin fishing; Dad thinks it's for the lazy man. He's the real deal. Compared to him, I just pretend."

He smiled. "There's plenty of time to talk shop, Quinn. I want to know why you're still fishing when you've already caught one."

I looked at him.

"Your words, not mine."

"I really don't know," I said.

"You don't know?"

And I didn't. Why was I there in this apartment with this strange boy making small talk when I had a keeper at home?

"He's a great guy," I said, "but . . ."

And in a rare moment, this lawyer-to-be had nothing to say. I wasn't being coy, or trying to appear mysterious. This wasn't about sparing him details about another man, or theories I had on the trajectory of relationships. The truth was I didn't know why I was doing this. Whatever it was I was doing.

"You don't have to justify it to me," he said. "I get it. I dated the same girl through high school and college, Sally. A good girl. She and my mother were just waiting for me to get down on my knee and I couldn't do it. I knew there was something bigger to wait for. She just wasn't The One," he says. "And maybe your guy isn't either?"

"The One?" I said, and cringed. I didn't believe in The One or soul mates or any of these hokey, new agey, bullshit concepts. "Can we go back to talking fishing flies and pretend you didn't say that?"

He smiled. "Sorry, that's my mother talking. She checks in daily to see if I've encountered The One. She's itching for grandkids."

"Ah," I say. "A good old-fashioned mama's boy, I presume?"

"Guilty as charged, daddy's girl," he said.

I shrugged.

"Speaking of guilt and innocence, law school?"

"What about it?" I said.

"Any chance you're still fishing for a career even though you've already snagged one?"

I smiled.

"Scared to be in the company of a budding young attorney?"

"I haven't done anything illegal," he said. "Not yet at least."

"Banking?" I said. "Two can play at this game."

"I've always loved numbers. Math major in college. Do you know how many times I've been invited to Vegas because I'm good with numbers? Banking's just like gambling, really."

"So, it's not about the money, then? The cuff links and summer homes?"

"The money can't hurt," he said, unbuttoning his shirt, peeling it off, folding it, and placing it on the floor.

"Only if you let it," I said.

He looked at me, perplexed.

"Let me guess: only child?" I said.

He was silent for a moment. Looked down. Traced a broad stripe on his faded comforter—no doubt a relic from college days—with his fingertip.

"I am now," he said.

In that dark and silent room, where moonlight mingled with the green glow of his clock radio, I waited for him to elaborate. But he didn't.

"You are now?" I asked, and suddenly chubby little boy faces—two of them—were cruelly crisp in those sparkling silver frames.

"I had a brother named Henry," he said, his voice crackly and soft, his Southern accent suddenly more detectable. "He was six years younger."

"Was," I say, and nod.

And though I wanted to know what happened, why he used that brutally simple past tense when talking of his brother, I didn't ask. But he told me anyway.

"It was Christmas Eve. I was sixteen and he was ten. We

were hanging lights on the fence around our property. Henry started at one end and I started at the other. Our plan, like every year, was to meet in the middle. I was faster than him, close to that middle spot when I saw it happen. The black car, the loud music, the faint and familiar scream."

"Shit," I said.

Sage fought tears. "The ambulance came, but it was too late. My father tried everything, CPR. But he stood up, covered in Henry's blood, Christmas red, and stared at my mother and me. He never said so, but I know he blamed us. Still does. My mother for not watching us. Me for not protecting my kid brother. Me for not catching the numbers on the license plate as the car sped away. I'm obsessed with numbers. Have a photographic memory. I could remember the exact number of fence posts we snaked lights through, the song that drunk bastard was playing, but I didn't even think to look at the license plate."

"You were just a kid," I said. "You can't blame yourself."

A few tears escaped those beautiful eyes, innocent and blue, and his cheeks glistened.

"It happened over ten years ago," he said. "You'd think it would get better."

"It will?" I said lamely, as if I had a clue about this kind of thing.

"I go home on his birthday every year," he said. "In August. My mother makes his favorite blackberry pie."

I nodded and rubbed his back.

"She hasn't been the same since. She started drinking when it happened. To escape, I think. And my father basically disappeared when Henry did. He's barely home. He works, he travels, makes money. She bakes and gardens and goes to church on Sunday. I worry about her. It's as if she has nothing to live for."

And though I'd never met this woman and barely knew this guy, in that fragile moment I said something, something that seemed to comfort him. And something that couldn't have been more true. "She has you."

Sage nodded. And curled up on his bed. Pulled me down next to him, draping a strong arm around me, holding me tight. And I lay there, happily trapped by a boy's tears and a man's muscles.

"Sage?" I said, before nodding off next to him.

"Yes?"

"How many fence posts?"

"Eleven," he said. "Eleven posts."

"What song was playing in the car?" I asked, hungry for this detail. I'm not sure why I needed to know these things. Maybe I wanted to know everything about this guy. Or maybe I knew that this was my chance. That this was the last time he would talk to me (in a very long time) about Henry.

" 'Silent Night,' " he said. "It was 'Silent Night.' "

"Oh," I said. "I love that one."

"I did too," he whispered as his eyes, still damp, drifted shut. "I did too."

I woke up the next morning, my cheek itchy. I looked down at the pillow and there it was. One of those little white rectangular labels that said "Sage McIntyre" in bold black type. I smiled and folded it back inside the pillowcase. I felt like I was back in camp.

"She still irons labels into my things," Sage said, sitting up, rubbing his eyes. "She can't sit still. She clips coupons every

Sunday and never uses them. Doesn't need to. You should see our garden."

I smiled. Thought of my own mother, how she sent me off to camp with a Sharpie in case I felt the urge to mark my things. How she killed every plant that we ever brought into our home.

I stood and gathered my things. My high heels, my angel wings.

Outside, the autumn sun climbed through the buildings. A new day.

"Do you have any bacon?" I asked. "A Bloody Mary?"

Met with a befuddled grin, I tried again. "How about coffee?"

"That, I think I can do."

Only when he left the room did I study the pictures in the polished silver frames. Of two blond boys, one tall and one small. Matching smiles and matching haircuts. In one, they were very young and peered over the edge of a bathtub. In another, they wore baseball uniforms. And in another, they wore fishing gear. And in yet another, they flanked a beautiful woman, petite and blond, same oversized smile. His mother.

In the tiny kitchen, Sage fumbled nervously with a box of coffee filters and grabbed a bag of grounds from the freezer. From his bedroom door, I watched him putter around, wiping down the counters, chucking his roommate's box of late night pizza.

I ducked into the bathroom. Noted the clichéd trappings of the twenty-something banker breed along the slim countertop—the medley of colognes and razors, the pile of dirty towels, the empty toilet paper roll crushed in the corner.

Only when I looked at myself in the mirror, at the broad smile I hadn't worn in a while, did I think of Phelps. I pictured him at my apartment. Beginning a new day just like it was any other.

And then I waited. For the guilt to wash over me. But curiously it didn't come.

I hadn't slept with another man. Hadn't even kissed him.

But even so, I knew there was no going back.

I walked into the kitchen. Sage smiled. Handed me a mug that said, "Georgia: We Put the 'Fun' in Fundamentalist Extremism!" "I hope it's okay," he said. "It's my roommate's coffee. I'm more of a tea man myself."

"A tea man, huh?" I joked. "Is there such a thing?"

"Indeed, there is," he said, smiling.

The coffee was bitter, but I drank it.

When his phone rang, Sage skipped off to his room to get it. "Don't go anywhere," he said.

And maybe that's exactly what I should've done: gotten out of there. For there were plenty of those proverbial red flags. Lined up, clear as day, waving furiously in that figurative and foreboding wind. The way he said "*my* mother," for one, like she was his possession that I might steal. That he talked about his ex-girlfriend and dead brother in the first twelve hours. That he was an investment banker and a neat freak and a tea drinker and *Southern*.

"I'm not going anywhere," I said.

He returned a few moments later, wearing his fishing shirt from the night before, buttoned wrong over khakis.

"Who calls you at this hour?" I asked.

"My mother," he says. "She's an early bird."

"Mama's boy," I said.

He nodded, running fingers through dirty blond hair that

flopped over his eyes and made him appear all of seventeen.

"Daddy's girl," he said.

I drained my coffee.

He smiled, his cheeks pinked. He took the coffee mug from my hand and placed it on the counter.

I unbuttoned his shirt and rebuttoned it the right way. Then I opened the front door and took a single step into the hallway, long and beige. And Sage stood there, barefoot on the other side of the threshold. He reached out, took my hand. Pulled me closer.

And we met in the middle.

"Well, did you tell your darling mother that you found The One?" I said.

He smiled and pulled something from his pocket, slipped it in my hand. Then he cupped my chin, and studied my face. Looked me in the eyes. Kissed my lips gently and then pulled away.

"Maybe I did," he said, optimism plain in simple words. "All you need is one."

And as I traveled down that dim hallway, walking away but going nowhere, I opened my hand. And there it was.

A lone Tootsie Pop.

Chapter 5

Every morning, I let the terrorists win. Secret Service–cushioned Bush tells me to be defiant, to be a strong American. I know what I *should* do. I *should* skip defiantly down cracking concrete steps and take the subway. But I never do this. In my veins, paranoia runs deep.

Truth is, I have visions of an odd-shaped navy backpack on the evening news, smoke billowing from caves below city streets, charred morning newspapers and coffee cups strewn about, left behind. Something's going to happen down there one day and I'm not going to be there to live it.

A therapist would have a field day with me given the chance.

Most people can't afford that attitude, Sage says. And of course, he's right.

Well, we *can,* knowing just how awful I must sound. But we can.

Sage still takes the subway. He says it doesn't make him

nervous. Statistically, he argues, it's far safer than putting oneself at the mercy of some sleep-deprived crazy behind the wheel of a taxi. Plus, it's faster and important to stay grounded, to mingle with the masses. Even, especially, in the wake of disaster. And on top of all that, it's far cheaper.

So, my man doesn't let the terrorists win. Sometimes, I'm confident this has more to do with not letting *me* win than saving cash or safeguarding American freedom.

This morning's no different. I hail a taxi.

The cheery yellow is only on the outside. Today, my taxi smells like body odor and some kind of souvlaki. A dirty plastic dog bone dangles from the rearview mirror and swings violently as the driver—unsurprisingly named Mohammed—somehow jerks in and out of lanes of unmoving cars. He seems very young, twenty at most. A long, skinny neck props up his bizarrely shaped head that shouldn't be bald. He has a small, unidentifiable tattoo that might be a birthmark. His eyes are small and dark like raisins.

Never talk to strangers, Dad said to me before I took my first solo ride on the public bus. He and Mom were big fans of public transportation. I'm convinced this was an attempt to distract Michael and me from the fact that we were wealthy, to keep us innocent and unspoiled, a tough, if not impossible, feat in the world of Manhattan. The universal parental lecture was no doubt meant to keep me safe and sound. It was really that simple. Armed with this rudimentary wisdom and a mere decade of life, I was sent into a world full of strangers of different shapes and sizes, most of whom had no interest in talking to little me.

What Dad never told me is that we're always at the mercy of strangers—the strangers who make up our government's administration, the strangers who interview us for jobs, the strangers who fly our planes and drive our taxis, those who make our coffee.

And those who terrorize our days.

"I'm getting married," I say aloud, presumably to the perfect stranger in the front seat.

And Mohammed turns and looks at me like I am crazy. "Good luck, woman," he says.

For the remainder of the ride, I sit in the backseat, wrestling with my BlackBerry, fighting nausea, e-mailing my best friend, Kayla. I write: Engaged this wknd ☺ and hit send before I lose my breakfast. Never did I imagine sharing such monumental life news from a taxicab with a sentence fragment and an emoticon.

Mohammed is a polite man, but a vicious driver. Perfect combination. He doesn't smile in his license picture or in the front seat. But he gets me there. As we pull up in front of my office building, I scan the cracked leather seat, running my fingertips over the broken surface, curiously warm in spots. I trace the wrinkled stickiness of masking tape, making sure I have everything. I reach around my boots to find my bag, feel the remnants of yesterday's snow, and slice the palm of my hand on a broken and rusting umbrella. I wish Mom were here with her foolproof maternal memory to assure me I am up-to-date on tetanus shots. But she isn't here and there's no way I'm up-to-date. I find a royal blue condom wrapper and a business card for a man named Ralph who specializes in speedy patio renovation.

I slam the taxi door and push through the revolving glass doors into the lobby. My office building is on Park Avenue. It's one of those sleek and towering, marble and mahogany beasts that impresses camcorder-toting tourists on a daily basis and tingles the pride of parents who drop by for outrageously priced chopped salads with yuppie children.

Once upon a time, poking out above the Manhattan skyline was a good thing.

This year's tree is *still* up, blanketed in tiny white lights and blinding ornaments. Someone wants to stretch the Christmas cheer that never quite materialized this year. Each November, those of us lucky enough to escape for Thanksgiving return to the grand tree. Each year's tree surpasses its predecessor in girth and greenness.

At first, I wondered where the poor tree lived before being yanked to remind us of holiday cheer. Certainly, it was far too big to be one of the lush Douglas firs peddled by ruggedly attractive Canadian men who populate the city's pee-soaked pavement beginning each November. Eye candy for disgruntled wives and overwrought supermommies, these men slide into town in the darkness of night, take turns sleeping in blue vans with tinted windows, and gouge New Yorkers with prices we recognize as exorbitant, but prices we are simply too exhausted to bargain down.

"Where do you think they got this one?" I asked Kayla, in my moment of naïveté.

"On the Internet," she said. "It's fake, Quinn. Like everything else here."

"Well, at least there's a charitable aspect," I said. Donated toys—Barbie dolls, LEGO sets, Rescue Heroes—gathered in symmetrical heaps at its base.

"All part of the act," she said, pointing out a shiny red bicycle with the name of a senior partner emblazoned on the side. "It's all about competition."

"And the music?" I asked, hopeful there was some good

old innocent explanation for the string quartet that played in the lobby each afternoon.

"To remind us there's more to life than mergers and acquisitions," she said, giggling. What she meant: There's more to life than sex and money.

Just a couple months later, I see things clearly. The display reeks. Not of pine, but of pretense. Falsity. Irony. Ostensibly it is the embodiment of human goodness and Christmas cheer, but I have a hunch that even this year many of the men and women holed up in the offices above do not spend much time focused on the less fortunate, on the kids without a Santa Claus. I have a hunch because I'm one of them. No, we conjure Christmas lists of our own: summer houses in the Hamptons, the latest line of Louis Vuitton luggage, private school admissions for privileged tykes. For us, Santa no longer wears red and white, boiled wool and snow white fur, but pinstripes and cuff links. And his gifts are not slithered down a chimney, but directly deposited. Yes, I'm among the souls who salivate for the beloved Christmas bonus, that not-so-little "extra" that's scattered each year at a time when families gather without us and doubts set in.

10:01 A.M. I'm later than usual. I speed through the lobby, my heels clicking away on smooth white marble. My bag slips off my shoulder and dangles on one arm, digging deep into my flesh. I fumble my BlackBerry open in the other, shuffling my feet in fits and starts, slowing down as I check the messages that arrive in clusters of two and three. The blood on my palm has dripped down and around my wrist, making me look either suicidal or like a Kabbalah convert. I can't decide which would be worse.

Big-shouldered Javier waits at the turnstile, arms crossed in front of his broad chest, and smiles at me. He's my favorite of the countless guards garbed in maroon polyester who patrol the vast lobby space; security is understandably a lot tighter these days.

"Hey," I say, managing a discombobulated wave. Did he notice the ring? When I started here, Javier told me I looked far too young to be an attorney. What about a wife? Am I too young for that?

I swipe my law firm ID card and wait for the elevator.

The elevator arrives, and waiting bodies with fisted Starbucks scramble to pile in. It's too early for eye contact, so we shuffle in, looking down at the medley of sneakers and high heels, the dangling gym bags and just-in-case umbrellas. I press my button and stare at the small TV screen above the buttons. It tells me the alert level du jour, sports scores about which I don't care, and how the weather will continue to be shitty through the week. The elevator doors are inches from closing when five thin fingers with the palest pink polish reach through the gap.

Kayla.

"Hey, bitch!" she says, breaking the morning code of silence, pushing up against me. Born a redhead, she now has blond hair. In her khaki trench and South Seas pearls, she's mastered the art of corporate casual. "So," she says, staring at her BlackBerry, "*someone* had a good weekend, huh?"

Kayla is a Greenwich girl. She has the pedigree of a champ: All-American swimmer at Hotchkiss, Harvard for college, Harvard for law school. She'd be easy to hate.

"Decent weekend," I whisper, and smile. "In Paris."

Kayla grabs my left wrist, jerking my hand up toward her face. "Yeah, I'd say you had a good weekend. And all I get is a butchered BlackBerry message? A ring that size and you guys couldn't splurge on the international call?"

I pull my hand away and return it to my side, but she grabs it again.

"Oh, Q, marriage isn't going to be *that* bad. No need for such extreme measures." She points to the traces of dried blood on my wrist.

"Umbrella accident," I say, as if this makes sense.

Two women eye my ring—or wrist—and whisper. A third follows their glances and smiles at me. I think she's the one who slept with a bankruptcy partner after a summer associate caviar party.

"Congratulations. I must say I'm not too thrilled about the abandonment, though."

Kayla follows me off the elevator and to my office.

"I can't believe you are going wife on me, leaving your poor ringless slut of a friend behind."

The use of profanity is the hallmark of insecurity and low self-esteem, Mom once said. *Fuck insecurity. Fuck self-esteem*, I said. We both laughed.

"K, I'm twenty-seven. This is what people *do*. They get married. They have kids."

"Guess I'm way behind the curve, then. Thank God. The thought of one man, just one, gives me the shivers," Kayla says.

"Better than herpes."

Kayla laughs. "So what now? We surf for dresses that make you look like Cinderella?"

"K, I love you, but not now. I'm screwed—Fisher's on me for this research." *Screwed. On me.*

Maybe it is all about sex.

"So calm down and bill a few hours," she says.

And money.

I boot up my computer. My desk is a disaster. The faux-cedar surface is blanketed in papers, errant paper clips, parched yellow highlighters. Ten almost-finished bottles of Poland Spring stand in a line, transparent soldiers standing guard along the honey-colored corkboard where my desk meets the wall.

"Look at you. What an environmentalist—here with your water conservation efforts," Kayla says, fiddling with one of the bottles. "When did you get so neat anyway? Practicing to be wifey, huh?"

Kayla helps me in my quest for order, stacking documents, ditching random plastic spoons and empty packets of artificial sweetener. I chuck the Poland Springs into the garbage can under my desk, knowing I should recycle. I feel a violent surge of déjà vu. The dream. I was *here* in my dream. At this desk, working late. It was all too real.

"You're on another planet. Is this the little-known effect of diamonds? I must know," Kayla says, shoving binders into an overhead shelf.

"I'm just exhausted. This is all a little surreal."

"Whatever you say, but if you ask me, you don't seem happy."

Silence.

"His mother helped him pick the ring."

"Hmm."

"Am I paranoid to think she has taken the very first opportunity to insert herself into our marriage? I look at this ring and I think of her."

"Lovely," she says. "Well, if you're right, she could ruin everything."

"Huh?"

"He's a mama's boy, Q. You've said it yourself. This isn't an instance of fierce competition. This is an instance of no competition. She'll win every time."

"Cheers," I say, tossing an empty water bottle at her.

Kayla shrugs. "Remind me: How many times has he brought you home?"

"Never," I say. "But he hardly goes home. Just for holidays and his brother's birthdays."

"All excuses, Quinn." she says. "He's been trying to keep you two on opposite ends of the ring, but that might not be possible anymore. You know what that little bauble on your finger means?"

"What?"

"Round one," she says.

I shake my head.

"The past is the past," I say. Cliché. "It's time for a fresh start." Another cliché.

Kayla looks at me, silent for once, worry plastered on her forehead, which is unseasonably tan. She nods and continues stacking Post-its into rainbow towers.

"Well, you're going to have yourself a fresh start—at another firm if you pull this shit again."

Fisher stands in my doorway, red in the face, stubby hands resting on love handles no custom shirt could possibly camouflage.

"The client needs an answer this afternoon and you can't even respond to my goddamned e-mails?"

Profanity is the hallmark of low self-esteem, I remind myself.

Fuck.

Kayla turns, slides by Fisher, and disappears.

"I'm sorry," I say, softly like a little child who has lost her father and lost her way, not like a professional pushing thirty. The two words are weak and soggy, limp noodles of pseudo-regret. But right now, it's all I can manage.

Chapter 6

Once upon a time I didn't fear Fisher, a mere peanut of a man with a pregnant woman's belly. When I first started at the firm, I learned he would be my partner mentor. The lady from human resources told us mentors were there for support, to field questions. I quickly appreciated the one thing a partner mentor was good for: an outrageous welcome lunch.

So, on my first official day as a big-time lawyer, I had a forty-dollar slab of Chilean sea bass.

"Look at you. First day on the job and ordering the only endangered species on the menu. Bold, very bold. I like that," Fisher said from across the table at the overpriced four-star restaurant. These were his first words to me. Another partner, Miles Shannon, debatably albino, more rookie, rolled his eyes only slightly at Fisher, but kept quiet. Lisa, the other new associate, probably thanked her lucky stars she'd ordered the chicken.

Fisher, on the other hand, ordered the only red meat on the menu and chuckled with delight when the diminutive waitress, devoid of facial expression, placed it in front of him.

"You'll learn," he said, addressing the table in his crackly voice, his astonishingly short arms flailing about, "that we fall into two camps."

Miles Shannon smiled as he cut his chicken paillard into small bites.

"Yup, two kinds of partners that you will encounter at our firm: the Porters and the Poultry," Fisher said, sucking a massive piece of steak off his sparkling fork.

I shot a look of confusion at Lisa. Her hair was scraped back into a low bun. She wore too much makeup and terror in her eyes.

"Let me explain," Fisher said. He was halfway through his steak, but Lisa and I had barely touched our food. "It all started a few years ago with some goddamned summer class that had too much time on their hands. Well, they came up with the names and we caught wind of them and you know what? They were on to something. Confirms that we only hire the brightest, most intuitive souls here at Whalen," he said, and guffawed.

Lisa and I nodded.

"Anyway, some of us are Porters," he said, making air quotes, "named for the porterhouse steaks we *apparently* live on. We're the frat boys of the firm, schmoozing clients, driving fast cars. The Poultry among us—they're the clean-living folk, lean and mean. Poultry are often the quiet brilliant ones who fly under the radar. Isn't that right, Mildy?"

Very appropriately, Miles Shannon flashed a half smile, remained mute, and continued to make his way through his chicken, slicing geometrical pieces, chewing slowly, and checking his watch between every few bites.

"Well, you have a representative from each camp here, girls. Pardon me. *Young ladies*, I should say. It's imperative that I brush up on my PC speak. Can you guess which one of us is a Porter and which one a Poultry?"

I laughed. Even petrified little Lisa managed a smile. Miles Shannon's face pinked.

"What about the women?" I asked. "Can they be Porters or Poultry too?"

It was hardly a ridiculous question. After all, there we were, two rookie female associates being initiated into the ranks, and these men had failed to even mention their female partners.

"No, they're different. Don't quite fit the categories," Fisher said. "Let's get some wine, shall we?"

I should've predicted that life at the firm wouldn't be all jokes and vintage Cabernet.

Today, when I walk into Fisher's office, my hands are clammy, my heart is racing, and I have to force myself not to look down. Fisher sits in his throne of a leather chair behind his impossibly large desk. I'm convinced this is intentional; perhaps he believes he can obscure his size behind a well-placed slab of mahogany. His face has returned to its trademark pinky hue. He flips through a stack of envelopes and ignores me. I scan the pictures of his son and daughter that populate each shelf behind him and remind myself that he's not a monster. No, he's a father. A decent man.

Today, I get it. I appreciate how right he was on that first day; Fisher is no doubt the quintessential Porter. He has a ruddy complexion and chubby fingers. Swollen skin spills over the edges of a dulling gold wedding band that he wears most of the time. He's an overgrown boy, like the chubby frat kids in college who somehow landed pretty girls, gut and all. He atones for missing abdominal muscles by sporting extravagant ties and cuff links. Or by flashing his gold Cartier constantly. Presumably, such trinkets remind him and the rest of us that *he* has made it.

Like the other Porters, Fisher is a faux dieter, alternatively a South Beach or Atkins devotee. But with clients he convinces himself there are no carbohydrates in dirty martinis and creamed spinach.

"I want to apologize about this weekend and today," I say.

"Then go ahead," he says. He keeps flipping and does not look up. Under his desk, his shiny chestnut loafers swing back and forth, barely grazing the burgundy carpet.

"Sorry," I say.

"So, how was Paris?" His eyes remain fastened to his mail pile.

How does he know about Paris? God, they do monitor our every move.

"Good," I say, ignoring Mom's perennial admonition against one-word answers.

"For better or worse, this firm's like a goddamned country club. I heard the secretaries jabbering on and on about a certain *someone* getting engaged this weekend. Made me feel like a bit of a Scrooge for my angry outburst this morning. God, I need some carbs."

This is about as close as you get to a partner apology. I'll take it.

"That's okay. I should've gotten back to you."

"Yes, you should've. Our clients don't care if you're going to be a bride."

"I know," I say, twirling my BlackBerry.

Our clients, a string of condom companies, are being sued by a class of women, including a bevy of porn stars and prostitutes, who are allergic to the spermicide these companies refuse to eliminate from their products. Fisher, once dubbed Mr. Toxic for successfully defending tampon companies against a legion of toxic shock syndrome sufferers, has a new name in the firm: The Sperminator. Even without the genes of a feminist mother, I think at this point I'd begin to realize this man isn't the biggest defender of women.

Miles Shannon, the other partner of my fateful first day, sticks his head in the office, sees me, and leaves. And, again, Fisher was right. Shannon's the anti-Fisher: chiseled, borderline gaunt, a marathon runner in his "spare" time. His office is modest and more organized. He prefers buttons to links. His ties are tattered.

Miles Shannon doesn't look like a movie star, but, given everything—his position in life, the ungodly number of hours he devotes to his work, the sky-high stress level he endures on a daily basis—he's attractive and together. He likely has the same waist size he did in high school.

"Morning, Mildy," Fisher grunts at the now empty doorway.

In the hallways and conference rooms, partners put on a good act. They joke and laugh deeply like good old friends.

This is fake too. All a charade.

Partners are in constant competition. For the most bankable and flashy clients, even for the most extravagant office furniture—leather chairs, antique desks, tropical trees, vintage prints, even the occasional marble desk. There appears to be no limit on the manner in which a partner can decorate his professional lair. Essentially, many of these aging men (and, yes, the occasional woman who's either enviably super-human or has forsaken dreams of marriage or motherhood, or has hired a team to cater to neglected husbands and children) decorate their offices like living rooms—with Oriental carpets, turn-of-the-century prints. My guess is that this is because they are so rarely home.

On my first day at the firm, I was told I'd "share" my secretary, Wanda—admittedly a weird property-esque way of talking about another human being—with David Greenenberg, a corporate partner, a Porter with terrible hair plugs. This man spends most nights on his mocha ultra-suede office couch. Rumor is his socialite wife, Bunny, finally gave him the boot. One afternoon when he was away on business, Wanda showed me the dark drool stains on his couch pillows.

Vodka stains, Wanda said, and showed me his secret stash of booze under his desk. *He asks me to remove them, but every time I try, they get worse. Makes my day.*

When talking with the other secretaries, she refers to him as Lady Macbeth, which kind of surprised me because I didn't know secretaries read Shakespeare. Which is obviously a terrible thought to have and perhaps one I should not admit to having.

As I leave Fisher's office, I feel a bit better about things, but I'm thankful he's already written my year-end review.

I return to my office. Time to work. I'm realistic, though: Whatever I hand him will inevitably be miserably sub-par and a lousy start to the week.

But I remember something important: Partners do know a lot of things that associates don't, but the law isn't one of them. And yet the myth persists that partners comprise a wholly different breed, that they have a mastery of the law that transcends our spotty understanding of the legal landscape. With the help of time and a permanently cynical best friend, I realized it's all bullshit. If these questions were easy, the partners would tackle them themselves. Partners invariably know far less than we do. But as their associate minions, we're the little pawns who keep the blood of a case pumping by researching law, uncovering facts, and attending to the mundane details of any matter.

So here I am with yet another "query" that inherently eludes answering. It's my job to spin my little Ivy League wheels. The fact that I will spend hours searching, however fruitlessly, for an answer, will comfort Fisher. And cost the client. The fact that *someone* has billed some hours "toiling with the enigma," "wrestling with the puzzle," will scatter the responsibility of a potential misstep in representation. We lawyers never stop thinking about liability; it's our job, after all.

In no time, I'm immersed in yet another obscure research assignment. Our case has been brought in Texas court, a state full of notoriously sympathetic and conservative jurors, so it's my job to scour Texas tort law for arguments to save our executive clients from scores of women who've suffered for one reason: They've opted to have safe sex.

After an hour, I've pasted together snippets from cases that seem remotely similar to ours, bits and pieces of arguments we will expertly morph with the help of legalese to suit our purposes. I e-mail my vacuous summary to Fisher with my strategic hedges and the requisite parting line: "If

there's anything I can do to follow up, please let me know."
It's bullshit. But I hit send.

Just for fun, I do an Internet search for our lead plaintiff
in the class action: Crystal Sugar. In no time, I'm on Crystal's
Web site and she stares back at me through sad eyes of electric blue. She stands there, legs splayed, in the center of the
screen wearing nothing but an American flag–print thong.
We all need a little Sugar at a time like this, a sultry voice says.

I scramble to find the volume control on my computer.

She's probably my age. I wonder if two sane parents could
actually give a child this name and expect her to grow up
to be anything other than a stripper. But I assume that the
name's fake—just like her ginger hair, golden tan, and perfect breasts.

Dad told me never to talk to strangers, and this girl has
made a profession out of seducing them. She's selling herself.

I look around. Out the window. At the ringing phone
and the blinking BlackBerry. At the pinstripes, simple and
straight, running the length of my thigh. And for a moment,
I wonder if what I'm doing is really any different.

A few moments later, two e-mails arrive: one from Fisher
and one from Sage. I don't know which one I dread opening
more.

Fisher: *Impressive, O'Malley. I thought your mind would still
be in Paris. Your fiancé's a lucky man; he's landed himself an
efficient girl and a looker. Well done, indeed.*

And then I open the e-mail from Sage. A single question,
sweet and simple, waits for me. And makes me want to cry.
Will you be my valentine?

Chapter 7

When I was little, I hated restaurants. *It's not a restaurant, Prue*, Dad would tell me. *It's a pub.* Technically, the simple argument was sound; every Sunday, my family went to the Irish pub on our corner where the accents were thick and the beer was black. *Have a taste*, Dad would say, offering me a sip. And though I was young, a decade-plus from being legal, I would take that sip. A bit reluctantly because Mom hated beer and I figured this must mean it was terrible stuff. *It's not beer, Prue*, Dad would tell me. *It's Guinness*.

But I was a smart kid. I knew pubs were restaurants. The fact that paper shamrocks dangled from the ceiling for the whole month of March and that rugby games played on the little TV on the bar didn't fool me. I was still expected to sit still and behave. I was still expected to pick one thing from the menu and then eat it when it came. But I never wanted to choose. Because I'd order the potato skins, and when they came, steaming hot and smelling delicious, I'd want the grilled cheese.

And I knew that Guinness was beer. The fact that it was dark and frothy didn't fool me. It was a drink I wasn't supposed to have yet. But I think I knew even then that I'd grow up to love it and that I would always think of it as Dad's drink.

Despite my aversion to eating out, Mom and Dad vowed not to let me dictate; the O'Malley family would head out for dinner in hopes that my inevitable meltdown would be low on the Richter scale. Invariably, before the waiter finished jotting down our drink order, I'd do my trademark disappearing act, slithering down in my seat to hide under the table. Mom and Dad learned to ignore my antics; they'd talk to each other about the menu, whether to order the pork chops or the penne. They'd ask Michael about school and he'd seize the opportunity to talk about art class, how his watercolor was his teacher's favorite, how she said he was a talented painter.

There under the table, their words became gentle rumble, a familiar melody muffled by the paper tablecloth that protected me from the adult world above. I'd sit there, legs crossed, in relative darkness, and watch as my parents and brother crossed and uncrossed their legs, occasionally bumping knees. Sometimes, someone would lose a shoe and I'd return it to the appropriate foot. It became a game for me. At least once a meal, Michael would kick me, but not very hard and only in good fun. Periodically, Mom and Dad would peer under and ask me to rejoin them, but usually I ignored them. They'd never push too hard; I guess they figured an absent child was better than a screeching one.

They let me do my thing. I've decided this wasn't because

they felt helpless, or couldn't control me, but because they respected my decision to be alone, to sit in silence and contemplate things. At any rate, I'd always emerge when the waiter brought my Shirley Temple.

But one magical day, things changed. Restaurant meals became treats not torture. Portobello mushrooms were delicious not slimy. Birthdays were dreaded instead of anticipated. Valentine's Day was no longer about perforated Snoopy cards, but about prix fixe dinners and scheduled sex.

I'm not sure where my penchant for fine dining—for the freshest guacamole, the most delicate slices of sushi— is rooted. Maybe it's because I can't cook. Perhaps it's all about being in New York City—where good restaurants are as plentiful as deer in the suburbs. Or maybe it's my dear brother. After a brief stint in the fashion world, he's now in cooking school. His studies have only reinforced a feeling he's always had—that food is a religion—that needs to be studied and absorbed. Maybe his piety for the gastronomical wonders is contagious.

It has nothing to do with the food, Mom has said. *You were born an anthropologist. Even as a baby, you loved watching people. Why do you think I stopped breastfeeding you?*

Because I bit you?

No, because you wouldn't stop looking around. You were more interested in the people than my breast. And you'd fling that little head around exposing my nipple to the world.

Mom, you were a hippie. You never wore a bra. You loved nipple exposure.

Of course I initially interpreted this anthropologist talk as another of Mom's attempts to dissuade me from a career in the legal world, but she's right. I've always been fascinated with people, how they cut their steaks, how they giggle on an uncomfortable first date, how they treat the waiter who serves them, how they deal with an improperly calculated bill. I can sit at a restaurant for hours watching people come and go, wrestling with oversized strollers, getting doggie bags to go, watching an aspiring actress shuttle Bloody Marys and bread baskets to make her month's rent. I'm captivated by the body language of couples, why one pair doesn't make eye contact for an entire meal while another ignores the food completely, devouring each other instead.

Oh how one could interpret us now: the clichéd young couple celebrating Valentine's Day. What should be made of our stiff silence, the good food between us, the way we sip our complimentary Kir Royales a bit too quickly? Sage and I sit side by side on a banquette at Café des Artistes, one of the city's finest. This is the first time we've had dinner out together since Paris. The restaurant is packed with old people, refined regulars no doubt. Sage and I stick out. He's too big for the banquette; he keeps shifting around, his elbows on the table and then off again.

"We need to talk, Bug."

To me, this means breakup. He will tell me—over gourmet food and with the assistance of fine wine—that he's made a grave mistake, that he wants the ring back. That a little bit crazy is okay, even a good thing, but he underestimated me.

We need to talk.

To him, apparently this means: We need to talk.

"It's good to finally see you," he says, draping his arm around me. "I mean really *see* you. We have so much to talk about."

And suddenly I want to slink down in the booth, to go under the table and take a time-out like I did as a kid. Suddenly, I crave quiet. And solitude.

"We didn't need to do anything this fancy, Sage."

Tonight, it seems, our agenda is twofold. We will do our best to revel in this Hallmark holiday and we will discuss our future. It's a very efficient way to do things and my man loves efficiency. *No harm in killing two birds with one stone*, he has said. (This once gave me a naughty idea about the two pigeons who've made a home of our bedroom windowsill.)

"Your brother recommended this place, Bug. He said if we could get over the geriatric element, the food's pretty amazing."

"So the restaurant's a buy then? Long or short?" I should've known he'd evaluate this restaurant like he does the companies and stock prices he and his colleagues assess on a daily basis. "You've already got me, Sage," I say, dangling my ring in his face. "You don't need to impress me anymore." As I say this, I wonder if I actually mean it.

When I first met Sage, he was your run-of-the-mill guys' guy; he didn't know that edamame were soybeans, or how to pronounce foie gras.

"Terrific. So, I could have saved about two hundred bucks and you would've been a happier camper too?"

Somehow, it's always about money. He looks slightly amused, but mostly defeated. The waiter glides by with a basket of rolls. Sage opts for a pumpernickel roll and I take a slice of whole grain. The waiter slips a small dish of olive oil between us. He hands Sage the thick bible of a wine list, bows his head, and disappears. Sage opens the book and flips through the endless pages, closes it again.

"You pick," he says, surrendering the list to me. This is typical. I'm the wine girl.

There isn't a bottle under sixty dollars, and I'm not surprised. The waiter returns and I order a Sancerre. As I point to the bottle on the list, Sage peers over. When he sees that I've chosen a bottle that costs one hundred and twenty dollars, he slumps back in the banquette.

"And I suppose you would've been happy with beer, but since you're here you figured what the hell?"

Sage never says "hell." He said it once at age nine and his mother grounded him for a week and he missed two Little League games.

"Happy Valentine's to you too, sweetheart," I say, raising my champagne flute to toast his.

"Okay, what's going on? Is this what things are going to be like? Now that I've given you the ring, it's time to practice bickering like all the other crappy couples we know?"

I shrug. "I'm just exhausted."

Sage looks at me with tired eyes. "It's been a tough month for me too. We need to hire more analysts at the bank. There's just too much on our plate with the upcoming IPO."

I'm no expert, but I know this has nothing to do with an overpriced wine or the fact that his department at the bank is short on staff.

"If that's all, fine," I say, lying.

The waiter returns with our wine. I taste it. Nothing special. Should've ordered the Riesling.

"It's just . . ." he begins. "It's just that you've been so incredibly distant. And don't blame it on the job."

"Just like you tried to do," I say.

"We haven't even talked about the wedding and it's been weeks. Makes me worry." With this, he grabs my hand under the table, looks at me for a second, and then away. This is the beauty of sitting side by side; you don't have to face the person you're with.

I take a gulp of my wine. And then another. "You know

I'm not the prissy type who obsesses over her wedding."

"I'm not asking you to obsess, Bug. I'm asking you to *acknowledge*."

He has a point.

"Okay, okay, I promise. We'll start planning." I squeeze his hand.

"You've been weird since I asked. I thought this was supposed to bring us closer."

Fear and relief wash over me. He's noticing me, the gulf between us, the unspoken uncertainty that maybe, just maybe, plagues both of us. Thankfully, there are limits to his quintessentially male oblivion.

I scoot closer to him on the banquette. "How much closer can we get?" I say, proud of my timely pun, and kiss him on the cheek.

"*Much*," he says, smiling, and squeezes my thigh.

But even as the wine flows, and we wordlessly anticipate a night of predictable-but-delicious Valentine's Day sex, it occurs to me, a sobering and subversive truth: There might just be things that alcohol and sex can't solve.

In Paris, the morning after we got engaged, Sage and I left our room to hunt for food. Hand in hand, we walked the length of the dimly lit hotel hallway. Nibbled croissants and orange pulp-coated glasses waited on trays outside closed doors. "Ne Pas Déranger" signs dangled from brass doorknobs. The carpeting was tacky; deep red, flecked with gold leaves. Gilded sconces lined pale striped walls. We reached the elevators, and Sage pulled me close and kissed me.

"You're going to be my wife, Bug. Bug McIntyre . . . that has a nice ring to it."

When the elevator came, we walked on, fingers woven. The

car was packed with a medley of fashion types and affluent tourists. Momentarily, all eyes were on us. This made me only a bit uncomfortable; the attention was kind of red-carpet cool. We stood at the very front of the elevator, pressed up against the large gold doors, Sage behind me, his arms linked tightly around my waist. Every few seconds, he kissed the back of my ponytail.

We reached the lobby and Sage led me to the hotel dining room where they were still serving Sunday brunch. The room was grand—overly grand, cold and cavernous, full of reds and golds and purples, quintessentially regal tones. But predictable. The chairs had tall thronelike backs and ornate embroidery. In the corner of the vast room, a small table for two waited for us with a tiny arrangement of white flowers and a chilling bottle of rose champagne—my favorite.

Sage had arranged this.

What a romantic, I thought.

But then I thought: *It's pretty easy to be romantic in Paris.*

He pulled a chair out for me and I sat down, slipped the crisp linen napkin from a monogrammed sterling ring, unrolling that perfect roll, and draping it across my lap.

"This is a dream, Sage," I said, surprised by my own choice of words. "You didn't have to do all of this. I'm just so happy." I listened to myself speak; my words were distant and fake, artificial mumblings of Hallmark banality. I wasn't being myself.

Even so, his smile said victory. Maybe to him, my words weren't so empty at all. He seemed pleased he had pleased me. That was hardly a bad thing. He reached for the bottle of champagne, but a gaunt waiter in an ill-fitting tuxedo jumped in. His name tag read "Jacques." He was heroin-skinny and gesticulated on fast forward, flailing his pin-thin limbs about with startling aggression. He had the pointiest nose I'd ever seen.

"*Bonjour! Bon matin!*" His energy was exhausting.

Jacques poured a little champagne in Sage's glass. And instead of smiling, taking in this majestic morning, I thought: *Why does the man always get to taste?*

Sage sipped it, wrinkled his brow in contemplation, and gave Jacques a slight nod and a thumbs-up, as if the two gestures weren't redundant. Then he filled my glass. I waited for the foam to shrink and then tasted, letting it slowly roll over my tongue. I hoped it would soothe my head. It tasted good.

Sage reached across the table and grabbed my left hand in his. I've always loved his hands—they are big and manly and he keeps his nails short and clean. When he pulled my hand toward him, he forced me off my chair. He studied the ring.

"You like it, Bug?" he asked, knowing the answer he would hear, perhaps wanting to hear it anyway.

"I do," I said.

"I'm so glad," Sage said. "I just wanted to make you happy, and I'm so happy and relieved that you like it, Bug."

"It does look a lot like your mother's ring," I said.

"Well, she helped me pick it," he said. "You don't think I could've done something like that on my own?"

Then Sage started talking about the future.

"I just never imagined this, you know? Here I am in *Paris* . . ." he said, rolling his R, attempting and failing to attain a passable French accent, ". . . drinking vintage champagne with the woman with whom I will spend the rest of my life." That morning, his grammar was impeccable, as if he'd been practicing for the occasion. When I met him, Sage always ended sentences with prepositions; this "with whom" business was a huge improvement.

Before we even started drinking, Sage started talking and talking about things, things that seemed pent up until this moment. He admitted things. That he pictured fishing trips with me and two blond boys. And I couldn't help but picture those fateful framed photos. Of him and his brother. And I couldn't help but wonder whether we marry to move forward, or to go back. To heal wounds? To start over?

He said he couldn't wait to get a Lab or a Golden. *Painfully Upper West Side yuppie, but I don't care.* He told me he pictured birthday dinners around a large wooden table with cake and candles and party hats. And then he told me he pictured our wedding day, waiting at the head of an aisle watching a gorgeous woman (yes, me) walking toward him *cloaked in the purest of white.* Yes, he said these words just like that. Borderline poetic.

I smiled when he said these things, but couldn't find the words to contribute.

Sage ate a chocolate croissant in two bites and washed it down with champagne. I finished my first glass of champagne and poured myself another. Jacques jumped over, apparently offended by this manifestation of self-help. He shot me a fiery look of disapproval. Maybe I was acting very American.

While my endearingly disheveled husband-to-be appeared ensconced in dreams about our future together, I was hostage in the past. My dream was still with me, an invisible third wheel at our small table. Visions pierced through. Phelps's smile. The flower girl's tears. Victor's muscles.

But that champagne was a godsend. I not only felt better,

but good. The pounding dulled. Finally, I was there: relaxed and maybe even happy? When Jacques dripped the last trace of bubbly into my cobalt blue Fabergé flute, I gave Sage my best puppy dog eyes, which he knew very well meant I wanted more.

What would a body language expert say that morning?

There we were. Certainly, we must have been amusing to the outside eye. I would have loved to slink outside my skin and watch the two of us, to pick apart our fits of silence, the rapid rotations of champagne, the furrowed brow of our deeply irritated waiter. I would have loved to guess our ages, our professions, our passions, whether or not we genuinely enjoyed the French food on which we nibbled. I would have loved to slither down and sit under that small table as I did as a child, noting the increasing and decreasing distance between my feet and his. To some, we surely resembled that clichéd bedheaded couple in a coffee commercial, holding hands, weaving fingers, making soulful eyes at each other in the haven of an intimate European breakfast nook.

In truth, though, we were nothing but two kids sitting there, playing adults, gearing up for a new phase of our life together. We drank fancy champagne and buttered our croissants with Christofle's finest. Periodically, we studied the diamond on my left hand together, remarking on its magic, celebrating how the stone caught the soft light of the crystal chandelier that dangled above.

Sage wanted to make me happy. Maybe it was that simple.

I pinched off the corner of a chocolate croissant and put the rest of the pastry on Sage's plate: my cocktail party modus operandi.

The chocolate melted in my mouth and snaked down my

throat with a swallow of champagne. It was for me a timely panacea, working wonders, temporarily quieting the storm of memories, the waves of guilt that buffeted me, muffling the crash of that dream that started it all.

"I think November's perfect," I say, taking a bite of his pork. "Bird Lake's beautiful at that time of year. We'll do it before Thanksgiving."

Sage smiles as he chews. The waiter glides by and I flag him down.

"We'll have another of those," I say, pointing to our empty bottle of wine.

"The '89 Sancerre," Sage says, defeated. He pronounces "Sancerre" like it rhymes with "cancer" and I'm thankful he's not yet all polish. "You know celebration is possible without inebriation."

"Thanks for the news flash."

"Come on, don't do that. At this rate I'm not sure when I'll see you next," he says, and laughs, his words laced with humor and, unfortunately, truth.

We make it through the second bottle of wine before looking at the dessert menu. Sage's cheeks have grown pink, which they always do when he drinks. The wine has worked its magic; before I know it, Sage and I are talking wedding colors and honeymoon destinations.

"What do you think? Should we get an after-dinner drink?" I say as the waiter drips the last drop in my glass.

"Check please," Sage says.

The waiter disappears into the back of the restaurant, leaving us alone in silence. Sage puts his arm around me and I can't stay mad. I cuddle up.

"Quinn, you're mute. You've never been an introspective drunk. Don't start now," Sage says, and smiles.

"I'm not drunk," I say, and smile back. "Okay, I'm a little buzzed, but that's legal, right?"

"Just as long as you're happy."

That word again. Happy. What the hell does it mean to be happy?

"We're engaged; no brooding allowed. At least pretend you're happy until the wedding and then you can go back to the real you, mood swings and all."

Pretending. I'm beginning to think I'm pretty good at that.

"Very funny. I *am* happy. This is all so surreal though. A month ago, I was your girlfriend and now I am a *fiancée*. It's great, just a lot to process. Just give me some time to let this all marinate," I say.

"Marinate, I like that."

"There's one thing that I'm really going to have to get used to though."

"What's that? That you have the good fortune of waking up next to me for the rest of your living days?" Sage says.

"Yes, that and the word 'fiancée.' I hate it. Really, it's so silly. I'm a girlfriend with a promise. I don't know why I have to refer to myself as anything more."

"You are a girlfriend with a promise and a neat piece of hardware, I might add."

"True. Did you think it all through? That you would shroud me with such a ludicrous French name in Paris?"

He nodded. "I have to admit it did occur to me."

"Fiancée—the word's just awkward on the tongue."

"We'll just have to practice then," he says, smiling.

"Practice makes perfect, huh?" I say as a joke and realize I might be on to something. "Maybe everything—even being happy—is something you have to practice at."

"Something at which you have to practice?" he says, and smiles.

And I smile too. "Point taken, counselor."

"Guess now is as good a time as any," I say, pulling my gift, hastily wrapped in leftover Christmas paper, from my bag. I hand it to him.

"Has my Bug been recycling?" he says, smiling, fiddling with the red paper with white snowflakes.

"Well, it's red and white and it's still winter," I say, shrugging, suddenly feeling guilty that I didn't make a special trip during my lunch hour to pick the perfect holiday-appropriate paper.

He rips the paper and pulls them out: a pair of white boxer shorts covered in red fishing flies.

"I love them," he says, smiling, and kisses me. "My turn."

He pulls out his gift for me. It's wrapped in the same snowflake paper.

I smile.

The box is flat and curiously heavy. I peel away the paper. "A waffle iron?" I say.

"A *heart-shaped* waffle iron," he corrects me.

I look at it, this odd contraption. "But I don't eat waffles," I say.

"But our kids might," he says, grinning, and grabbing my hand.

"Are you pregnant or something?" I ask.

Our kids might. I finish Sage's wine in one gulp. And smile. And say thank you. And kiss him. Because this is a sweet gesture, right? Because he's doing it again, thinking about our future. Picturing holidays with our children.

Because this is what you do, right?

You get engaged.

Get married.

Have kids.

Make heart-shaped waffles.

"Eightieth and Amsterdam," I say to the cabdriver, clutching my new waffle iron.

"But that's not where we live," Sage says.

"I know," I say. "One quick stop."

And I drag him into the pub. The same Sunday night pub.

We sit at the bar. And an old man, vaguely familiar, smiles big and tosses two shamrock coasters at us.

"Two Guinnesses, please," I say.

"Coming right up," the man says, his Irish accent thick and sturdy.

Sage and I sit there quietly, side by side, twirling on wooden stools, watching a rugby game on mute.

"What are you thinking about?" he asks, his eyes sparkling.

"Honestly?"

"Of course honestly," he says.

"Mr. Nolan."

Met with a look of confusion, I elaborate. "My fourth grade teacher."

"Okay."

"He gave me a hard time because whenever he asked me a question, I always said, 'I don't know.' Even when I knew the answer. Finally, he got fed up and said: 'When you're standing at the altar on your wedding day and the officiant says, Prudence, do you take this man to be your lawful wedded husband, are you going to say, I don't know?'"

"And what did you say?" Sage asks.

"I said: 'I don't know.'"

Sage smiles, fiddles with that cardboard four-leaf clover. "Well, I'm beginning to feel quite lucky you said yes when I asked you to marry me."

I nod and smile and sip my Guinness, as bitter and delicious as I remember. And suddenly I feel lucky myself. I look over at the booth where my family used to sit, the table under which I used to hide out. And for a brief moment, I do the unthinkable: I envision the future. I picture us there, Sage and me, laughing and pleading with screeching and slobbering kids who slurp Shirley Temples, enjoying the quiet promise of a new week.

Chapter 8

"Goddamned groundhog," I say, looking out Whalen's vast smudge-free conference room windows. The sky is gray. Weathermen are predicting snow. I feel the building swaying. Earlier this month, that glorified creature saw his shadow and crawled back in its hole. This year, people got all excited about Mr. Punxsutawney Phil—and here in Manhattan our local celebrity rodent Mr. Pothole Pete—doing his little weather-predicting dance because the date was 02.02.02. I'm not sure why people get all hot and bothered by repeating numbers, but unsurprisingly, Sage, my number-loving man, was among the masses.

Shit. I'm not sure I can handle more winter, I said on the morning of February second.

You know, he's seen his shadow eighty-five percent of the time. It doesn't really mean anything. Spring will come when it comes, Sage explained. *It's like saying Quinn or Prudence. They mean the same thing. One just has a more foreboding ring to it.*

"You're boxing me out, O'Malley. I knew you'd do this. I knew you'd retreat into your own little wedding world," Kayla says, walking into the conference room to meet me. Growing up with all brothers, Kayla acquired a litany of athletic references, ones that come in quite handy here at the firm where sports metaphors are tossed about all day. Weeks have passed since I got engaged and Kayla and I haven't taken the time to sit down and talk.

Here, we gather for the mandatory Words from Whalen Women, an annual lunch where we'll be educated—in a very efficient ninety-minute block of time—on the issues facing women, particularly mothers, in the legal world.

"You going to take notes?" Kayla says. "I mean this could be you in a year. Wearing maternity pinstripes. Or who knows—if you and Sage get going, you could even be checking your BlackBerry for messages from the nanny."

We pass by platters of fluorescent orange curry and overstuffed sandwiches.

"I'm not boxing you out. I'm completely swamped. I've barely seen my boyfriend," I say.

"Your *fiancé*. Remember you now have a fancy label."

"*Right*. Cheers."

Kayla and I find a table in the back of the room. Kimberly Crane, a senior associate, sits at the far end. She's been at the firm for more than eight years and there's no question that she's been gunning for partner. This fall she "off-ramped" temporarily to give birth to her son, Harry. We all saw photos of her adorable and chubby-cheeked baby on the firm's announcement page. In any event, Kim wasted no time getting back to work. Only two months after his birth, she had a Filipino nanny holed up in a closet-sized bedroom in her two-bedroom York Avenue apartment.

"Now that one, she makes me sad," I say, nodding toward Kim.

"Why?" Kayla asks.

"Her office is wallpapered with pictures of her baby." I've worked with Kim only briefly, but long enough to know her story.

Kayla checks her BlackBerry. "So? Everyone around here partakes in progeny plastering. It's perfectly par for the course."

Kayla's right. This is my favorite part of visiting a partner's office (which can often be a stress-inducing activity because otherwise a phone call or e-mail would suffice): getting the chance for the inconspicuous once-over. I love looking at the art on the walls. Some partners have framed black-and-white photography, some have Audubon prints, and some just have their diplomas and bar certificates. But the partners I like always have many pictures of their kids on display throughout the office. Often they have notes from their kids or artwork propped up on their shelves. I love it when a partner catches me looking at the pictures and at the crayon masterpieces and starts telling me about his or her kids, their ages, their love for horseback riding or T-ball.

"I know," I say. "I love seeing the pictures. Reminds me that these people are human."

"All part of the act, my friend," Kayla says, typing away on her BlackBerry. "If these people really cared about their kids, they wouldn't be lawyers."

"Not true," I protest. "Some people, *most* people, have loans. People need to make money, Kayla."

"Oh yeah. Decent point," she says, and giggles. "That's sad."

"She's different, though. Look at her," I say, pointing to

Kim, who I pray hasn't heard our admittedly obnoxious, en-titled exchange.

Kim tries futilely to hide her postpartum belly under solid-colored twin sets. She's developed a very sad habit. "I heard that every morning, she takes a Polaroid picture of her baby boy and tapes it to her computer screen when she gets to work. She says she does this so that she can *watch Harry grow up*."

"Shit. That *is* sad," Kayla says.

Someone taps a microphone. The room grows quiet.

Linda Maxwell is the first to speak. She's a plain-faced and diminutive litigation partner in her fifties. She rotates through her gray, navy, and red pant suits with alarming pre-cision and manages to keep her silky black bob an inch above her shoulders at all times.

"I'm here today to tell you my story—which I warn you might be as boring as I am," Linda says in her deadpan voice. The room erupts with laughter because this woman *is* very boring.

And Linda tells her tale of being a female attorney in a jungle of men. Of how she never planned on becoming a partner, but it just happened. And before the music plays and she hands off that mike, she thanks her stay-at-home husband and her twin girls.

"Note to self: Marry a pussy of a man and wait until my eggs have near-rotted to pop one out," Kayla whispers. "Or *two*, as the case may be."

The next on the panel: Henriette Young. She's a new cor-porate partner. She's giddy and speaks too loudly, spitting into the microphone.

"I suspect a pre-panel Red Bull," Kayla says.

"My name is Henriette Young," she says, and giggles, "but call me Henri."

"Note to self: Find masculine nickname," Kayla continues her play-by-play.

Jolly Henri has oily hair and puffy eyes and tells us, enthusiastically, that she wakes up at 4:30 A.M. to read contracts before her kids wake up. That she often conducts conference calls in the evenings while bathing her "little critters."

"If the guys are Porters and Poultry," I say, "then what are the women?"

"Pastries," Kayla says. "Fine and flaky."

"Sweet as pie," I say in my best Southern accent.

"We *are* tasty little tarts, aren't we?" Kayla says, and giggles. "Sweet as pie, but topless. Well, *some* of us are at least."

She nods toward Sandra Friedman, a trusts and estates partner, not so tasty, who begins to speak to the now-dwindling lunch crowd. She's a lot less glowing about the mommy-career balancing act.

"Every night when I get home to my house in New Jersey, my kids are asleep. I go through their hampers to see what they wore to school that day," she says, her voice shaking.

"I don't mean to interrupt," Linda says, interrupting. "But New Jersey is your problem."

"I want my kids to have a backyard, Linda."

"Frankly, they'd rather have a mom than an acre of grass," Linda says.

And just when the truth starts coming, when things get a little less sweet and flaky, it's as if the men can hear it and the alarms start blaring. Fire alarms. And emergency lights flash on the ceiling.

And I look around. Everyone is in slow motion. Unfazed. Checking BlackBerrys, stacking papers, discarding lunch plates.

But I stand, grab my things, and run. Down the carpeted

hallway to the emergency exit. I take off my heels and throw them in my bag. Barefoot and alone, I cling to my blinking BlackBerry and run. Down countless flights.

I reach the lobby where people have begun to gather, where security guards usher us outside. Shaking and sweating, I step back into my heels and cross the street to the small café where Kayla and I often grab lunch. I find a small table in the corner and sit.

I pull out my cell phone and call Mom.

"They just evacuated my building," I say when she answers. "But I'm okay."

"You're okay," she says.

"You should've seen me," I say. "I ran so fast."

"Good for you."

Silence.

Still catching my breath, I say: "Mom, do you think maybe if he ran, if he didn't hesitate . . . He was such an athlete."

"Prue, we can't afford to play that game. He's gone. We can't change that."

"I know," I say. "I just wanted to let you know I'm okay."

"I love you, Prue," Mom says before hanging up.

Kayla finds me.

"Just another bomb threat," she says.

I nod. *Just another bomb threat.* I look out the window at my colleagues who gather on the sidewalk, talking and texting, smoking cigarettes, rolling eyes at this latest inconvenience, at the annoyance of billable minutes lost. And I wonder if I'm the only one whose heart pumps furiously like this and feels like it's breaking all over again. I wonder if I'm the only one who's fighting tears.

"The engagement. Tell me everything. I deserve details," Kayla says, kneading a piece of everything bagel between her slim fingers, rolling it into a small ball. Poppy and sesame seeds scatter on the faux granite surface of our wobbly little table.

"Details are overrated, K," I say.

"Nice try. How did he propose?"

For some reason I don't want to tell her.

"It happened Saturday after a delicious dinner at a four-star restaurant in the Left Bank. He got down on one knee in our hotel room," I say, and pause.

"And?"

"And he read me something. It was Plato," I say, looking down into my salad of wilting spinach.

Kayla laughs. "Plato? So, Banker Boy is a closet philosopher too?" Kayla makes fun of the fact that I was a philosophy major all the time. She was an economics major. While she was studying market forces, I was contemplating the cosmos.

"Very funny. I knew you were going to laugh. I shouldn't have told you."

"Don't go soft on me, little Mrs. I think it's sweet. I'm just having fun," she says, backpedaling. I'm not sure if she means it. "Tell me everything," she says.

And so I do. I tell her everything I can remember . . .

Sage and I stumbled back from dinner after two bottles of '82 vintage red. I wore my violet lace camisole that Michael bought me at the Barneys warehouse sale. Sage wore his blue sport jacket, the one with the gold buttons that his mother bought him for church. It was the first time he wore it. Once in our room, I grabbed his hand and pulled him toward our mountain of a bed, but he resisted me. He walked to the corner, keeping his back to me the whole time, and then I heard the pop. Champagne. He tipped the bottle and poured slowly into twin crystal flutes and floated a lone strawberry in each.

I asked him if we were celebrating something and he smiled. I asked him where my birthday cake was, but he ignored me. His eyes grew wide and focused. His lower lip trembled. He reached in his pocket and pulled out a scrap of paper. As he unfolded it, his hands shook. He glanced at it only once, folded it up again, and then spoke.

"*So ancient is the desire of one another which is implanted in us, reuniting our original nature, seeking to make one of two, and to heal the state of man. Each of us when separated, having one side only, like a flat fish, is but the tally-half of a man, and he is always looking for his other half . . .*"

Plato. We both began to cry. And Sage grabbed a small box from behind the ice bucket. His lips trembled faster now and he lowered himself on one knee, paused and looked up at me, and said, "Prudence Quinn O'Malley. I'm done fishing. I knew from the moment I met you. You're my other half. Will you marry me?"

And I didn't even look at the ring, but said yes, screamed it actually, and tackled him to the ground, knocking the box from his fingers. We rolled around the carpet laughing and crying. Side by side, pressed into one another, we stared up at the embroidered ceiling and the soft glow of the miniature chandelier. Sage reached for the box, popped it open, and I saw it, the ring. He slipped it on my finger.

But the next morning was different. It was one of those mornings that began quietly, but with startling confusion. The world was peaceful, and yet brutally foreign. There was a faint knock on the door. Panicked and sweaty, I shot up in bed and looked around. I scanned the room desperate for clues. I was naked—and hostage under a mess of powder-soft ecru sheets. A deep burgundy velvet canopy with braided gold tassels loomed above. A petite mosaic table lingered in the right corner of the small room between a pair of over-stuffed chairs covered in fading red toile.

Finally, thankfully, I spotted something familiar—the canary yellow label of a kicked bottle of Veuve. It was capsized, swimming in silence in a silver monogrammed ice bucket full of water now warm.

I was in Paris. I began to remember.

I grabbed a plush robe from the mahogany closet and tied it around my bare body and answered the door. A man in a hotel uniform hugged a vast arrangement of flowers. I took them from him, placed them down, and read the small card: "Congratulations to my Sage and his lady! À bientôt! Mama."

I looked over at her Sage, his ruffled tuft of dark blond hair peeking out from the top of the sheets. I bent over him, planting a soft kiss on the back of his head. I slid off the bed, trying my best not to wake him. My head was pounding.

Our small room had a bow window framed by lush gold drapes, with a half-moon seat covered in thick tapestry. When I peeked through the drapes, light bounced in and there it was: the Eiffel Tower. Sun shimmied through lace curtains in front of twin French doors opposite our bed, casting spiderweb shadows on beige carpet. I tiptoed over, jimmied the antique iron key in the lock, and slipped through out onto the tiny balcony. The streets were quiet and the air was cold. A faint aroma of cigarette smoke came and went with the strong January wind. A truck or two ambled by.

The Tower stood tall and quiet, a lone soldier, only yards from me. Even in the early morning, guards swarmed like ants around its base, protecting it from evil. I'd seen it before— while on vacation with my family, on my European tour with the girls after high school graduation, but that morning it was different. It wasn't the cliché, the trite image stamped on one too many postcards displayed on twirling wire racks. No, unlike my disoriented and shivering self, it was full of power. It was a symbol—of human accomplishment, and of national pride. Its shape was simple and exquisite, phallic. It was at that moment—when I found myself comparing France's national treasure to the male anatomy—that I relived the night before.

Sage had proposed.

The stone on my finger caught the light of the rising sun. I remembered the words. I remembered how it all happened.

The balcony was an icebox in the air. Goosebumps spread over my skin. Wind blew my robe. But I couldn't stop staring at the stone; I was mesmerized. At twenty-seven, I was as captivated as I was at six when Mom and Dad caved and bought me the Easy-Bake Oven for Christmas. Maybe Mom, forever paranoid, was scared of exposing her little girl to fire. More likely even, the feminist in her did not want me to tread the domestic path at such an impressionable age. But I already had a little lawyer in me even if my powers of persuasion had only just begun to bloom. I begged my parents to the point of sheer annoyance and wrote a surprisingly articulate letter to Santa begging him too. My persistence paid off.

I went back inside. Shifting sheets marred the perfect silence. Sage curled up—a lovable lump under the pile of sheets—and shielded his eyes from the sun I had ushered in. In that moment, as he bridged the worlds of night and day, I loved him more than ever.

Sage was still sleeping. He was a gorgeous creature that morning, even more so than usual. He had picked me. Proposed to me.

He stirred, stretching in the canopy bed, limbs poking out from sheets. Through the thickening fog of my obnoxious hangover, I flashed back to the night before. He had looked into my eyes with a new brand of love.

Even forever had a beginning.

His touch had been softer and his lips, sweeter. His strokes were gentler, his grip on me protective. *This is it*, I'd thought as I felt his strong body move on top of me, two halves becoming whole. For the first time in too long, I felt safe.

The reality of it all was daunting and delicious. He'd take out our garbage. I'd wash his smelly gym socks. Well, maybe. He'd father my babies.

"You, my pretty pastry, can tell a story," she says, handing me half of her black-and-white cookie.

"Well, there's a footnote to that story," I say. "An important one."

"Do tell."

"I had a dream that night. After he proposed," I said. I told her about the dream—the bizarre courtroom wedding, the lineup of grooms, that diminutive bailiff in black.

It was that dream that tugged at me, a detectable tarnish on the beautiful morning. Immediately, I chalked it up to my hangover. Even then, though, I knew in the back of my aching mind, my symptoms wouldn't vanish with Excedrin and carbohydrates.

I plunked down on the burgundy velvet chaise that ran the length of the window, pulling my knees tight to my chest. I stared out the window, this time past that Tower. I was worried. I'd always preached to Sage and my cynical friends about the importance of dreams, about how they reveal bits and pieces of the truth, shadows of feelings we all try to bury.

While Sage showered that morning, singing Johnny Cash's "Walk the Line," tone deaf as ever, I found a stack of hotel stationery in the precious little antique desk and scribbled away. Every detail of the dream I could remember.

"Quinn, it was a goddamned dream. Relax," Kayla says, and takes a sip of her coffee. "All of a sudden you're a believer? You think psychic powers are tingled during REM?"

I shrug.

"Look, I'm sure this is all very normal. I hear everyone freaks out when they are getting married. Hell, I would break out in permanent hives. It would be very sexy," she says. "If your dream was prophetic, can I have one of the leftover grooms? Phelps, preferably?"

I laugh. "Sure, he's all yours."

But something in me still thinks: *No, he's all mine.*

"Good, I'm going to hold you to it," she says. And then she's quiet for a moment and sadness creeps over her perfectly lined eyes. "I thought I was your other half."

I smile.

Kayla looks at me now, searching my eyes. "What are you so scared of?"

And I hate her and love her for this question.

"Being trapped," I say. *In a career? In an office building? In a marriage?*

"Hence the sublimely symbolic handcuffs," she says, nodding. "You know, Q, people spend their lives trying to find the right person to trap them, to stand still with."

"You're right," I say, nodding. Because maybe she's right. Maybe there's a fine line between feeling trapped and feeling safe.

"So, the sex is still good?" Kayla says, killing our silence.

It's snowing outside now. I think of that little groundhog

and how good he has it. If he sees his shadow, if he senses bleak and uncertain times, he can just crawl back in that hole and wait for brighter days.

"Yes," I say, no doubt blushing. "Sex has never been an issue."

"Can't build a good marriage on a foundation of bad sex," Kayla says.

"Since you're the authority?"

She ignores this one. "Bet the sex in Paris was more unbelievable after he gave you that ring," she says. She'd be right at home at my gym's locker room.

"Well, yes it was as a matter of fact."

"Figures. Who knew? Diamonds and guilt bring out the little sex kitten in you," she says.

"Guess so," I say.

"So, what's the problem then?" Kayla asks, slurping the rest of her coffee. "Good sex, good ring. Good man who is pussy enough to quote Plato."

"K!"

And suddenly the dire fog has lifted and I'm no longer fixated on the alarm bells of a bomb threat and an unwelcome reverie. For a brief and delicious moment, we eat bagels and cookies and giggle like girls.

Until now, I haven't noticed the man next to us. He stops fumbling with his crumbling croissant and stares at us now, seemingly shocked by the candid and colorful exchange between two preppy lawyers cloaked in basic black.

Chapter 9

Can't beat the white stuff," Kayla says, sniffling.

A few months ago, this statement would've alarmed me. Kayla had a brief but intense fling with Cap'n C (her stealthy code name, not for Cap'n Crunch) when we started at the firm. Said it kept her going. I opted for coffee.

Tonight, it's snowing. Times Square, the rainbow mistress, is momentarily cloaked in innocent white. Kayla and I wind our way through clusters of tourists, dodging the usual rush hour behemoth. Normally at this hour, we're at our desks, hunkering down for a night of document review or due diligence, debating delivery options. But tonight, we're out early heading to our firm's Winter Party.

"Dad always said they ruined this place when they got rid of the strip clubs and Disney-ed it up," I say.

"Who knew Daddy O'Malley was a fan of the vintage peep show?" Kayla says, and smiles.

For a brief moment, the streets are charming. Hardly Main Street, U.S.A., but still. I take a calculated risk and share my thought with Kayla. "Snow is magic," I say.

She smiles. "Someone woke up on the right side of the bed this morning."

"You have a choice," I say, rubbing a few flakes between gloved fingers. "You can see this as a nuisance, curse the traffic, the soaked clothes, the ruined heels. Or you can see it as a reminder of nature amidst the man-made. Plus, everything looks good in white. Even this hell." Days ago, I was cursing that little groundhog for the prediction that this stuff would fall. Now it's bringing out the poet in me.

Kayla looks at me like I'm a Martian. "And while we're at it, a sign that maybe global warming ain't that bad, huh?"

It all depends on how you look at things, really, and I've decided to experiment with something new and foreign, decidedly less dangerous and less sexy than Cap'n C: optimism. Sage's drug of choice.

Everything in moderation, right?

After all, my life is hardly a sob story. I'm healthy. I'm financially secure. I have a man willing to put up with me for a lifetime.

So, tonight, the seedy haven is hot-cocoa-and-marshmallow innocent. The swarms of wide-eyed tourists wielding guidebooks and camcorders and fanny packs are welcome guests. Their infestation is a good sign. Mere months after disaster, the city is back. A concoction to drink in. Not a poison to avoid.

Tonight the flashing fluorescents are beautiful and dramatic, beacons of light and hope, casting an effervescent glow on the mosaic of faces. Not a sign of commercialism-gone-mad, epilepsy-waiting-to-happen.

Tonight the gigantic stock ticker is a reminder that here we are in the financial capital of the world. Not evidence of our obsession with the bottom line, the dollar. Or yen. Or euro.

Tonight the streaming headlines are bold symbols of truth and information. (This is Times Square, after all. Named after the best paper in the world.) Not clues that the world as we know it is beginning to crumble.

Tonight the American flags—flashing and flying—are emblems of unity, of patriotism, of national pride. No, the ubiquitous stars and stripes aren't bizarre tokens of a premature and permanent Independence Day, a proclamation that we're the best; not a red-white-and-blue screw-you to the other nations out there.

"If you ask me, this place right here," Kayla says, pointing around us, "*this* is why they hate us."

I don't have to ask her who this "they" is. Most people wouldn't dare say something like this to someone whose father that nebulous "they" so recently killed. But Kayla isn't most people. And, even in this moment, I love her for it. It's First-Amendment-all-the-way, no-censorship-crap with this girl.

Kayla and I wait on a corner for the light to change. A tall man in a long black coat carrying a vast black suitcase sneaks up behind us and mumbles something only a New Yorker could decode. "Louis Vuittons."

He opens the suitcase a crack and I see the telltale brown and tan logo. He's selling fakes.

"Very authentic," he says, his breath condensing in the night air.

"They're either authentic or they're not," Kayla mutters. She grabs my arm, but we've missed our light.

"No thank you," I say to the man, and he disappears. Kayla looks at me as if I've committed a crime by being polite to this man. "He's just trying to make a living."

"Ah, Project Optimism," Kayla says. "Guess NYPD has bigger fish to fry these days."

"Indeed."

"Now, *that* makes me optimistic. *Yum*," Kayla says, pointing to the tan Adonis on the corner wearing nothing but tighty-whities and a cowboy hat. The Naked Cowboy. He's become quite the cement celebrity.

"Selling sex in the snow," I say. "How precious."

"He's just trying to make a living," she says, and smiles.

Tonight, Kayla is an endearing girl trying to find herself, unwittingly airing insecurities about love and sexuality and life via constant cakey cynicism and *Sex and the City* chatter. Not a selfish debutante who dabbles in the law and who has been given unfair quantities of money and education and intelligence.

Tonight, we are two friends, bantering, laughing, strolling the streets, taking our city back. Not two overworked, overprivileged bottle blonds following the scent of free booze.

The streets swirl with bits and pieces of conversation, sirens, fading cologne, and roasting chestnuts. Trash cans overflow with crushed Starbucks cups and mangled umbrellas. A homeless man crouches on the pavement in front of a newsstand. I drop a twenty in his shoebox, and tell myself that he will use it to buy food or to find a job. Not to fund addiction. Just as I'm really beginning to enjoy this new view of things, I see a little figurine of the Twin Towers in the window of that newsstand. Written in black ink on a little index card: "Remember what was."

All of a sudden, I'm nauseous. About to faint. I sit down on the pavement, next to the homeless man. He moves his bag of soda cans to make room for me.

Kayla turns and sees me popping a squat by a bum and presumably thinks I'm just taking this exercise in optimism a bit too far. She grabs my hand and pulls me up.

"You okay?" she asks.

"Yes," I say, unsure if I mean it. I don't tell her about the little Towers. That she can make comments about 9/11 and hatred for the West and Dad liking porn, but that I see a little index card in the front of a bodega and I'm about to turn into a faucet.

"Maybe you need to eat more. You're looking kind of thin," she says, rolling a calculated compliment into her expression of concern. She stares deep into my eyes where tears begin to gather. But she knows me. Knows now's not the time. "Good thing there are calories in wine," she says with a smile.

We arrive at our destination, a vast midtown hotel. Young men wearing matching long black coats, maroon ties, and newsboy caps jog into the street and back again trying to hail cabs for a bulging line of bundled hotel guests. Frustration is plain on rosy red faces as traffic inches by, kicking up yellow slush in its slow-forming wake.

"Future actors of America," Kayla quips.

"One of them could be the next Brad," I say. Because this is true. Here, everyone has a dream, a talent, another self just below the surface. No one is just a bellhop or bartender.

The lobby carpet is deep purple and smells of stale smoke. I think of Paris. And Sage. And smile. Elevator music crackles over the sound system. Tired families with plastic bags from Niketown and Macy's congregate on couches. In the far corner, a baby cries. A very old man in a wheelchair sleeps and snores. He wears a navy sweatshirt that says "New York" across the front in silver italics.

"Maybe he needs the shirt to remind him where he is," Kayla says.

"Or maybe he likes this place and wanted a souvenir," I say.

"Could be, Optimissus," Kayla says, and links her arm in mine.

We ride to the hotel's top floor. In the corner of the elevator, a tall blond woman in a magenta coat chats with a woman in short red leather skirt and fishnet stockings. The blond woman has impossibly long nails, with painted stars and rhinestones on the tips. The women are vaguely familiar. It takes me a minute, but I realize that they are secretaries from our firm.

As the large silver doors part, we hear music and muffled voices.

Tonight, the Winter Party is a time-out from the grind, a chance to celebrate for celebration's sake. An all-personnel event, so everyone is here. We're one big firm family tonight; lawyers and secretaries, catering staff and maintenance workers. Tonight, with a few top-shelf cocktails, the sharp hierarchy will go blurry. No, the party's not a part of the executive committee's plot to cut a fat check and make us forget. About our often miserable jobs. Or the fact that we rarely see our own families. Or about what happened a few short months ago.

Typically, this annual attempt at blending Whalen personnel is defeated by one thing: wardrobe. Partners arrive in freshly dry-cleaned pinstripes. We associates stick to the prudent palate of safe and boring shades—grays and blacks and navies and tans. Tonight, the nonlawyers among us are bold as ever, and we have a rainbow of leather, a sprinkling of short skirts, stacked heels, and blue eye shadow. The color is a welcome change, a sign that not everyone is obsessed with conformity, with convention. Not a blatant attempt to catch the wandering eye of partner.

Kayla and I hand our things—our coats and scarves and bags—to a man with a mustache hostage in the small coat check station.

"Keep your BlackBerry," Kayla says, holding on to hers.

Dad's wine-fueled words of wisdom find me now: *Don't become one of them. A Berry Baby.*

"Not tonight," I say, and this baby abandons her Berry, stuffing it in the inside pocket of my coat, feeling wonderfully rebellious. Now the man smiles.

"Let's get you some pinot," Kayla mumbles.

Kayla links her arm in mine. *You know every man fantasizes about two girls*, she's said. *Even old saggy lawyers.*

Truth is, however lubricated one is at these events, awkwardness reigns. In the office, professionalism is the rule. Decorum disguises idiosyncrasies. When you add party dresses and alcohol to the mix, things get more interesting.

In the corner by the bar, a group of fifth-year litigation associates gather.

"Ahhh, the Little Gators," Kayla says. "Waiting to bite."

Each is dressed in a black pantsuit. These girls are always dressed in black pantsuits. Each balances a skinny flute of champagne in her right hand.

"Look at them," Kayla says. "Hovering and gossiping, their skinny asses in their matching little suits. I bet they're trying to get a good look, trying to estimate the wattage on your hand. They are the kind of chicks who are probably holding out for five carats, waiting for their prince investment banker to come along, so they can quit this bullshit. Those girls would give their pinky fingers to have a wedding announcement run in the *Times*," she says.

"Is that the way you look at Sage? My i-banking prince?" I ask.

"No, of course not, Quinn. Sage a prince? Hardly," Kayla says, and giggles.

At one point, I was hopeful that there would be no room for cattiness in the working world. But I learned. And fast. In this world, cattiness would only be more defined, and its perpetrators, only better dressed.

But tonight their faces are friendlier, the impasse between us silly, simply a matter of age and relative legal experience. The competition, the dirty looks, the sizing up—all natural, nothing more than good old Darwinian survival of the fittest.

I smile at them.

And, shocker: a chorus of smiles in return.

Nancy Finnerman raises her glass and walks over. She's a Boston native, quite preppy, and refreshingly kind. She lives alone in a brownstone apartment in the West Village and writes poetry in her spare time. I worked with her on a recent case. On September tenth, the night before everything happened, Nancy and I spent hours holed up in a conference room, cocooned in a sea of cardboard boxes, delirious, laughing, bingeing on Mexican food, rifling through mind-numbing financial reports and e-mails looking for the smoking gun we knew we'd never find.

How quickly things can change.

I got taken off the case. Replaced by someone who would be more focused. I haven't talked to her since.

"How are you?" she says softly, her voice condescension- and fakeness-free, putting a hand on my shoulder.

"Hanging in there," I say. And pause. "I'm getting married."

She smiles. "Good for you. That's incredible news."

Kayla returns and hands me an overflowing glass of pinot. "I made it a double," she says.

Nancy clinks my glass with her flute and excuses herself.

"My family money radar is going crazy," Kayla says. "Did you see those diamonds?"

"Nope, didn't notice."

"I want my friend back," Kayla says. "Seriously, the bling, the brownstone, the easy-breezy attitude. It's a no-brainer. She's a trust fund baby."

"Takes one to know one," I say.

Kayla smiles. "Cheers," she says, and clinks my glass. It's half full.

The ice sculpture is massive. It's shaped like a snowman and it must be five feet tall. It towers above us at the center of a long rectangular table dressed in cranberry silk. The table is covered in silver trays of miniature desserts; éclairs, cheesecake, individual soufflés in little white cups, and white chocolate–covered strawberries. Every time someone grabs something from the table, a waiter with a bow tie and a sandy-colored ponytail scurries by and replaces whatever has disappeared.

"That table," I say, as we watch the feeding frenzy, "is just like our firm."

"How so? Bad for the waistline and bad for the heart?" Kayla says. "Snow is magic. Law firm like a pastry table. What's up with you?"

Whenever an associate leaves—for another firm, to soul search, to start a business—he or she is almost instantaneously replaced. Offices are refilled, cases are restaffed.

Firm directories, updated. Associates, like party pastries, are fungible.

But tonight that's a good thing. That I am a number, a cog in the big corporate machine, means that I can focus on other things. Leave early on a random night to have dinner with Sage. Even quit if I feel like it. Tonight, the firm is a lovely and golden revolving door. Not a chosen hell, a fire pit a human being can endure for only a limited time.

I hear someone say: "They spent two hundred and fifty dollars per person this year." She's probably not that far off. Sure, they could've canceled this year's party and given the money to the victims of 9/11. Or the fight against AIDS. But instead they chose to spend it on *us*. To tell us they appreciate our work and devotion.

The bartender is a handsome bookend to a mundane day. He manages to look grungy in a tuxedo. Impressive. Kayla has noticed him too; we share the same taste in men. She wastes no time flirting. She grabs a pen from her purse and jots her cell phone number on a green cocktail napkin and hands it to him as he passes us our refills. His name tag tells us his name's Jake.

"Looks like you two are up to no good." The voice is deep and male. It's Fisher. He stands behind us, swinging an empty martini glass. Tonight, Fisher is an overgrown boy with a winning smile.

"Hi. Yeah, the party is fun," I say. I feel my cheeks redden. *The party is fun.* The sentence is beautifully simple in a kindergarten kind of way.

I watch, half horrified and half awestruck, as Kayla places her right hand on Fisher's shoulder and smiles. "Yeah, why not? You never know where you are going to meet someone these days. I prefer this to that online crap, you know? And I figure we young lawyers need to loosen up a bit. Agreed?"

Unbelievable. Tonight, her confidence is legendary, enviable. Tonight, she's a spicy footnote in a boring book. Not the predictable ending to a formulaic story.

"Agreed. Have we met? You cannot be in the litigation department. I'd surely remember such a spitfire," he says.

I'm mute.

"Kayla Waters," she says, setting her wine on the bar and extending a manicured hand. "Unfortunately for you two . . ." she says, pointing at Fisher and me, "I'm in the department that actually brings in the dough so we can afford events like this."

Fisher laughs. Not a cocktail party cackle, but a deep belly laugh. "Don't count us litigators out. They call me Bill for a reason."

Kayla has practiced mingling with powerful people since she was a little girl. Training for life as a Stepford Wife started early; her mom dressed her in party dresses and pigtails and made her carry around trays of egg salad sandwiches to her parents' guests who drank hot toddies and mint juleps on their Connecticut porch. I doubt Mrs. Waters envisioned her little girl as an attorney at a big firm, flirting with a high-wattage career and a middle-aged man.

"Nice talking to you. Have a terrific evening," Kayla says to Fisher, taking a delicate sip of wine, morphing back into the professional and polite associate she is by day. She walks away and leaves me standing with Fisher at the bar. I'm not moving at full speed; I think I'm still in shock.

Fisher looks up at me. I'm blocking the bar and I have nothing to say. He smiles, perhaps sensing my discomfort.

"Have a terrific evening," I say. A sad copy of the original.

"These events require a three-martini minimum," he says

under his breath, to no one in particular. And, I think: *This man is fun. The life of the party*.

I find Kayla on the other side of the dance floor talking with Cameron Stone, a corporate associate in our class. Cameron's a boys' boy, a frat guy all the way, a Porter-in-training despite his good build. He went to UVA for undergrad and law school, and you can tell. His side-parted blond hair and caramel-smooth Southern accent have helped him with the ladies. I'm confident that he has bedded most of the paralegals in the corporate department.

"Hey guys," I say.

"Hey girl," Cameron says, and smiles, his Southern accent strong between sips of whiskey. "We were just talking about you."

"Really?" I say, and look at Kayla. She smiles and shrugs her shoulders.

"I was just lamenting the fact that you're off the market," he says. "I guess congratulations are in order."

"Yes, it's a sad time for the male species," Kayla says, looping her arm through Cameron's.

The music is loud. Carlisla, the quiet lady who works the graveyard shift at the document center, is in the middle of the dance floor, really getting down. She is wearing a short red crushed velvet dress that's very tight. As she shimmies to the music, she grabs the bottom of her dress and slides it up and down her thighs. She sings along to Chubby Checker.

We laugh. Good for her.

"Look at her go. Now that is impressive," I say.

The crowd roars. Bill Frank, a real estate partner, now dances with Carlisla. He is easily two feet taller than she is. And not a very good dancer. Apparently, very limber though. He bends backwards, places his hands on the floor as if to do a back walkover, and then he thrusts his body up again. Beads of sweat line his forehead. Carlisla seems to love the attention. She grabs his waist and grinds up against his bony thigh.

"What do you say we give 'em a run for their money," Cameron says, and takes my hand.

"I don't dance," I say, trying to pull my hand from his. "Not a talent I have." I think of telling him how Sage calls me Jitterbug, but decide against it.

Cameron brings my hand up to look at my ring.

"Not too shabby," he says, smiling.

He lets go.

So the party's a success, a success in the most contrived and plotted way possible, but still. There they are: a forty-something partner—Wonder bread white—who probably commutes from Bedford in his Mercedes SUV, and a single mom of three (I'm guessing here, probably not so PC)—of the whole-grain variety—who probably makes only a bit more than minimum wage. They dance together, not a care in the world, against a backdrop of American flags and spirited colleagues. The picture is both superficial and lovely. It would make for a very good picture in a firm brochure if such a thing existed.

It's getting late. I look around.

The party is winding down. The bartender has run out of Ketel One. The glorious snowman is melting.

For a moment, smiles outnumber frowns. Everyone appears happy. In my own haze, genuine optimism finds me and I smile.

I think of those little Towers, that little reminder in a random store window. I think of Sage at home in our bed, cuddling our cat, falling asleep to *Conan*. I smile. A real smile.

Everything will be okay.

"Let's jet," Kayla says, grabbing my arm, spilling wine. "The after party is at Swank. It should be decent. I hear they are going to open a tab."

"I read somewhere that partying with colleagues helps the career. I like the theory," Cameron says, draining his whiskey. "That and the one that says red wine is good for the heart." He pounds on the wrong side of his chest.

And here I am laughing hard and drinking harder. Enjoying life. Like I should. And even as I stand here, smiling, flirting, I'm proud of myself for moving on. Because that's what I'm doing; moving on, relishing the precarious and precious present moment. And maybe it's the wine, but for the first time since everything happened, I can picture Dad, his vast and goofy smile, his yellow teeth. He always liked a good party. Never turned down an opportunity for just one more drink and a little Irish debauchery.

Tonight the image of Dad doesn't make me cry, but smile. Tonight it fuels me, emboldens me. Because he's not gone completely. Never will be.

And the thought is cheesy and trite and all of those things, but I feel it now: Dad's part of me, part of this reluctant Berry Baby. I have his pale skin and stubbornness and love of late nights. I have his eyes and his irreverence.

I'm my father's daughter.

"So, a few more drinks tonight might get me something more than a hangover?" I say, smiling.

"If you're lucky, girl," Cameron says, lingering on his last word, "grrrrrlllllll," looking into my eyes and staying there for a moment, wordlessly luring me into a staring contest I quickly lose.

Chapter 10

We're among the last to leave. Abandoning subtlety, hotel employees in ill-fitting maroon tuxes herd us through the vast ballroom doors and tell us to have a good evening even though evening is long gone. Before those big doors slam shut, I see the lights snap on; people buzzing like bees, collapsing tables, stacking chairs, vacuuming carpet, getting ready for the next gala for disgruntled strangers.

A man starts hacking away at that ice sculpture, decapitating the cocktail hour's robust snowman into flimsy chips and water. Easier to discard.

The coat check man waits for us, tonight's variety of privileged stragglers that lengthen his nights. He hangs over his stable door, staring us down with bloodshot eyes, fingering his overgrown mustache. He stands as we get close and I hand him twin plastic tags—mine and Kayla's—and in return he shoves a pile of black cashmere at me, leaving me hugging what seem to be our coats. I spot Hula hairs on one and hand Kayla the other and float two crumpled dollar bills into his little wicker basket, which is about as empty as this man's eyes.

"Thank you," I say. He looks at me, presumably another fungible face in the night's endless string of lawyers, tugs one end of that mustache, but doesn't respond. He removes the bills from the basket and smooths them out one by one, folds them down the center, and places them in his front pocket.

"Get a fucking razor," Kayla mumbles as we walk away. "This isn't the seventies."

We pack onto a waiting elevator, ignoring the conspicuous fire marshal's warning of a maximum capacity we vastly exceed. Bumping bodies, accidentally brushing fingers, we descend one floor at a time.

A centipede of lawyerly black, a parade of pinstripes, we troop through the lobby, quiet now but for saccharine swells of smooth jazz and empty but for clusters of boozed-up tourists and a single homeless man in the corner who tries to escape notice and stay warm.

We leave through the doors we entered hours before. Under the hotel's soiled and wind-whipped canopy, I wait with other associates of assorted shapes and sizes and one-size-fits-all drunkenness for a legion of preordered Town Cars to pull up, funeral-style, to take us somewhere where we can continue our collective binge.

"This Swank place is supposed to be *the* hot spot," Kayla says, her words muffled by a massive black scarf that hides all but her eyes. She links her arm with Jeff Brice's, a corporate associate, fellow Greenwich kid, and friend of Cameron's. "Who knew meatpacking would become the mecca of cool?"

"Meatpacking. God, it just sounds so gay. *Meat. Packing*," Jeff says, lighting a cigarette.

"They used to pack meat there," Kayla says.

"I'm pretty sure they still do," Jeff says, guffaws, and strokes his balding head.

"How's the Propecia treating you?" Cameron asks, and laughs, stroking his hand through his own thick hair.

"Fuck off, Stone," Jeff says, smiles, and takes a drag.

"Hot spot, K?" I say. "Maybe if we're really lucky we'll spot some celebrity slipping in a pool of her own vomit."

"Or forgetting to tip the waitress," Kayla says.

"Or having a dance-off with another celebrity," Cameron says, no doubt referring to a fallen pop princess and her estranged soul mate.

"Ahh, someone likes the gossip mags. And I thought readership was limited to those without a Y chromosome."

Cameron's face reddens. "Sue me. I have a sister."

"Sure you do," I say.

"Meatpacker," Jeff says, flicking ash.

"This one's got a phobia," K says to Cameron, and points at me, and I wonder which one she's thinking of.

"Is that so?" he says, looking at me.

"I've got plenty of them," I say. "I'm a New Yorker."

"She doesn't like the subzero set, the nocturnal skinnies who prance around these places."

"Well, that makes two of us," Cameron says, looking me up and down. Thankfully, my coat, my cat hair–covered cashmere, hides my body. "We'll have to stick together then."

"Deal," I say.

"A little meat is a good thing," Cameron says, his Southern accent echoing with the howling wind.

"Meatpacker," Jeff mumbles.

"On the bones," Cameron says.

Kayla and Jeff walk away arm in arm and leave me talking with Cameron. I slide in the backseat with them, and before I can shut the door, Cameron grabs the door, holding it open.

"Want to be on top?" he says, ducking down and smiling. He holds his hand out. His breath condenses on the tinted car window.

"Get in the front seat," I say, and smile. "You're dirty when you're drunk."

The driver starts moving things from the passenger seat; a phone book, an empty bag of Cheez Doodles, a tattered blanket.

"And she's flirty when she's drunk," Kayla mumbles to Jeff, but I hear.

Cameron hasn't moved. He stays there, propping the door open, letting the cold wind slice through the backseat. The driver in the car behind ours honks the horn.

"Goddamn it, Stone, get in the fucking car," Jeff says.

Cameron forces himself into the backseat, sits on me, and slams the door as we pull away. "Have it your way," he says. "I've never objected to riding a pretty girl."

"*Dirty*," I say.

Cameron reeks of sweat and whiskey. He braces against the window so as not to crush me with his two-hundred-plus pounds. Under his weight, I feel warm, trapped, and secure. As the car shifts and turns, Cameron shifts his weight, rubbing up against me.

"You okay under there?" he asks.

"Yes," I say. "Thankfully, I've got some meat on my bones."

"Just the right amount if you ask me," he whispers.

"I didn't," I say, and hesitate. "But thank you."

I look over at Kayla. She fights the weight of her eyelids, barely keeping them open. "Whore," she says to me, and smiles.

"Yo, man. Will you pump up the radio?" Jeff hollers.

The driver—small, quiet, potentially Puerto Rican—turns and looks back at us. He squints his beady black eyes as if to say, *Who do you think you are?* Frankly, a very good question if he is in fact thinking it. But the man humors Jeff, turns a knob, and rap music pours from rear speakers.

"Thanks, man. You da bomb," Jeff says, and I wonder if that term of endearment is PC these days. "What's your name?"

"Don't be a punk, Brice," Cameron says. "He's a punk," he says in a whisper to me.

"Juan," the driver says. "My name is Juan."

"Juanny, man, nice to meet ya. We're celebrating a cool twenty-K," Jeff says. "How much do you pull in driving this boat around?"

"Brice, don't be a dick, man," Cameron says, flipping his cell phone open.

"But Cam, man, I *am* a dick, and my mama always told me to be myself," Jeff says, laughing, spraying vodka-drenched saliva, playing with his watch.

"This isn't the place, mama's boy," I say.

"What, O'Malley—the bonus means nothing to you now that you've found yourself an i-banking knight?" Jeff says.

"Something like that," I say.

"Knight, huh?" Cameron says. "That's tough competition for a measly little lawyer."

"Not so measly," I say, trying to revive my legs.

"Some of us," Jeff says, burps, and pinches his fingers together, "have these little things called loans."

"Cry me a fucking river, Mr. Rolex," Kayla pipes in.

"Why not just a regular river?" I ask.

"Because sometimes it's not just a river, but a *fucking river*," K explains.

"Got it," I say.

"My buddy from law school works at legal aid and he just got word that his loans are being forgiven. Hell, I need some forgiveness too."

"He's *helping* people who need it," I say.

"So are we," Jeff says. "So are we."

"Yeah. We help people," I say. "Rich men and some rich women. We help them get rich and stay rich. We help partners work their way to a second home in the Hamptons or the Vineyard. We help executives who've dabbled in insider trading, or set up offshore accounts, or defrauded shareholders."

"So much for Project Optimism," Kayla says.

Not too long ago, the executive committee, the team of rich and powerful, circulated a memorandum announcing our year-end bonuses. The announcement came three weeks later than it usually does because our firm had to wait and see what the "market" did. What that means is our firm waited to see what Cravath did. So, when Cravath decided to fatten first-year associate paychecks by a whopping twenty thousand dollars, our firm matched the number.

When I got that memo, I was happy too. Of course. Jeff's right; I don't have loans, but money is always a nice thing and I do feel that sense of satisfaction that in some way, in some small way, I'm being rewarded for my hard work even though I know all too well what we all should know: My bonus has nothing to do with the work I have done.

The snow has stopped. The streets have lost their temporary magic. The traffic isn't terrible, though, and with little Juan at the wheel, we zoom through the streets, weaving in and out of other late night traffic, speeding through lingering yellows and stopping short at the occasional and sudden red. We bounce around, the four of us, packed like sardines in the pine-smelling backseat of this car chartered for our convenience.

Cameron still fiddles with his phone, thumbing blue buttons that flicker like fireflies against the dark windows. Even as the car jerks and he readjusts his body weight on my numbing legs, his fingers remain still, in control, as he text messages someone.

"So, where's your girlfriend?" I hear myself ask.

"Which one?" he says.

Sirens slice through the rap music and an ambulance flies around the corner, nearly grazing the front of our car, which Juan manages to halt just in time, lurching all of us forward, and sending that little phone flying from Cameron's hands.

He reaches down to retrieve it from the dark slushiness by our feet. Feeling around, fishing for his phone, he brushes my leg with the back of his hand, and I hope that my stockings will somehow disguise the fact that I haven't shaved in weeks.

"Got it," he says, slowly coming up again. The car hits a pothole. "Shit. Lost it again."

I feel a hard object slide toward me on the seat, wet against my inner thigh, and then Cameron's big hand comes crawling for it. I feel as his hand settles around the small phone. His hand stays down there, on the edge of the leather seat, motionless for a second or two, in the dark. I don't move. The music pumps on, seems louder all of a sudden.

"I don't have a girlfriend," he whispers in my ear.

"Good."

And then I feel his fingers moving around, gently tracing the length of my thigh. Those fingers stop where they shouldn't. He rests his fingertips there, firmly, against me, that spot—warm, hidden to all, now moist.

Thankfully, there's a fortress of nylon when I need it; control top pantyhose all of a sudden takes on a new meaning.

I think he waits for me to slap him.

But I don't.

His fingers flutter, tapping me, one finger, now two, now one, and then stop.

Now I reach my own hand down there, to find his, to stop this. I grab his hand, large, warm, now still. He grabs my hand as if he's been waiting for it the whole time, patient bait. He holds my hand in his and then moves my fingers where his have been only seconds ago, pressing my own fingers there, firmly against myself, as if to prove something that's already been proven. He loosens his grip on my hand and then laces his fingers in mine, pulling both of our hands out from under my skirt. Before he lets go, he traces the outline of my diamond, slowly, carefully, and gives it a gentle tug, spinning it on my finger, so the stone faces in and not out. Then he closes my hand in a fist around it.

Cameron *Stone*.

Finally he pulls away, slush-slicked phone in hand, and mumbles, in words presumably clean to all but the two of us, "Did I get you wet? I'm sorry."

Chapter 11

I wake up in my own bed. Good sign.

Teeth chattering, covers to my nose, I fight a spotlight of sun. My head throbs. My thoughts jump between Sage and Cameron before landing with a thud on the control top pantyhose I'm still wearing, apparently the only thing I've slept in. Still damp. Full of runs.

Sage pulls the covers back, crouches at the end of the bed, and starts tugging at the toes of my stockings.

Snow has accumulated on the bars outside the window. Only in Manhattan would you shell out a million for prison bars on a bedroom window. All of a sudden the white stuff doesn't seem so pure and innocent. This morning, the frost is ominous.

"I'm frigid," I say. *Hardly.*

"I'm not surprised," Sage says, and laughs. His hair sticks up. "Sexy PJs, Bug, but they aren't going to keep you very toasty."

"Apparently not."

Did I get you wet? I'm sorry.

Cameron. His words come back to me now.

In one final yank, Sage separates me from my pantyhose and drops them to the floor. They land in a sad moist beige pile. Hula sniffs them.

"No undies?" Sage says, flashing a wicked grin. "Now we're talking."

I don't tell him that this isn't part of a special plan of morning seduction, but simply that hose and panties are redundant.

Sage nuzzles his nose between my legs. He gives me a sweet little peck down there, naughtiness at its most innocent, and I push him away. I push *him* away, the man with whom I've agreed to spend the rest of my life, and yet hours ago, I spread my legs in the backseat of a corporate car and let a relative stranger play me like a piano.

"What's wrong?" he says, staring up at me. I've never been one to turn away this kind of attention.

"I just *can't*," I say, running my finger along that deep red groove those dreadful hose have left around my waist.

I look at him, his pleading blue eyes, his straight nose and strong jaw. Mom says he has the bone structure of a Disney prince.

I don't deserve him.

"You're killing me, Bug," he says, smiling, fiddling with his boxers, reminding me of all those silly jocks in college and their blue balls conspiracy.

Mom taught me about blue balls myth. The night before I left for college. It was a footnote to her respect-your-own-body speech.

Dad's advice was not about sex—that was Mom's

territory—but tolerance. For an atheist, the man sure could preach. College—and then the real world—would be filled with different kinds of people, he said. *No kidding.* Different races, cultures, religions, socioeconomic brackets. *Yup.* I wouldn't always understand everyone I encountered, but I should respect them nonetheless. *Blah blah blah.* I nodded my head at the banal and very un-Dad-like words of wisdom he seemingly collected from some send-your-kid-to-college guidebook. He ended his homily on tolerance by becoming more like the dad I knew, by addressing the tolerance I'd in no time confront and repeatedly ignore.

Know your limits, Prue. Now, those limits might be quite high, he said, smiling. *You are an O'Malley after all. But a limit is still a limit,* he finished, forcing away that grin that wasn't appropriate for such a sober matter.

Amen, Father, I said, and that smile of his returned as he poured the three of us a glass of wine.

"Please, no references to death," I say to Sage, unconsciously pulling that good old bait and switch. And cry. Big, fat, salty tears.

He wipes my eyes, staining his fingers with last night's mascara, and kisses me on the forehead. He doesn't say anything. I know he thinks this must be about Dad. My father died mere months ago and I'm allowed to have my moments.

"You look like a raccoon," Sage says, presciently comparing me to that nocturnal creature known for being clever and mischievous.

"He hated raccoons," I say. Dad was an animal lover, but never fond of the little critters who ruined his camping trips.

"Well, they *are* mischievous little fucks," he says, and I laugh, because hearing him swear sounds so wrong and he's just described the woman he's due to marry: a mischievous little fuck.

I look at Sage, the genuine concern plain in his eyes, the blond stubble on his chin, his chapped lower lip. He smiles, trying to get me to do the same.

I cry a little harder.

"A very beautiful raccoon?" he adds, and hugs me tight as Hula chews my discarded hose.

We sit in silence and watch snow fall.

"He loved the snow though," I say. "We used to make snow angels in Central Park the weekends he wasn't on call. They were the only angels he believed in."

Dad was wary of religion. Said it caused more harm than good. When one of his patients miscarried, he'd never say things like *That was God's will.* No, he'd say, *Things happen.* He told me all about natural selection and survival of the fittest before any teacher did. The man had a way of explaining most occurrences in the context of the natural world. *We think we're above it,* he said. *But we're not. We're animals, in the business of surviving and dying.*

"Everything will be okay, Bug," Sage says, hurling that vague promise at me. He hops up from the bed. "You know what you need?"

Alcoholics Anonymous? A chastity belt?

"Bacon," he says, hopping off the bed, pulling on jeans. "Bacon can fix anything."

"What about Wilbur?" I say, and smile through new tears.

Sage smiles. "Even he'd approve this time."

Dad read me *Charlotte's Web* when I was six. One chapter

a night, on that old porch swing at Bird Lake. I immediately fell in love with Wilbur, that fat old pig awaiting his demise. And the little spider who saved him from his bacon fate.

But then I grew up to love bacon.

What about Wilbur? Dad would ask as I stuffed one strip after another into my mouth.

I'd shrug. No good answer for his good question.

But isn't this what happens? As children, we care deeply about a fictional pig. As children, we dream big, nurture great ideas; we practice musical instruments and collect things. We play the what-do-you-want-to-be-when-you-grow-up game, and no answer is too silly, or impractical, or indulgent.

Then we grow up. We spend spare time watching TV, dying our hair blond, working out. We become doctors and lawyers and bankers. We dream a bit smaller—hoping that nothing disastrous happens, that we'll be reasonably happy, that the stock market won't crash, that our country won't be attacked again.

"I'll run out and get some," Sage says. "Now, *this* is what the city's good for. A package of bacon thirty seconds away." But his optimism isn't so contagious this morning and I immediately think of the things we give up in exchange for convenience: grass, affordable housing, smiles from strangers.

Before he walks out our bedroom door, he turns and looks at me. "Okay, now you're a goth raccoon. You'd scare even a friendly spider away."

He leaves me, and I can't help but think of Dad, that rusty old swing, the little story he read to me in his gravelly voice between tears he probably thought I never noticed. Leave it to Dad to enlighten a six-year-old on the fundamental fact of lingering mortality. But when Dad talked of death, he talked of nature, of life cycles, of ecosystems. He said death was not bad or scary, just a fact of life.

I decide to clean up while Sage is fetching bacon. On the way to the bathroom, I trip over my heels. I look at myself in the mirror above the sink. My eyes are puffy, and corners crusty. My hair is a forest of knots.

I attack my teeth and gums with my electronic toothbrush and think of Dad and his anti-technology rants. The thing stops buzzing, but my tongue still tastes like wine.

I don't remember. I don't remember coming home.

I walk into the kitchen. Three empty beer bottles are lined up on the kitchen counter.

Did I drink those? I don't remember. I swirl my tongue around my mouth to see if I can locate the taste of Coors Light. It's unlikely that I drank these. I don't like beer. But the truth is I really don't know.

The last thing I remember is drinking wine and talking to Cameron. After that, it's blank. I feel sick.

Did Cameron drink the beers?

I imagine bringing him home to our apartment. I picture us drinking beer and canoodling while Sage sleeps in the next room.

I pace around our apartment trying to think of all the things I should do today:

Work out.

Pay bills.

Pick up dry cleaning.

Figure out whether I've cheated on my fiancé.

And all of a sudden, I'm in a shame spiral. I can't drive. My thighs are fat. I have a drinking problem. I am dishonest and self-serving. I am superficial and shallow. I am mean. I am

a fake. I am a fake blond. I am a cheater. I am a disappointment. I am a bad fiancée. A bad sister. A bad daughter. I will
no doubt make a horrible mother one day.

But then I have an idea. A great one.

Frantically, I throw open the kitchen cupboards and look
for it. And there it is, still in the box. My heart-shaped waffle
maker.

I pull it out and plug it in, squint to read the small print on
the back of the box. I pour waffle mix in and press down.

And wait.

It seems I wait too long.

The smoke alarm sounds as Sage walks in carrying two
brown grocery bags. He always chooses paper over plastic.

I don't deserve him.

He looks at me, fanning smoke that pours from his Valentine's gift, and laughs. He hops up on the kitchen island
and pulls the smoke alarm from the ceiling and removes the
batteries.

I look up at him. "I wanted to make you breakfast," I say.

He hops down, pulls a package of bacon from a grocery
bag, and kisses me on the forehead. "We both know that
making breakfast is better left to the expert."

The smell of smoke fades slowly and I stand in the kitchen
watching our little flat-screen while Sage cooks. Bacon crackles. Wolf Blitzer pontificates.

We spend the morning fighting each other for space on
our striped couch, that prudent love seat the perky chick
from Pottery Barn insisted wouldn't show spots, my head
on one end, his on the other, our legs intertwined under our
navy cashmere blanket, a big plate of crisp bacon and our cat
balanced between us.

Sage lets me watch silly television, weekend gossip roundups, and a *Saturday Night Live* rerun. As I begin to doze off, he turns the channel to some nature program.

"What time did you get home? I didn't hear you come in."

I don't have an answer for him. I fight back tears. "Late," I say, trying to be casual about it, awaiting further inquisition.

"My little party animal," he says, and tickles my foot.

"I think I drink too much," I say, crying, competing with a family of grizzlies for my fiancé's attention.

He looks at me and pauses. "I think you might be right."

"That's not what you're supposed to say," I bark, sitting up straight. He's been coached for these situations. "What about *Yes, Bug, you drink a lot but you're Irish?*"

"What about honesty?" he says. "What about telling it like it is instead of following a self-serving script?"

I am silent.

"She lost one of her cubs," he explains, pointing at the screen.

"Maybe she's an alcoholic," I say. "Ergo a delinquent mother."

"You slept in a pair of damp nylons and have a hangover, Bug. It's not the end of the world," he says, choosing his words clumsily or, perhaps, all-too-honestly, rubbing my back, watching those grizzlies bound through the woods.

"I just wish I had more control over things," I say. "I wish I could have done something."

"Things happen that are out of our control and all we can do is react," Sage says, sounding a little bit wise and a little like a fortune cookie.

"Thanks, Confucius," I say, and force a smile.

Things happen.

Things happen that are out of our control and all we can do is react. I think of Cameron's fumbling fingers. I think of Dad, his untimely last swallow of espresso. He loved espresso; the tiny cup, the no-nonsense unfluffy blackness. I look at the lost cub, a lone shaking blob of black amidst a sea of green.

Maybe Dad had it right all along. We're animals. Am I really any different than that scared little cub?

We're in the business of surviving and dying.

My phone rings. Sage hands it to me. "It's Kayla," he says.

Kayla. My brain does a U-turn.

"I'm not in the mood," I say, and let the phone ring.

In the kitchen, I check my voice mail. Kayla's message blares from my phone

"Quinn, my friend, um, just calling to see if my little bitch is alive and kicking this morning after last night. It seems like you were enjoying yourself with your new, um, friend. Call me. Need to know. Don't leave me hanging or I'll track you down. Love ya."

Sage stands there, in the door of the kitchen, looking at me. I'm pretty sure he heard the message. "Everything okay?"

"Nothing a few strips of bacon won't solve," I say, and force a smile.

He looks at me for a minute and then gets up and walks toward the kitchen. Hula follows. He stops and turns. "Get dressed."

I love being told what to do. Like a child. It's easier that way. It's not just men who crave instructions. We all do.

I don't ask any questions. I escape to the bedroom and pull on a pair of his plaid pajama bottoms and my boots, grab my coat and hat.

Outside, it's still snowing.

"We should shovel the sidewalk before someone sues us," I say.

Sage ignores me, takes my hand, and drags me down the block. Children with pink cheeks are laughing and crying, dragging sleds, throwing snowballs.

We stop at the corner and wait for the light to change. An older woman stands next to us, her graying blond hair peeking out from a knit cap. She looks at me and then Sage and smiles. Maybe strangers *do* smile. Even here.

When we get to the park, he drags me to a virgin patch of snow—pure, white, untouched—and he pushes me down to the ground. The snow, a soft pillow, catches us. He kisses me, his lips cold, his whiskers rough.

"It's a good day for angels," he says.

And here we are, two adults acting like kids. Tummies full of bacon, heads free of worry, we flop our arms and legs about in freshly fallen snow.

Chapter 12

It's Monday again. I can no longer deny there's a world out-side my door, a world that might house an answer or two I don't want to hear. I must shower and dress like a normal person, a person who's not suffering a cancerous breed of guilt.

This morning is business as usual. We juggle the carton of one-percent between our respective cereal bowls and coffee mugs, and trade newspapers after ten-minute intervals.

Out the window, across the street, schoolchildren wearing precariously low-riding pants wait for school to start. They gather in clusters, clutching greasy paper bags from the cor-ner deli.

Sitting here with my mate, swimming in international news and stock quotes while drinking fancy coffee, I feel painfully adult. I long for the days when I would trek down the street to school, eager to show the girls my new pair of cowboy boots, nervous for my algebra quiz, eager for my af-ternoon soccer game versus our biggest rival.

We don't speak much. But this can be very normal for us.

This morning, though, our silence is loaded. I am taking it all in and trying to wake up, to soak in the new day, the new beginning.

"I hate Mondays," I say.

"Everyone hates Mondays," Sage says, and sips his coffee.

Sage's phone rings, and it's his mother. He answers, goes into the bedroom, and shuts the door.

The thought of going to work makes my stomach turn. Most Monday mornings, as dreadful as they are in their capitalistic yuppie monotony, at least I know what to expect: streets crowded with people in the mild throes of low-level misery, people sleepwalking their way toward a corporate destination somewhere in the morass of midtown, loading themselves with enough caffeine to float them to Tuesday.

But today's different. I imagine the worst: whispers in the hallway, gossipy e-mails bouncing around the office like an invisible and deadly boomerang.

Gossip is fun. Really fun, sometimes. Okay, most of the time. But gossip is not fun when it's about you. It just isn't. Sure, it's a release from the plague of seriousness that has swept over us in the corporate, responsible world. *Gossip is rooted in ancient forms of storytelling*, Mom told me once when I caught her with *Star* magazine. I think it's even fine to talk about Britney Spears, even sink as low as engaging in the breast implant debate. It's all an innocuous breather from the stress of our wrinkling existences.

Before he leaves for work, Sage kisses me on the forehead. I'm still in my robe. "Have a good day, Bug. Say hello to Kayla and your *new, um, friend*." He looks me in the eye, searching for something I won't yet give him.

"I love you," I say, as if these three words, like bacon and snow angels, can patch a shredding moment.

* * *

When I walk into my office, I see a single rose floating in a plastic cup. A purple Post-it is stuck to my desk next to the cup.

"I had fun." That's all it says. The three words are hardly cryptic, but intriguing in their English-as-a-second-language simplicity.

I feel a hand on my shoulder.

Cameron. He towers over me, managing to look masculine in his wrinkle-free lavender button-down. For a moment, I'm living in my own little purple nightmare.

"Quinn. How are you?" he says, looking past me.

"Fine, you?" I say, and wish he would go away and come back in ten minutes so I could prep a little. Come up with a few witty one-liners, a clever way to figure out what happened between us. But he's not going anywhere.

Unfortunately, you cannot prepare for life like you can a deposition.

"Nice flower you've got there," he says. And just as I think I hear his voice crack and conclude that he's just as nervous as I am, he starts singing "Every Rose Has Its Thorn." And not quietly either.

"Gotta love Poison," I say.

"Gotta love red roses," he says.

"Guess I have you to thank, cowboy?"

"Not me," he says. "Guess you have more than one admirer. One smarter than me, what with the sub rosa Post-it. Genius. Did you know the Post-it was an accidental invention? And that guy is loaded. Beats this shit."

I study the handwriting on the Post-it. *Kayla*. Why would she do this? This isn't funny.

"Oh, I know who's behind this. She's perfectly insane," I say.

"Kayla?"

"Yeah. How did you know?" I ask.

"She came by my office this morning and was joking around with me about how obliterated we all were and how I was being a bad boy. She said that you were pretty shaken up and that I should come talk to you."

"So here you are."

"Here I am," he says.

Leave it to Kayla to meddle. Leave it to Kayla to orchestrate the postcoital "discussion," where we make only intermittent eye contact, where we hurl meaningless sentence fragments back and forth at each other waiting for it all to end.

"Don't worry. Nothing happened," he says.

"Good. The end of my night was, well, kind of fuzzy. When Kayla said that we left the bar together, I guess you could say I panicked . . ."

"Yeah, we did leave together. You wanted to go to Mc-Donald's. So we went across the street from the bar. You gobbled up a Happy Meal and drank my milk shake. It was very sexy," he says, chuckles, and runs his fingers through his blond hair. I'm pretty sure he blows it dry.

"Nuggets?" I ask.

He nods. He can't be making this stuff up because it sounds just like me. For some reason when I drink I crave my childhood favorites. Mom used to take Michael and me to McDonald's when Dad was on call.

Momentarily, I feel better about things. Nothing happened.

"So nothing happened?" I need for him to say it again.

"No. You went on and on about Sage, about how much you love him, how he is such a terrific guy, and how you think he will be a good dad someday. It was pretty inspiring, actually. Don't tell the guys I said any of this. I will lose my manly edge if they find out that I spent the night having a heart-to-heart with you, acting like your sorority sister listening to you sap it up. It would be very emasculating. There I was thinking you were having naughty thoughts about me and you jabbered on and on about another guy," Cameron says, smiling.

"I've never quite thought of my fiancé as another guy. Guess that's a good thing," I say. "I owe you a milk shake though."

"I'll hold you to that. And no regrets. There are worse things than spending a night in the company of a pretty girl," he says, and smiles. Flirtation was probably taught at his high school.

Cameron turns to leave. "Well, I better get going and get some work done. I'm hoping to escape for poker night with the guys."

"Better go then," I say.

Just as he's about to disappear, Cameron returns. "Oh, I forgot one thing that happened."

"Oh?"

"At McDonald's, you kept talking about some fishing boat and kept saying one thing."

"What's that?"

"That you miss him," Cameron says, and looks down. And no doubt assumes I was talking about Dad.

And maybe I was.

Chapter 13

S pring in Manhattan is like breasts in a sports bar;
longed for and bound to arrive—at some point. You
never know when, but if you wait long enough, it will
come. And it might not hang out, but sure enough it makes
its cameo.

Scarves hit storage. Smiles reappear. Bundled and sleepy
New Yorkers begin to buzz again, to trade in deep glasses
of cozy Merlot for oversweetened mojitos, puffy parkas for
blazers of suede, hot coffee for iced.

Another Monday. I walk to the gym and sense someone
behind me. I turn and see Avery. She sips water, smiles big,
and skips over to me.

"Time to get serious," she says and hugs me. "No one likes
a bride with fat arms."

"Good point," I say. And wonder how a human being can
be so damned chipper at this early hour, so infused with

optimism about life and commitment and, well, *everything*, even toning up flabby arms (which she doesn't even have).

We walk toward the gym. People are already sporting sandals.

"It's a bit early for toenails, don't you think?" I say. The toenails tell it all; who's on her game. Are they yellow and gnarly? An inch too long? Or polished with the season's most vibrant coral for their reveal?

Avery shrugs. "I don't know about that. I'm all for embracing the new season."

And she's right. It's a shiny new season. Restaurants set up outdoor dining, lining up rickety plastic tables and chairs and erecting precarious and soiled umbrellas. Ice cream trucks park on select street corners, ring with childhood bells, and remind us of warm weather delights we once had time to appreciate.

White snow disappears and yellow slush melts and cherry blossoms perk; a snapshot of nature amidst the ubiquitous man-made.

"I feel queasy," I say. "I never knew you could be hungover for two days."

And Avery, perfect and happy Avery, emits a string of judgment-free giggles.

Together, we walk into the gym, childhood friends, two brides on a mission.

The locker room is filled with new bodies. Everyone wants to be skinny by Memorial Day and they've pinned all their hopes on this place.

Avery affectionately squeezes my biceps, reminding me that my arms aren't Madonna-buff yet either, and disappears to her corner treadmill.

I take a few large swigs of my coffee, burnt but drinkable,

and scan the gym for Victor. I spot him by the Cybex machines and walk over. He loads weights onto the machine.

"Hi," I say, gulping coffee, begging the caffeine to start flowing through my floppy limbs.

Victor looks me up and down and doesn't do a very good job of concealing his disappointment. His glare speaks volumes; it's spring already and I've only lost two pounds.

"What?" I ask, hoping he goes easy on the honesty. He hands me a forty-pound barbell.

"Dead lifts," he says, ignoring my question.

"Why are they called dead lifts?" I say, lifting and lowering the weight to the ground.

"Because if you do them the wrong way, they'll kill you. But if you do them the right way, they'll *kill* you."

"Lovely. Seriously, why are they called dead lifts?"

"Someone took a curiosity pill," he says, resting his hand on my lower back. "If you really want to know, they're called that because you're squatting to pick something off the floor, a dead weight."

"I liked your first explanation better," I say, finishing my last rep.

"It's a very functional, practical lift. They say it prepares you for 'real life,' for picking up groceries, a laundry basket, a child."

"Screw practicality and *real life*, prepare me for my wedding day. I don't want muscles to scoop up a toddler. I want to look good."

"Do you really?" Victor asks.

"What the hell is that supposed to mean?"

"Nothing. It just seems like you're more a fan of the forklift these days."

"Cheers," I say. But he's right.

The gym is packed. Bodies have emerged from hiding. Winter flab is no longer kosher.

"This year's seventeen-minute members have arrived," Victor says, looking around at all the new faces. These creatures think a short spin on the stationary bike will make the swimsuit look better come summer.

"Sometimes I think life would be so much easier if I were delusional like that. Having a firm grip on reality is exhausting."

Victor laughs. "You are plenty delusional."

"What does that mean?"

He doesn't answer.

"Speaking of delusions, I had another dream."

Victor pulls a knot out of a rubber jump rope. His eyes light up. "A sequel? Do tell."

"Don't get too excited. You don't have a surprise role in this one," I say.

So, I tell him about the dream. We were back in Paris. Sage and I sat across from each other at a small table covered in white lace. We waited for more champagne. But the waiter wouldn't come. Finally, he came by but it wasn't the waiter. It was Phelps. He smiled big when he saw me. His teeth were whiter and straighter. Phelps studied me, then Sage, and then laughed a shrill laugh. He kept bringing new bottles of champagne and refilling the basket of croissants. Sage kept saying how efficient the service in France was. Each time I took a bite, my thighs tingled and expanded slightly. And each time I took a bite, Sage slumped down in his chair, appearing to shrink the littlest bit. Each glass of champagne had more bubbles than the last, and every time I took a sip, Sage's face grew blurry. His features softened. But I kept eating and drinking. Couldn't stop. Finally, I blinked and Sage was gone. The seat was empty and Phelps sat down. He said it was nice to see me. I told him I was engaged. He said he didn't see a ring. I looked down and my finger was bare. I panicked. Looked around. At the edge of the table, I saw the stone. It rolled away from me, off the table and onto the floor. And then I was under the table, feeling around in darkness, fumbling with carpet for my lonely diamond. There were four legs, not two. Phelps's legs were intertwined with another pair. I heard laughter above.

And then Phelps said to someone: "Always pay attention to dreams." I came out from under the table without my stone and found my seat. There was a girl on his lap now, facing him, ringlets of red snaking down her back. She cupped his broad jaw with her thin fingers. They kissed, but only for a minute, and then the girl turned around. It was Kayla. She was made up like a 1940s housewife with bright red lipstick and a candy cane smile. "We're engaged," she said, and held out her porcelain fingers. And there was the ring, my ring, nestled snugly on her finger. She shifted her weight and moved, lifting the shadow from Phelps's face. But it wasn't Phelps. It was Sage.

"That's an easy one," Victor says. Insinuating that, duh, I'm fat. Ergo, reveries about fat.

"What the hell is it with you today? Bad one-night stand this weekend?" I ask. Guys like Victor make me relieved I'm in a committed relationship. He sleeps with women as casually as I shop.

"Things with the ladies are just fine," he says. "Better than fine. You know that."

"What then?"

"It's just that . . . I'm not a miracle worker, Quinn."

"Miracle worker?"

"I can't wave a magic wand and poof—get you in the best shape of your life. You've got to work with me. Why do you think you are having panic dreams about expanding thighs?"

Oh, I'm fat.

"Fuck you. I'm sorry I canceled last week; I was at the office until almost 2 A.M. every night. Toning my biceps didn't seem quite as crucial as getting some sleep, and my mom is coming to town and his mother is coming too," I say, blaming the job like I always do, scattering excuses like seeds. He hands me the jump rope and I contemplate boycotting. "And don't you think that dream is about a bit more than thighs?"

Victor doesn't bite. "What about the diet? How's the diet been? I'm hoping those croissants are only in your dreams."

"The diet's fine."

"Do you want to look *fine* on your big day or *perfect*?"

"Let me sleep on that one," I say.

"What about carbs? Nothing is going to happen unless you reach a ketogenic state."

"I've been limiting them," I say.

"Drinks?"

"Sure. When?" I say, but he doesn't smile. "What about them?" I ask. Victor doesn't drink. I can't fathom how he swings these one-night stands when sober.

"You're not going to lose weight if you keep boozing," he says.

"You're not going to be a world-famous photographer if you keep spending your days training delusional and fat and spoiled souls like me. Souls who spew excuses and profanities. I haven't been drinking much anyway," I say.

"Well, you smell like alcohol this morning. Your body is sweating it out because it is *toxin*."

"I think *you're* the toxin," I say. "Maybe you should try that sometime—have a few, it'll loosen you up a bit. The ketogenic state is overrated."

"Protein is a better crutch than booze," he says.

"Last time I checked, I am paying you an arm and a leg to tone my arms and my legs, not lecture me on my extracurriculars," I say.

Victor punishes me; I lift impossibly heavy dumbbells, but still he stands behind me while my shoulders begin to quake on my last few reps. I run suicides down the slender walkways between treadmills. I sweat in embarrassing places.

After a long and uncharacteristic silence, Victor stuns me with a simple question. "Are you happy, Quinn?"

I don't answer him. Because I'm not sure I know the answer to this one. Maybe happy people don't drink every night and let colleagues seduce them. Maybe happy people don't pay muscled strangers to listen to their problems. Maybe happy people don't begrudge mothers who pick rings and send flowers and love their sons.

"Are *you* happy?" I ask.

He looks at me, sarcasm and pride missing from his eyes. I wonder how often he's asked this question, this scary and simple question, no one who is honest really knows how to answer.

"As a clam," he says, nodding, looking away. "Happy as a clam."

Silence.

"Why do people think clams are happy?" I ask. "Because they're always smiling?"

"No, that's not it."

"Does Mr. Trivia have an explanation for that phrase?

How do we know if clams are happy? It's hard enough to tell if people are."

Victor's eyes light up because he knows this one. He's a trivia guy. Which to me has always been a sad sign. What is trivia but a distraction from what matters? Who appears on *Jeopardy!*? Middle-class folks who focus on random tidbits, study useless information to distract themselves from pre-dictable lives, the mortgage payments, the birthday parties, the sexless marriage, the thinning hair. Or maybe trivia is an antidote for those who feel insecure about their intelligence. They stock up on trivia as a defense, as ammunition. Sure their grammar might be shaky, their spelling atrocious, their common sense off-kilter, but *they* know how many yards there are in a mile, how many species of bats there are in North America.

"The real expression is *happy as a clam at high tide*," Victor explains. "Clam digging must be done at low tide. At high tide, clams are relatively safe from hunters and able to feed because they are covered in water."

"I guess you could just say everyone's telling me it's finally high tide, but I'm still scared," I say.

He nods and smiles and stretches my left hamstring.

"Well, if this dream thing turns out to be a trilogy, I'll be very disappointed if I don't reappear. I could wear some colorful Lycra and show off these goods," he says, stroking his abs and chest. "I'd be the superhero trainer who saves those thighs of yours," he says, and laughs.

"Oh Victor, you already are."

He smiles, pinches my thigh. "That, my dear Prudence, remains to be seen."

Chapter 14

N ever set foot in a heart-shaped hot tub," Phelps said once. We were both nineteen and had just finished our freshman year of college. His hair was longer that summer, losing his mother's blondness and gaining his father's curls. His skin neared that caramel brown of summer. My guess was he had grown at least an inch or two over the past year.

"What is *that* supposed to mean?" I asked. "Who was talking about hot tubs anyway?"

Our parents sat only a few feet away, conversing in hushed, civilized tones. They sipped martinis. Dad said something about his martini being "dirty," and Mom and the others laughed.

"No one was talking about hot tubs, Quinn. That's not the point." Phelps sipped his Bud Light slowly and dramatically, concentrating on each drop, as if it were potential poison. Our parents decided that this summer it would be okay if we drank. If it was okay for kids our age to fight in combat, then certainly it was okay for us to have a beer or two, they reasoned. A logical thought indeed.

My parents knew I drank. I'd spent a year at college and they weren't clueless. But condoned public drinking was another thing. The funny thing is that Phelps's parents were Lake Forest WASPs through and through; no one doubted that alcohol flowed like water in that household and that little Phelps had been drinking for some time now.

But appearances were big.

"Why the non sequitur warning then?" I asked. Phelps and I had been talking about college, the ubiquity of marijuana and Ecstasy on our respective campuses, whether each of us would go Greek, our potential majors. What we didn't talk about: the dance-floor kisses, the hookups and crushes. This was our rule. It wasn't prudent to put life on hold, especially during our formative college years. But when we were together, we were *together*.

Only a nineteen-year-old would think this could work.

"Non sequitur? Good to see you're getting some mileage out of those SAT words," Phelps joked. "The *point* is that predictability is a plague."

"Huh? Now you have lost me," I said. Phelps's eyes glinted with the setting sun. Birds chirped lethargically. Bullfrogs gulped.

"All I mean is that . . ." He paused, took a big, bold swig of his beer. "We have to make sure not to become one of them."

"One of *them*?" I said, motioning to our parents, creatures who guffawed with practiced laughter, legs politely crossed, swirling colorless drinks with pinky fingers.

"No, Quinn. *One of them*. Part of the crowd. The cliché. What's expected of us."

"What is *expected* of us?"

"No, what's expected of *us*." Phelps said, motioning his beer-less hand between us, quietly like a secret.

I nodded.

"Why do you think they drink like that?" Phelps said. And then he did something he often did. He answered his own question. "They drink because they're bored. Booze adds spice."

I nodded again.

"There's nothing wrong with it," he said. "It's simply adaptive behavior. Darwin's ideas in action."

And I didn't realize it then because I was young and blinded by his undeniable glow, but Phelps had a pathological fear of boredom. It manifested in a spoken reverence for paths dark and difficult. He had a taste for rebellion, for originality. He was determined to dodge the clichés that litter life's path. But the irony (and I'm never sure how to use that word) was that in his steadfast efforts to avoid predictability and prudence, that's what his life would become: predictable and prudent. And that's who *he* would become: a hardworking doctor, a predictable and prudent soul.

"Did college transform you into an intellectual big shot?" I asked. "Maybe you should contemplate the philosophy track too."

Phelps shook his head. "I'm not going to spend my days digesting the pretentious musings of bearded men whom history has arbitrarily chosen to revere."

"History hasn't chosen anything. *People* have chosen. People like us. And history can't choose anything unless you are speaking of the poetic device metonymy."

"Poetry, Quinn?" he said disapprovingly, dragging out the simple word, enunciating each of the three syllables. "Po-et-ry?"

"Yes, Phelps. Poetry."

"Why bother? Life is about more than iambic pentameter and rhyme. There are plenty of disciplines that actually have some consequence, some practical consequence, but poetry isn't one of them. It's an indulgence."

The vast majority of our conversations were like this one: undeniably intelligent, unabashedly indulgent, both predictable and youthfully profound. A competitive, passionate pulse throbbed beneath these exchanges, one that would unite us at the time and divide us down the line.

"Poetry is art," I corrected him. "It's daring. To capture everything—and nothing—in a few chosen words."

"Impossible," Phelps said, drinking his beer.

"Exactly," I said.

Our conversations were everything we were: smart, pretentious, smacking of privilege and naïveté. Full of a shared and practiced cynicism only college could polish. Full of fancy words we used for the most part correctly. Full of nascent confidence and inchoate insecurity.

But if you listened closely to our words, the ebbs and flows of our own brand of flirtation, if you took the time to trace the flimsy contours of our banter, you'd realize that every conversation we had was really the same. Over and over, we talked, debated, dreamed aloud and together, about one thing, one impossibly nebulous thing: who it is we'd become.

Because for the most part, we knew who we were up until that point. Or we were foolish enough to think we did anyway. We were two kids. Good kids. Smart kids. Kids who liked learning and fishing. Who loved each other. Because love each other, we did. I've come to doubt many things, arguably everything, but this I've never doubted.

I loved him for his smile, for his abundance of confidence, for his arrogant displays of control. I loved the way he took something complicated—like fishing, art, love—and rendered it in simple strokes. Fishing was sport. Something to be good at. Art was beauty, impracticality. Love, according to his gospel, was what we had.

Some things defy articulation, Prue, he said. When shrouding me with his most lofty musings, he called me Prudence or one of its diminutives. *You can't capture it in words. And it's not worth trying.*

And at the time, this was nothing short of bliss. Of romance. But as time went by, I wanted him to try. I wanted the words even if they were clumsy or insufficient. I wanted him to attempt the impractical. Do the impossible.

But, alas, he was a fan of efficiency and prudence and possibility. It never shocked me when he declared ambitions to be a doctor. To leave a stamp. To make a mark on this world.

And, at the time, this was heroic and responsible and lovely. I imagined the sandy-haired boy in a white coat with all the trimmings. I imagined him gripping hands of sick people, sharing that winning smile with those who were losing life.

When I thought about the future, my future, he was in it. His white coat flung on an armchair by the door. His stories of pain and perseverance relayed over home-cooked meals like the ones I'd relished growing up.

Phelps and I spent many long, languid, wine-soaked nights, talking about my future. When I mentioned going to law school, his eyes lit up as if I had uttered something deeply genius and not utterly predictable. I reminded him that many people, too many people, went to law school because of concurrent uncertainty and desire to achieve paradigmatic success.

But he swatted my doubts away like mosquitoes and told me there was nothing wrong with success. That success is what makes the world go around. That people like us were bred to be successful and there was nothing wrong with that. And as he said these things, I nodded. In part because he had an intense and intangible power over me and I believed him. In part, because I wanted to believe him. But even then I knew that this man, this smart-thinking, success-bound man, was worlds different from the boy on that old porch swing.

But I chose to believe him. And that deep in this ambitious creature lingered the dreams of youth. And I went to law school.

"It's just too easy," he said, seeming to enjoy his newfound cryptic aura.

"What?"

"Doing what our parents want. We go to school, we get good grades. We send our grandparents birthday cards. Being good kids. It's just too easy."

His words were laced with fear. Fear that our parents had blueprints for how they wanted us to turn out and that it was up to us to fight this, to be ourselves.

"What's so wrong with being good, Phelps?" I asked.

"Nothing is *wrong* with being good. But being good can be boring. Before we know it, we'll be engaged, get married, honeymoon in small town, U.S.A., make love in a heart-shaped hot tub infested with germs of mediocrity, wake up with three blond-haired kids who eat only Cheetos and Wonder bread, and have a lease on a minivan."

At the time, I nodded, swallowing his musings whole. If

only I could go back and say: *Chances are we will get married, honeymoon in Asia, and make love in a private plunge pool infested with germs of privilege, wake up with three blond-haired kids who eat only edamame and soy crisps, and have his and hers Range Rovers.*

"*We* will be engaged?" I asked. My heart danced, a rookie ballerina, bouncing softly, uncertainly.

"No, Quinn. Don't be silly. We *will* be *engaged*, though. Both of us. In a matter of years. And our mothers will phone each other up to talk about centerpieces and ceremony music. About whether to serve mint juleps with the lemonade during the procession."

"Oh."

Phelps finished his beer in one proud gulp as if it would make him seem more of a man. Mine was still halfway full.

"Well, my kids aren't necessarily going to have blond hair. And who knows if I will even give them Cheetos or Wonder bread. Did you have a bad experience with a heart-shaped tub, Phelps? You're being weird." It was a soggy comeback, but honest.

"No." He smiled and took a swig of his beer that was already empty and blushed.

"Spill it."

"Spill *it*?" he said, shaking the empty bottle.

"*Spill* it. Where is all of this ridiculous hypothesizing coming from?"

"Okay, okay . . ." he said. On the lake a mother loon swam, her five babies trailing behind.

"Yes?"

"Okay, I admit it. I heard my parents talking on the ride here. They were talking about the heart-shaped tub in their hotel room when they went on a road trip in college."

"You're hijacking your parents' stories, buddy?"

"Shut up, Quinn," he said, embarrassment plain on his tanned face. "I'm going to get another," he said, holding the beer bottle in front of me. I looked down the nose of mine, into the bottomless amber darkness. I still had some left. "Want one?"

"Sure," I said. In retrospect, not because I wanted more beer. But because I didn't know what it was I wanted. Because when life gets quiet or uncertain or loaded with that dampness before truth, there was always something to fill it in. Because we can always sip instead of think.

Before he left to find beers, Phelps looked at me, studied me, looped a strand of hair around my ear, and asked me a question he'd come to ask me many times, too many times: "Am I boring you?"

At this, I smiled sweetly, and said something that was true at the time. "You couldn't bore me if you tried."

"Am I fat?"

It's not even eight in the morning.

"No," Sage answers. He races around our apartment, coffee cup in tow, cleaning up clutter. Both of our mothers arrive in a few days. Typically, I get more than this, more than the one-word response that he must utter as a man who wants to survive.

"Victor thinks I'm fat."

"Of course he does," Sage says, flipping through a thick stack of bills we haven't paid.

"What do you mean by that?"

"Well, if you start realizing that you're in good shape, that you are far from fat, you just might not need him anymore. And that wouldn't be good for little Victor's bank account."

"He's not little, Sage. And why does everything have to be about money to you? Not everyone's a banker, all hot and bothered by the bottom line. Some people care about other things, like helping people for instance," I say.

"Like my super-charitable wife-to-be who spends hundreds of dollars a week sculpting her figure when she could donate it to some worthy cause?" Sage's eyes wander to Katie Couric, who gesticulates wildly while talking to George Clooney about his ever-baffling bachelor status.

"What? Katie deserves your undivided attention, but not your future wife?"

Sage is quiet. He runs his fingers through his hair. It's gotten a bit long. "Yes, actually. She actually talks about *things*; it isn't all about her. Self-obsession gets stale."

"It's Katie's *job* to talk about things. She has a freaking script and now I'm the self-obsessed one? And I hate to break it to you, but Ms. Couric has a *team* of Victors. How do you think she gets those legs that apparently hypnotize you?"

Sage doesn't take the bait. He continues his efforts to bring order to our chaos.

"Too bad Katie's too old for you. Though you never know these days. She'd probably love your new surfer dude coiffure," I say, running my fingers through his hair. "And a little Botox here, Restylane there, and she could pass for thirty."

"Isn't that fascinating?"

Hula curls up on top of the pile of mail, frustrating Sage's sorting efforts. He purrs, apparently oblivious to the brewing storm in his midst.

"If you spent half the time you spend with Victor learning to drive you could get a license like the rest of us human beings. You're *twenty-seven*. You have a law degree, a mortgage, we're *getting married*, but no license."

"Barbara Walters doesn't drive. And no one's knocking her. And she's doing just fine, isn't she?" I say. "Why is it always the driver's license, Sage?"

He doesn't understand that New Yorkers don't drive, don't need to drive. When I hit the landmark age of twenty-one, I began carrying my big navy passport to bars.

"It's just symbolic. I love you, Bug. But you're in so many ways a child, refusing to grow up. My own little Peter Pan." Suddenly, he flashes a bright and conciliatory smile.

"*Petra* Pan," I say. "As if that's a crime."

I'm quiet. I don't have the energy to argue with him.

The silence stretches on and I fill it in with those three words we say when we're scared of silence. "I love you."

"I love you," he says back.

Suddenly, these words seem strange. Suddenly, it seems as if we are reciting lines from a script, a predictable script. And maybe we are.

"I know you think it's boring, but one of these days, we're going to have to grow up, start paying these bills . . ." he says, waving them about, "and stop drinking like nineteen-year-olds. After a certain age, it's not cute to be irresponsible."

Sage has cleverly substituted the royal "we" for "you," but I can see through it; this is about me.

"You used to love that I drink like a college girl," I say. "Here I've been convinced that it was one of my most alluring features."

I laugh, but find no echo.

"You're right," I say, and he is. Time to grow up. "But it all strikes me as boring. Responsibility can be boring."

As I say these words, I think of Phelps. Of course I do. Because they are his words. Practically his mantra.

"Is that the rumor these days?" Sage stops what he's doing

and looks at me. "Are you getting bored with me like you did with him?"

"No," I say, a bit too quickly. "Of course not." I grab the bills out of his hand, place them on the counter, and hug him.

"You know something?" I say. "*He* liked that I drank."

"Or maybe *he* didn't care," he says. "Maybe he was afraid of what would happen if you dried things out. Of what you might say and learn and become. *I'm* not scared."

And these words, these simple words, slice me. Because they might just be true.

"Marriage will no doubt transform me," I say, nodding. To him. To myself. But even as I utter these words, I know they are weak. Marriage doesn't transform people. It just brings them together and they transform each other. Or try to. I know that in life there's no silver bullet. There's no happily-ever-after. Evolution does not occur with a simple exchange of saccharine vows. But still. Sometimes I want to believe that marriage will change me.

Sage looks at me, eyebrows arched, skepticism clear in tired eyes.

I nod. "Once your wife, I will all of a sudden drink like a twenty-one-year-old."

As Sage smiles, those eyes, those bright eyes, glaze over with amusement and defeat.

And it hits me. Here I am. In the tub. Caught in a passing storm of predictability. Living in a world of clichéd confections: of bankers and lawyers, of diets and trainers, of Eiffel Towers and dark chocolate truffles and champagne, of bickering and boredom, of paying bills and missing an ex. Of meaningful silences peppered with platitudes and profanities and clumsy jokes.

Chapter 15

There is something about mothers. Whether your own or someone else's, whether Northern or Southern, liberal or conservative, they spill bits of wisdom as they walk. They just know better. Depending on the day, this can be infuriating or enlightening.

Our mothers are both in town. Today, Sage and I will each spend the day with our own mother. Tonight, we will all come together for dinner. And hope for the best.

"You can't hide behind that mountain of mascara," Mom says, gripping her glass of sangria with both hands, studying my eyes. "At least not from me."

I've never been comfortable with Mom's stare. *Toughen up. Grow a thick skin.* As a little girl, she hurled these clichés at me. To this day, the woman can still see right through me.

We sit in Cilantro, the small Mexican restaurant on my corner. The walls are deep red and the bar boasts an impressive array of tequilas. It's quiet at this hour. The bartender rests up for happy hour, leaning elbows on the bar he periodically wipes down to appear busy.

"Frida Kahlo, now *that* was a real woman. She didn't live by the rules; took life by the horns even though she had polio. Slept with men and women, was wined and dined by Picasso, a fan of good tequila and raunchy jokes," Mom says, speaking as if she knew this woman, as if she was a friend from college. "You know she had an affair with Leon?"

Met with my blank stare, she clarifies. She means Leon Trotsky, the Communist leader. "She was even arrested for his murder."

"She had a *unibrow*, Mom," I say. What I don't say is that this is about all I know about this Frida Kahlo, that she failed to pluck in that important place. Oh, and that Salma Hayek played her in a recent movie.

"Yes, that was her trademark . . . her way of saying fuck you to conventions. And people thought she was *beautiful*." Growing up, my parents didn't swear in front of us. Only behind closed doors and only once in a while. Certainly, we weren't allowed to swear. Since Dad died, Mom has embraced profanity like a long-lost friend.

"So if I had a little less mascara and some renegade eyebrow hairs, you'd approve?"

Mom smiles, shrugs her shoulders, and takes a Frida-sized sip of sangria.

April's coming to a close already, but it's the first time I've seen her since Sage and I got engaged. It's just us girls—mother and daughter—catching up over chips and guacamole and a deliciously illicit pitcher of red sangria. I've decided this is well within the firm's nebulous definition of "personal day."

"I like my makeup, Mom. This is New York City, not Wisconsin. We do things a little differently here if you hadn't noticed, or don't you remember?" I say.

The makeup thing has always been one of Mom's biggest buttons to push. As a teenager, I layered on thick foundation when I was mad at her. I lined my eyes with harsh black smudges. Mom said she hated this because she said makeup hid the dusting of freckles on my nose that darkened each summer, *the spots that made me ME.*

Today, Mom's face is clean-scrubbed with hints of childhood freckles, faded and few, freckles I've inherited in unfair quantities. Her smooth skin belies her age; after almost six decades, it's milky white and very close to wrinkle-free, thanks to a daily regimen of SPF 30, well-placed umbrellas, and a collection of impossibly vast sunhats.

And she, like me, has two very distinct eyebrows.

I know very well that Mom isn't launching an intervention about my abuse of cosmetics, but I'm trying to put off her inevitable—and inevitably astute—analysis of me.

"Oh, don't I know. Even though we lived here for thirty-odd years, this place never ceases to amaze me. And I'm beginning to see you really belong here. I never really felt like your father and I fit here," she says, wiping her lips with a green paper napkin. A shred of napkin sticks to her upper lip, but I don't tell her. "But you . . . you and your brother are different. You're becoming quintessential New Yorkers, I daresay."

"Despite good intentions, Mom, you've produced a pair of New Yorkers," I say. "This probably could've been avoided by not giving birth to us here, or, say, raising us here. If you wanted us to be Midwesterners, you should've stayed put in Michigan."

Mom's right about one thing: She didn't fit here. As she would have it, she chose not to. She was never like the other private school mothers—coiffed creatures dripping in pastel cashmere and diamonds who wintered in Palm Beach and summered in the Hamptons, stick figures who'd mastered the affected cocktail party guffaw. I went to school well before the Botox-and-pocket-dog wave, but these women no doubt have both today. Mom wasn't the prototypical outsider though; she claimed to be more of an amused observer who never quite penetrated the inner circles of dinner parties and gossip and said she never wanted to. She nurtured strong opinions of the world of privilege in which she and Dad raised us, a world they at once shunned and embraced. The world they chose for us.

"Mom, I'm a New Yorker. It's not a crime."

"Point taken, counselor. I still cannot get over that ring of yours. It is gargantuan," she says, masterfully changing the subject, grabbing my hand for at least the third time to pull it closer to her. Her comment's not exactly a compliment.

"I know what you think of big rings," I say. "But don't blame the boy. His mother picked it. Same as hers. It's like she wants me to morph into a copy of her. You will witness tonight why that is a scary notion."

Mom nods and smiles.

"I bet Frida didn't even wear a ring," I say.

As she studies my ring, I study hers; a thin gold band and a small round diamond. It's beautiful. Even though I was a tomboy, I asked to try it on every once in a while. Each time, staring into that diamond, that diamond from Dad, I was mesmerized anew. Mom never wore the ring while teaching; presumably being the happy wife didn't jibe with her rants on feminist independence under the law. She would put it on each night, though, when she got home. Now that she's retired, now that he's gone, she wears it all the time.

"I don't even want to know what kind of money he spent on this, this, um, little bauble," she says, running her finger around her sweating glass and laughing. Her laugh—deep and gravelly, purely contagious—is a relief.

"Does he make you laugh?" she asks. "We get older, we can't help that, but we don't ever have to stop laughing."

"Do I seem laughter deprived to you?" I ask. *Am I laughter deprived?* I try to think of the last time I laughed so hard I couldn't catch my breath. I can't.

Mom has always preached about the power of timely humor. So many people, she's argued, glorify wisdom and accomplishment, financial integrity and social status, but that the real gem is humor. "So few people have it, I mean, really have it. The gift of funny, the ability to laugh loudly and deeply and make others follow suit," she said.

Well, Mom has it. That much is for sure. And sitting here, halfway through a pitcher of sangria and a basket of tortilla chips with this woman, my mother, a generation older and wiser and funnier, I hope that her humor, even a fragment of it, is tucked away in my genes.

"Mom, none of this is important. I should've known that you would come here and throw a feminist wrench in my happiness. And now this lesson on laughter? I should've known this wouldn't be easy."

"Easy's never good," she says.

"Is that necessarily true? Maybe good things are often simple."

Mom smiles. The sangria has stained her teeth. She's never had braces. "Life isn't a fairy tale, Prue."

"Sage bought me a beautiful ring and he wants to marry me. Can you believe someone wants to spend his *whole* life with your daughter, your crazy little Prudence?"

"I love it when you call yourself that, Prue. You threw your dad and me for a loop when you changed your name. Now I kind of understand it, but it hurt a little—as if you didn't want to keep the first gift we gave you, your name."

Frankly, I hadn't even realized that I called myself Prudence. I haven't referred to myself that way in ages, and usually it's when I'm at an airport handing over my passport. I've never legally changed my name, which always gave the parents a modicum of hope. I've chalked it up to laziness.

But now, sitting here with Mom, the woman who carried me in her belly, the woman who nurtured me through all my phases, I'm not so sure. Maybe I held on to my name for a reason. Maybe it's a name I will grow into one day, something I have just saved for later. Until I'm ready for it. And maybe this was all part of the plan. Maybe Phelps was right after all. Maybe parents have blueprints for us, for who we will become.

"Oh, Mom. I thought you'd gotten over the name thing," I say, knowing very well that she's never gotten over it. Parents don't get over these things.

"I know, I know. But you will always be Prudence to us, to me. And it's just that . . ." she says, looks down, and pauses. The calm before the storm. I know Mom.

"What?"

"You're getting married. Knowing you, you'll probably change your name. You'll be Quinn McIntyre. Born: Prudence O'Malley. Died: Quinn McIntyre. It makes me sad. It's like you are leaving us behind. Finally, leaving us behind." Her eyes are glossy with tears. She avoids my eyes.

"Knowing me? What does that mean? In case you don't remember, I'm the one who changed her name when I wasn't

supposed to. What makes you think I will change it when I *am* supposed to?"

"Your rebellions, Prue, they're so predictable. You spend so much time trying to be different, but . . ."

"Like mother, like daughter." I say. "Last time I checked we were both lawyers. And you're more of a housewife than I'll ever be. Don't go calling me the cliché."

Mom's silent. She pushes a glob of guacamole, now a faint brown, across her small plate.

"Plus, even if I do take his name *like you did when you married Dad*, you have to admit you love the name Quinn McIntyre. Mom, it couldn't sound more Irish. You are going to have freckly little grandkids one day."

"Who drink like fish," she says. Her laugh slices through tears that have begun to glide down her pale cheeks.

"Like Frida," I say.

Another moment saved.

I ask Mom if she wants more guac and she nods. The waiter, the little Mexican waiter with a postcard mustache, appears with the guacamole cart. Call it good service. Call it good old-fashioned eavesdropping. Mom and I watch as he grabs two avocados and swipes them into thin slivers with his big knife. Now, he slices the slivers the opposite way, rendering the avocados—once beautiful imperfect spheres—into tiny cubes.

Mom and I are transfixed. He drops the cubes into the little black pot, adds tomatoes and peppers, and begins smashing away, clobbering green with stunning aggression. I wonder if there's anything behind that energy. Maybe he is just good and quick—efficient. This man spends his afternoons smashing while I spend mine hunched over my desk on a veritable IV drip of Diet Mountain Dew trying to get an assignment done so I can get home and watch primetime TV on TiVo.

"Avocados—are they fruits or vegetables? I can never remember," I say.

"I say both," Mom says. "Why can't they be both? We humans are so hungry for labels, for order. We are so quick to categorize, to box things up."

"So maybe, just maybe, I can be both Prudence and Quinn?"

She doesn't answer this one, but I see it: a faint and fleeting smile.

"Pretty impressive. How quickly he does that," I say.

"Definitely. A real art. There are so many arts that go unnoticed in this world, so many that fly under the radar of the socially noticed and accepted. On the Food Network, the other day, there was this special on a man. I forget his name, but he was a latte designer. That's right; the man makes a living swirling milk and foam into designs. I think it's fascinating," Mom says.

"A latte artist? Now, that's crazy. But cooler than being an attorney," I say.

"Isn't everything *cooler* than being a lawyer?" Mom says. Her smile fades, a quiet departure from the sunny afternoon. Her face grows taut; she has something to say. Mom always looks older at moments like this when she contemplates something big.

"It's remarkable, Prue . . . you haven't changed a bit," Mom says, and downs the rest of her sangria. "You might have two decades on the little pigtailed brat at the dinner table, rolling her eyes in disgust at my trademark tuna casserole, but I can see it in those eyes of yours. Sure, now you wear more makeup. A little too much, if you ask me . . ."

"Yes, I got the memo, Mom."

"You know what I've always said about masks."

"They hide everything but the eyes," I say.

"Yes. Masks are for Halloween. Don't wear one now," she says. "Not with me."

Again, this isn't about makeup. Or masks. Or metaphors.

"You know that goddamned cliché—that some people wear their heart on their sleeve . . ." she says, "but, you, my girl, you wear it in your eyes."

She's told me this before. When I was a little girl, she and Dad worried about taking me in public because I would roll my eyes and make faces at everything—the punk teenager with the blue hair, the old lady in the wheelchair, the young woman with skin darker than mine.

After a long pause, she pours each of us another glass. "I was hoping that we could talk."

"Isn't that exactly what we are doing, Mom? Talking? I took a personal day so we could talk. I left my BlackBerry at home so we could talk. And here we are, talking."

"We lawyers are well-schooled in the art of bullshit. It comes so easy. The rub is that it's possible to go hours, even days, possibly a *lifetime*, without saying anything. I don't want that to happen to us. I don't want to talk about makeup or the art of chopping avocado. You're getting married. That's something we should talk about."

"You have something on your lip," I say.

Mom licks her lips. The speck of green disappears into her mouth.

"Something's off. I see it in those eyes of yours. Yes, you have a nice big ring on your finger and that might distract the rest of the world. They might miss the telltale gloss—of sadness, of fear? But not me. There's something going on in those eyes," she says.

"Nothing's wrong. Did you travel all the way here to try to shake things up, Mom?"

"Maybe, if that's what I need to do. I came because I love you . . . Prue, you're getting married. And I needed to *see* you. Is that so bad? You can't tell anything over the phone. Certainly, not over e-mail, the Devil's creation," Mom says.

"Well, here I am. Look at me all you want. Although it sounds like you don't like what you see. Too much makeup, an extravagant ring. I bet you think I'm wearing too much black, right?" I say.

I *am* wearing too much black, *all* black in fact.

A New Yorker indeed.

"Do you love him?" she asks.

"I do," I say. "That much I'm sure about."

She nods. "But you're not giddy."

"Am I supposed to be giddy, skipping on sidewalks like a chick in a hair commercial? Sorry to disappoint you. This is not the countdown to college. This is *marriage*. I'm not looking at freedom from the parental hold, ubiquitous booze and boys, tailgates. I'm looking at an institution no one seems to understand. I'm moving toward something society tells me to covet and crave, but a reality no one really shares. All we're told with certainty is that half of them end in divorce. Half of them end. Does it make sense to be giddy about something that fizzles or fails fifty percent of the time?" My heart is racing. I finish my sangria.

Mom looks at me. Smiles big. "No. No, it doesn't. But I just hope you have giddy moments. Moments when you smile because you have no choice. Not because a smile is expected or appropriate. I want you to have moments where the world, this gray world, is rainbow again."

"I want those moments too. But I'm overwhelmed. I'm scared. I have these doubts." I cry. As I wipe my eyes, eyeliner, my excessive dose of eyeliner, comes off onto my hands.

"Good," she says, crunching an ice cube. "Good."

"Good?"

"Yes, *finally* you're making some sense. I was beginning to fear that diamond had stripped you of your O'Malley reason."

"I love him. I do. I want to marry him. I do. It's just, I don't know, it feels different, *bigger* than everything else. Everything up to this point, Mom."

"It is."

"And . . . I had these dreams. They *got* me. They feel like warnings," I say.

So, I tell her about the dreams. I tell her everything I can remember—which is almost everything: the wedding in the courtroom, the tearful young me as flower girl, the multiple grooms, the faceless judge. I tell her about the swelling thighs and missing diamond, about Kayla and Phelps.

Mom listens. And through the fog of my furious retelling, I glimpse her face. She appears more riveted than concerned. She digests each word, lets each of my sentences saturate. It seems this matters to her.

"Wow," she says when I finish. "That would make for a great novel or screenplay. And no, I don't mean that as another jab at your career—*our* career. It's just so *cinematic*, so real and yet so *fantastical*."

"Mom, this isn't a screenplay. Not a novel. These are not actors. Not protagonists. This is my dream. My *life. Me.*"

"Yes, of course it is. But admit that it's amazing that we can retain such creativity, such nuance in our dreams even when we shirk creativity in our waking life."

Another unappreciated knock at my career in the corporate law world.

"So? What do you think?"

"I think you're getting married."

"Genius," I say.

"Marriage is a big deal," she continues, undeterred. "I don't know what the consensus is in Manhattan these days, but where we come from, it's forever. You have an amazing ability to love, to be loved, Prue. You always have. It makes sense that while contemplating your future, your forever, you revisit your past. To find out how you got here, right?"

And she dissects my dreams like a seasoned surgeon and like a mom, telling me that the three grooms represent my past, present, and future. Victor could have been anyone really, she says, he's just a future face. There will be infinite faces in my future—ones who will tempt me.

"You will be attracted to other people. You will flirt, have crushes," she says, and I think of Cameron. "You don't stop being human, Prue."

She tells me the judge's face was blurry because we don't ever really know who the final judge is. Is it society? Our parents? Ourselves?

"Most important I think is that little flower girl, that beautiful soul who can't stand the thought of growing up and making big decisions. You are that girl, Prue. Growing up doesn't just happen. It's not a fact; it's a decision. You have to decide to grow up and you're doing that now."

She makes it sound so simple, so poetic. This is what mothers do. They tidy chaos. They offer translations.

"What about Phelps?"

"You loved him, Prue. You may never stop. But you also left him. That means something."

"But I didn't really have a reason," I say. "I was bored, I met Sage. I didn't really have a reason to leave him."

"Sometimes the best decisions don't require reasons. Or good ones, at least. Truth be told, you had a reason and you just might not know what it was. You'll figure it out. Reasons reveal themselves over time. Often, after the fact. If we waited for reasons to materialize, we'd never move forward."

Something clicks. I've spent my whole life stockpiling reasons—for why I should go to law school, or become a litigator, or become a wife. Maybe some things don't need justification to be right. Maybe instinct is the best measure.

"And about those doubts . . ." Mom says.

"Yes?"

"Let them live. Nurture them. Doubt can be a beautiful thing. Embrace it. Let it teach you."

"So, you had doubts about Dad?" I ask, not sure I want to know the answer, but somehow needing to.

"Up until the very end. Sometimes I'd look at the man when he was hunched over, cross-eyed, trying to tie a fly, and I'd think, *This is it?* I think you doubt the things you love most. You don't have doubts about things that don't matter. And don't ignore them—the dreams. See what they mean to you over time. You owe it to yourself, Prudence. And to Sage."

That night, Sage, the moms, and I go out for sushi and there's no dream talk. Mom, ever the wonderful contradiction, delivers a diatribe, both artful and empirically sound, about the dangers of eating raw fish while sampling my tuna sashimi. She tells us how they have begun selling edamame in the frozen section of their supermarket in Wisconsin, and that maybe she will throw a sushi dinner party for her friends out there, bring a little Manhattan back to the woods.

Mrs. McIntyre is on her best behavior. When there is a pause in conversation, she places her hand on Mom's and whispers, "I'm so sorry about your husband. There are no words, so I won't try."

Mom nods and sips her drink. "Thank you. Where is your husband this weekend?"

"On business," Mrs. McIntyre mutters, sipping tap water. "They don't have to be gone to be gone."

Sage and I hold hands under the table, witnessing this miracle.

"You sure you don't want a splash of sake?" Mom says.

Mrs. McIntyre pauses and says, "Why not?"

And Mom pours far more than a splash. She holds her glass up to the table. "To mothers!"

Mrs. McIntyre smiles. "To sons and daughters."

We clink glasses.

"Quinn, dear," Mrs. McIntyre says, "I've been meaning to ask you. Will you please come to Savannah with Sage in August?"

For Henry's birthday.

"I would love to," I say, smiling.

"Now, let's talk business. We have a wedding to plan," Mom says.

Dreams are not necessarily bad things, I'm beginning to realize.

We laugh and sip sake. There's no mention of the ring, of how much makeup or black I'm wearing, of those dreams and doubts that made me cry in my guacamole only a few hours ago.

Every now and then Mom catches my eye. For once, I don't

dodge her glance. I don't look away. For the first time, I feel as if I don't have anything to hide.

"I was thinking that instead of numbering the tables, we can name each table after a fishing fly," Sage says, smiling, poking me with his chopsticks. "We can have the May Fly, the Woolly Bugger, and of course the Hula Popper and the Jitterbug."

"That's a *splendid* idea," Mom says, and grins.

"And we can have a little picture of a fly on the top of the invitation," he says.

"You're obsessed," I say. "Are you going to get married in waders and a BuzzOff shirt? The attire can be angler casual. My veil can be made of fishing net," I say, and laugh.

And it's a good moment. Stuffed with love and laughter and life.

"Well, we've taken care of that part, haven't we, son?" Mrs. McIntyre says.

"What part have *we* taken care of?" I say.

"We bought Sage the most darling tan suit today. We're having it tailored," she says.

We.

The giddiness is gone. I slip my hand from Sage's.

In my mind, I see it now. That vast black-and-white of Mom and Dad, barefoot, sporting goofy grins, just married— at home on our coffee table. Dad in his tuxedo, crisp black and white against the white cloud of Mom's dress.

"I thought *we* decided you'd wear a tux," I say to him as Mom pours all of us an emergency round of sake.

But Sage isn't the one who answers.

"Nah, a light-colored suit's far more appropriate," Mrs. McIntyre says, and smiles, rubbing her son's back. "Isn't it, son?"

Chapter 16

I 've never liked dresses.

In fifth grade, my friends got girly (think: skirts, sparkles). It made sense, I guess. For the first time, there was talk of tampons, and boyfriends, and bras. But I went in the opposite direction (think: baseball caps, basketball jerseys). I nurtured a sudden passion for the Boston Celtics, which was odd since I was a New Yorker and swimming in a sea of budding Knicks fans.

"Mom, your little tomboy's all grown up," my brother says. "On a mission to buy a wedding dress."

Mom laughs. "Don't think 'tomboy' was ever an adequate label for this one," she says, patting my thigh. I think Mom was thrilled I wasn't a priss. No, like her, I was a toughie. In those days, people didn't worry like they do now. The fact that Michael was the one stealing her lipstick didn't faze her.

"Did you ever think this day would come?" I ask her.

"I feared it might," she says through a smile. Our cab flies through the park, nearly flattening a young mother and her twin toddlers. As we bump along, I attempt to check my BlackBerry.

"God, Quinn, if you were a kid today, you'd be put on a regimen of Ritalin with your Flintstones," Michael says, flipping through a slim stack of wedding magazines.

He's right. I'm not sure I even have the attention span to shop for my wedding dress.

"She doesn't need Ritalin, Michael. She needs to get rid of that device," Mom says, gripping the door handle for dear life, as if she didn't spend years surviving these rides.

"Mom, it's a BlackBerry. You know what it's called," I say.

"I still think it's ludicrous that they would shroud such an evil piece of technology with such a sweet, natural name. That thing has the ability to wreck human interaction," she says.

"Point taken, Dad," Michael says. And Mom's eyes dilate with sadness for just a moment before brightening again. Michael throws his arm around Mom. "Nothing wrong with carrying on the Luddite legacy. Let Q finish her stuff and I'll swipe the sweet little Berry from her when we get to the store."

"So, you ready to choose your very own princess costume?" Mom asks.

"Princess costume?" I ask.

"That's what you called them when you were little. You asked why everyone dressed up as a princess when they got married. Wondered whether it was like another Halloween. I assured you that if you chose to marry, you could wear whatever you wanted."

I smile. This sounds like me. "Did you picture me walking down the aisle in a Larry Bird jersey?"

"Wouldn't that be a sight?" Michael says, "Cue the quartet. Here comes the butch bride."

And in this little yellow haven, we forget political correctness. And laugh. Hard.

"Need I remind you, Michael? You told me *you'd* wear a princess costume on your wedding day," Mom says. "Thrilled your father to imagine his only son in a dress."

Avery and Kayla wait for us outside the boutique. Avery's the picture of Saturday morning fresh in her perfect ponytail and flats. Kayla, on the other hand, appears to be wearing her outfit and makeup from last night. Kayla talks. Avery appears to listen, but I know better. She checks her pearl-encrusted watch at least twice as I approach.

"Nice of you to join us," Kayla says, unapologetic about her display of morning cleavage. "Frankly, this isn't how I usually choose to spend my Saturday mornings."

"You don't say!" I joke.

Avery hugs me.

"What do you think of this one?" Michael asks, pointing to a sleek number made of banded satin in the window. It's draped on a pipe cleaner of a mannequin, arms akimbo.

"Pretty, but not exactly right for a Bird Lake bride," I say. "Though that's exactly how I plan to look on my big day— bald, emaciated, snow white, about to run for the hills."

Laughter erupts, and buoys me through the spotless glass door of the small salon.

So far, so good.

"Good answer, kid," Michael quips. "I just read about that one. Vera made only one. It's a size two and costs a mere sixty-K. Exclusivity's a bitch."

"Good to see my daughter still has good taste. And good sense," Mom says, and smiles.

"So this Wisconsin thing's a done deal?" Kayla asks, linking her arm in mine. "There's nothing we can do to make Fisherwoman Barbie come to her senses?"

Three stick figures in matching charcoal skirts perch behind a tiny antique desk and shower us with matching disapproving glances.

Kayla fingers a crystal champagne flute on display next to a conspicuous sign that reads: "Please do not touch."

"Can you believe this is *it?*" Avery asks, grabbing my hand. "On the hunt for your *wedding dress.*" Her smile is vast, open.

"Simmer down," Kayla says. "It's not like she's choosing the groom."

"I know. Some of us have already taken care of that part," Avery says.

"I think you, my friend, have had your noggin buried in *Martha Stewart Weddings* and *The Knot* for a little too long," Kayla says to Avery.

"*Someone* is rather schooled in the names of wedding magazines," Avery says, and laughs.

Kayla, usually immune to the punch of humiliation, forces a smile as her face grows pink.

Avery sticks her hand out and stares at her engagement ring, a veritable carat overload, and makes sure Kayla sees it.

"Not too shabby," Kayla says, looking at Avery. And we have ourselves a timely truce.

A sulky girl named Marisa ushers us up a winding staircase, her stilettos stepping softly on fluffy beige carpet. Upstairs, Marisa points to a white leather sofa. Everyone plops down except for Michael, who disappears into white horizons. Marisa balances a clipboard in her left hand, pen cocked, ready to take my vitals. Location. Head count. Vision.

"Vision?" I ask. "Not great. I wear contacts."

"What kind of bride do you want to be?" Marisa asks, ignoring my failed attempt at matrimonial humor. And I half expect her to hand me a menu.

"The kind who gets married and gets on with her life," I say.

Avery frowns.

Kayla nods.

And Mom smiles. "That's my girl."

"Okay. Let's start over. Are you familiar with the rainbow?" she asks me.

"No. I'm a rookie."

"Well, you have antique, ivory, eggshell, ecru, blush, champagne . . ." she says.

"And then you have the fun stuff," Michael says, reappearing. "The jewel-encrusted tiaras, antique brooches, supersized bows, oddly placed strings of pearls. Some of the dresses this season even have color, Q. Touches of eggplant and turquoise, splashes of bright burgundy and rose."

And finally, we have a smile from Marisa. "Thankfully, *someone's* clearly done their homework."

"*His* homework," I correct her. "Guess you don't need good grammar to sell a princess costume," I whisper to Mom.

"Quinn!" Avery chides.

"How about ivory?" I say. "How will ivory look with a *tan suit*, one surreptitiously purchased by a very thoughtful mother of the groom?"

"The battle rages on. Why not pure white? Is white a little too pure for our little bad girl?" Kayla pipes in, eyes glued to the tiny screen of her BlackBerry.

"Brides historically never wore white," Mom says. "Not until Queen Victoria. The white-as-tradition thing is another Western myth. Like the one that equates diamonds with love."

"Ah, the big bad De Beers conspiracy," Michael says.

"No complaints here," Avery says, flashing that ring again. "A Diamond Is Forever."

"More like A Diamond Is for Now," Kayla says. "Thanks for the history lesson, Mrs. O'Malley. What color was your wedding dress?"

Mom doesn't answer.

Now Michael grabs Mom's left hand. "And check out the rock," he says, pointing to Mom's engagement ring, the lone diamond, still sparkling after all these years.

Mom shrugs her shoulders. "More like a pebble."

We all laugh some more.

"Lace?" I say, lamely. Back to business.

Avery smiles big. "Ooooh, I always imagined you'd wear ivory lace. There is something so classic and timeless about that," she says. Avery's wedding dress is ivory lace. "Yes, I pictured you as a classic and timeless bride. Sure, antique lace is a bit old-fashioned, a tad grandmotherly, but in my daydreams as a little girl, that's what I envisioned."

"I didn't daydream about my wedding as a girl," I say.

"Start now then," Avery says, smiling.

Michael and Marisa leave us, divide and conquer in the quest for ivory lace. They return under ivory piles. Marisa comes into the dressing room with me and stands there as I undress. Up close, I can see the wrinkles around her over-lined eyes, the rebel strands of gray amidst coiffed hair. I see for the first time that she doesn't have a ring of her own.

She helps me into the first dress, a simple strapless number. It barely closes in the back, pinching my skin.

"Bridal sizes run very small," she says, a scripted assurance, as I attempt to breathe.

I come out of the dressing room. All eyes on me. Good practice for my wedding day.

Marisa tells me to stand on the white wooden box in front of the vast mirror, so I do. On this pedestal, I stare at myself in the mirror. The faces behind me blur and blend. And there I am, in sharp focus.

A fucking princess.

All of a sudden, I'm light-headed.

"Let me fix you," I hear Marisa say.

"Please do," I mumble.

Before I know it, Marisa is crawling around on the carpet and under my dress. "Adjusting the tulle," she mutters.

"I didn't get a chance to shave this morning," I apologize. "Or this month."

"You know my theory about shaving," Kayla says, her voice distant.

"Huh?" Her words nick me like an errant dart in a crowded sports bar. I catch a glimpse of myself again in the mirror. Confusion contorts my face, now pale, rearranging my features. For a moment, I don't recognize myself.

Mom perks up. She loves theories. "Let's hear it."

"It's never a good sign when you stop shaving with a guy. Means the chase is over. Time to sit on the couch, take turns with the remote, and get fat," Kayla says.

"I'm sure she shaves other important places?" Michael says, looking in my direction.

"Don't think it's overly appropriate to discuss pelvic grooming in such an institution," Avery says.

A thank-you emerges from under my massive skirt.

"Plus, I think it's the opposite. There's nothing wrong with becoming comfortable with a man. It's good to relax, not worry about every hair. It shows confidence, if you ask me, that something as silly as stubble isn't going to make him walk," Avery says, defending me. She chooses not to mention the weekly waxing sessions she's kept since high school.

"What's this obsession with shaving?" Mom says. Should've known this was another ripe opportunity to peddle feminist ideology. "Society's goddamned preoccupation with returning to prepubescence? Hair is natural, a sign of maturity."

Michael nods as Mom talks and then he lifts her pant leg, running his hand along her calf. "Smooth as silk." Then it's back to business. "Not so sure about the lace," he says.

"I think I agree," Mom says. I'm beginning to wonder if this haven of femininity is traumatizing her. Or whether she, in all her smooth-shaven, diamond-wearing glory, secretly loves it here.

"Well, I think you look beautiful," Avery says, wiping a tear from her eye. She's a crier. "I mean, *look* at you."

Kayla slips her BlackBerry into her bag and looks at me. "A little prissy if you ask me," she says, and shrugs. "A shred predictable."

Mom nods.

"I hate to say it, but Special K has a point. Lace seems drab and boring. You don't want to be drab and boring. You want to be a contemporary stunner, an edgy sophisticate," Michael says. "You want heads to turn."

"I do?" I say, and think of my dream. The swiveling heads on bodies, convened for me, cloaked in white. "Oh yeah, I do."

Michael continues his commentary, his voice animated. "Lace isn't you. You aren't on the fast track to becoming a muffin-baking Martha Stewart. In fact, I think you'll dodge that fate at all costs."

"That won't be hard," I say. My cooking repertoire—

college-honed—amounts to boiling eggs and burning toast. "Too bad skinniness hasn't been a by-product of my inability to make a meal," I say, still sucking in.

Skinny Marisa pops out from under my dress and surrenders another smile.

Michael won't stop with the arguments. "Lace is fitting for platinum blond twinset-sporting country clubbers. The bride in lace was probably a respectful child who wore pigtails and ruffle socks and who didn't put up a fuss about an early bedtime. The lace bride will be the coiffed and well-balanced wife and mother who is expert at juggling kids and work and has a warm meal on the table and manages a lipstick smile even at the end of a hard day."

"Can I suggest something?" Marisa asks.

"You *may*," I say.

"You should try on many different types of dresses, even ones you never thought you'd like. That's really the only way to know what you want."

A rational suggestion. I'll buy it. "Bring it on," I say. In the mirror, I see that some color has returned to my cheeks.

Within minutes, I've hopped in and out of duchess silk and antique pointelle, blush and champagne organza. Finally, I emerge from the dressing room in a gown symmetrically smattered with stark black velvet embroidery.

"I saw this one online," Michael says. "The model sashayed down the runway in tattered black cowboy boots."

"I wonder what kind of little girl grows up to wear a gown that dangerous," Avery says. "I wonder what kind of wife *she* will be?"

"Probably a tomboy who went through a passing punk phase, who's pierced at least two body parts before reforming her ways. She'll probably keep her husband guessing. She'll probably have a secret box under the bed full of naughty things. Like, say, handcuffs. White ones. Quinn, this might be your dress," Kayla says, smiling.

At this reference to my dream, Mom stares at me and smiles, eyes tellingly wide, sparkling.

"You know what, K? You can wear this one when you get married," I say.

"Shall we put it on hold?" Avery says.

"Ouch," Kayla says, fingering the dress. "I think Sage would like this. Actually, I am pretty sure he'd find it hot. Perfect for our little tasty tart here."

"You know," Mom chimes in. " 'Tart' wasn't always a derogatory term. Used to be a term of endearment, short for 'sweetheart.' And then it took on the meaning of an opinionated bold woman. Nothing wrong with a bold woman."

"Like Frida Kahlo," I say. "Bet she would've loved this one."

I emerge from the dressing room one last time, happy to be back in my jeans.

"So, what's the verdict?" Kayla asks.

"I'm requesting an adjournment," I say. "I need a drink."

"I'll grab you some water," Marisa says. "FIJI or Pellegrino?"

"Not that kind of drink," I say.

"She needs de beers," Kayla says, and laughs.

And Marisa's deceptively simple words echo in my head. And it occurs to me that finding a wedding dress is not unlike finding a groom. It's a matter of trial and error. A process. Not something you do in a day.

"Not ready to commit?" Kayla says, linking her arm through mine.

"Not yet anyway," I say as we descend the swirling staircase of boring beige.

"Promise me one thing, Q," Kayla says, as the others walk ahead.

"What's that?"

"That you'll shave those legs of yours on your wedding day."

"We'll see," I say. "Promise me one thing, K."

"What's that?"

"That you will never again talk about white handcuffs."

Kayla flashes a ponderous, impish smile. And as we walk back through the hushed haven of femininity and grace, she pauses by the door and then turns around and retraces her steps. She approaches the women at the counter.

"Excuse me. I see here that you sell wedding shoes and tiaras. But what about white handcuffs? My friend is looking for the most stunning pair of white handcuffs."

Giddy, we giggle, and run. At the front of the store, I ignore the delicate gold handle. Instead, I place my sweating palm on the door and push hard. Strong platinum collides with fragile glass as I leave smudges on what was once perfectly clear.

Chapter 17

I did shave my legs the morning of January twelfth. My twenty-seventh birthday. The day of Dad's memorial service. I'm not sure why. We were all at Bird Lake and I decided to shower in Mom and Dad's bathroom in our cabin. Michael and I have our own bathroom, but still, Mom didn't say anything when I asked to use theirs. Now, hers. Just that there was an extra towel on the hook behind the door.

So there I sat, holed up in the tiny bathroom Dad never finished remodeling, naked, at the bottom of the bathtub, dragging cheap pink plastic over furry white legs. Hot water sprayed from the old showerhead, pelting my back. Dad's bottle of Head & Shoulders rested on the edge of the basin; Mom hadn't thrown it out yet. But then again it had been only a couple months since he died and I figured this shampoo's days were numbered. Dad was the only one with dandruff. And Mom wasn't like those other widows profiled on the morning shows, the ones who left everything the way it was before their husbands died, who refused to throw away the half-eaten bag of potato chips, or the toothbrush that would never be used again.

As the room steamed up and the mirror above the sink fogged, something became clear to me. This wasn't how I pictured the end.

No one's supposed to imagine her parents' decline. But I did. Maybe it's the realist in me. Maybe it's that Dad was never afraid to talk to us about mortality, to explain the limp and lifeless body of a young bird on our front porch, or the lineup of glass-eyed trout in the rickety old icehouse. Maybe it was that goddamned trusts and estates seminar in law school where our bow tie–clad professor pummeled us with prudence: It's never too early to plan for death.

Whatever the cause, I thought about these things. About losing Mom and Dad. I pictured Dad, an extraordinary man, exiting this world the ordinary way. I envisioned the generic grays of a hospital room, a quiet good-bye punctuated by faint rumblings of some kind of medical machine. I even imagined living the euthanasia debate, arguing with Mom and Michael over whether Dad would want to live like this, prisoner to exactly the kind of machines he despised and knew intimately from his decades as a doctor. I envisioned debating whether to bury or burn, whether my dear dad would prefer to spend eternity in a box in the earth under a pricey slab of stone or scattered over the lake he loved.

But it didn't happen like this. I never got that hospital room. I never got to see the big man who was my father cloaked in a paper-thin gown. And we never got a body. Or ashes.

A timely pragmatist, Mom embraced the benefit of having no body or ashes: no logistical restraints. "Well, we can do it anywhere then," she said of the service. "He'd want it at the lake."

So there we were, shivering, arranging folding chairs on the big screened-in Clubhouse porch, mere yards from the vast old oak where Mom and Dad baptized me with lake water, gathering to celebrate Dad.

That morning I stood with Mom as people arrived. Soon, we were surrounded by the characters from his stories, the faces from his grainy photographs. The football teammate who threw the winning pass against Michigan State. The med school classmate who said fuck it and did the unthinkable by trading prestige and power for a stab at happiness. He now ran a surf shop in California. Yes, there they were, his colleagues and friends, graying, bespectacled, rattled.

"He didn't even want to go," Mom said.

I nodded and rubbed her back, but for a moment, I wasn't sure what she meant. Certainly, he didn't want to die.

"He hated those power meals. He hated discussing money."

"I know, Mom."

"He was a Cheerio guy," she said. "*My* Cheerio guy."

Then Mom cried. There were very few times I'd seen her cry: that winter evening when I told her I changed my name, on September eleventh, now.

A lawyer must have a thick skin. Never let them see you weak, she told me the night before my first day at the firm. I was never sure whether these clichéd words of wisdom were meant for the courtroom or for life. Or, likely, both.

But there she was. A self-proclaimed feminist, a wannabe Frida, presumably wondering (for the first time perhaps) whether she was all talk. All of a sudden, a legion of strangers with visions of virgins and eerie precision had challenged her to live without a man, without *the* man who made her laugh. Without the man upon whom she perhaps secretly and totally depended.

As kids, we pester our parents with one question: "Why?" And, dutifully, they muster answers and explanations. It's only when we grow up when they can be, perhaps must be, honest. And tell us when they don't have the answer. Or when, simply, there isn't one.

That morning, Mom had the courage to reverse things, to ask that same question I asked her so many times as a little girl. "Why?"

And I had the courage to answer her. "I don't know."

She nodded. And then the tears were gone. And real life sliced through. "I can't believe she had the nerve to come," Mom said, pointing to a petite brunette only yards away. "Virginia Brookstone, his ex. Hippie slut. She tried to convert your father to Buddhism."

"Ah, Mom. You won him."

"Yeah, lucky me. I'm the widow," she said, and smiled. "Speaking of exes . . ."

As if I needed another reason to grieve. There was Phelps. It was the first time I'd seen him since we'd broken up. He looked better than ever; a mature, seasoned version of that precocious boy in the rowboat. He'd lost the weight he put on in medical school and wore his hair military short. The stunning blond on his arm didn't help things. Her smile was open and friendly, her eyes held the appropriate level of sadness for the day, for the memorial of a man she never knew.

As Phelps approached, he looked down. Not at me.

But I looked down too, at their intertwined fingers, the braid of tan skin and the flash of gold. A ring.

They were married. At least that's what it looked like.

Before he said anything, he hugged me. The way he used to; no holding back. A big bear hug, a hug that said a mixture of *You're safe with me* and *You're going nowhere*, a hug that promised everything would be okay.

I wondered if she got those hugs too.

For the first time that morning, the tears came.

"I'm so sorry," he said, through his own tears.

I'm so sorry. These were words I'd said to him at the end. Over and over. *I'm so sorry.* We said these things. As if these words could stitch a threadbare heart, or bring back a dead father.

It's okay, I wanted to say. But I couldn't and it wasn't.

I'm okay, I wanted to show him. But I couldn't and I wasn't.

Phelps pulled away, gripped my shoulders with his big hands, and finally looked me in the eyes. I looked into his. The same baby blues framed by new wrinkles. The same long lashes, the same eyebrows, wonderfully unkempt, threatening to touch. He ran his fingertip under my eyes, stopping the snaking mascara like he always did.

"*Your canthus*," he said. Every night before bed, he taught me the silly scientific name of another body part. This was one of our favorites.

"My canthus."

"Waterproof would've been prudent on a day like this," he said, and smiled.

A hand on my waist. Sage walked up behind me, threw his arm around me, pulled me close. I gripped his sweater.

"This is Sage," I said to Phelps. His blond still hid behind him.

Sage held out his hand and Phelps grabbed it between both of his and shook. The exchange seemed genuine. This wasn't how I envisioned their first meeting; I pictured a testosterone-propelled fistfight. At the very least, a thrown beer. But instead: civility. The boys in my life were acting like men.

"This is Phelps," I said. As if Sage didn't know.

A few too many moments passed before Phelps introduced the blond. God, she was skinny.

"This is Carter," he said. "My wife."

"Congratulations," I said, that easy word escaping me before I could orchestrate some better ones. "You didn't tell—I didn't know."

"It all happened very fast," Carter said, and smiled, extending her hand toward me. And her words are still crisp in my mind. *It all happened very fast.* Even in the haze of grief and longing, her words struck me as odd. Is marriage something that just happens? She uttered these words and her right hand came at me, but my eyes stayed fixed on the left. On the modest but brilliant diamond that rested on her bony finger.

"Well, congratulations," Sage said, his smile the biggest.

"Yes, congratulations," I said. Again.

Sage left us. He and Michael walked with Mom to the front of the chairs. The service was about to begin.

Carter excused herself too. She said she needed to use the bathroom.

"She pees all the time," Phelps said. And then turned red.

"Good to know. Well, you're not wasting any time. Let me guess: no heart-shaped tub on the honeymoon? What's next? Cheetos-eating towheads?"

Phelps smiled.

And we stood there for a while without speaking. Shrouded in an unrelenting, rich silence.

"Why didn't you tell me?" I said.

"I don't know." Again that honest, lackluster trio of words.

"She seems nice," I said.

"She is," he said. Carter walked toward us, her navy skirt shifting in the breeze. And then he put his lips to my ears, the ears on which he used to nibble, and whispered: "But she's not you."

I smiled. And as I walked away from my past to find my future, a hand grabbed me.

And Phelps bent over and whispered something in my ear. Something I thought he'd maybe forgotten.

"Happy birthday, baby," he said.

Chapter 18

For two and a half years, I've waited for this day. And dreaded it. Sage and I are going home. To Savannah, to his childhood digs.

I've spent an embarrassing amount of time imagining his house (Georgian of course, spotless windows, enveloped by a perfect little garden) and how his mother decorates it (ginghams and chintzy florals, lots and lots of pillows, perpetually fluffed). In my visions, it is always clean and quiet and the lawn is permanently mowed and sweet-smelling. I picture friendly neighbors, all blond—authentically blond—with perfect matching teeth thanks to the same town orthodontist. Neighbors who, depending on the season, drop by with muffins or pies or roasts.

It's Saturday morning and what would have been Sage's brother's twenty-fourth birthday. Sage and I motor through LaGuardia Airport, dodging screeching toddlers and motorized carts that beep ominously and tote old people, trying to make our flight. Outside, the sky is gray and a summer storm looms.

Sage wears that symbolic sport coat, the one he wore on our Paris trip. The one from his mother.

"I still don't understand the sport coat," I say, "on a Saturday in ninety-degree August heat?"

He smiles and shrugs and shoves our boarding passes in the front pocket of said coat. I choose not to make fun of the fact that he stayed up last night ironing it.

"And I still don't understand the cookies," he says, pointing to the white box I'm carrying. "Don't you think they have dessert in Savannah?"

"Black-and-whites are very New York," I say. "I wouldn't dare show up empty-handed and I thought it would be nice to bring a little city to your parents' house."

"Look at you," he says, flashing a mischievous grin. "You're *nervous*."

"Guilty as charged," I say.

"You're wearing a polo shirt," he says. "A green one."

"A *mint green* one," I say. "A mint green *Lilly Pulitzer* polo *your mother gave me*."

"Well, you do look good in color," he says.

"I still think it's weird that you've never invited me home," I say. "Kayla thinks it's a red flag."

"I think Kayla's a red flag," he says. And then he grabs my hand, kisses it.

"It was very nice of your mother to invite me this year."

On the plane, I clutch Sage's arm and order a Bloody Mary. As we climb into a slate sky, Sage's mood dampens and he grows quiet, losing himself in the pages of an American Airlines catalogue.

"Anything interesting in there?" I say.

He looks at me, and then my drink, bloodred, melting fast. Then looks away.

Now his sadness is palpable, present in glossy eyes, suddenly distant, and in his uncharacteristically parted hair. In the way he squirms and sweats inside that sport coat he refuses to shed.

"So, he would've been twenty-four today?" I say.

He nods, but doesn't look up.

"What do you think he would be doing?" I ask. "Do you think he would have beaten us to the altar? Do you think he would be banking too?"

He shrugs.

"Are you okay?" I now ask him, grabbing his arm.

He nods, flips a page, and studies a mechanized self-flushing litter box on sale for ninety-nine dollars and ninety-nine cents.

"Well, I wish you would talk about him more," I say, sipping my drink. "It's not healthy to do this."

He looks up from the magazine, finds my eyes. "I wish you would drink less. It's ten in the morning. It's not healthy to do this."

And so we dance.

For the remainder of the flight, he talks even less.

And I drink even more.

At the airport, his mother perches by a pillar at baggage claim. She is darling and diminutive as ever, clad in pale peach; her smile is vast and her arms, outstretched. Those skinny arms swallow her much-taller son whole. She studies him. "Handsome as ever," she proclaims.

She plants a delicate kiss on my cheek. "What a lovely shirt, dear."

"Thanks," I say.

Sage escapes to find our bags. And I hand his mother the box of cookies. She peeks inside the box. "Black-and-whites?" she asks. And in her wispy voice, I detect a shred of accusation.

Or I'm being utterly paranoid. It's a distinct possibility.

"Yes," I say. They are cookies, for God's sake. Not an invitation to debate race relations.

"You shouldn't have," she says. And I wonder if she's being literal.

Sage musters a smile.

We ride in her car, a white Range Rover with tan leather interiors. Celine Dion whines faintly. Sage and his mother sit in the front seat and I have the backseat to myself. I study the backs of their heads. Their hair is the same sandy shade and they have the same gentle waves. They speak to each other in fractured words I can't hear very well over Celine, exchanging smiles.

We pull into the driveway. The house is just as pristine as I imagined it. Bright white. Big, but not offensively so.

As we unload our things, I can't help but study the perfect lawn, mowed and sweet-smelling just as I envisioned. And there it is: the spot where the grass meets the road. The meticulous white picket fence. And though it's a hot morning in August, I can see it now. That night. The barren trees, the trickle of Christmas lights along the road.

Inside, I am overwhelmed by the generic smell of baked goods I can't identify, the shimmering of silver frames and crystal chandeliers, and the gentle hum of central air-conditioning.

"Sage, honey," his mother says. "Why don't you show Quinn to her room?"

My room? In any other setting, the laughter would be

immediate and loud. But here, on her turf, I manage uncharacteristic deference and decorum and trail my thirty-year-old fiancé up a set of grand stairs to the home's second level.

"Separate rooms?" I say softly. "She knows we live together, right?"

Sage ignores me, huffing audibly as he wrestles my suitcase, embarrassingly large for an overnight stay, up to a place where she can't hear us.

I follow him down a hallway, dimly lit by mirrored sconces, walls blanketed in familiar black-and-white photographs of two blond boys. Sage stops at a door, opens it, and pauses before going inside.

"She's redecorated five times in the last ten years, but she won't touch his room," he says. "Or mine."

So, my room is Henry's room.

The room is dark. I look around. At the twin bed in the corner, dressed in eighties plaid. At the tattered teddy bear reclining on the pillow. The baseball posters. The bookshelves filled with encyclopedias and trophies. The small window with curtains drawn.

We head downstairs. Sage's mother sets platters of pastries on a massive dining table more suitable for a board of directors than a family of three. Sage's father sits in the living room, muttering to himself between sips of fresh lemonade, cursing at some golfer who has apparently missed an easy putt.

Sage grabs my hand and walks me toward his father. "Guess they can't all be Tiger," he says, standing. "Good to see you, son."

Sage and his father shake hands like business partners. Which is exactly what Mr. McIntyre hopes they will be. He

owns a local bank and continually hints about having his only
son join him one day.

"Welcome, Quinn," he says, putting his hand on my
shoulder.

"Hi, Mr. McIntyre."

And I pause there. Discreetly, I study this man whom I
hardly know. This man who has bequeathed to Sage his ski-
slope nose, his skin tone, his love of baseball, and his quintessentially male inability to excavate emotional soil.

I wait for Mr. McIntyre to say something else. I haven't
seen him since my dad died. I haven't seen him since his son
proposed to me. I half expect him to take me into his arms,
to tell me I still have one father. To spout some combination
of those well-meaning platitudes I've ingested in excessive
quantities. I expect words like "condolence" and "sympathy"
and "thoughts" and "prayers."

But no.

Instead, this is what I get: "Have you tried my wife's lemonade? It's tart as hell."

But brunch is lovely. We nibble on scones, spoon egg salad onto mini baguettes. His mother pours chamomile from
a blue-and-white pot. "My mother's Spode," she says, and
waves a manicured finger our way. "If you two behave your-
selves, you might have this set someday."

I smile. "Lucky us," I whisper.

But I think: *I might be here to win something, but it's not your
mother's Spode.*

We talk about work. Sage's father has been busy starting
up a new branch of his bank in West Virginia. "West Virginia
of all places," he says, guffawing, a renegade dollop of egg
salad escaping the corner of his mouth. "But people need
banks there too."

He stands, tosses his napkin down on the table, and walks to the kitchen. "Sage, son," he says, his deep voice bellowing from the other room, "I got you something."

And naïve me thinks: *An engagement present. Something heartfelt, meaningful.*

But no.

Mr. McIntyre comes back into the room clutching a plastic bag. "You're going to love this one," he says, pulling a blue mug from the bag. "West Virginia: We're One Big Happy Family . . . Really!"

We all find smiles.

Suddenly, I have a flash of our future kitchen cabinets: silly mugs with offensive slogans mingling with heirloom Spode.

"Isn't that just precious?" Sage's mother says, eyes smaller now. She gently steers the conversation to something equally irrelevant: her flower garden. Apparently, the lilacs have had a good season. And the deer have been extra pesky this year.

Then we talk about the weather. How a thunderstorm is predicted.

We talk about everything that doesn't really matter.

Everything but Henry.

Sage and his father take to opposite sides of the couch, and mumble about golf. I follow his mother into the kitchen. I help her wash dishes and collect crumbs from the table.

"While the boys are golfing, we can have a girls' day," she says. "I've been looking forward to it."

When Sage and his father leave, Mrs. McIntyre perks up. "Let's go blackberry picking before it gets any hotter out there."

She disappears and returns with two big hats and two pairs of gloves.

Mrs. McIntyre drives us to Bamboo Farm & Coastal Gardens. She parks the car, balances a hat on her head. Pulls gloves on. I follow suit.

And soon, I am following her around, ducking and standing, examining berries, meandering through the branches.

"Watch out for the thorns," she says.

"Thanks for the warning," I say politely, gingerly making my way through the "bramble"—which is a word I never knew before. I don't tell her that it's not the stains and scratches I'm worried about.

"And pick the ones without the hulls. If the berries still have hulls, it's too early to pick them. They're immature and they'll taste tart."

She plucks a berry and marvels at it. "They say that blackberries are especially good at protecting us from cancer, fighting inflammation, and possibly even preventing a type of brain damage linked to Alzheimer's disease."

"Is that so?" I say.

"That's what they say," she says, and resumes plucking.

Too bad these little suckers can't ward off a terrorist attack or a careening car.

Abruptly, she stands. All five feet, two inches of her, arms waving. And I wonder if she's been stung by something?

She mutters one word over and over: "Sally!"

And I look. And there she is, across the bramble. Sage's ex. Long-lost Savannah Sally. She's tan and blond and wears a hat just like ours. Her smile is wide and her teeth are perfect.

She walks toward us, basket in one hand, and her other hand linked to a trio of toddlers, all blond and absolutely adorable.

Suddenly, they stand before us.

"My goodness," Sally exclaims. "You must be Quinn. *The* Quinn."

I smile. Extend a hand. She shakes it.

Her children look up at me, matching blackberry-stained smiles.

"I always tell them to wait to eat them until we get home," she says. "But kids will be kids."

"Isn't that the truth?" Mrs. McIntyre says, fiddling with her hat. "Isn't this sun positively ruthless, Sally?"

"Sure is."

"Well, lovely seeing you and the little ones. We must get back to business. We have a pie to make."

Sally nods solemnly. And I wonder how many of Henry's pies she's tasted.

"Lovely to meet you," Sally says. "You're a lucky girl, Quinn."

And with that, Sally turns and walks away, her three precious ducklings trailing behind.

So while the boys are soaking up the sun on the other side of town, swinging clubs and sipping beer, here we are in what might as well be Easter bonnets and white gloves, delicately plucking black fruit from thorny branches, delicately making small talk with the girl who would've gifted Mrs. McIntyre with the grandchildren for whom she salivates, dancing around the one thing that might just unite us: We have both lost someone we love.

I want to ask her about Henry. What he wanted to be when he grew up. How often she thinks of him. If any of this truly does get better with time. Or whether that's just something people say.

I want to ask her about Sage. What he was like as a boy. Why she didn't let him eat the candy on Halloween.

But I don't ask these things. Instead, I do something I'm very good at. I play it safe.

At home, we bake pie.

Mrs. McIntyre stands in the kitchen, reading the recipe from the back of a postcard. A postcard with a picture of Paris.

"We went to Paris on our honeymoon," she says.

And it all makes sense.

"You have beautiful handwriting," I say. "You should see mine. All of these years on a computer and I barely remember how to hold a pencil."

"Penmanship is a lost art."

I stand by, ready for orders.

I pull ingredients from the fridge, line them up along the counter.

"This reminds me of that nursery rhyme about blackbird pie," I say.

"Oh?"

I don't know where I muster the courage, but I start singing. "Sing a song of sixpence, a pocket full of rye . . . four and twenty blackbirds, baked in a pie . . . When the pie was opened the birds began to sing . . . Oh wasn't that a dainty dish to set before the king? The king was in his counting house, counting out his money . . . The queen was in the parlor, eating bread and honey . . . The maid was in the garden, hanging out the clothes . . . When down came a blackbird and pecked off her nose!"

"That is a strange one indeed," she says.

"My dad used to sing it to me. And I would laugh so hard at the thought of birds in a pie. Mom hated that one because she said it was subversive and sexist—the king was counting his money while the queen was eating bread and honey."

"For the most part, we avoided nursery rhymes in this household. They appear innocent, but do you know that most of them are very subversive? They say Ring Around the Rosie's really about the Black Plague."

And I find myself wishing that nose-pecking blackbird were standing by.

And I don't ask her about another precious nursery rhyme that plays in my head.

> *Miss Mary Mack, Mack, Mack*
> *All dressed in black, black, black.*
> *With silver buttons, buttons, buttons*
> *All down her back, back, back.*
> *She asked her mother, mother, mother*
> *For fifty cents, cents, cents.*
> *To see the elephants, elephants, elephants*
> *Jump over the fence, fence, fence.*
> *They jumped so high, high, high*
> *They reached the sky, sky, sky*
> *They never came back, back, back*
> *Till the Fourth of July, July, July.*

But suddenly this simple string of childhood words isn't so simple. No, suddenly, this song is an ominous warning about mothers and money and fences. But I keep my observations to myself. Of course I do. I don't tell her about her cameo in my dream. That in my reverie she didn't wear innocent pastels, but all black with those subversive buttons all down her scrawny back.

When the pie is in the oven and the pork chops are warming, we sit there at the dining table. She shines it. Checks her pearl watch.

"The ring looks nice on you," she says, suddenly grabbing my hand.

"Thanks," I say. "Thanks for helping Sage choose it."

Playing it safe.

"I will never stop helping my son," she says. "That's what mothers do."

I nod.

"Well, the boys won't be home for a bit. That'll give us some time to talk."

I nod.

"Follow me," she says.

And I do. Just like I've been doing all day.

She glides up the stairs. Down the hall. Into Henry's bedroom. "You know I'm the only one who comes in here anymore?" she says.

"Is that so?"

And for a moment, I foolishly think I've underestimated this woman. In here, in this bittersweet haven, she will open up to me. Tell me about her lost son. How everything has changed. She will apologize for clinging so tightly to Sage. Show me pictures, old yearbooks.

But no.

She leads me into the bathroom. Points to a stack of freshly washed towels. "I bought you a few things in case you forgot them."

A few things = a razor, a bottle of the perfume she wears, lotions, emery boards, ring cleaner. I wonder if I should remind her that we are just staying the night.

On the way out of the room, she pauses. "One more thing."

She walks to Henry's desk, pulls out a drawer, reaches in, and fishes out a bottle of white wine and a stack of little Dixie cups.

"Nothing wrong with a little cocktail while the boys are away," she says, flashing a sad smile.

And just like that we're making strides.

Mrs. McIntyre moves Henry's teddy bear to the nightstand and we sit side by side on his bed, feet dangling to the carpet below. We sip wine rapidly, with shared urgency, and keep refilling.

"Isn't Sally a lovely girl?" she says.

I nod. "And what darling kids."

"I always thought Sage would end up with her."

Silence.

"Is that so?"

"Maybe once you have kids, you two will come back here?" she says, pinning me with a look of hope.

"Maybe," I say.

Not a chance in this tarty Savannah Hell.

"You should start soon," she says.

"Start?"

"Thinking about kids," she says.

"I just started my career," I say.

"Well, you never know. Sage's father and I didn't have an easy time. I miscarried several times. It's terrible to keep losing your children."

I nod.

"And I can tell my son's homesick," she says. "He might be *happier* here than in that city."

Dixie cups are not big enough.

"He's happy," I say lamely, uncertainly. "We both are."

She nods, holds out her soggy little cup, and like a good daughter-in-law-to-be, I fill it up.

"Quinn," she says softly, placing her hand on mine. "I know you are a go-getter. I know you have a couple of fancy degrees. I know you thrive in the cutthroat world of New York City. But I do have some advice for you."

"Yes?"

"Don't be foolish and turn this into a competition, dear," she says, shaking her head, pursing her lips, "because you're not going to win."

A car pulls into the driveway and Mrs. McIntyre swigs the last of her wine and hands me the cup. Straightens her apron. "Would you mind?" she says, pointing to the bottle we've finished.

"Not at all," I say, gathering the evidence. "I'll be down in a minute. I'm going to freshen up."

In the bathroom, I spritz her perfume. It smells like peach.

Downstairs, Mrs. McIntyre is on fast forward, scurrying around the kitchen, wearing her evening smile. She looks at me with glassy eyes and winks.

Sage comes up to me, his face tanned. Kisses me on the cheek. "You smell good, Bug," he says.

After dinner, we eat blackberry pie.

Mr. McIntyre chews with his mouth open.

Sage stabs his slice delicately, deep in thoughts he won't share. Now. Maybe ever.

Mrs. McIntyre pushes her slice around her dainty dish, black blood running from smashed cancer-fighting fruit.

No one mentions Henry. That this was his favorite pie. That he is why we are all here, together, looking down, not at each other.

But I am no different.

Here I sit. Drowning in thoughts of my own. Thoughts of family dinners, artfully strained. Thoughts of rooms filled with the clanking chaos of dishes, and that breed of quiet heavy with all the things left unsaid. Thoughts of childhood, and its precarious aftermath, of silly nursery rhymes and the words that stick with us. Of blackbirds singing in a pie.

Here I sit. Next to a boy. And on his other side is a woman. A mother. One who can't let go. Of the son she's already lost. Of the blackberry pie neither he nor the rest of us can honestly taste or enjoy. Of the boy she still has, the one who lives and breathes and hopes and dreams. The one who believes he is growing up by giving a ring to a girl. As if it is that simple. The one who perhaps intends to let go, but might never have the heart to stop eating that childhood pie.

"Another slice, son?" Mrs. McIntyre says sweetly.

And two words fill the Savannah silence: "Sure, Mama."

Chapter 19

That night, I hole up in Henry's bathroom. I scrub my face with lavender wash until my skin stings. I drop my ring in the little plastic jar full of chemicals that smell toxic and good. A few minutes later, the ring comes out sparkling.

And I stare at that ring. Study it. And my mind takes a delirious, poetic detour. If only there were relationship cleaners like there are ring cleaners. If only you could take a good relationship, one that is in fact quite beautiful and robust, but dulled in spots (because of a lost brother or father, or a meddling mother) and just drop it in and wait. And then it would come out glittering and new. Because real life tarnishes even the most stunning gems. If only.

I climb into bed, Henry's bed, and in no time I am asphyxiated by panic and peach perfume. The room spins.

I stand up. And wander aimlessly around the small space.

I sneak over to Henry's desk, flip through the graded papers, the yearbooks.

I pull my BlackBerry from my bag and sit down again. I read about pregnant celebrities and drug busts and terror alerts. I scroll through my address book. I land on the only number I ever had for Dad—at the office where I'd call him, and his chipper and ancient assistant Val would say the same thing every time: "Kindly hold for your old man," after which Dad would hop on and say his crackly and singsong "Hi, hi." I loved that I never just got one "hi." It was always two.

I stare at that string of numbers and hit delete. I will not be like Mrs. McIntyre.

I will let go.

I banish my Berry to my bag.

I will let go.

I stand again and go back to the desk. I open another bottle of wine from Mrs. McIntyre's secret stash and take a swig. I part the curtains and look outside at the grass, at that lonely white fence standing guard. At the parked car and scattered stars.

I keep drinking and scan Henry's shelves. And there they are: the books I loved as a kid, the Choose Your Own Adventure series. Mom loved these books, she would later tell me, because they were written in the magically gender-neutral second person. She would sneak the simple language of cause and effect into our daily lives.

If you decide to drink your milk, you will grow up to be big and strong.

If you decide not to drink your milk, you will be short and stumpy and go to bed early.

But I loved these books for far simpler reasons, reasons

that had nothing to do with superior literary points-of-view
or academic theories of free will and causation. I loved them
because you never knew what would happen next and it was
up to you. Michael and I could read the very same book and
it would end differently for each of us.

But to a child, the variety of possible endings wasn't
alarming.

Some endings were happy.

Some endings were tragic.

Other endings were satisfactory, blah, ambiguous—neither
perfectly good nor perfectly bad.

Sometimes, a set of choices would send "you" into a loop
where "you" would repeatedly end up on the same page and
the only option would be to start over.

I pull out my favorite one: *Inside UFO 54–40*, a book
about the quest for a utopia that no one can actually reach.
Buried in the book is a single page that describes "you" finding that dream world, that sought-after paradise, and living
happily ever after. But the thing is, none of the choices in the
book actually led to that page.

I remember Mom explaining this one to me. And I remember not quite getting it. "You can only reach the perfect
ending," she said, "by ignoring the rules, by flipping through
the book at random. And when you get there—to that perfect ending—you are congratulated for realizing how to find
that paradise, that happy ever after."

Could it be that happiness, true happiness, can only be
reached by aimless wandering? That paradise will only welcome those who live their lives without it as a destination?
That the path to happiness about which we are all conscious-
ly or unconsciously preoccupied is not a linear set of prudent

choices, but a smattering of random decisions, a haphazard adventure?

Or is it that ultimate happiness doesn't exist?

The only thing I know is that without choices, without decisions, without actions, there are no stories and there are no endings, good or bad or perfect.

So what do I do? I make a choice. I stop playing it safe.

I choose my own adventure.

I open the door a crack and tiptoe into the hallway. I sneak into Sage's room. And there he is, a boy of thirty curled up in his childhood bed, feet dangling off the end.

I sit next to him, and his eyes open.

"Hey," he says.

"Hey."

"My mother's going to hear you," he says, sitting up.

"We are *engaged*," I say. "What's she going to do? Withhold Grandma's Spode?"

On his shelf, I notice Sage and Sally's prom picture.

"What's the deal with Sally?" I say, plucking the picture from his shelf. His hair is long and shaggy and his smile is goofy and young. But even as an awkward teen, he looks good in a tux. *He will wear a tux at our wedding*, I remind myself. In the photo, Sally is as skinny and blond as ever, wearing a powder blue dress at least a size too big. She clutches Sage's arm.

"Huh?"

"I met her picking blackberries," I say.

"Wonderful. And?"

"She has three beautiful children," I say.

"So I've heard."

"Your mom thought you'd marry her."

"Yes, she did," he says. "But I'm not. I'm marrying you. Don't make me regret that decision."

"While you boys were at the club indulging in a lovely round of golf, your mother attacked me, Sage. She said that I am the reason you aren't coming back to this charming hamlet to bring the family back together . . ."

Sage succumbs to his pillow. "Quinn, *my* mother wouldn't say those things."

And those two words, those simple words "*my* mother" sound just like they did the night we met. But that night was just the first page of our story. That night, everything was brand new and unsullied. That night, it was sweet that he mentioned his mother.

Many pages later, things are a bit different.

"I travel to this place, this Stepford town, the Hostess City of the South. I say words like 'lovely' and 'precious' and 'darling.' I wear mint green for God's sake. I follow her around in a freaking Kentucky Derby hat and debutante gloves in the blistering sun. Picking fruit for a pie for your dead brother," I say. "Because I love you. And I'm *trying.* And what does she do? *Your* mother? She waxes poetic about that baby-factory ex of yours. Tells me how we should start thinking about having kids. How you are *homesick.*"

"Keep your voice down," he says. "This place means something to me, Quinn. It's my home. And did you ever stop to think that my mother is trying too? That *dead brother* you so nobly picked fruit for? Today was his birthday. And we loved him and he is gone. I would think *you* of all people would understand what that's all about."

"Don't make this about Dad," I say.

"Don't make this about *my* mother," he says.

"But it *is* about her. It's about how she can't let go. None of you can."

"Don't you tell me how to grieve," Sage says. "Should I try your tactic of anesthetizing myself with alcohol?"

"It's worth a shot. Has to be healthier than pretending he's still around and having a birthday party for a boy's ghost," I say, glaring at him. "You know something? *Your* mother should do herself a favor and convert these little bedrooms into closets for her pastel wardrobe because your brother is not coming back here. And neither are you. And if you are, then you better tell me and fast because I'm not coming with you."

"You've been drinking," Sage says.

"Yes," I say, standing, walking toward the door. "Yes I have. And not nearly enough. And so has *Mama*."

"Bug," he says, standing now and walking toward me, grabbing my wrists. "Tell me what you want. Tell me what to do and I'll do it."

I think of Avery's words of wisdom, that men need instruction manuals.

"I don't know, but one of these days, you are going to have to grow up and be a man and stand the fuck up for me."

He nods, a little boy scolded, and says words so diplomatic, so measured, so emotion-free, they at once pacify and enrage me: "We'll talk about it tomorrow. We have plenty of tomorrows to talk about all these things, Bug."

But I wonder if we do.

Defeated, boiling, scared, I retreat, almost tripping on his old baseball glove.

I tiptoe across the soft carpet. As I pull the door behind me, I look down the hall, past the blond bowl cuts and toothless grins, past the glittering glow of innocence and antique sconces. And peering out from her own room is his mother. I can't tell whether I see a smile or a scowl, or a bit of both. But toward me, her words float faintly, sweetly as ever. But they're unmistakable and dreadfully crisp, like that foul peach perfume we're both wearing. Down the corridor, here they come as I disappear like a little girl well seasoned in the ways of hide-and-seek. Words loud enough for her beloved son to hear: "Good night, dear."

And then the night is silent. A silent night indeed.

Chapter 20

And that silent night is followed by a silent morning. And a silent plane ride home. And a silent week.

Sage and I avoid each other. This is not exactly a tough feat when working twelve-hour days. At home, we take turns in the bathroom and sip our morning coffee in silence. We share custody of the cat.

There's no mention of our thorny trip to Savannah. There's no mention of his mother. And there's no mention of the fact that we are supposed to marry in a little more than two months.

Couples, perfectly healthy couples, have these mini cold wars, I tell myself.

Another New York summer threatens to slip away. Kayla and I leave work early, hop into one of the countless waiting Town Cars, and head down to the water for our firm's end-of-the-season celebration, the Summer Sail, which will take place aboard a soiled and sad "yacht" named *Destiny* of all things, a boat that spends long days tooling tourists along the Manhattan skyline.

Those who've been around awhile call it the Summer *Sale* because for a few hours our focus is not on billable hours, but on selling this world, this life, to a bevy of optimistic, impressionable souls. It's our job to make sure they accept the full-time offer they will each receive tomorrow morning as long as they make it through the night without sleeping with a partner's wife or saying something terribly racist.

We wait to board when I hear him.

"Nothing beats an old school booze cruise," Sage says, appearing by my side, grazing my cheek with a kiss.

I force a smile. "Nothing beats a surprise cease-fire."

"Who said anything about cease-fires? I figured it was time I get a firsthand peek into your little lawyer world," he says.

"Peek away," Kayla says, putting her hand on his shoulder. "I just hope you've come prepared to drink."

Onboard, I look around at the summer associates, the future freshman class of the firm, who've now spent a few months apprenticing. And drinking heavily. They started in the middle of May, sharply dressed, eager to please. A couple months later, they are bloated and bleary-eyed like the rest of us. They cluster in small groups, little islands in a rough professional sea, shifting back and forth between stocked bars and lavish buffets, periodically exchanging well-cooked pleasantries with partners and associates who pretend to care.

"Talk about a captive audience," I say.

"No kidding," Kayla says. "Why do you think this shindig's on a boat?"

"So we can blame the existential nausea on the rocking?" I say.

"An odd choice among lawyers," Sage says. "Gotta imagine the liability's greater on a trip like this. Certainly the suicide risk's higher than at a hotel ballroom."

"Don't give me any ideas," Kayla says, smiling.

"Might as well be the Fourth of July," I say. Fat partners wipe brows with American flag napkins.

"Cheers to patriotic prom," Kayla says.

In so many ways, life at the firm is just like high school: the cliques of catty attorneys, the copycat haircuts, the palpable social hierarchy. Gossip bounces through hallways and conference rooms. We even have a cafeteria, for God's sake.

But this time there's no epidemic of acne, no limp corsages on bony wrists, no legion of nervous virgins. And at this soiree, alcohol isn't taboo. There's no need to raid a parental liquor cabinet, to stash mini bottles of booze in backpacks.

Here, wine flows.

But conversation doesn't.

Sage's gray polo is tucked halfway into his slacks. And he wears that same goddamned sport coat from his mother again, but it's still wrinkled from our trip.

"Did you make an extra effort to be disheveled tonight?" I whisper to him.

"Only for you, Bug," he says, glaring and grinning.

"Hey Banker Boy, let's round up some real drinks. Champagne's for pussies," Kayla says, grabbing Sage's arm.

"Goose on the rocks," I say as they disappear.

All of a sudden I'm alone and I do the predictable: I reach for my BlackBerry, scroll through messages, look busy, avoid eyes. But as I pretend, the thing actually buzzes. I have a text message. From Phelps.

> **Phelps:** Know what tonight is?
> **ME:** Thursday.
> **Phelps:** Our anniversary

And I feel hot. And nauseous. It's the anniversary of our rowboat ride, our first time. My very first booze cruise.

> **ME:** How's the wife?
> **Phelps:** About to pop :(

And it all begins to make sense. I remember his words on the day of Dad's service. *She pees a lot. It all happened so fast.*

Moments later, I feel a hand on my waist. My heart races. I slide my BlackBerry into my bag.

"That was quick," I say.

"I'm anything but quick," a voice says. It's Cameron.

"Thought you were someone else," I say. "He's getting me a drink."

"Getting his lady a drink? Wow, I guess the courting phase isn't over for you lovebirds." He smiles big. His teeth are impeccably straight, too white. He pulls the plastic sword from his drink and chews on it. Kayla returns, balancing drinks. Sage is a few steps behind.

"So, he's pretty romantic I hear. A Parisian proposal and Plato?" Cameron says.

Kayla shrugs. "Big mouths run in my family," she says. "Luckily for the male population."

"Well, I can't compete. All I've given you is a Happy Meal and a panic-inducing blackout."

And Sage is back. Next to Cameron, he appears small, unpolished. "I come bearing gifts, Bug," he says, handing me a vast glass of vodka.

I take a large swig and then do what's necessary. I introduce them. Their handshake lasts an eternity. All the while, Kayla is smiling, eyes twinkling, courting disaster.

"Only good things, man. Only good things," Cameron says to Sage, still fiddling with that little plastic sword.

"Good to know," Sage says, draping an arm around me.

"Well, it was a pleasure to meet you. Now, I have some pressing business to tend to. Last chance to tap some summer ass," Cameron says, pointing to a group of blonds in the corner. He and Sage laugh deeply. And I should be offended.

"Quinn, don't forget," Cameron says.

"Forget what?"

"You owe me that milk shake," Cameron whispers. And I'm not sure whether Sage hears him. Sage pulls his little sword from his own drink. And I imagine a duel with plastic cocktail weapons.

"Well, if it isn't my two party girls."

It's Fisher. He clinks our glasses with his.

"What, the bartenders at this party aren't handsome enough?" he asks, looking at Kayla. "Not number-worthy? If you want, I can submit a complaint to my buddies on the executive committee.

"So, you must be the future Mr. Quinn?" Fisher says, reaching to shake Sage's hand.

"Nice to meet you, sir," Sage says, shaking Fisher's hand.

"No need for 'sir'—I'm not a dinosaur. Just call me Fisher."

"All right, sir."

"What did I say?" Fisher laughs. "I guess you can take a man out of the South but you cannot take the South out of the man, huh?"

"Something like that," Sage says. He's heard this cliché one too many times. So have I. "Cheers." He clinks Fisher's glass.

"You must be very jealous that I'm whisking your girl away on a romantic jaunt to Dallas?"

And reality slices through. Fisher and I leave in less than two weeks for depositions in Dallas.

"Nah, she'll come back to me," Sage says. "A few days of buffalo wings and beer will do the body good."

"My kind of guy," Fisher says, nodding, looking at me.

"So relieved you approve," I say.

"Special delivery." Kayla reappears and hands Fisher a fresh martini.

"Well, thank you," he says. "Now, this is what the gals used to do in the good old days. They'd bring us coffee. Those were the days."

In the corner, the blonds drape themselves over Cameron, giggling, gulping wine. I wonder whether much has changed.

"Well, aren't I a throwback then?" Kayla says, putting her hand on his shoulder.

"In the best possible way. Thank God there are no movie star waiters here because that means more attention for me, right?"

"Absolutely. I am beginning to think that ex comm knows exactly what it's doing," Kayla says.

"Well, Sage, you're a lucky lad. You've hooked yourself one of our prized associates."

"Prized associate who screws up from time to time?" I say, nudging Fisher, finishing my vodka.

"Little secret: We partners would be lost without our young colleagues. You grow older, you make your first million, they give you a corner office with views of the water, but you still fuck up. That never ends," he says, guffawing.

"To fucking," Kayla says, extending her glass. Her eyes are glossy and distant. "Up . . . to fucking up." She laughs and spills the rest of her drink down her shirt.

Talk about fucking up. I try to facilitate a fast exit, a trip to the bathroom, anything. But to no avail. On this rocking boat, Kayla's feet stay stubbornly fixed to her little plot of carpet.

"I'm going to take her for some fresh air," Sage whispers to me. He manages to drag Kayla away, and puts his sport coat around her as they head outside.

"That's a real gentleman you've found yourself," Fisher says.

I nod. And slip my BlackBerry out of my bag again.

"I love your generation," Fisher says, crunching ice. "Always plugged in."

"Gotta love us BlackBerry kids," I say, and glance at the tiny screen.

Phelps: You there?
Phelps: I miss you.

The boat sways. Music roars. Summer associates get frisky with each other on the dance floor.

All of a sudden there's a loud rumbling and the boat stops. Most people are too drunk to notice. The lights go out, and the music stops. In no time, we're all sweating and heading outside. Fisher and I join Sage and Kayla at a table on the deck. Kayla drools on Sage's shoulder.

Cameron reappears, carrying five overflowing shot glasses. "What's a party without shots?" he says, putting a shot glass in front of each of us.

"Civilized?" I say.

"Strike out with the rookies?" Sage says, brandishing his little blue sword.

"I haven't done a shot in twenty years," Fisher says, fingering the glass.

"Dinosaur," I say, and smile and picture Phelps holding a tiny baby.

"SoCo Lime. Easy," Cameron says.

"Who is going to offer a toast?" I ask.

"I think the lady should," Fisher says. And I assume he's not referring to Kayla.

"Was this another part of female associates' job description in your heyday?"

"No," Fisher says. "We didn't let them talk."

An eruption of male laughter. Again, should be offended.

"Okay, then give me a second."

"Only a moment, Quinn. You know, a good litigator must be able to think on her feet."

"Ahhh, the pressure."

I don't know where I find the words, but I find them. "To putting love first, the law second, and prudence dead last," I say, clinking their glasses, looking at Sage, a beautiful and oblivious creature, a bemused visitor in a strange land.

"Yeah, forget prudence," Cameron says, and I swear those teeth glow in the dark. Maybe I imagine it, but I think he grabs my thigh under the table before tossing that shot back.

"Fuck prudence," Fisher echoes. Kayla's eyes open. She smiles before drifting away again.

And for a few moments, we sit in silence under a starless sky. A glass or two breaks. BlackBerrys blink.

And all of a sudden there's a piano and a piano player. Summer associates who can still stand gather around the baby grand and sing "Life Is a Highway."

Sage whispers something from across the table. "I didn't know you drank milk shakes."

"Apparently I do," I say, and shrug.

I miss you.

"Know what I want to do later?" he asks, his blue eyes bright even in the dark.

"What's that?"

"Fuck Prudence," he says, and laughs.

"A mama's boy and a fucking gentleman," I say. "Lucky me."

And we're all a little too fucked up to see the irony. Here we are, Manhattan attorneys—and those brave enough to love us—older, but not necessarily wiser, than a bunch of high school prom dates, living dangerously within padded walls. Being spontaneous in predictable ways. Spouting profanities and platitudes. Drinking in a curious mixture of warm booze, authentic laughter, and artificial emotion. We're sloppy advertisements for lives we struggle to enjoy, fates we should've perhaps dodged. And the stench of success and sweat and sewage embraces us all aboard a stalled vessel named *Destiny*.

Chapter 21

The standoff continues. Days pass. Weeks. We barely speak. It is time for me to leave for Dallas. My suitcase is packed, and parked by the door. When I am about to leave, Sage walks toward me.

And eagerly I wait for the peace negotiations to begin. For the hug. The apology. The declaration that we've both been impetuous and silly. That everything will be okay.

But instead, he says: "We have a package."

He pulls the cardboard box onto the counter. It's addressed to both of us, blanketed in stickers that say "Fragile." And I wonder if it's an early wedding gift?

"Let me guess," I say. "The contents are fragile?"

He doesn't laugh.

And there it is, snug as a bug in bubble wrap: his grandmother's fucking Spode.

Now Sage smiles. "See?" he says. "*She's* trying."

"*This* is trying? No. *This* is a game. I'd rather have a white trash mug from every state in the fucking union from that lug of a father you have than this," I say, unwrapping a gravy boat.

"I'm glad I went sailing with you. I'm beginning to realize it's not my mother. It's not me. It's not your dad. This job is making you selfish bitch."

"A selfish *alcoholic* bitch, no?" I say.

"You said it."

"Didn't you get the memo that selfish alcoholic bitches make better lawyers?"

"No, but I did get the one that said they make lovely wives," he says, gingerly placing a teacup on the counter.

"Don't get ahead of yourself. I'm nobody's wife yet."

"Thankfully," he mumbles.

I look down at my hands, shaking from anger, the ragged nails and chipped polish, the pale fingers still clutching that goddamned boat from which we will one day be expected to pour gravy. And, yes, I do it. It's a scripted move, straight from a formulaic and flop-worthy movie, but I do it. I wind up and hurl it at him.

I close my eyes and brace myself for the shattering and screams. But I get something else.

My fiancé, my handsome ex–baseball player fiancé, doesn't flinch. He extends his big hand like a baseball mitt and catches it. Places it down on the counter next to the lineup of teacups.

"Nice save," I say, reaching for my suitcase.

And now Sage approaches once more, this time sporting a sad and conciliatory smile. He kisses me on the cheek and says, "Have a good trip, Bug. Live big. Have endless cocktails. Enjoy some time away from this incurable mama's boy who can't seem to do anything right."

And in this fragile and fleeting moment, I want to tell him that as much as I hate him, I love him more. But instead, I act like the proud and selfish lawyer I am. I grab my suitcase and say: "You know what? I will."

After a four-hour delay, Fisher and I board our plane.

"Those assholes really fucked everything up," Fisher says, checking his Rolex as we settle into our seats. "The airlines are never going to recover."

And then he must remember that *those assholes* did a bit more than cause airline delays.

"I'm sorry," he says. "That wasn't appropriate."

I don't say anything. I roll my coat up and stuff it in the overhead compartment. People look at me like I've just flashed them.

"Ah, a business class virgin," Fisher says, standing, retrieving my coat from above, smoothing it out and handing it to the waiting flight attendant. "They take care of you here. Right, Candy?"

Candy nods and smiles.

"It's important to know people's names, to say them as much as you can. Throw them in at the beginning or end of a few sentences. It makes them feel important. Even if they aren't," Fisher whispers. "But I don't know what the hell is wrong with people these days. The names they give their children. Candy? Might as well be Bambi. Don't tell me her parents thought she'd grow up to be anything other than a stewardess or stripper with that name."

"Like our very own Crystal Sugar?" I say, referring to our sexy nemesis, one of the lead plaintiffs in our case.

"Exactly," he says.

"So Quinn passes muster, I hope?"

"A little unorthodox for my taste, but sounds distinguished. It is a boy's name though," he says as if this is a news flash. "But that's not a bad thing. Especially in a man's world."

"My name's actually Prudence," I say.

"Ah," he says, nodding. "Now that makes sense to me. Good old Irish name for a smart, savvy girl. A maker of sound decisions."

"My parents were just big Beatles fans," I explain.

"Whatever you say. Truth is, parents have agendas," he says as if he knows something I don't. "Anyway, it's a big name. You'll grow into it someday."

I nod.

"Let's hope this plane fares better than that sad excuse for a yacht," Fisher says.

I laugh nervously. I'm way too young to die.

"You okay?" Fisher asks.

"I will be. Not a great flier," I say.

"More babies drown in mop buckets every year than people die in planes crashes," Fisher says, appealing to an odd statistic in a clumsy effort to comfort me.

"Good to know."

"It's nothing a little sauce can't solve," Fisher says, and flags down Candy. "A little Grey Goose for the lady, Candy."

He knows my drink.

"A good lawyer pays attention to details," he says.

He orders himself a bourbon.

"Here comes the plebeian parade," Fisher says, nodding toward the front of the plane.

The cabin fills up. People shimmy past each other, dragging bags and books and kids. Luggage is loaded below us.

And for a moment, I wish I could slip into line with them, follow them to the back where I could be anonymous, where

I could read a gossip magazine and fall asleep on the shoulder of a stranger. Where I could be scared. Where I could take a break from pretending.

We take off. The plane climbs high into a slate sky. Reaching for clouds and beyond. The upward hike is always the bumpiest; Mother Nature tosses us around a bit, screwing with us. When we reach our cruising altitude, she'll give us a break and we can pretend that we're not pushing our limits, hanging high in the sky where we don't belong.

The vodka helps. Here we sit, divided by a generation, getting sloshed.

"So, you ready?" Fisher asks.

"I think so. I'm going to read over my notes and I think I'll be okay," I say, pulling a folder from my bag.

"No, Quinn. For marriage."

"Oh," I say. "I think so."

Fisher nods. "I took one goddamned philosophy class in college. And all I remember is Plato's parable on love and marriage," he says, pronouncing "parable" like it rhymes with "barbell." "Do you know it?"

"Rings a bell," I say. Of course I know it. I don't tell him I was a philosophy major. Partners aren't interested in LBL, life before law. And, more than that, they like to hear themselves speak, and feel like they are teaching us.

But of course I remember the classic story.

Plato asks his teacher to describe love. And the teacher tells Plato to walk through a field and find the best stalk. When Plato comes back empty-handed, he says he found a great stalk and didn't pick it because he didn't know whether there were better ones out there. So, the teacher says that is love. You only realize love's worth once it's gone.

Then Plato asks his teacher to define marriage. And the

teacher says to go into the field and chop down the tallest tree. Plato comes back with a tree that's neither healthy nor tall. The teacher asks Plato why he brought back such an ordinary tree and Plato says because of his earlier experience. He didn't want to come back with nothing. The tree was not bad, so he cut it down. And the teacher says that's marriage. Love's an opportunity, but marriage is a compromise.

"I only remember the gist," Fisher says after a big gulp of bourbon. "Love is like a beautiful wheat field, but marriage is like a dying tree."

"Ah," I say, nodding. Guess now's not the time to ask him about his wife.

"So, you want a family?" Fisher asks, casually, like he's asking if I want another drink.

"Sure," I say, perhaps a bit too quickly. I wonder if he's trying to gauge how many years he and his partners can get out of me before I pop one out.

"So did I," he says. And I can picture the kids from the pictures in his office.

"You have these dreams," he says, swallowing. "But the problem is they come true."

A baby cries.

"Got a mop bucket handy?" Fisher says. And I can't help but smile.

The hotel lobby is packed.

"What's the commotion, Cindy?" Fisher asks, eyeing her name tag as we check in.

"A medical malpractice conference," the lady behind the desk says.

"Better than Candy," he mumbles to me. "But still no Prudence."

"So here we are in the throes of a malpractice conference, huh?" I say.

"Doctors and lawyers. Lethal combo," Fisher says, and asks for directions to the cigar bar.

The cigar bar?

"Too late to work," he says. "Let's grab a bite."

I follow him, noticing for the first time that we are wheeling the same efficient little suitcases. His is just an older model. We travel down a carpeted corridor toward music and the smell of smoke. And I find myself missing Giuliani and his smoking laws.

In Fisher-talk, grabbing a bite apparently means ordering cigars and booze. He orders two Bloody Marys and two cigars. He hands me one of each. I thank him, shove the cigar in my bag, and think of poor Monica Lewinsky. The little place is packed. It's ironic that a bunch of lawyers and doctors are sitting around smoking and drinking, bantering about professional responsibility and malpractice.

"How do you like it?" Fisher asks as I sip my drink.

"Not spicy enough," I say.

Through the fog of smoke, I see Fisher smile; the lineup of imperfect teeth glistening with chandelier glow.

In the corner, a fat man and a girl who could be his daughter huddle and laugh.

"That's not his wife," Fisher says, instructing me on the obvious. And I mine his words for judgment, for disapproval, but I don't detect any. "Don't blame him. Probably has a witch of a wife at home. Let the guy have a little fun."

"And who are we talking about?"

Fisher shrugs. "You're young. You'll learn. Can't live life with the dying tree. Sometimes you've got to visit that pretty little field again."

And I don't have to check my handbook on sexual harassment to determine that this isn't the portrait of appropriate.

I should be offended. Mom would probably throw her drink, or slap a cheek. But I stay put, sipping red vodka, breathing in his precarious words with his cigar smoke.

"Did you always want to be partner?" I ask.

"Hell no," he says, taking a drag, laughing deeply.

"So how did you get here?" I ask.

"American Airlines Flight 759," he says, pointing to my glass. "Or have you had too many to remember?"

I smile.

"It just happened. The guys and I started as summers. Worked a little, partied a lot, went to Yankee games, accepted our offers in August."

I try to imagine a younger Fisher. A little more hair, little less belly. But my imagination fails me and all I can see is the aging boy of a man in front of me, reclining in a deep velvet chair, desperately inhaling cigar smoke in August, numbing the pain that's evident, quieting dreams forgone. Flirting with the closest thing to him, a person who will listen or pretend to, who will nod at appropriate times and even laugh at a bad joke.

"Before I know it, I'm a seventh year. I have a wife. And she's pregnant," he says. "Time to grow up. Time to provide. An inspiring tale, huh?"

And I think of Mom's words. *Growing up is not a fact. It's a decision.*

"Almost as profound as Plato," I say. And drink some more.

"Don't squander it," he says, patting my knee, pulling himself to stand, leaving his dying cigar in the gold ashtray, and heading to the bathroom. "Don't do what I did. Don't let this job suck the life from you."

"Okay," I say. And wonder if it's already too late.

My BlackBerry buzzes. And for the first time in too many hours I think of Sage. I didn't call him when we landed, which is something I always do. The little screen lights up, a small beacon in the dark cave of a bar. And it's a text message. And not from Sage.

> **Phelps:** What are you up to?
> **Me:** Not too much. You?
> **Phelps:** In a smoky bar, getting my drink on. Missing you.

My heart jumps.

> **Me:** Oh.
> **Phelps:** Purple is a good color for you. Or is it navy??

I look up, scan the small room, and there he is at the bar, mere yards away, grinning behind a glowing pint of Guinness.

Fisher returns, rescues his cigar. "You and that thing. You chatting with your man about this creepy old geezer?"

"Something like that," I say.

> **Phelps:** Ah, so you traded up? ☺

I smile.

> **Phelps:** Room 547. Maybe I'll see you later when u lose the old man?

After billing a few more drinks to our clients, we stumble to the elevator, pulling two generations of suitcases behind us.

He walks me to my room and waits as I find my key. "Shall we have a nightcap?"

I look at him, the bloodshot eyes, the stray mustache hairs probably left over from a hasty morning shave.

"Better not," he says, answering his own question, looking down. "Could be trouble."

Before turning to go, he kisses me on the cheek. "Good night, Quinn. You're a good kid." And he disappears down the long hallway, the nutty smell of cigar smoke trailing behind him.

Once he's gone, I retrace my steps. Back onto that elevator and press 5. I walk slowly, 553, 551, 549 . . . 547. I knock softly, as if this is any less of an action.

"I knew you'd come," a voice says. And then he opens the door. And he's mere inches away, smiling like nothing ever happened.

"Still not lacking in the confidence department?"

"Guess not," he says.

Silence.

He insists I come in for a drink, that we hardly got a chance to talk in January. Knowing I will blame everything on the cocktails, I enter.

Phelps heads straight for the minibar and fiddles with the little key. "It's one of those ones with a motion sensor that charges you for everything you touch," he says. "The curse of technology."

"Then don't touch," I say, looking around the dark room.

But he already has a fistful of mini bottles and a Toblerone bar. "Nothing wrong with a late night snack," he mumbles.

"Don't need the calories; I'm getting married soon," I remind him.

"Screw calories. You look incredible," he says, handing me a bottle of Jack Daniel's and a square of chocolate.

I look at the little bottle, start peeling away at the black label. "Who *is* this Jack Daniel? Wouldn't it be cool to have a drink named after you?"

"I know it would be delicious," Phelps says, smiling. "But would it be The Prudence or The Quinn?"

Before I know it, most of the minibar contents are scattered between us on the beige bed; a tin of cashews, a jar of gummy bears, bottles of water and champagne.

Phelps feeds me a pretzel. And before I finish chewing, he's kissing me. And I'm kissing him back. He rolls on top of me, kicking bags and bottles to the carpet below.

And we're naked. This doesn't feel as wrong as it should because I've been here before. So many times. Like a memory. Like a dream.

But real.

"You still on the pill?" he has the prudence to mumble.

Before I have a chance to answer, his tongue is back in my mouth and it seems he's presumed a positive response to his romantic question.

When we're finished, we lie there like we always used to, toes touching, staring up at the ceiling. There's a crack running between the two overhead fixtures we never turned on.

"When is she due?"

"Any day," he says, looking away.

"And here you are," I say, looking at him, searching those eyes for sadness, for remorse, for love.

"Here I am," he says.

"Good thing you inquired about the birth control situation. Did you ever think to ask her that one?"

"I do love her," he says, and all I can think of is dying trees and lonely stalks.

"I'm sure you do. You don't have to justify it to me," I say. "And I love him."

"I'm sure you do. You don't have to justify it to me."

"Why did you do it?" I ask. "You didn't have to marry her. It's practically in vogue these days to have a baby out of wedlock."

He doesn't answer me. "Why'd you?" he asks.

"Why did I get engaged?"

"No," he says. "Why did you leave?"

Why did I leave him? And I don't have a good answer for him. Or for myself. Perhaps because boredom settled like fog over our yuppie existence? Perhaps because it isn't prudent to waste time on a first love? Because we all know first loves don't last. Or do they?

"I don't know," I say, and as I say it, I wonder if it is a copout, or simply the truth. But then I think of Mom, her wisdom that reasons often manifest after the fact, that the architecture of decisions is often only perceptible in retrospect. So I qualify these words. "I don't know *yet*."

And then he asks me the question he's never asked: "Had you already met him?"

I look at him, at his pleading blue eyes, the scar above his lip where I snagged him on that fateful fishing trip.

"Do you want to know the answer to that?" I ask him.

"I guess I have it," he says. He looks down and plays with his ring finger. No ring.

"Where's the ring?" I say.

"I wear it most of the time," he says, still staring down, playing with that finger.

"Just not when sleeping with women who aren't your wife?" I say, climbing out of bed, shielding my naked body—the body he's seen countless times before, the body he's just consumed along with a mini fridge full of junk—with a filthy hotel bedsheet. "Might as well be a heart-shaped tub."

He buries his head in his hands.

"The good husband," I say.

He throws his legs over his side of the bed, facing away from me, collects his boxers from the carpet—Brooks Brothers, plaid, an old birthday gift from me—puts one leg through and then the other. "Yes, the good husband."

There's nothing wrong with a late night snack.

But I fear that an ex is like that state-of-the-art minibar. No harm in looking. But if you touch, you'll have to pay.

Chapter 22

I open my eyes. Phelps sits next to me on the bed, staring. Like he always used to.

"You still sleep with your mouth open," he says. "You look like a trout."

"Trouble sleeping?" I ask.

"No. Best sleep I've gotten in years," he says, standing, opening drapes. Summer sun slices in on us. "Hard to sleep through your pocketbook symphony though. That thing's been buzzing all morning."

"Shit," I say, checking my watch, scrambling for my things.

"Let me guess. Hot coffee date with the old man?"

"Something like that," I say, escaping to the bathroom. The lights are harsh, highlighting every smudge and wrinkle. I splash cold water on my face. I scan the countertop and see the familiar lineup. Old Spice, shaving cream, Q-tips . . . Ro gaine . . . I grab the bottle and take it out to him, smiling.

His cheeks turn pink and he grabs it from me. "She doesn't want me to be bald," he explains.

"I wouldn't care if you were bald," I say.

"I know," he says, looking down. "That's the problem."

When I leave his hotel room, he follows me out, onto that same elevator, a few floors down. He trails behind me as I find my own hotel room door, the one I never opened. And he walks me inside.

"You can go now," I say, avoiding his eye, heading for the phone on the bedside that's blinking red.

He ignores me. "Your room's exactly the same," he marvels, looking around.

"They're all the same," I say. "They always are."

As I dial down to the front desk, Phelps grabs my hand, squeezes hard, and whispers, "No regrets."

"No regrets," I say back. And wonder if I mean it.

And then he's gone.

A guy at the front desk answers, "Good morning, Ms. O'Malley. It seems there's been an incident."

No shit. For a moment I wonder how this clerk knows about my latest indiscretion.

"Mr. William Fisher was taken to a local hospital a few hours ago," he says. "He asked that we contact you."

I hang up. In the small bathroom, predictably blanketed in beige marble, I splash cold water on my face. And cry. And as I cry, I wonder why exactly I am crying. Is it because I have just ruined my future by dipping into my past? Is it because my boss has been hospitalized? Is it because I am finally seeing the true reflection of a pathetic creature? Is it perhaps simpler than any of these things? Or is it all these things—the confluence of adult crises—commitment and infidelity and sickness and loss? Is it the realization that there is no going back?

In the lobby of the hospital, I buy two coffees.

A nurse leads me down a dim corridor on the cardiac floor. "He's in there," she says, pointing to a door that's slightly ajar.

I hesitate and knock. For a moment, all I hear is the buzzing from some machine and a toilet flushing in the distance.

"Come in," he says in a strong voice, those two words I've heard so many times when I've knocked on his office door.

But this time when I walk in, he's not behind his vast desk, clicking his fancy pen. This morning, he's a different man. No pinstripes or designer tie. The color's gone from his face; he's horizontal and hooked up to a number of tubes.

His cigar bar wisdom finds me now. And the pat and predictable words, bequeathed from one generation to another, echo in my head. *Don't do what I did. Don't let this job suck the life from you.*

"It's a good look, huh?" he says, managing a laugh.

"Not bad."

"A few cocktails and one bloody cigar and see what happens?" he whispers, smiling. "The gods are punishing me."

"The price you must pay for being King Porterhouse," I say. And together we laugh—mine high and nervous, his deep. But the harmony ends and we're left with a vulnerable expanse of quiet. I stand next to his bed, put my hand on his arm. "You okay?"

"Sure thing, kid," he says matter-of-factly, a bit too quickly, with the detectable defiance of a seasoned attorney who's not quite telling the truth. Or who doesn't quite know it.

What he should say, it seems, what we so rarely have the courage to say: "I don't know."

"What's wrong?" I ask.

And now Fisher really laughs, shaking in his bed, making those tubes dance. And I'm relieved to see some color again in his cheeks.

"What's wrong? Where do I begin? Today, nothing but a little old-fashioned heart attack," he says. "They've been mumbling about bypass."

He says these words without much affect, as if he's delivering the facts of a case.

"Are we double fisting again?" he says, nodding toward the twin cups of coffee I'm still grasping.

I hand him a coffee, which is likely an imprudent beverage for a cardiac patient. "Half and half, two sugars."

He smiles and nods.

"A good lawyer pays attention to details," I say.

"Channeling the lady lawyers of latter day," he says. "Good girl."

I think he catches me staring at the tubes that snake across him, and the small black and green screen, the ever-changing peaks and valleys of a threatened vitality.

Don't let this job suck the life from you.

"*You* can get out of this god-awful state. You aren't trapped here like I am," he says, tugging on his IV.

"I think I'll stay awhile," I say, smiling, settling into the fake leather armchair in the corner, the one patently meant for husbands and wives. I scroll through my BlackBerry, and offer a clumsy joke: "Any chance we can bill this time to the client?"

A nurse pops her head in, tells me to turn off my phone. "It might interfere with our equipment," she says.

"Isn't it fascinating that we are more worried about machines interfering with other machines than machines interfering with us?" Fisher says, a timely philosopher with a profound point. And if I closed my eyes, it could be Dad talking.

"*This* machine's okay apparently," Fisher says, turning on the TV that hangs precariously from the ceiling. We both sip coffee and settle on a channel that's airing reruns of *Law & Order*. But exhaustion overwhelms. He is tired because he's been up all night fighting for his life. I'm exhausted because I've been up all night fighting for mine.

I wake up when the door swings open. A small woman with frizzy dark hair flings herself at Fisher. The wife.

"Billy," she says through fresh tears.

And with this, I can suddenly picture him as a boy. Billy Fisher. Not the cutest boy in class, but funny, and irreverent. And lovable.

"Mary," he replies, and hugs her. He buries his face in her chest and I can't see his eyes, but I think he's crying too.

"I'm going to be just fine," he promises her.

"What happened?" she asks, pulling away from him, wiping her eyes. And I wonder what these words really mean; if it's the first time she's dared ask such a dangerous, honest question in decades. And in his eyes, I see distance disappear.

"It seems your old Billy goat has a big bad broken heart," he says, his voice both strong and cracking.

His wife giggles, awkwardly for a woman her age, and perches on the edge of his bed.

And I'm caught in the corner of this small room, an untimely impostor, witnessing a moment I shouldn't. A moment of—dare I say it—love. Not perfect, but palpable. No sparkling wheat field. But no dying tree either.

I stand. And his wife turns and sees me, half her age, sporting bedhead, smudged mascara and all.

"My name is Quinn," I say, offering my hand. "I work with your husband."

She shakes my hand limply and searches my eyes for an answer I can't give her. "I'm sure you do," she says.

And it occurs to me that I am just another one. We're all the same really. Sure, at one time we had our natural hair color and quirks and hobbies. But now we all have good manners and good highlights. We wear gray and navy and black, drink too much coffee and booze.

Interchangeable, really.

Then she takes the coffee cup from his bedside. "Are you allowed to have this?" she asks sharply, a simple question sprung from not-so-simple depths, fear and anxiety and anger dancing in her breath.

And Fisher becomes Billy, a little boy who's in trouble but doesn't know why exactly. He shrugs, catching my eye only briefly as I sneak out.

I book a flight for early the next morning. I go back to my hotel. To my room. For hours, I lie on that bed, that beige bed I should have slept in. For hours, I lie there alone and cry.

At the airport, the security line is long and moves slowly. Tired souls scrutinize photo IDs and tell us to remove our shoes. We fill plastic bins with machines—phones and computers and video games. We don't speak. But we eye each other, sizing each other up, trying to smell evil among aromas of stinky feet and fast food.

"They should rename this the insecurity line," a wise stranger mumbles.

At the newsstand, I stock up on tabloids and gummy candy. For once, I linger. I take time to look at all the silly items I usually breeze by, the cheap souvenirs that guilty husbands bring home for waiting wives and kiddies. Out-of-season snow globes, pens that light up, aprons with the shape of Texas emblazoned up front. I see a mug and grab it.

"The Best Way to a Fisherman's Heart Is Through His Fly."

I stop at a little sports bar and find a stool. Under the baseball game, a ticker reminds us that the alert level is orange. A bartender sidles up, and without thinking of it, I order a Bloody Mary. "Extra spicy," I say, and think of Fisher and his Mary, that small hospital room that looks like all the others. And it occurs to me that hospital rooms are just like hotel rooms are just like us lawyers. We serve a purpose, yes. But we're fungible. Each one of us is expensive, a generic copy of the next, sadly waiting to be filled.

I pull out my BlackBerry. For once, it doesn't blink.

I take a large sip of my drink and type in "bypass."

To avoid (an obstacle) by using an alternative channel, passage, or route.

I board the plane and walk to the back, past the forest of sad and aging men. I take off my jacket, roll it into a ball, and shove it overhead. No one says anything. The man next to me pulls out a weathered copy of *Moby Dick*, and flips to the middle.

The flight attendant reminds us to shut off our cell phones. And, happily, I comply. As if wireless signals are truly our biggest foe.

And as I dive into the rainbow pages of a gossip magazine and chew a fluorescent worm, bypassing brewing blockages and emotional malpractice, still gripping that porcelain mea culpa, a little baby cries.

Chapter 23

I follow the smell of bacon to our front door. As I fumble for my keys, I hear the hum of Saturday morning inside: Hula's scratchy meow, the clanking of dishes, Wolf Blitzer's Saturday morning growl.

Never before have I so appreciated the mundane sounds of a new day. And mere feet from him, on the other side of a door to which I have the key, I miss Sage more than ever; his sandpaper whiskers before he shaves, his toenails scratching me under the covers, the way he squints when he thinks hard about something.

I walk in, silly souvenir mug in hand, ready to pounce and surprise him, full of new stories and new remorse, ready to start over, to do this right, to prove old Plato and Fisher wrong. To let the tree thrive.

A giggle. I turn. Red toenails. Bare skin.

Kayla.

She wears Phelps's old flannel, my secret souvenir, and

leans against the kitchen island, drinking coffee, stroking my cat.

Sage hovers in the background in our sun-blanched kitchen, looking stunned. He wears nothing but those boxers with the fishing flies I gave him on Valentine's Day.

Surprise.

I drop the mug and it shatters.

"Nothing happened, Bug," he says, coming toward me as I turn to leave.

"Nothing happened," she says too, harmonizing his lie.

It must be a lie. Because this is what we do. We betray. And then lie.

Hula hops down from the island and follows me to the door.

Anger would be the appropriate emotion. But it's as if this emotion has been used up in me and instead anger's not-so-distant cousins, fear and sadness and longing, stand in. Instead of sizzling like the bacon my fiancé cooks for another woman, I'm floating. A lonely island in a suddenly rough sea. Lost, unreachable.

When I reach the corner, I look back. Sage stands there, frozen on our front stoop under an unforgiving spotlight of September sun.

You can only go so far in bare feet and boxers, I tell myself.

On the way to the gym, my BlackBerry dances in my bag, buzzing with explanations and apologies waiting to be heard. And I turn off the device and keep crying, my mind somewhere between Texas and here, muddled by vodka and shock and guilt.

But, suddenly, a thunderclap of relief. I'm not evil. Just weak. Imperfect. Human.

And so is he.

Two wrongs don't make a right. The clichéd words float in my head, mocking me, undermining my new and fleeting sense of comfort. Two indiscretions don't cancel each other out. Even when they're simultaneous.

But wait a minute, I tell myself, we're not talking about raising a good kid, one who doesn't yank hair, or bite. We're talking about vastly more complicated things. Life. Love. Maybe, in these situations, childhood tenets simply don't apply.

When I walk through the gym's front door, a strong arm grabs me.

"You're home early," Victor says.

I nod.

"You look like you've seen a ghost," he says.

"I have," I say, shaking.

Like he's done so many times before when spotting or stretching me, he grabs my arm. But this time his grasp is gentle, concerned. He walks me to the gym café. And orders me a coffee.

We sit at a small rickety table blanketed in someone else's crumbs. I sip bitter coffee and stare out the vast window as people march by holding hands, carrying groceries, pushing strollers. I wait for Victor's questions, but they don't yet come. Perhaps this man knows exactly what I need: time.

Among the swarm of strangers, I spot a familiar face. Avery. She walks in and doesn't seem to see me, but waits patiently on line and orders a green tea. Her eyes are red and puffy.

She turns and catches my eye. I smile. She hugs me, nods at Victor.

"Sit," I say. And she does. "Buff Brides must be getting intense these days, huh?"

She blows on her green tea and takes a delicate sip. "No more Buff Brides for me," she says, lifting her left hand, splaying thin, ringless fingers. "It's off."

"I see that," I say.

"No, the wedding. Goddamned lawyers. He wanted a pre-nup."

"I didn't even know he had money," I say. As far as I could tell, Jonathan was like all the other preppy guys I went to law school with. Intelligent, ambitious, eager to make the money he never quite had.

"Neither did I," she says, shaking her head. "Neither did I."

"Who would hide the fact that they have money?" Victor asks. A fair question. "Most of us work hard to hide the fact that we have none."

"Less than a fucking month before our wedding, he wanted me to sign on the dotted line."

"You never say 'fucking,'" I say.

"Only in emergencies," she says.

"Maybe he wanted to protect you?" I say.

"From what?"

"Money can ruin people, Avery," I say.

"It can also buy dinners out. It can also pay for private school tuition or an apartment," Avery says. "The bastard told me we'd have to wait years to have kids because of his *loans*. He has no loans. Just millions. Millions that now he wants to protect from me. Since I'm *obviously* such a gold digger."

She sips her tea and looks down.

"Well," I say, looking at them both. "Men are animals."

With this, Victor takes my coffee and Avery's tea, stands, and drops them into the garbage. "Girls, this animal is getting you out of here. I think we need a real drink."

"You never drink," I remind him.

He links his arms in both of ours. "Only in emergencies," he says, and leads the way. And like two little girls lost, we gladly follow.

Cilantro is buzzing with a Saturday brunch crowd, but we find a table in the back corner. Michael has responded quickly to this morning's text SOS and zips through the front door as we settle in. The waiter pours our first of many pitchers of sangria.

"Did you know 'sangria' comes from the Spanish word 'sangre,' which means blood?" Victor says, sniffing the crimson liquid, fishing an apple cube from the surface.

"Does that make us vampires?" Avery says, and a smile glides across her face.

"Okay," Michael says, taking a swig. "Why the sudden vampire convention?"

And now it's my turn to talk about my animal.

"He cheated," I say.

I tell them all about my morning. About Kayla barefoot and giggly in Phelps's shirt in my kitchen with Sage.

"Slow down, Quinn," Avery says. "It's entirely possible that nothing happened." And it's good to see that a certain goddamned lawyer hasn't drained her of her optimism.

I nod, eager to believe her. Maybe nothing did happen. Maybe I'm so drunk with guilt and remorse, I'm assuming the worst.

Michael and Victor look at each other and roll their eyes. A moment of male communication.

"She wasn't wearing pants," I say. "Hardly the portrait of innocence."

"Okay, so it's unlikely," she says. "But you never know. I

never did trust that girl. Speaking of trust . . . lawyers. They just fuck everything up," she says, glaring at me, letting fly that word again.

"Ah, the clichéd prenup dilemma," Michael says, catching on. "So, he has money. That's a nice late-breaking development, right?"

"I don't want his money. I want him," she says through fresh tears. "I *wanted* him."

With more sangria comes more courage. And truth.

"I saw Phelps," I say. "In Texas."

"You saw him from afar?" Avery says. "Or you *saw* him?"

"I *saw* him," I say. "It just kind of happened."

But even as these pathetic words escape me, I know better. Indiscretions, like marriages, don't just happen. We make them happen.

"Hence the flannel shirt hidden away in the depths of your dresser," Michael says in dramatic tones. "The leftovers of love."

Glasses down. Eyes on me.

"Monogamy might not be my thing," I say. "I'm not very good at it."

Avery glares at me. "Wow. Lawyers *do* fuck everything up."

I spare them the details. The gummy bears, the mini bottles of alcohol, the missing ring and pregnant wife. But I do tell them the pertinent details. The most important part. That I am immoral and lost and pathetic.

And for the first time in hours, our table is quiet and I hear the din of New York brunch, the snippets of conversation hurled back and forth between hungover lovers, parents pleading with a toddler to stop throwing food.

"Well, you're not married yet," Michael says. "There's a reason people get engaged first. Monogamy takes practice."

"Practice all you want, but you need to tell him," Avery says. "Even if it turns out he's no Boy Scout himself. Lies are never good. A last-minute confession beats a noncon-fession."

"But it was an accident," I plead. "And accidents happen, right?"

But even as I say these words, I know I don't mean them. Again, I know better. There aren't any accidents. For the most part, we do things intentionally, don't we? Like choose the people with whom we surround ourselves. Here I am with my brother who must love me no matter what. Avery, an old friend who keeps me honest, and optimistic, even in the throes of her own despair. And Victor, my trainer and so much more, with his surprisingly muscled mind and pro-foundly simple take on things.

Victor shrugs, looks at all three of us, and fills the silence. "This is just what we do."

And even in my own liquored fog, even in my haze of guilt, I note a nuance in Victor's wise words. He doesn't say *men*, this is what *men* do. He chooses his words more care-fully, it seems.

This is what we do.

Because it's not just the men who are animals.

I sip sangria, nod, and realize that monogamy is like ghosts. Some people are fervent believers, they tell stories, point to examples. But the rest of us are maybe a little less convinced.

Avery and I stumble back to her apartment.

"I'm sorry about the mess," she says, flipping the switch as we walk in. And for a moment, I wonder which one.

"I'm allowing myself a few days to grieve, but then I need

to get organized. This is pathetic," she says, slurring her words only slightly, clinging to her trademark decorum that another drink would surely snatch. She gestures toward her living room, a forest of pink florals. The books on her shelves are color-coded. Mail lingers in organized piles on a glass coffee table.

But the floor is littered with boxes and bags, gifts she's prudently left unpacked. "I'm beginning to wonder if I knew it was going to end, that I'd have to return everything," she muses.

In the small and spotless kitchen, she flips another switch and the dishwasher purrs. She uncorks a bottle of wine and pours two glasses and hands me one.

She steps over boxes and opens her coat closet. "You would have looked so pretty in this," she says, holding up my bridesmaid dress. It's periwinkle, a color that's pretty and safe, predictable for an early fall wedding, one that looks good on most skin tones. A color I've always hated.

Despite the boxes that litter her rose carpet, the apartment, like my friend, is peaceful. She lights twin lavender candles on the coffee table. I notice she still has pictures of Jonathan and her all over the apartment—a picture from their scuba trip where they sport matching sunburns and snorkels. A picture from the day they got engaged, mere minutes before she called me and could barely choke out the words through tears of joy.

"That's my next project," Avery says, apparently aware of my eye's path. "Getting rid of the reminders—the pictures, the letters, his light beers in my fridge. I *never* drink beer."

And I wonder if you can get past something like this by tackling projects, and methodically moving down a to-do list.

Avery stops stacking boxes, takes a sip of wine, and sits

down at her dining table. I sit too. She moves the vase of fresh pink roses that stands between us.

"From him?" I ask.

"Yeah, I've been getting them every day. Men and their flowers. So pathetic," she says. "Why do they think a nice-smelling bouquet is going to fix things?"

"Ever notice when people buy flowers? When a person or a relationship is dying. When it's already too late," I say.

But then, miraculously, a flame of optimism flickers in her again. "Or when people marry. Or when a baby is born."

Undeterred, I continue to theorize about men and flowers, bozos and botany. "Maybe," I surmise, "he wants to remind you of life when everything threatens to die."

Avery shrugs and takes a large sip. "One day I'm going to meet a man who is going to love me enough to be honest."

"Of course you will," I say. A timely assurance, a potential lie.

"Someone like . . ." she says, and pauses. And we both know she was about to say Sage.

"Someone like who we thought Sage was? A good guy, a what-you-see-is-what-you-get kind of guy? Someone who wouldn't sucker punch you right before your wedding day?"

She nods.

"I'm beginning to wonder if these guys exist," I say.

And she nods again.

"Someone who is honest," she says. That word again. "Is that too much to ask?"

"No," I say. But maybe it is. Maybe honesty is just another one of those things we strive for and banter about, a glittering cliché like prudence, which necessarily eludes us. "Maybe dishonesty is part of the game. Maybe it's just part of who we are. Good people can be dishonest."

"Not about big things," she says. "Quinn, I'm not talking about a cute little white lie. This guy's been saying we can't have kids for years because we can't afford it, and he has millions locked up somewhere with his name on it."

"I think good people can lie about most anything," I say, thinking primarily, egotistically, of myself.

"Don't get all philosophical on me," she says, and giggles.

I find the bottle of wine in her fridge, and look through her cabinets. I grab a box of Cheerios and bring it back to the couch.

"Remember when things were simple?" Avery says, pinching a lone Cheerio between slim fingers. "Such a simple shape. So childish and wonderful, nothing complicated about it."

"Cheerios are round with holes," I say. "So kids don't choke."

And here we are, drinking and pontificating the night away, in ponytails and pastel PJs, choking on reality. Just the girls. Like it used to be. My ring, boxes of wedding gifts, the only evidence that we aren't little girls anymore.

After a few more hours of hypothesizing about happiness and commitment we pluck stray Cheerios from her carpet, blow out the candles, and call it a night.

I climb into her bed, on Jonathan's side. Like I always used to do before we gave our beds up to boys. And then to men.

We say good night. And Avery turns off the light next to her bed. "You're going to tell him," she says. "You've got to tell him. Secrets are toxic."

"I don't want to lose him," I say to her, and admit to myself.

"If you really love him, you'll tell him," she says. "You'll find a way."

Before she nods off, and surrenders to the deep snoring

I only now remember, she says: "I know you love him. And you're not a bad person."

"Thanks," I say into the pillow, wishing she had chosen her words a bit differently, but knowing why she hasn't. There's a big difference between not being a bad person and being a good one.

Chapter 24

The next morning, I find Avery in her living room hunched over a cup of coffee watching cartoons.

"Too much wine," she mumbles, peeling her eyes from a little girl with a round face and a bowl cut, a little girl who jabbers impressively in English and Spanish.

"Looks like I might not be the only one having a hard time growing up."

"Dora the Explorer," she says. "My students are obsessed. Every episode, she goes on a new exploration, to either find something or help someone."

"Charitable tyke," I say, watching the little girl bounce along. And then her bag begins to talk.

"That's Backpack," Avery explains. "A gift from her mom and dad. It helps her complete all her tasks. She can find whatever she needs in there."

"I see that," I say, as Dora pulls a ladder from Backpack.

"And she also has Map," Avery says. "Gives her directions to get wherever she needs to go. Jonathan thought it was so silly that I watched this, but now I can watch Dora whenever I want. I can even TiVo it."

"That's the spirit," I say and pause. "She's pregnant."

For a moment, Avery's face crumbles. "Dora?"

And we laugh the way you laugh when your brain isn't working properly. "Now that would make her a stellar role model, huh? I guess she could ask Backpack to fix that too?"

Avery shrugs. And stands. "Let me make you a latte," she says.

And so I let her.

She fumbles around her kitchen, spills milk, then wipes it up.

"Kayla's knocked up," I say. "Or so the story goes. Apparently, she showed up at our apartment freaking out. Forgot that I was in Dallas. Sage said she was a wreck and my Boy Scout of a fiancé insisted she stay over."

Avery's eyes sparkle as she nods, stirs my coffee, and hands me the cup. "Now *that* makes sense."

"It does?" I ask, taking a sip.

"It does sound like Sage, right?"

"It does," I say. An odd mixture of relief and disappointment rolls through me. "Do I really want to be with a guy who turns our apartment into a fucking bed-and-breakfast for wayward pregnant women the second I leave town?"

"She's not a wayward pregnant woman. She's your friend. Sage is a caring soul. And yes, speaking from experience, you are lucky to be with someone who's a good person. Someone who's not only good to you, but good to your friends."

I nod. Because this is all true.

"If he's such a good person, why do I feel nauseous?" I ask, staring down into my latte. "What if it's his baby?"

Avery grabs my shoulders, looks me in the eyes. "We are both nauseous because we drank a senseless amount of wine last night. And it is *not* his baby. You know that, Quinn."

"It's not?" I ask.

"There's no way," she says, shaking her head.

And I nod because I want to believe her. "There's no way."

"Has it occurred to you that you might be nauseous because of Phelps?"

I nod. "Maybe. It's just that for a moment I thought I wasn't the only one who messed up."

"Everyone messes up," she says, placing her hand on my arm. "You just seem to be particularly good at it."

"Thanks."

"Nobody's perfect," she says.

"Not even you?"

"Not even me," she says, smiling. "I'm obsessed with fairy tales. But they don't exist. I watch cartoons. I have a wedding dress in my closet that I will never wear and I don't want to return it. No, I want to be able to look at it. Just seeing it makes me believe. So, no, not perfect."

There are tears in her eyes now. "It's okay to believe. I wish I could believe a little more," I say.

"Well, it's good you talked to him," Avery says, guzzling latte, eyes following that bouncing little girl once more.

And I nod. But I didn't speak to him. Just read his words and Kayla's, woven together, corroborating today's truth, on my sweet little BlackBerry.

"How's the latte?" she asks. "I have more sugar if you want it."

"It's perfect," I say to her, lying a bit. It's too sweet.

And it hits me: I never make coffee for other people.

"When you and Jonathan traveled, who held the tickets?" I ask.

Confusion contorts her face. "Why?"

"Just curious," I say, swallowing her latte.

"I did," she says, confirming my hunch. "Always."

I nod. This makes sense. The one who holds the tickets is the caretaker, the protector, the adult.

"Who holds the tickets when you travel?" she asks.

"He does," I say. "Always."

I have an idea. A good one. A fantastic one.

"Get dressed," I say. "We're going out."

And like a little girl, she listens.

Before we leave, I open her closet door and grab the vast garment bag.

"What are you doing?" she asks.

"I'm being a friend."

We walk into the small salon. Avery trails behind me, but I'm all business. I walk to the front and say, "We need to make a return."

The petite saleslady looks past me at Avery. At diminutive, ashen Avery. "I'm sorry. This dress has been altered. We can't take it back. It's our policy."

I think of Fisher. His wisdom about names. I look at the saleswoman's name tag. Jasmine. And suddenly I morph from best friend to litigator. "Jasmine, ostensibly you are in the wedding business, and that means that you are well-acquainted with the sad statistics that some unions are not meant to be?"

Stunned, Jasmine nods. "Sure."

"Well, every now and then an individual, a smart individual, has the insight to end things even before they begin. And we should applaud that. Not make it more difficult by instituting inflexible policies about dress returns."

"Well. If I let everyone return—"

I cut her off. "Jasmine, don't get all Kantian on me. Not everyone returns her dress. No, most people cling tight to that dress just like they cling tight to the belief in happily-ever-after."

"My, my. A negotiator and a philosopher?" a voice says.

"Liv," the saleswoman says. "I'm sorry. I didn't see you there."

I turn. A young woman stands there, clutching a stack of dresses.

"My God, are you returning all of those? You're killing my point," I say.

"No," Liv says, smiling. "I'm selling them. I designed them."

"Oh," I say. Avery lingers by my side.

"Let me guess. You're a lawyer?" Liv says.

"Guilty as charged," I say. "It does come in handy sometimes. Like, hopefully *now*."

"I was a lawyer back in the day. Jumped ship to, well, live," she says, and giggles. And then she turns to the saleswoman. "Let this poor girl return her dress and I will give you a discount on these delicious confections."

Jasmine nods, takes the dresses from Liv, and one by one holds them up. She smiles. "You have yourself a deal."

Avery and I watch her study each dress. The final dress is a simple sheath. On the back, I see a tiny splash of color.

Liv takes the dress from the clerk and explains, "I like to let the bride add a little something to the dress. Here there's a sunflower. But it could be anything. I don't think wedding gowns should be fungible. I think they should be playful and unique."

I smile. "Can I hold it?"

Liv hands it to me. Avery's eyes light up.

"It just so happens I'm getting married," I say.

"And *soon*," Avery adds.

"Try it," Liv says.

"I think I will," I say, and slip into the tiny dressing room. I step in. It fits perfectly. I look in the mirror. And smile. A giddy, goofy, girly, nonlawyer smile.

I step out of the room. And I'm met with three more smiles.

I turn and look at myself in the bigger mirror. "I like it because I'm wearing a wedding dress, but I don't look like a bride. I look like *me*."

Maybe finding a dress *is* like finding a groom. You don't do it overnight. And it doesn't happen when you are looking. It happens when you are living.

"Exactly," Liv says. "And if you need this soon, I can remove the sunflower and add whatever it is you want to add."

Avery runs in place. "This is so exciting. What would you add?"

This is an easy one. I run back into the dressing room and find my phone. I dial Sage.

"Bug," he answers. "I'm so sorry. Nothing—"

"I believe you," I say. "I need you to do me a favor."

"Anything."

"Do you still have that fishing fly from our first night? The Parachute Adams?"

"Of course I do," he says.

"Will you bring it to me?"

He doesn't ask why. Just takes down the address of the small bridal salon. And, like a good boy, he arrives and waits outside. While Liv pins the hem of my gown, Avery steps outside to get the fly from him.

She walks back in, clutching it. "Perfect," she says. "This is perfect."

I take the fly from her, turn it over in my hand, study it. The imperfect white wings. The brown hackle. The sharp and delicate hook. Outside, I can see Sage pacing. I see his sandy blond hair and smile. And then I hand the fly to Liv. "This is what I want. This is my thing."

She smiles. "You've got it, counselor."

Outside, Avery hugs me hard. "Thank you, Quinn. Thank you for this day." And then she hops in a cab. Before it pulls away, I see her, her little-girl nose pressed up against the glass, watching us. Still eager to believe.

I grab Sage's hand. "I found my dress," I say. "You're going to love it."

"Not as much as I love something else," he says. And looks up. His eyes are red, still wet. "I've been calling you."

"I know."

"And e-mailing," he says.

I nod.

He hugs me, suffocating me with his strong arms, burying his head in my chest. "I was so scared," he says.

"So was I."

We don't talk much. But begin walking. Toward home.

And I have so much to tell him. About things he doesn't know: a heart attack and a betrayal. About my new theory that monogamy is a sport that takes practice, but that I'm willing to work at it. That he's worth it, that we are. And I want to tell him that even the very moment I saw them together, I wanted to forgive him. That in that moment, I glimpsed myself in him. That for a split second, the imperfections he typically camouflages so expertly were right there, ruefully raw and exposed. That in that moment, I saw the fear I'd been fighting gloss his eyes too. And maybe this is self-serving and narcissistic, but all this made me love him more desperately than ever.

But I don't say these things.

Instead, we walk and walk. Hands linked. Silent.

"Avery called her wedding off," I do say as we walk into our apartment. For it's easier to talk about other peoples' pain than your own. "This whole time Jonathan had these trust funds and didn't tell her. He's been lying for years."

"Wow," Sage says. "Never did like the guy, but still. She must be devastated. That girl was born to nurture."

Yes, an old-school latte-making, ticket-holding goddess.

"Born to nurture," I say, nodding. "Unlike me, right?"

And just like that, we're back. Being the people we are, bickering about the people we'll never be.

"You only need one nurturer in a relationship," Sage says, smiling, pulling two mugs from the cabinet. "I think I've got that part covered."

We make a wordless pact to enjoy the silence of a new day. He pours me a cup of coffee. And, though bitter, I drink it down.

"Bacon?" he asks.

"Nurture away," I say.

And as I'm mustering the courage to say things, precarious things, impossible things, my BlackBerry buzzes and I reach for it.

Ladies and Gentlemen of Whalen Stanford,

It is with deep regret and sadness that we members of the Executive Committee inform you that our dear partner and friend William Fisher passed away yesterday during emergency heart surgery. Details about services to follow. Please join us in sending prayers to Bill's family.

The Executive Committee

Sage looks away from the sizzling bacon when I start to cry. "Fisher died," I say.

And I'm not sure whether these words make immediate sense to him, but Sage abandons the crackling pan and hugs me. He does what he can to comfort me. Which, frankly, is not much.

But I do what I'm supposed to do. Something I'm not very good at: I let him try.

He rubs my back in small circles and feeds me bits of bacon. And when my tears run dry, he points to a beautiful vase of flowers. Like him, they've been wilting, waiting for me to come home.

"They're beautiful," I say, robotically, wondering how many bouquets Fisher gave his wife over the years. Whether she was optimistic or naïve and loved them, tried to keep them alive. Or whether she did what was expected of her, what she was supposed to do, and said those two words ingrained in us so early on: *Thank you.*

"God, Kayla must be scared," I say. "I don't know what I'd do if it were me."

"Sure you do," Sage says confidently, gripping my hand between both of his, tracing the diamond he gave me. "You'd have our gorgeous little baby."

I smile. Because in this moment, this delicate moment, the image of a baby, our baby, brings joy. Happiness.

This is how happiness comes—in small moments, in fierce flashes. It's not a state of being, not remotely permanent.

"We're going to have kids one day," I say. "Can you believe it?"

"Yes," he says, grinning. "I sure can."

"Promise me one thing," I say.

"Anything," he says.

"Promise me that when the time comes we don't have to name our poor child after a fishing fly."

And before I lose myself in those strong arms again, I study his eyes. And I see happiness there too, mixed in with the blue, and I think that maybe this is what we can both hope for and achieve; moments when everything seems okay, even a bit better than okay.

Chapter 25

F isher's memorial service is held on the morning of September tenth. Sage, more of a teddy bear these days for predictable reasons, asks if I want him to come with me.

And though I do want him to come, I say I don't and hope that he still does. Insist this is something I can do on my own.

A test.

One he fails.

The service is, fittingly, just like Fisher was: a bit fat, important, over-the-top. Full of pomp and circumstance. Exotic flowers burst from every seam of the vast chapel, where he was a significant donor, no doubt. Bursts of color amidst a dark sea of mourners.

There's a program printed on thick parchment, and on the front, in strong cursive letters, is written: "Porter William Fisher, Jr. (1954–2002)."

He was a Porter after all.

Like me, he went by his middle name.

And he was a junior. He came from someone. I remember our discussion about names, and his cryptic words: *Parents, like the rest of us, have agendas.*

Lawyers and clients and family fill the large chapel, hordes of black. And I think a dangerous, inappropriate, Fisher-esque thought: I wonder how many people are here because they loved this man, because they knew him, really knew him, knew about more than his stellar litigation record, his predilection for big steaks and double martinis. How many of these people knew the story behind his name, the octaves of his laughter, the depths of his regret?

How many people showed up to make business connections? How many people showed up, like we so often do in life, because they thought they had to?

And then there are bagpipes and plaid. And "Amazing Grace."

And, suddenly, I'm back at Bird Lake on that January afternoon, huddled with family and the other faces from Dad's life, listening to this worn-out and lovely Christian tune that on that afternoon played from Dad's old boom box.

Once we're seated, Fisher's wife walks down the center aisle, holding the hands of two teenagers. An impeccable family, a united front. Today, her hair is straight and her eyes are red. The kids are dressed in black too, and they share a dazed expression. Periodically, they lift their gaze from the floor and look around into the masses, people their father has touched in some way, people who pulled him away and demanded his time.

Mary Fisher and her kids take a seat in the front and peer

back as six strong strangers dressed in matching black carry the coffin forward.

The beautiful box, like life, is full of sharp corners and blurring detail.

The music fades and Fisher's daughter, a skinny girl with glasses, stands and climbs the steps to the podium. Her mother rubs her back as she walks past, and sends her off with an encouraging nod.

Her little girl unfolds a piece of loose-leaf paper with the scraggly edges, stares blankly into the sea of strangers, and looks down. "I loved my father very much," she says.

Her mother nods. *Keep going. Do him proud.*

"Even though he was very busy a lot of the time, he came to my cello recitals and helped me with my homework."

At these simple words, people around me start crying.

"He loved us. I know because he told us all the time."

And I think: *This is not how I want my kids to know I love them. I want them to know because I am there, holding a hand, cutting the unwanted crusts off a grilled cheese. Because I read them stories as they're falling asleep, or make the rubber ducky quack during bathtime.*

Mary Fisher nods proudly, but a frown overtakes her pinched face when it seems her little girl goes off script.

"I wish he was around more."

She folds her paper and returns to her mother, who has no choice but to throw an arm around her brave and honest girl and squeeze tight.

Miles Shannon is the next to speak, Fisher's ostensible good friend, the partner who accompanied us on our first-day lunch.

"Bill was a good lawyer and good man. He had the power

to light up a room, to argue any point and win, to make believers of us all. His track record speaks for itself. He was an asset to our firm and he will be sorely missed."

Good. Power. Argue. Win. Record. Asset.

Mildy speaks slowly, deliberately, enunciating clearly and carefully like the good litigator he is. His words are economical, well-chosen, entirely impersonal. He speaks as if he is before a jury.

And maybe he is?

Listen to me, folks. This man meant well, he worked hard, you will mourn him.

I look around and think: *Who's next? Who'll be the next to get the life sucked from him by this world?*

And I see Cameron. His caramel hair, carefully parted, neatly combed. On his face is an expression of unadulterated worry, as if this day is some sort of warning for him.

Or for us all.

Next, an old man climbs to the podium. He wrestles with the microphone, and stares out at us all with a look of confusion and wisdom. His father. The original Fisher. His words are simple, woven with sadness and wonder. "It's amazing how you can raise your son into a person you no longer recognize. I never understood the desire to be a lawyer. But I respected him . . . I should've seen it coming though. The boy could argue. And manipulate. When he was fifteen, he crashed the family car. Before I had time to punish him, he said: 'Remember to focus on the fact that I'm okay. Not everything's about money.'" His voice trails off and laughter thunders in the vast chapel.

And part of me thinks: *It's unfair that some people live so long. Years are things that should be doled out equally.*

But then I think: *A father shouldn't, it seems, survive his kin. Or see them die.*

And I think of Fisher, horizontal and lifeless in a box custom designed for his exit, and wonder if he can hear all this: the fact that his little girl mourned him even before he died, that she called him Father and not Dad. That his partner stood and carefully quoted bland statistics like he was reading from the back of a baseball card. That his own father, his namesake, no longer knew his boy. Can Fisher hear these words—some canned, some truthful—about the man he had, perhaps unwittingly, become?

Eyes fixed on the thousand or so faces, I miss the one suddenly next to me. "Losing the tree for the forest?" Kayla says, slipping in, late as usual. She wears black too. Missing from her eyes is her trademark glint, that sarcasm waiting to burst.

"Hi," I say.

"Hi," she says. "A law firm gathering without booze is like a car without wheels. Very sad, going nowhere."

Her metaphor is as mixed up as she is.

"Guess I'm going to have to get by without the sauce for a little while anyway," she says, rubbing her belly.

"It'll be worth it," I whisper, and grab her trembling hand.

She nods. "I guess so."

Then she reaches into her bag and grabs something and slips it to me. That little figurine of the Towers. From the little newsstand in Times Square.

"I thought you'd like it," she whispers.

"I do."

And in this gathering where we bow to death and mourn one end, swimming in there, somewhere beyond her prudent cloak of practical black, is a tiny reminder of life, of another chance, of a new and unexpected beginning.

And soon the music will stop, and some charity will be announced in Fisher's name. And that coffin will be whisked away. And all these people will scatter like ashes. Go back to their days, as if this was just a lengthy and last-minute conference call, a blip on a finely tuned schedule.

Or maybe not. Maybe they will take the day, go for a walk. Call a family member. Maybe they will realize that life isn't carved in six-minute increments of billable energy, but lived in more meaningful units—in moments, in days, in years— that aren't unlimited.

Chapter 26

H ome that night, I uncork a pinot grigio and pour myself a glass. I swallow fast and keep the bottle close.
And soon, everything is in slow motion.

And it hits me: *This* is why I drink. For this feeling. When
things are speeding and spiraling, when things are out of my
control—and aren't they always?—the blurry buzz saves me.

The voices on the TV drone on and on about one word:
tomorrow.

And I wonder what's worse: pain or the anticipation of it?
Or whether these things are really the same.

The phone rings. Sage. Do I want him to come home early? Yes. Obviously. This is no night to be alone.

"No," I say to him as the tears come. "I'm fine."

Another test.

"Okay, Bug," he says as an aria of male laughter swells in
the background. Bob Marley croons "No Woman, No Cry,"

and foolishly, I decide those words must be meant for me. For them, it's just another night at the office.

I hang up. Drink more.

Another call.

It's Mom. We talk about little things: the unseasonable weather, my wedding registry, how bad the bugs are in Wisconsin. We chatter on, nervously dancing around the conspicuous reason for her call, pausing only to refill our respective wineglasses.

"I wish you were here," I say. "Or that I were there."

"Why?" she says quickly, defensively, as if convening on the anniversary of Dad's death would be ludicrous. "Why is tomorrow any different than any other day? He'll be no more dead tomorrow than he is today. The goddamned media is so obsessed with anniversaries, hell-bent on stirring things up right when they're beginning to settle."

"I guess," I say.

Are things settling? Do we want them to?

When asked if she wanted to read his name during the televised memorial at Ground Zero, her answer was unsurprising, and so very Mom. *No, I don't want to wait in a line of strangers to read aloud the name that floats through my head every day, the name I no longer call out when I'm on the toilet and there's no paper left, or when I'm buried in a wonderful novel and need a refill of wine.*

Dad was the nurturer.

Tonight, her voice is alarmingly crisp and calm like those September minutes before it all happened, her words calculated, practiced even, braided with anger and pain she refuses to admit.

And I think: *I will have to do this someday. I will have to be strong, pretend I'm okay when I'm not, to protect someone.*

"So, how's everything there?" she asks.

"Okay," I say. "I found my dress."

She laughs. A cork pops. "A dead father, a pregnant bridesmaid, a rendezvous with an old love, the untimely death of an esteemed colleague, and we're talking organza?"

"I see Michael has given you a news flash," I say.

And here we are, separated by a generation, swallowing the silence with our white wine, doing the same thing on opposite ends of the line; drinking through our denial of a day that has no choice but to arrive.

"Things *will* be okay," I say.

This simple change of tense sparks something in Mom. "That's my girl," she says. "And they will. You're the pilot."

More silence. More swallowing.

"I still wish you were here," I say. "*I* could bring you toilet paper and keep your glass full."

"I love you, Prue," she says. "And so did he. So did he."

"I know," I say. And as our TVs buzz on in the background, we both cry and gulp wine. And the calmness cracks, finally cracks, and sadness snakes through.

"Let's talk tomorrow," I say.

"It's a date," Mom says. "And Prue?"

"Yes, Mom?"

"I can't wait to see your princess costume. I just wish he were around to see it too."

"Me too," I say. "Me too."

We hang up. And keep drinking.

Sage walks in.

"You're home early," I say.

One test passed.

"Of course I am. I'm no dummy," he says, eyeing the wine

bottle on our coffee table. "Thirsty, huh? How many have you had?"

"Not nearly enough," I say.

"How was the day?" he asks me, his words one-size-fits-all, plain. A sobering—or is it comforting—thought: *I will hear him utter this question every night for the rest of my life.*

"Fine," I say. A quick, thoughtless reply, not untrue. I don't tell him about the sad faces of good people. How you can tell a lot about a person when she crumbles, when the tears come. How grown people blend and look alike until they cry. I don't tell him about Kayla, her pallid face and shaking hands.

That little figurine of the Towers sits on the table next to Mom and Dad's wedding picture. Sage picks it up.

"From Kayla," I say. "A peace offering."

I pour another glass of wine. He sits next to me on the couch. The TV blares in the dark room. Indecisive, I flip channels. Men and women wear pinstripes and appropriately ominous faces and American flag pins and say it over and over: *tomorrow.* They talk about freedom and the vitality of the American spirit and a downtown man who is holed up in a studio apartment with his potassium iodide and particle mask.

"Have you talked to your mom?" Sage asks me, expectantly.

I nod.

"How's she holding up?" he asks.

"Fine," I say. That word again.

He doesn't pry, but sits there with me, his breath heavy.

"Are you still going to the gym in the morning?" he asks.

"Of course I am. Why wouldn't I?"

Fuck. I *am* my mother.

He lets me pick where we will get takeout. Queen for a day. Lucky me.

As I pour another glass, he grabs my wrist gently. Takes the glass away. Walks into the kitchen. And I follow. He dumps the wine. Rinses the glass. Looks at me.

"I'm not going to let you do this anymore," he says. "Put your shoes on. We're going out."

I hold his hand and follow as he pulls me through the streets of our neighborhood under a starless September sky. We walk by our local fire station where framed photos of nine men, young and smiling, perch on windowsills. Votive candles flicker on the sidewalk beneath.

When he leads me down the concrete steps to the subway, I don't fight him. Oddly, on this night, my paranoia doesn't swell, and I'm not scared. Tonight, this isn't about letting terrorists win or lose, or letting my future husband win or lose. No, tonight is about something far bigger than winning and losing.

On the platform, an old man plays "The Star Spangled Banner" on his saxophone.

When we get off at Vesey Street, Sage stops in a bodega and tells me to wait outside. In a few minutes, he returns with two cups of coffee in trademark paper I ♥ NY cups and hands me a new souvenir mug for our growing collection. On this mug, above a picture of the Towers, it says, in words painfully trite and true: "Gone But Not Forgotten."

I clutch that mug and through fresh tears I say, "Beats Spode any day."

Sage nods and kisses my forehead.

I sip bitter coffee, sweetener-free, and clutch my new gift as he walks me to the site. To Ground Zero. And there they are: the sixteen barren acres I've heard all about on the news. The footprints of the Towers that just one year ago stood proudly and peacefully, hours from collapse.

The debris is gone. So are all the posters.

We pace around the so-called Pit, apparently six or seven stories deep, an abyss of mud and darkness. We stand there, hand in hand, on the sidelines of the cemetery where Dad is buried. The cloying smell still lingers. Tomorrow, this place will be baptized in tears. Tomorrow, people will gather, read names, fly flags. Politicians will make cameos and offer well-cooked sympathies while proclaiming battle.

"*This* happened," he says, gesturing around us. "Nothing—getting a kitten, getting married, drinking buckets of wine, or fighting me is going to change that, Bug. *This* isn't something you or any of us should ever let go of or try to escape."

I nod, clutching my new mug, burying my head in his shoulders, holding on to him. And I look at him through the salty blur of tears and wine and say, "Thank you."

Because away from here, even only one year later, 9/11 has been packaged and prodded like an event from an American history book.

Tonight, I don't see things, this gray gash in the side of the city, as an American. It's not about religious freedom and equality. It's not about economic opportunity or political choice. It's not about safeguarding our lives and democracy.

Tonight, I don't see things as a lawyer. It's not about the law of intent and consequences. It's not about guilt and innocence. Or chaos and order.

Tonight, I don't even see things as a New Yorker. It's not about hometowns and pride and souvenir mugs. It's not about there being a conspicuous hole in our glorious skyline.

But tonight, finally, I do see things as a daughter. It is about

Dad. It is about the fact that he is as gone as those Towers. It is about the fact that he will never again answer the phone when I call. That I will never again hear his "Hi, hi."

"Life will go on," Sage says, marring the silence of this bittersweet moment, this melancholy and beautiful moment, his unsullied optimism breaking through, "if you let it."

And as the clock strikes midnight, ushering in that new and dreaded day, I clutch tightly to this boy, this man, my future. And something strikes me: Maybe you can hold on and let go at the very same time.

Chapter 27

I wake up and find Sage in the kitchen cooking bacon.

"Morning, Bug," he says like he does every morning. And I'm thankful he hasn't written a special script. He leaves the pan long enough to kiss me on the forehead.

He hands me a cup of coffee. And as I empty the sweetener into it, he looks at me disapprovingly.

"Don't say it," I say. "I know it'll do me in."

He nods.

"What is the point of monitoring our intake of sucralose or aspartame or wine when boom, just like that, we can be sitting there sucking smoked salmon off a sterling fork and, bam, it's just *over*?"

"Sweeten away," he says, fear in his eyes.

And for a moment I wish there were something—artificial, carcinogenic, I don't care—that I could sprinkle to sweeten bitter moments like this one.

"Drink up and wake up," he says. "We've got work to do."

"We do?"

We sit side by side on our Pottery Barn love seat. It's years old, but newness still seeps from those synthetic stripes. We hunch over our coffee table, stuffing envelopes with wedding invitations, passing the small roll of American flag stamps back and forth.

And on the television, Katie sits there, nervously twisting her legs like pretzels, talking to someone, so very euphemistically, about "the events that occurred a year ago."

Sage and I lick our last stamp at the same time.

He dangles an envelope in front of me. "Want to leave this one out?"

It's addressed to Phelps and his wife.

"If you don't feel comfortable . . ." I begin.

He laughs. "I'm kidding," he says. "I won you, right? No worries here."

"Am I a prize? A piece of property? A trophy? Is this ring your brand?" I say.

He pauses, sips coffee, collects words presumably.

"I'm willing to be your fucking punching bag today if you need me to be. Because I love you," he says. "But not forever."

I recant, retrace. "It's just that his family and my family are so close," I say. "You know this is all about Dad. I'm sorry."

"Stop the fucking rationalizing," he says.

And I think: *But this is what I do.* I search for reasons. Collect them like stamps. Reasons for everything that happens, big and small. Reasons for why I became a lawyer (*it will open so many doors, the pay is good even if I don't really need it, it will screw with Mom, I don't know what else to do*), why I'm so scared of becoming a wife (*fear is normal, this is a big step, finality is daunting, maybe matrimony and career are not friends*).

I take the envelopes from him and place them down next to mine: little twin towers of a new beginning. I kiss him hard. Straddle him. Katie chirps away in the background as Sage pushes me down onto those stripes—those prudent stripes that the saleswoman promised wouldn't show dirt.

I keep my eyes open, looking into his. The television flashes to a split screen of memorials at Ground Zero and the Pentagon. Crowds of people—mothers and fathers, sons and daughters, sisters and brothers, husbands and wives—huddle together, tears commingling, cloaked by a collective grief that maybe only time can dissipate.

As we both let go, Sage holds me tight and I wonder how many beginnings there were on that day when everything seemed to end.

We walk hand in hand to the corner.

People buzz about, gripping coffees, pushing strollers.

And I'm pleased to hear a cabdriver fire a good old "Fuck you" to someone who crosses on his light. We're coming back.

As the fighter jets fly overhead and the sun beats down, Sage grips my hand tight. And for the first time in too long, I feel safe.

My BlackBerry buzzes.

A message from Phelps. No doubt the first of many messages I'll receive today making sure I'm okay.

I open the message.

> Carter and I proudly welcomed Phelps, Junior
> into the world at 2:13 this morning.
> He weighed in at a hefty 8lb 2oz.
> and is tall like his daddy—22". We are all doing well!

At the bottom of the message is a small image of a pink face with Phelps's nose and trademark dimple.

Parents have agendas.

Another junior. Another poor kid stripped of his own identity on his very first day. Welcome to the Heart-Shaped Tub Club, little dude.

At the corner, Sage and I drop the invites into the fat blue mailbox.

Before parting, Sage takes my face in his hands, looks into my eyes, and says, "This is an impossible day. And it isn't going to be easy, and I don't really know what I'm doing, but I love you and I'm here and I'm trying."

And though his words are hardly poetic, they are honest and humble and confident and patient. And, most importantly, they are his.

He loves me. And unlike a certain other man who loved me this much, Sage is still here.

"See you tonight," I say.

"Our cozy couch, say 8 P.M.?" he says.

"It's a love seat," I say.

He smiles. "It sure is."

And I watch him go, striding confidently, shaking the change in his pockets like Dad used to do. On the corner, he trips on the curb, and I'm happy to see he doesn't look around to see if anyone's watching.

When I walk through the glass doors of the gym, it all comes back to me. I was here. I was on the elliptical machine watching Britney's new video on VH1. In a single moment, we went from strangers, to New Yorkers, to Americans. One by one, televisions were taken over by breaking news. And those images of a plane flying into a building were played over and over. One by one, we shed earphones and looked around, stunned, searching, catching the eye of the person next to us.

What's happening? Eyes and voices and news anchors asked. And bits and pieces swirled: Twin Towers. A plane. Another plane. The building collapsed. And the sirens blared on TV and outside those glass doors.

And for a while, I was just one of them. A New Yorker, scared, devastated-at-a-not-so-great-distance.

In the locker room, I tried calling Mom. To tell her that I was okay.

It took a while to get through. But when I did, she said, "He was there."

"Who was where?" I asked.

"Dad," she said. "Having breakfast with our banker. On the top floor."

And just like that, I was in a different category.

I huddle in the back corner of the gym locker room, crying into a fresh towel that smells, predictably, of almonds. My fits of sobs are drowned out, I hope, by the buzz of hair dryers and gossip and music that's meant to soothe. Naked women chatter about diamonds and preschools and Labor Day barbecues.

"I can't *believe* it's been a year," one woman says.

"This city's remarkable," says another. "The way we New Yorkers have rallied. And everyone thought we were selfish bitches."

A chorus of laughter muffles new tears.

"You okay?" a voice says.

I look up, and through the salty blur I see the kind face of an older woman, round, vaguely familiar.

She offers a sympathetic smile. "Today must be hard," she says.

Instinctively, I nod.

She hesitates and then says, "He loved you very much, Prudence."

I squint dizzily, trying to place her. I've seen this woman before. This supposed stranger. Who knew him. Who knows my name. Who knows too much. And it hits me—this is the woman from the street corner, who smiled at Sage and me, as we frolicked our way to Central Park, the woman who watched me from the bike she pedaled furiously while going nowhere.

"Caroline Lewis," she says, her eyes watering, grabbing my hand. "I was your father's—your parents'—next-door neighbor for twenty years. Your brother used to play with my son Sam."

"Oh," I say, nodding.

Her tears fall harder and faster. And she does not let go of my hand.

And it doesn't take a JD to put two and two together.

And for mere moments, here we are, crying, longing for the same yet different man, for understanding.

And, again, just when I need it, the anger's run empty.

I look into her eyes, dark and wet. And my thoughts are those of a little girl. Brilliantly naïve. *But you aren't my mother. But my dad would never do this.*

And like a little girl, I run away, carrying with me the silly belief that I can leave something like this behind, with the shallow hope that this moment, like this day, like Dad's death, isn't already part of me, of who I will become. But still.

My escape is a blur of cellulite and breasts and tan lines.

That night before Sage gets home, I call Mom.

I want to ask about that woman, her neighbor. But I know

I can't. And it occurs to me. It goes both ways. Sometimes parents need protection too.

"How's Sage handling all this?" she asks.

"I don't think he knows what to do," I say.

"Men never know what to do," she says. "They aren't perfect, you know."

"You don't say? Good thing *we* know exactly what to do. Good thing we're perfect," I say.

"Anger's a perfectly appropriate emotion at a time like this," she assures me. "It can actually be very empowering. There's more agency in anger than sadness. If you're not careful, though, anger can give way to sadness, and sadness can be pathetic."

Enough with the lecture. I'm not your student. I'm your fucking daughter. Or am I both?

"Good to know," I say. "How's your wine?"

"Doing the trick," she says, and laughs. "And yours?"

"Scrumptious," I say.

Silence.

And I think: *One day we will be able to talk about this, not around it. One day we will have this conversation sober. One day we will stop theorizing, stop ranking emotions and talk about what we are actually feeling.*

"I am angry," I say, "but I'm sad too."

"Of course you are, Prue," she says. Pauses. "And I don't like it very much, but I'm sad too. I have been for a while."

It's a start.

Sage walks in carrying flowers. Red and white roses in blue cellophane.

I see them and start to cry.

Men never know what to do. They aren't perfect.

"Dad was a . . . fucking cheater," I say.

Sage approaches me gingerly, cradling those terrible flowers, fear in his eyes.

I tell him about the woman in the gym. And he's rational about this because men always are about these things and he tells me that I don't know the circumstances.

"Why would he do this?" I ask.

"I don't know," Sage says. "But he was your dad and he loved you. And you loved him," he says.

All true.

"But he wasn't the guy I thought he was," I say.

"We never are," he says.

Genius.

"He was human, Bug," he says. "He fucked up. Plenty of good people, really good people, do."

Yup, I'm one of them. I'm my father's daughter. Not only do I have his smile, his taste for Guinness, but I have his gray morals, his ability to betray.

"We're about to get married, Sage. And now this? How am I supposed to believe in marriage when my own father couldn't keep it in his pants?"

"Because you are not your father," he says. "You are you. And we have our own shot at things."

And I nod. Because he's right. We have our own chance. To get this right. Whatever that means.

"This isn't going to change things," I say, trying to convince myself. "Dad was flawed, but he was a good person. And my parents had a good marriage even if it was far from perfect."

Now it's Sage's turn to nod. "That's the spirit," he says.

At 9 P.M., W stands there, and the leader of the free world is a little boy, little Georgie, that little clichéd deer in the headlights.

At 9:01 P.M., he speaks. About strength and salvation. About life and death. About good and evil.

"Don't you think there must be something between good and evil?" I ask.

"I don't know," Sage says.

"I hope there is," I say. "There must be."

Buried there in the piles of sugarcoated hubris, one line grabs me:

"September 11, 2001 will always be a fixed point in the life of America. The loss of so many lives left us to examine our own. Each of us was reminded that we are here only for a time, and these counted days should be filled with things that last and matter."

"I think she forgave him," I say.

And maybe it's the little Christian boy from Savannah buried deep in this man I've snagged, but he nods and says, "I think forgiveness is underrated. There's nothing wrong with forgiveness. It's basically noticing and accepting that other people make mistakes, just like we do."

And I swallow Sage's words and nod. And I hear what I want to hear because I'm allowed to do this today. I have a free pass. I hear: *I forgive you, Quinn, but I'm not going to forever.*

I don't thank him for the flowers, but for something else.

"I love that you've started saying 'fuck,'" I say. "It makes you a little less good."

Sage shrugs and smiles, and a beautiful glimmer of mischief flickers in those incandescent, innocent eyes. "Well, then: fuck, fuck, fuck, fuck, fuck . . ."

And on this day when tears are predicted, we choose a different catharsis. Good old childish laughter.

Chapter 28

On Halloween morning, Hula's sandpaper tongue grazes my lips and nose. He balances like a seasoned surfer on my chest as I shift under him. He stares at me.

I'm convinced that today will be better than most days. For today's my bridal shower, and this is supposed to be exciting, a delicious taste of what's to come. Kayla's hosting at Cilantro. She sent out invitations on thick tangerine parchment. The theme is "Trick or Treat"; guests are to bring lingerie (tricks) or goods for the home (treats).

Strong October sun slips through the shades to find us under the covers. Now that we're stirring, Hula chases his tail around the foot of the bed. This morning, the light is curiously welcome; I don't yank the sheets up over my eyes to escape the glow.

We hop out of bed and pull up the shades. I hold Hula and scrape the crusty sleep from his eyes. Barefoot, Sage and

I stand there for a moment, side by side in the morning's silence, and take turns cradling our cat before the inevitable wriggle and drop. He kisses me on the forehead.

"Happy Halloween, Bug," he says. "You excited for your shower?"

"I guess," I say. "I'm thirsty for sangria."

"Well, *I'm* excited," Sage says.

"Why's that? Because you're getting rid of me for a few hours and you can watch football in peace?"

"That and the fact that after today you have no excuses."

"Excuses?" I ask.

"You are going to come home today with piles of lingerie and cookware. After all this time, I'm going to get me my sex-kitten cook. Just in time."

"Very funny. Your sex-kitten cook?" I say.

We retreat to the bathroom to brush and shower. We fidget for space, expertly shifting, imperfectly avoiding one another.

I step on the scale and smile. I'm down five pounds. So far it is a Happy Halloween.

That evening, the doorbell rings. Kayla.

She walks in, carrying orange flower arrangements and bags of gifts. "I figured you could use an escort," she says.

"How thoughtful," I say.

Sage is home early from work too and busies himself in the kitchen. "How are you, Kayla?" he says, talking over the vibrating espresso machine.

"Getting fatter by the day," she says. "Thanks for asking."

And we leave to walk to the corner.

Thank God for morning sickness. Waves of nausea have left her pale and willing to flirt with reason. Powerful exhaustion has etched dark circles under her bright blue eyes. Impending motherhood has in no time wreaked havoc on my dear friend, the formerly unflappable Kayla.

I follow her, walking the length of my block in slow motion, crunching leaves under high heels, sweating from nerves and fading sunlight. I give myself a timely pep talk. If I can survive the bar exam, I can survive a bridal shower.

"After all these years, I'm finally being punished for being a thoughtless slut," Kayla says, playing with her newly snug waistband.

"I wouldn't call you thoughtless," I say.

She smiles, but stops short of her trademark guffaw. "That's all I've got, Q. Full-on laughter requires too much energy, energy I apparently no longer have in unlimited quantities. Good to know I have twenty-eight more weeks of this shit to look forward to. Did you know that pregnancy is actually ten months and not nine? I feel duped."

I didn't know this, but it seems I better learn. Without the support of her mother and with no man in the picture, she's tapped me to come to her prenatal appointment next week.

"K, I think the forty weeks is supposed to be the easy part. After that things get tough. After that, you are going to have a mini version of yourself to keep alive."

"Fantastic. Good to know my stellar judgment has sent my life on fast forward down the proverbial toilet," she says. "I still think it's criminal that you're not having a bachelorette party and that I'm letting you get away with it. Here I am, your maid of honor, and what do I do? I spread my skinny-ass legs, open the floodgates, get knocked up, and worse still, morph into a reasonable person, a pussy for the first time in my life."

"Your legs aren't so skinny-ass these days," I point out.

"Fuck off," she says, and smiles.

Anyway, I'm thankful this pussy's given up on the clichéd bachelorette, the weekend of high-gloss strippers. I'm all for letting loose, for drinking a senseless amount of alcohol, for celebrating the last days before my freedom is snatched by the institution of matrimony. But I can do without the genetic mutants, high on creatine and self-tanner, with practiced gyrations and come-hither glances. I don't need to lose my precious dollar bills in the elastic of some lost soul's fluorescent banana hammock.

"I know you're a modern woman, K, but even you don't want to expose your dear fetus to the throbbing and thrusting. Give the little bugger a few decades to find the filth on her own."

"Whatever you say, prudent one. Deep down, you're just a Jurassic feminist like your mother—no strippers, no leg shaving. I'm on to you, O'Malley. Anyway, you know I'll make up for it at the shower," she says, scattering wedding cake–shaped confetti. "Just because I can't wear the slutty stuff anymore doesn't mean I'm going to spare you. Consider yourself warned."

And soon I'm swimming in a sea of unseasonable pastels. Two generations of women buzz in and out of each other, trading cheek kisses and making wispy small talk, rearranging towers of gifts tightly wrapped in pale floral papers. For a moment, I linger in the corner and absorb the ordered chaos that is my initiation into the ranks, unsuccessfully escaping notice of these women, my friends and family, who are here for me, to prepare me for life as a wife.

"Maybe I shouldn't have worn black," I say to Mom, taking stock of the faded rainbow that engulfs us.

"Oh, please. I didn't get the Easter egg memo either," she whispers, squeezing my arm. She's head-to-toe in smart navy. "We're in this together, Prue."

"Mom, I don't cook and I don't wear lingerie," I remind her.

"Just pretend," she says. "We're good at that."

Sage's mother approaches. She wears a gingham suit in the softest of pinks. Her ashy blond bob just grazes her delicate shoulders. "Quinn, dear," she says, her Southern accent thick and guttural. She stumbles as she always does on the one syllable of my name. She hugs me with all her might, which isn't much, momentarily displacing Mom. She frames my face with her fingers, cold, bony, meticulously manicured. "How are you, darling?" she asks, pinning me down with her doe eyes.

"Fine," I say. "Good."

And here they stand: my two mothers, more or less the same vintage, but still worlds apart. Their interaction is genuine, if strained, and they acknowledge each other with a polite nod and mumbled pleasantries. Despite their differences, these women have one important thing in common; each wishes I would get over the Quinn thing. Of course Mrs. McIntyre wishes this. Far from a closet Beatles fan, Mrs. McIntyre is a religious creature. *Prudence is such a beautiful name and such a wonderful virtue*, she's told me more than once. I've never taken the bait.

The moment Sage told his parents about me there was trouble. Not because I was a Yankee, a city girl headed for a high-wattage career, not because I didn't spend my Sundays at church. There was trouble because this little woman thought, if only for a few terribly confused moments, that I was a man. *I've met someone, Mother*, Sage told her, three short weeks after we met, as I curled up on his lap and listened in. Sage's mother, hungry for grandchildren, had been waiting for this proclamation from her only child for almost a decade. *You're going to love Quinn. Quinn O'Malley.* His mother was quiet, very quiet, so quiet Sage feared a lost phone connection. *I'm not gay, Mother,* he assured her mere moments later, knowing his mother and her primal fears. *She has a beautiful and unusual name. Plus, her real name is Prudence.* This fact, it seems, rejuvenated his wilting mother; there was hope.

Kayla stands in the corner with her own mother, a slight woman clad in pale purple. Thanks to Botox, her face is devoid of wrinkles and expression. Mrs. Waters has always liked me, or so Kayla says, because she thinks I'm a good influence on her wayward daughter. The fact that I'm within a week of marriage surely confirms my utterly sensible nature; the fact that I, unlike her daughter, do things in order, abiding by the schedule society has for us.

Kayla sees me and seizes the opportunity to escape her mother's orbit. Unlike the others, she's dressed for the season, in the brightest of oranges. This notorious color, which washes out the vast majority of its wearers, only brightens Kayla's complexion and highlights her slight bump. In the sunlight-filled Mexican restaurant, the dark circles have disappeared and the color has returned to her cheeks. The ten pounds she swears she's gained is suddenly nowhere to be seen, except maybe in her breasts, proudly displayed by a brazen dip in her bold sweater. She pours a tall glass of sangria and walks over.

"Well if it isn't the bitch of the moment," she says, as always a bit too loud, and hands me the sangria. She grabs at my black sweater. "What, are we mourning the death of your freedom?"

Mom smiles and Mrs. McIntyre looks stunned.

"I'm afraid you're going to need some booze to make it through this frilly fest," Kayla says.

"Amen," I say, and take a big swig. Outside, children dressed in costumes race by, and parents, as if on invisible leashes, half jog behind them, and race ahead when they get to a crosswalk. Sometimes, the parents join the fun wearing a witch's hat or mask. One day, I'm going to be one of these fun parents.

Avery and her mother walk in. Avery looks exhausted, and holds the sleeves of her shirt over her hands.

"Has someone developed insomnia?" Kayla says.

"Has someone developed a fetus?" Avery says, and flashes a smile. "Nice to see you, Kayla." Her eyes drop to Kayla's ample cleavage.

"Just doing my best to steal the bride's thunder by going the push-up bra route," Kayla says, shrugging. "I figured I'd test drive one of Quinn's gifts. Admittedly, a bit tacky, but who's counting?"

Avery hugs me, but avoids my eyes.

"You okay?" I ask.

"Of course I am," she says, nodding. It's then that I notice the reservoir of tears in her eyes. "I will be."

Avery's mother appears and throws a protective arm around her daughter, who's downed her first drink. "Everything's going to be fine," her mother says. "Just a hiccup for my beautiful daughter."

"Your beautiful daughter, it seems, needs another drink," Kayla says, appearing with a fresh glass of sangria, and hands it to Avery.

Avery doesn't try to hide her tears. "Thank you, Kayla."

"Not a problem," she says. "Alcohol can cure most anything. I wonder what my dear mother over there is trying to medicate with the sauce." Kayla's mother talks to a waiter in the corner and convinces him to bring her a glass of Chardonnay.

"I'm not a fan of the fruity cocktail," she explains to the man in an audible whisper. "Keep them coming."

Avery laughs and wipes her eyes. I grab her hand and interlock my fingers in hers. Her palms are clammy and cold. We sit down just as a waiter places a pot of fresh guacamole between us. The wooden table is blanketed in pastel candy corn. We each grab a handful.

"Time for the tricks and treats," Kayla says, standing by the piles of gifts. "Stop feeding your face, Q. Don't you have a wedding dress to fit into in a few days?"

"*She'll* fit her dress fine. It's you I'd be worried about," Kayla's mom mumbles over her disappearing glass of wine.

I abandon the guacamole.

Everyone pulls chairs into a circle around me.

In no time, I'm buried under boxes, holding up nonstick pans and thong panties, twirling spice racks and sheer teddies. A graceful pretender.

Leave it to Mom to give me books. I open the first; it's a cookbook. *The Practical Woman's Guide to Cooking.* The final book is not a cookbook, but *The History of Lingerie.*

"Forgive me, I'm a professor," she says. "I think it is nice to know the history behind things. Fascinating to know the genesis of those little strings you girls wear between your butt cheeks."

Sage's mother blushes and smiles.

"Brilliant, Mrs. O'Malley. Are there instructions on how best to burn a bra in there too?" Kayla says.

Next, Kayla hands me her gift, two boxes. I open the first and pull out four pairs of thong underwear with Sage's name on the crotch. "Just thought it would be nice to give him directions," Kayla jokes.

"Maybe I should get you some of those with a stop sign," Mrs. Waters mutters.

The next box is thin; I open it and pull out a thick white certificate. It's not a gift card to Williams-Sonoma or Tiffany's.

"Dance lessons?" Mrs. McIntyre guesses. "That would be terrific. Despite our best efforts, our son isn't the best dancer."

"Yes, this is for dance lessons," I say, my face no doubt turning magenta, and look at my troublemaking maid of honor.

"Striptease lessons," Kayla says. "If you're going to do the forever thing, you need to keep it interesting."

"Why don't you just put up a stripper pole in your bedroom and call it a day?" Mom mutters, audibly to all. One generation laughs; the other's eyes widen.

"Not a bad idea," K quips.

Sage's mother is a good sport about this. A good sport about the skimpy lingerie and the mystery cookware. She sits on the edge of her seat, thin legs folded underneath her, balancing a chipped teacup which I can see vibrating. When things get raunchy, her eyes fall, she looks down into that teacup that must be empty by now, and feigns a delicate sip until it's safe to look up again. Every now and then, a nervous laugh escapes her thin pink lips.

Kayla hands me another gift. I recognize the lovely loopy handwriting. It's from his mother.

I open the card first. Read her words. Words that I will read over and over in the future.

Quinn dear,

We are lucky women. To have him in our lives. And what different lives we lead. But with him in them, in whatever capacity, they will continue to be blessed lives. Like most people, I have my share of regrets. About things done and left undone. About things said and left unsaid. But I look at him—my boy, your man—and I know I have done something right. Please know that I don't care if you cook a single meal or bake a single pie. Whether you practice law or pick blackberries. But what I do care about is that you are kind to him, that you hold his hand—as I have done until now—when he needs it most. When and if you have a child, you will understand something: how questions of money and career and geography fade the moment you hold your own. One day in the future you will know what matters most, your child, cradled in your arms one day and then in the blink of an eye, cradled in the arms of another. Letting go is hard. Not something I'm doing gracefully. But please know I'm trying. Because let go I must. For him. For you. For all of us.

All my love,
Mary

PS—For better or worse, mine was not a child-hood of nursery rhymes. But when I grew up and met Sage's father, my mother, a glorious

*woman with a sharp sense of humor, couldn't
stop singing it, mocking me. Is it a nursery rhyme
or a song? Mrs. Mary Mack, Mack, Mack all
dressed in black, black, black . . .*

And it doesn't matter whether it's technically a rhyme or
a song, but the words echo in my head . . .

*Miss Mary Mack, Mack, Mack
All dressed in black, black, black.
With silver buttons, buttons, buttons
All down her back, back, back . . .*

I look at his mother, meet her eyes, and smile.

"Now you know why I always wear pastels," she says.

And I keep smiling as I slip my finger under the pale floral
paper, opening the gift wrapped tight.

"Hospital corners?"

She laughs.

And there it is, a pie pan. And inside it is that postcard
from Paris. And on it, the recipe. For Henry's pie.

"I figure you and Sage won't be able to make it South every
August," she says. "Nor should you."

And it occurs to me why I've been so scared of his mother.
It's not because she's an evil and predatory woman, a bailiff
of a mother who runs the show, a vulture who won't release
her claws.

Rather, I've feared her because she like the rest of us is
exquisitely flawed and essentially good. She is a woman, imperfect and loved and lovable. A woman who has lost too
many children. A woman who was once young like me and
probably thought things would be different. A woman who

fears many things: poison in candy, and symbolism in songs, and losing another child.

I've been scared because we want the same thing.

We want his love and his loyalty and his smile.

We both want him.

And like we did in kindergarten, we're going to have to learn to share.

"Thank you, Mrs. McIntyre," I say.

And then she does it. She says those words, pat and predictable, that I thought I'd never hear. "You can call me Mom."

I smile. And I won't call her this. Because I have a mom already.

"How about Miss Mama Mac?"

It's a start.

The final gift is from Avery. First, there's an apron. Across the front, it says "Mrs. McIntyre" in pink cursive writing.

"Now, *that's* darling," Mama Mac says.

Mom doesn't do a very good job at hiding her cringe.

There's a second part to her gift: a doll. A Dora doll.

"There's a card too," Avery says.

I open it. "Two gifts. Because we're growing up, but we'll always be girls."

"I love it," I say, and hug her. "But I would've appreciated that Backpack and Map."

She nods and says, one lost little girl to another, "Me too."

Outside, autumn sun glistens and fades. Trick-or-treaters swarm. A pumpkin and Wonder Woman stop briefly at the window, press pink button noses against the soiled glass, and look in at us. Then they continue on, disappearing into the night.

And here I am, all grown up, past my days of going door-to-door in search of mini Snickers and Tootsie Pops, past my days of holding Mom's hand and absorbing her motherly wisdom. Here I am, neither young nor old, accumulating a new string of costumes so I can pretend to be an adult.

Yes, you get older, but you never stop pretending.

That night, I walk into my apartment, flanked by two mothers, trailing a rainbow of ribbons, lugging boxes and bags. Sage waits for me. He's wearing his waders and vest and his fishing hat, popping Hershey's Kisses into his mouth.

He takes the gifts from me, places them on the counter. And he hands me those wings, those flag-print wings.

"We're going out for a bit," he announces to our moms, who sit on that prudently striped love seat.

He takes my hand and drags me to my parents' old block. Where kids gather and giggle. And we join in for a few houses, collecting candy, drawing some incredulous stares. But far more smiles.

On this Halloween, he's not going to let anyone tell him he can't eat the candy. And on this Halloween, I think I'm finally happy choosing only one.

Chapter 29

T he Thursday afternoon before my wedding, the day on which Sage and I fly to Wisconsin for our big day, Kayla and I leave work early and head to her ob-gyn. First, we stop at her building, which is only a block away from her doctor. I leave my suitcases with her doorman.

As we walk that block to her doctor, Kayla reaches into her purse, pulls out a vial of pills, and pops one. For a moment, I'm horrified. "Prenatals," she says. "It's all about the folic acid, Q."

I nod.

"This whole thing is turning me into a reasonable creature," she says. "It's a bit worrisome."

"No kidding."

"I even made a list during our client meeting this morning," she says, and pulls out a legal pad with the name of our firm up top.

She rattles off questions she will ask her doctor:

When should I hire a baby nurse?
When can I find out the sex?
What are the chances I will get stretch marks?
Can I really not eat tuna?
Is one cup of coffee okay?

As she utters these questions, I can think of only one, one that I haven't had the courage to ask thus far.

"Kayla, whose is it?" I say, pointing to her belly.

She looks at me, disappointment plain in over-lined eyes. "Well, fuck you."

I shrug. "Seems relevant."

"It's *mine*."

I nod. And part of me thinks: *Good for her. She's a modern woman.* But another part of me, maybe the bigger part, thinks: *At least I had a father.*

"I know you're pretty talented, but you didn't cook that up all by yourself," I say.

"No, I didn't," she says, and flashes a smile. "I had some very handsome help. And I'll tell you when the time is right."

"Fair enough."

A young mother pushes a stroller by us. "I think I want a black Bug," Kayla says.

And even I know about the Bugaboo, the nine-hundred-dollar monstrosity, the SUV of strollers, ubiquitous as black Labs on the Upper West.

I look around us and think: *Even Manhattan looks innocent in fall.* Leaves change on planted trees. Every now and then, a kid walks by wearing a Halloween costume a week after the fact, hand attached to a defeated and fashionably disheveled mother or a nanny on her cell phone.

At the front desk, Kayla signs in. Behind her mop of red frizzy hair, the doctor's assistant flashes a gummy grin, and hands Kayla a small blue cup and utters in a Russian accent: "You pee now."

Kayla hands me her jacket and bag.

"Good luck," I say.

Kayla grins and disappears into the small bathroom.

I take a seat in the waiting room. A young couple sits in the corner flipping through a book on prenatal nutrition. The wife is absorbed, but every few moments her husband looks up and around the small room, nerves apparent in his darting eyes.

And I think: *This will be Sage and me—crouched together, fearful and excited, full of questions, eager for answers, walking hand in hand toward our biggest, most important roles.*

A woman waddles in, clutching a belly that looks as if it might drop off, and jokes with the nurse about how she is past due.

I flip through an album of birth announcements. Pages and pages full of little pink faces captured in the first moments of life, faces beautifully contorted from ungraceful entrances. Pages and pages full of names in pink and blue. Pages and pages full of those aesthetic statistics—height and weight—that are for some reason important even from the very beginning.

I think of Phelps and his little son. I try to imagine him as a father, cradling a crying baby, changing a diaper. I admit these are things I've imagined before. But now when I picture things, one thing's different: It's not my baby.

There are stacks of books scattered about, and depending on how you look at things, this office is a haven of hope and new beginnings—baby name books, books showing the gestational development from fertilized egg to kicking infant, books showing portraits of prenatal yoga poses. But if you look a little closer, things aren't so bright; books on Down syndrome, on cystic fibrosis, STDs, and breast cancer.

Kayla returns. "That's one skill law school doesn't teach you," she says. "You'd think that if I can hammer out an ironclad contract in hours I'd be able to get it all in the cup. Not so."

She's still smiling.

Kayla fills a plastic cup full of water from the water fountain. "Hydration is key," she says. "Amniotic fluid."

And so the seminar continues.

"Have you thought of names?" I ask.

"Not yet," she says. "I have plenty of time for that."

Kayla's name is called and she stands, tells me to follow. So I do.

They weigh her. "Up two pounds," the nurse mumbles.

"What happened to those ten pounds you said you gained?"

Kayla shrugs. "Well, I never have been able to gain weight."

We wait in the small, sterile room for the doctor to come in. There's a framed photograph of condoms artfully arranged.

"I hope I get another sonogram," she says. "Did you know Sub-Zero fridges aren't magnetic?"

The doctor walks in and, instinctively, I sit up straighter. She's perky. Her pixie cut is endearingly mussed, and she is impeccably dressed in a smart camel suit and tasteful gold jewelry.

"So, how are you feeling? Last time you were here you were feeling pretty rotten, I recall," the doctor says.

"Yeah, I was. I am actually feeling a lot better. I have been for the last couple of weeks. I think it has something to do with that new prenatal vitamin you prescribed."

"Well, you're entering your second trimester. We like to call it the safety zone because from this point on, the chance of miscarriage is pretty much nil."

Kayla smiles, looks at me.

"That's great," I say.

I'm following along just fine, but then I'm somewhere else. Kayla and her doctor banter in a language I'll one day speak fluently. About platelet levels and blood types, rubella and gestational diabetes, fundal height and spilling protein.

"The next thing we must discuss is testing for abnormalities. We have the nuchal, CVS, and the amnio," she says as if she's reading from a menu.

"I think I want the most information I can get," Kayla says, nodding, looking at me for approval. I nod. "The more information the better, right?"

The doctor nods. "That's how most of my patients feel," she says, making a small notation in her chart.

"Time for the fun part," the doctor says, stands up, and walks toward Kayla, handing her a thin paper sheet. Kayla stands and shimmies out of her pants and underwear and hands them to me. She hops back up on the table and spreads her legs under the sheet, placing each heel in the appropriate metal brace.

"Now slide down," the doctor says, and Kayla does. She slides an instrument inside my friend.

And there it is. As the doctor moves around inside her, the picture on the small screen changes rapidly. Finally, a shape appears. Kayla sees it and smiles. And I see it. The big head, the smaller body, curled like a comma.

Her baby.

"Oh, look at that," Kayla squeals.

The doctor stops moving.

"Hold on," the doctor says, squinting, still staring at the screen, not looking at Kayla.

I grip Kayla's thigh, tearing the thin protective paper.

"I can't find a heartbeat," the doctor says, stripping plastic gloves from her hands.

Kayla giggles, looks at me and then the doctor. "Well then look a little harder."

In that moment, the silence is unrelenting and cruel.

I look at my friend, who still clutches that list of questions. She begins to shake and her face goes white.

But suddenly, there it is. The thud of life. The baby's heartbeat. Loud and proud and strong.

I wipe a tear from under Kayla's eye. The doctor smiles. "Sometimes it's hard to get the heartbeat right away. But there it is. Everything looks perfect."

The doctor slips out and I stay with Kayla as she dresses again. She bends down to pull her heels on and starts to cry. I crouch down on the floor next to her. "Are you okay?"

"I thought I lost it," she says. "The first good thing that's happened to me. The first pure thing. And I thought it was suddenly gone."

"It's not gone," I say. "It's inside you. Growing. With a strong and perfect heartbeat."

She nods, wipes away her tears. "I feel like it's a girl. I kind of hope it is."

"A little *you*," I say.

"I hope not," she giggles.

On the sidewalk, she grabs my shoulders and looks me in the eyes. "You're getting married in two days. I'm having a baby. What is happening to us?"

"We're growing up," I say.

And she grabs my hand, yanks me down the street. Back at her lobby, I ask her doorman for my suitcases.

"Leave them there for a bit and come upstairs. I know you have a flight to catch, but you have time for one glass of champagne."

"I do?"

"Yes, you do."

As we walk toward her apartment, her cell phone rings and she looks at it.

"It's *him*," she says. "Calling to see how the appointment went."

"Well then, answer, but I'm not getting on that plane unless you identify this mystery man."

She picks up the phone and as she whispers, the tears come again. "The doctor says things look perfect."

She hangs up. And her smile is different.

"You're in love," I say.

She smiles. "Remember the Winter Party? That gorgeous bartender Jake? Well, he called."

"It seems he did a little bit more than call," I say. "Why didn't you tell me?"

"I don't know. Because I was embarrassed. He's no i-banker. I am a lawyer. He is a bartender."

"Who cares? Plus, no one in Manhattan is just a bartender," I say.

"Exactly," she says. "Turns out he plays the trumpet in a jazz band. He is away for a gig in L.A. this weekend. They just signed a record deal."

For a moment, she disappears into the kitchen, and returns holding a glass of champagne in one hand and clutching something in her other hand.

"This is my baby quilt," she says, clutching a faded pink and green blanket. "My grandmother made it when my mom was pregnant. I'm going to give it to her."

At this display of uncharacteristic joy, I smile. At the fact that she is so determined it is a girl simply because that is what she hopes for, I smile. "So, let me get this straight. A few months ago, you were a cynical and pin-striped power-house and poof!—you're going to have a gorgeous little girl and a man who plays her jazz lullabies and then fixes you perfect cocktails? Not bad."

"I will still be a pin-striped powerhouse," she insists. "But a pin-striped powerhouse-plus. I will have it all. The job, the man, the baby. I'm allowed to believe that's possible for now at least."

I nod. "Of course, you are allowed to believe," I say. And she is. "K?"

"Yes?"

"I don't think I've heard you swear once today."

She pauses. "Maybe when you're happy, *fucking* happy, there's no reason to swear."

We laugh. Hard.

Together, we sit on her floral couch. She plays back an episode of *Oprah*. The woman herself stands at the center of the flat-screen TV, her body stretched, vast diamond ear-rings flashing in the camera. Her lips move, but we don't hear what she says.

"Her teeth are illegally white," Kayla says.

"Totally," I say, and smile.

I look around her apartment, the complementary floral patterns and gingham pillows. The botanicals hung in per-fect lines, the well-chosen antiques scattered about. Kayla swears her mother decorated it.

Oprah talks about alcohol abuse. That forty-three percent of Americans misuse alcohol, and it's for a variety of reasons—to suppress emotional pain, to self-medicate, to cope with loss, to quell anxiety, to make life more euphoric.

I nod and sip my champagne. "*Cheers!*"

On tomorrow's *Oprah*: women and bra size. Some eighty-two percent of American women wear the wrong size bra. I wonder if I'm one of them.

Outside, the sky grays, preparing for night, and windows on the tall buildings turn on and off, a crossword puzzle of light.

"K, I should go," I say. "I have a plane to catch."

I stop off in her bathroom. And I see them there on the counter. A tall stack of wedding magazines. I pick them up and carry them out to her. "Is there something you have to tell me?"

"Not yet," she says. "But hopefully soon."

I smile. It's good to hope. It's good to believe.

"Q, I want to thank you," Kayla says as I gather my things.

"For what?"

"For coming with me today. For putting up with me. For being a good person. For being a good friend," she says. "I don't deserve you."

"What are you talking about? Of course you do," I say.

"No, I don't," she insists, taking a small sip of my champagne. "I'm sorry."

"Why are you saying that?"

"Because I mean it," she says.

"What do you have to be sorry for?" I ask.

"Sage. I always had this crush. I think I was envious of you, how much you have. It only happened once, I promise."

"It?"

"It was just a kiss. And it happened a long time ago."

"*When?*" I ask.

"At my birthday party last year," she says.

Kayla's birthday is on September fifteenth. When the Towers came down, she canceled her table at a nightclub and opted for a "quiet gathering" at her apartment. And while I was with my mother and brother uptown, Sage "stopped by on our behalf" to drop off a bottle of champagne.

"Let . . . me . . . get . . . this . . . straight . . ." I say, my voice eerily calm like those September minutes before everything happened. "While I was uptown comforting my insta-widow mom, processing the fact that my *dad* was buried under a pair of buildings, you were staking your claim?"

And then my friend, my exceptionally clever friend, says two exceptionally unclever words, "I'm sorry."

"I'm sorry too," I say, and stand. Chug the rest of the champagne and slam the glass down. "Cheers."

I turn to leave.

"It was one kiss," she says. "One meaningless kiss. Don't go."

"That one kiss means something to *me*," I say. "And, yes, I have to go. There's a wedding this weekend in case you don't remember? One to which you are no longer invited."

"Q, you don't mean that," she says.

And maybe she's right. Maybe I don't mean it. But I say it. And leave her there clutching her belly and her baby blanket. Before I walk out the door, I turn and look at her. And for the second time in one day, I see her cry.

Chapter 30

Toward my future, the cabbie drives fast—honking, swerving, cursing. A gold cross dances dangerously on the windshield.

I look at his license. His name is Bob.

It's rush hour and the traffic's a bitch. "I'm not sure you're going to make it," Bob says from the front seat.

"Me neither," I mumble. "Me neither."

It only happened once.

And suddenly I'm hungry for details. Did he run his fingers through her hair? Tug her earlobe when he kissed her? Cup her chin as he pulled away? Was it just a kiss?

The more information the better.

Maybe not. Maybe a little mystery will save us.

Words convene mercilessly.

Phelps: No harm in a midnight snack.

Victor: This is what we do.

Sage: Good people fuck up. Forgiveness is underrated.

Mom: Men never know what to do.

Me: Good people can lie about most anything.

Bob pulls up to the terminal. "That was faster than I thought it would be," he says. "You have plenty of time."

But all I can think is: *Do I?*

And Sage stands there waiting for me, flanked by our matching suitcases, an early wedding gift from his aunt, hugging a white garment bag.

My wedding dress.

The man behind the desk looks at our photo IDs. "No license?" he asks, scrutinizing my tattered passport.

"No," I say. "Maybe someday."

Sage smiles. "One of these days, she'll grow up," Sage says to the man.

The man prints boarding passes and Sage reaches for them.

"I'll hold mine," I say.

It's a start.

On the security line, I clutch my dress and look around. At the babies and old people, the bald heads and ponytails.

"Statistically, forty-three percent of these people drink away their demons and eighty-two percent of the women wear the wrong size bra," I say.

And this is the beauty of trivia. We talk about things that don't matter when avoiding the things that do.

"Fascinating," Sage says.

We take off our shoes. Arrange electronic devices in soiled gray bins. I lay my dress down on the rolling black rubber and watch as it appears on the other side.

At the sports bar, we find three bar stools. One for each of us, one for my dress.

"We had this magical afternoon," I say. "I sat there with her as she saw her baby. And she's so happy. She's in love. I think she's looking for a fresh start."

"That's good, right?" he says.

"In theory, yes," I say. "But in practice, for some people having a fresh start sometimes entails admitting things. She told me about her birthday."

He looks down.

"Nice birthday present, but I think the Veuve would have sufficed," I say.

"You know something about fishing when you've already snagged one," he says.

The bartender sees my dress and smiles. "Good luck," he says, and hands us menus.

Thanks. I think we'll need it.

Sage sits there, sad and defeated, sipping Guinness, the black beer Dad used to love. Fear overtakes those blue eyes.

And just as I am about to wind up and let him have it, really let him have it, I have a flash of Phelps. Naked. On top of me in a cheap and generic hotel room. And then I say words that perhaps surprise us both. Words that Sage once said to me. "Life will go on. If we let it."

Sage's eyes widen. Those pupils dilate. "Huh? You deem my mother the devil for giving us her mother's china. I kiss your friend and I'm off the hook?"

I nod, slowly but surely. "Enjoy this moment of temporary insanity while it lasts," I say. But what I think of is those books I loved as a child, full of stories simple and profound. Despite the decisions and mistakes we've both made, we are both here, on the very same page. Maybe, just maybe, this is the way it was supposed to happen.

I shred a cocktail napkin into tiny pieces. And think of that night we first met. When everything was new and untarnished. When I wore those wings. "Sage, I'm sure you know this by now, but I'm no angel."

A captive audience. A pseudo-confession.

He nods. "Neither am I."

Our silence is filled with sudden and imperfect understanding, the conversation of others, a blaring basketball game, a weatherman predicting unseasonable snow.

It's then that my future husband orders two more pints of Guinness and finally asks me: "Are you happy, Quinn?"

I pause. Think about this. "I want to be," I say.

He smiles.

"Me too. Do you think it's possible?" he asks. "To be really happy?"

"I don't know," I say.

"Maybe happiness is a herd ideal," he says.

And just when we are getting somewhere, finally getting somewhere, really getting somewhere, he quotes another philosopher.

"Borrowing from Nietzsche?" I ask.

"From him and from you," he says, reaching into his bag for something.

He pulls paper from his bag.

"You gave this to me when we first met. When you were in law school," he says, waving those sheets of paper. "You said it was proof you wouldn't become *one of them.*"

And then he reads some words from it.

"Nietzsche said, *It is* not *the satisfaction of the will that causes pleasure, but rather the will's forward thrust and again and again becoming master over that which stands in its way.*

The feeling of pleasure lies precisely in the dissatisfaction of the will, in the fact that the will is never satisfied unless it has opponents and resistance. 'The happy man': a herd ideal.

"Then you wrote this which I love," Sage said. "*The good struggle had become a way of life and it wouldn't end at graduation. The JD would bring a new herd to abandon one day. Moving on would usher in a new cast of opponents and a fresh stock of resistance. Nietzsche's 'forward thrust' would continue and they hoped, they knew, that they could manage. Stronger, rookie masters of the struggle that is life, they knew deep down that somehow, someday, they would just do it. Even when the real 'it' still eluded them all.*"

I smile. I wrote that. Even then, I knew. "The good struggle," I said. "Then it was theoretical. Now it's life. Our life."

He nods, clutches those papers. "I've held on to this because it makes sense to me. The best things in life are never easy."

Buzzed, we board our plane.

"When did you know about me?" I ask him.

"The night we met," he says. "The freckles, the playful irreverence. I just knew. You asked me the next morning if I had any bacon and I didn't. I kept bacon in my fridge from that day on. You were different. You weren't like the others."

And I can't help but notice that he speaks in the past tense. *You were different. You weren't like the others.*

"The night you proposed, I had a dream," I say.

I pull that crumpled stationery from the Ritz out of my bag and hand it to him. And I watch as he reads my words, scribbled down the morning after he asked me that all-important question. I watch as he reads about the trinity of grooms, and the jury, and his mother, and the blurry-faced judge. I watch as he reads about the disappearing father and the screaming little girl.

He finishes reading, and maybe he sees the worry in my eyes because he smiles and says, "Bug, it was just a dream."

I nod because I want to believe him. But still I wonder if it's ever just a dream?

He doesn't ask who the other guys were. Maybe he knows, maybe he doesn't care. Maybe it really doesn't matter.

"I just hope that on Saturday, you choose me," he says.

And we take off.

The stewardess's name is Victoria. She asks if we'd like a drink.

"Keep them coming," Sage says. "We're struggling to celebrate."

And as the plane stumbles upward into darkened skies, I say, "I'm not sure I want to go back there." To New York? To the law firm? To our sad and predictable dance of mutual deception? "Might be time to start over."

But I think: *Can you ever really start over?*

"Ah, so you have your new herd to abandon?" he says, and laughs. "Just do it then."

"I want to write a story," I say.

"Just don't start with a dream. Too clichéd. You'll end up in the slush pile."

And I think: *We are a cliché.*

"What? A post–9/11 New York story about a privileged Petra Pan who returns from her honeymoon and quits her high-paying job, jumps ship, and writes in an effort to find clarity is a bit cliché?"

"Not at all," he says facetiously, smiling big.

"And don't write things like 'the air was thick and smelled

like peanut oil' or 'crucified the deep silence.' Too pretentious."

"But I am pretentious," I say. "And messy. And difficult . . .
Are you sure you want me?"

"I do," he says, smiling. "I do."

And for a moment, we sit there silently, stirring drinks
with our pinky fingers like my parents used to do. And the
engine hums.

"You can't write a story about the law when you've barely
set foot in a courtroom."

"Of course I can," I say.

It would be a story, not researched, but dreamed and lived.
Full of bits and pieces gathered. It, like the slush pile that is
life, would be formulaically seasoned, peppered with predictability and profanity and platitude. Because real people
are often stereotypes and stereotypes are often real. Because
at one time or another, we all struggle and swear and stumble. Because life is never a fairy tale no matter how much we
want to believe.

This story would also have fierce flashes of rawness and
honesty. Its characters wouldn't be perfect people, but gor-
geously flawed Nietzschean souls. Souls who individually,
and collectively, dance that fabled forward thrust. Souls who
have no choice but to live the good struggle that is life.

I imagine coming home married. There would be chatter
about my leaving the firm. Colleagues would whisper words
of prudence: "Wait until bonuses. That's a lot of money even
for someone who has money."

But I'd think of all the people in those Towers who sleep-
walked their way to work that morning, who counted down
the days until they would allow themselves to do something
else, to be someone else. Mortgage and tuition payments,

fear, or apathy, I-don't-know-what-else-I'd-do-with-my-life thoughts kept them there.

And then it all ended.

At the firm, they'd encourage my plan, though. "Writing a book? Good for you," they'd say while thinking obvious thoughts: *Why did you go to law school?* and *At least she's not going to a competitor.* To them, this would all be code for taking a breather, setting up house before popping one out. Or maybe they'd assume that it was hard after everything that happened for me to keep up in this world. Anyway, I'd be just another woman full of untapped potential who opted out, leaving room for another generation of Porterhouses and Poultry to float to the top.

So very predictable.

They'd throw me a departure party like they do for all the associates who bow out. They'd serve the same shrimp curry and the same white wine, and those people whose lives I'd glimpsed would approach me gingerly, ostensibly wishing me luck, but really pleading that I be kind in characterizing them, and this world they for now can't, or don't want to, escape.

And I would giggle heartily, swallowing the generic well-wishes with the bad white wine. And I probably wouldn't say it, but I'd want to; that they have nothing to worry about. That I have nothing to vilify, that if I was going to rip anything apart, it would be a world far bigger than the four walls of this firm, a world of excessive ambition and privilege, of sadness too often camouflaged by designer clothing, and profanity, and booze, and distance. A world I could study and observe, of course, but one I couldn't myself escape if I tried.

I would pack up my office. The pens, the parched highlighters, the prudent stock of Excedrin ready to combat the inevitable late night headaches. I would scatter good-byes and a few awkward hugs.

"See you on the bookshelves," a few would say.

I'd turn in my BlackBerry, my best friend and biggest foe.

And I would travel down in that elevator once more, eyes fixed on the little TV that reminds us of the life—and death—beyond this vertical grind.

I would click away on the marble floor and spin through the revolving door once more. The fresh air would feel different this time.

These thoughts zip through me like lightning, and momentarily, I'm empowered. High in the sky, I'm neither here nor there; this feeling is electric.

This is up to me.

Or maybe this is just another dream. It rivets as long as it lasts.

We sip drinks and talk. About how the most we can strive for is to be real, imperfect, honest. We talk about happiness. What is it? Is it attainable, or is the fruitless search for it what really makes people unhappy? I tell him about my theory that happiness comes in flashes. He doesn't use fancy words, but his own words. His grammar is less than perfect, but not bad. But for the first time in so long, it's his voice that carries. His own words. Not Plato's. Not Nietzsche's. Not our parents'. Not society's.

And I think: *We are judge.*

I look at him, those impossible deep blue eyes. The tears waiting, just waiting, to break free. And I see that fly fisherman on Halloween, that boy I first met.

"I miss him," he says.

I nod.

"I miss him too," I say.

And it doesn't matter that we're talking about two different people, two people who will never see us walk down the aisle. Or grow up.

Our best men.

And the plane bumps along. For the first time, the turbulence lulls me. It's normal. Nothing but a reminder—at once humbling and oddly comforting—that we are always up against something bigger than we are.

"Sage," I say. "I don't like flowers."

He nods and smiles. "Okay. Anything else I should know?"

I pause. "I'm not your other half."

He nods, and it seems he needs no explanation. "I know," he says.

His smile says: *You are that girl I met.*

"Now I have one question for you," he says.

Cruelly, he pauses, and fear rushes through me. I do what a well-trained attorney does so naturally: I contemplate answers to questions not yet posed.

"How does this hypothetical story of yours end?" he asks, those blue eyes brimming with hope and fear, promises and apologies.

I look at him and leave him with those words a good lawyer knows not to utter too often, those words my fourth grade teacher deplored: "I don't know."

Chapter 31

I 'm losing my freckles," I announce from the bathroom.

"Congratulations, Bug," Sage says, laughing. "One less thing for you to complain about."

One less thing for me to hide.

He packs his things in the bedroom. Tomorrow is our wedding day, and per tradition, we're spending the night apart. Tonight, Sage will join the rest of the wedding guests at the Clubhouse, the rickety old lodge that perches on the edge of the lake. Modest rooms, ancient mattresses, communal bathrooms; it's just like camp.

"But they're being replaced by wrinkles," I say, studying my face in the mirror. "Lovely souvenirs from my past year."

"Wrinkles should merely indicate where smiles have been," he says.

"Thanks, Mark Twain."

"You're beautiful," he says, coming at me from behind, wrapping his arms around my waist. And as we watch ourselves in the mirror, he kisses my bare face, lingering longer than usual, pinning me with a look of pride and anticipation and victory. And for a moment, I'm envious of the seemingly effortless optimism that buoys him and I wish that it were contagious, that it could pass, like the common cold, through a simple kiss. Or that it were genetic like freckles. That at least our children, when and if they come, will more often than not see things brightly too.

He returns to the bedroom, grabs his bag, and pulls his tuxedo from the closet. And leaves something behind. That suit his mother got him, a milky tan.

Another peck on the cheek. "Until tomorrow," he says, grinning, drying his eyes.

"Don't go," I say, and grab him.

And on the night when we are supposed to separate gracefully, sleep in solitude, and contemplate a future of togetherness, I miss him even before he goes. Because as long as he's next to me, as long as I can see him, things are okay.

"A night free of my snoring," he says. "It'll be a treat."

I grab his face and memorize the blue of his eyes before he walks away.

"Make sure to steam it in the morning," I say, pointing to his tux.

He shrugs and smiles. "Nothing wrong with a few wrinkles."

"See you tomorrow," I say, coyly, casually, as if tomorrow's just another day, the logical consequence of today, just the next in line.

"Walk me out," he says.

So I do. I walk him onto the porch. Into the moonlight. As I lead him to the screen door, he resists. Pulls me in the other direction.

He walks me to the porch swing. Where Dad read me stories. We sit. Swing slowly. The lake glows.

"Quinn, do you remember the morning after we met when my mother called?"

"I do."

"You called me a mama's boy. And you were right. I am one. After I hung up, you jokingly asked if I told Mama that I'd found The One?"

I nod.

"Well, I didn't," he says. "But what I did tell her was that I found my blackberry girl. A girl whom I wanted to know, whom I wanted to know me, everything about me, even the difficult things. I wanted you to know about Henry. That's why I told you about him on that very first night. And I was right. You're not perfect. In fact, you're often quite a mess, but you're it for me. You're my blackberry girl."

"Your blackberry girl?" I say as the tears come.

He nods. Crying like that very first night. A little boy again. "And that's why my mother's had such a hard time. Because I told her you were it. I announced loud and clear that you were the girl."

"Your blackberry girl. I love that."

"Good," he says.

Something strikes me. Something silly and cheesy and true. "You know what, Sage? You are my Cheerio guy."

"Your Cheerio guy," he says. "I'll take that."

And here we are, late in the game, speaking our very own language. A simple, childish language. A beautiful language that's all ours.

But then Sage reminds me of something. "Blackberry girl. Cheerio guy. You know these are just code words for The

One, right? That concept you hate, Bug. These are also code words for other half. They all mean the same thing."

And I hate it and I love it, but he is right. Absolutely right. "We strive so hard to be original, but life is all one big cliché," I say. "But I think I can live with that."

"I have something for you," he says. He pulls a small fly box from the pocket of his khakis. He opens the transparent plastic top. And I peer in. At the Woolly Buggers and the Jitterbugs and the Hula Poppers and the . . .

Ring.

My ring. A ring he chose all by himself.

It's far smaller. A simple round cut.

He reaches for it.

He takes my hand. Holds it for a moment, studies each finger. He pulls the ring, the one his mother picked, from my hand.

"Will you marry me, Bug?" he says, his words so simple they are profound, so profound they are simple.

"Yes," I say, smiling at him, looking at the lake.

And miles from Paris, centuries from Plato, next to him, I feel a flash. Of happiness.

Mom and Michael are sleeping, and once Sage is gone, the only noises are those I make—clumsy footsteps fueled by bundling nerves, a hairbrush yanking through stubborn knots, the cracking of knuckles. Without these sounds, the silence overwhelms. Suddenly, I crave the city sounds, the staccato of sirens, drunken laughter floating from sidewalk revelers, snippets of rap music blasting from speeding cars, garbage trucks halting clumsily to cart away our trash.

In the living room, I boot up Mom's old computer. Black-

Berrys don't work here. I dial up and the connection is slow. Though I am a fan of speed and instant gratification and efficiency, tonight the slow motion is welcome, the rainbow images a retreat.

I type in "freckles." I learn what I pretty much already know: They are genetic, rare on infants, common on children, less common on adults.

I log into my e-mail and there's a message from Kayla. I open it.

Q,

Sometimes a kiss is just a kiss. Here I sit. Missing you. Your practical wisdom, your cautious laughter, your quiet, but unscrupulous judgment. Your willingness to listen to my nonsense, to swallow my bullshit when it doesn't matter. But to call me on it when it does.

You've been there for me through it all—the drugs, the men, the poor decisions. You propped me up even when I didn't deserve it. And now, certainly I don't. You held my hand when I thought I lost the first thing that really mattered and then when I saw that furious flicker of life.

I did kiss him. I was curious and jealous and desperate. You were not there. But when you are, I see the way he looks at you—proudly, with quizzical amazement and the deepest of affection. He revels in your neuroses and your accomplishments. He finds your imperfections delicious. In a moment of weakness (and there are too many), I wanted to taste what you get to taste every day, and wanted

to see if he would look at me that way too, if any-
one would. And when I kissed him, he was gentle
with me. He didn't slap me, or yell, or reprimand.
He pulled away and was polite. He didn't say it, but I
heard it loud and clear: "I'm taken."

And he is. He's all yours.

I wish more than anything you would forgive me
for my selfishness, for my constant insecurity mas-
querading as confidence. For the sadness I hate to
admit, the loneliness I've only now made worse.

Sometimes a kiss is just a kiss,

Your MOD (Maid of Dishonor)

Just then, a reminder flashes across the screen. It's the little paper clip guy with the googly eyes. "Today is your wedding day!"

I shut down, return to my room. I rummage through everything I've brought—the clichéd stash of honeymoon lingerie with tags still on, the box of thank-you notes I'll write on the flight, and I find it.

Phelps's flannel. I hold it up to my nose and inhale. One last time.

I wander out to the porch, sit on that old wooden swing where Dad read me stories, where Phelps and I grew up, where Sage finally spoke up, and stare out onto the lake. The lake Dad loved like a child, where we would've scattered his ashes if given the chance. Like me, the lake appears calm, and stone-still. But under its deceptively placid surface, chaotic currents roil.

And soon the haunting silence is filled in. Bullfrogs gulp good night. The whippoorwills croon their nightly lullaby.

I step into Dad's old wading boots that wait like they always do by the screen door on the porch.

The moon is bright and lights my way. Leaves crunch underfoot. And soon I'm there. At our spot near the dock, under the mess of scraggly branches. For some reason, I fold the shirt, out of respect for childhood firsts and fond memories perhaps, and place it down, on the damp ground. Where he will find it. Or won't.

I look at it, the small square of faded plaid on the dark ground. And I begin to walk away.

"Fancy meeting you here."

Phelps. He too is in pajama pants and fishing boots. He smokes a cigar and carries a plastic baggie of cheese curds and a bottle of red wine.

He waves the bag of cheese in my direction. "Wisconsin's finest," he says.

I shrug and take a curd. Pop it in my mouth and chew slowly, waiting for words to come.

"Why are you here?" I ask.

"For your wedding," he says, smiling.

"No," I say. "*Here*." I point around us.

"I come here sometimes," he says. "When I can sneak away. It reminds me of happiness. The kind of happiness before you know any better. When everything seemed possible. Why are you here?"

"To return something," I say, picking up that shirt again, handing it to him. "The problem with keepsakes or relics is that they work. They make you remember."

And it strikes me that we can try to control what we remember and forget but it doesn't really work this way. Some things leave us and some things stay. It's not up to us.

He smiles. "I like to remember." He holds the flannel, his

old shirt. In his eyes, sadness gives way to something different. He hands me the bottle of wine, and puts the sweating cigar between his lips. He puts one arm and then the next through the old shirt.

It still fits him. Barely. Differently. But still.

"That's not going to help me forget," he says.

"Good."

He smiles and walks toward the dock. I follow. To our boat.

Wordlessly, I climb in behind him and grab the anchor.

"Remember when we carved this?" he says.

"Of course I do."

And there they are, our clumsy initials scratched into the side of the aging and waterlogged fishing boat.

"It's interesting the lengths we go to make things immortal," I say.

The moon highlights errant strands of silver amidst the blond, the fading scar I left above his lip, the wrinkles, the bags under his eyes. And it occurs to me, foolishly for the first time, that he too will be an old man.

No one's immune to time.

"Congratulations," I say. "You're a daddy."

His smile is vast and proud.

"Didn't want to give the poor boy his own identity?"

He smiles again. "It's interesting the lengths we go to make things immortal."

And then he speaks a new and beautiful language, the words of which I imperfectly understand. That little Phelps was colicky at first. That he loves tummy time and to be swaddled. That his head is in the seventy-fifth percentile, but is a bit flat because they sleep him on his back for fear of SIDS.

"And he loves breasts just like his daddy," Phelps says, and laughs.

"He'll be drinking beer and fishing in no time," I say.

Phelps nods and rows to the edge of the lake, chasing the moon. And stops. "The scene of the crime," he says.

I look around. The same canopy of lilting trees, the same dark water, the same old rowboat.

But now, two different people.

He offers me another cheese curd and says, "Nothing wrong with a late night snack."

But this time I refuse.

Tonight he wears his ring.

"The good husband's back?" I say.

He smiles. "It's too easy being good," he says, clumsily quoting himself from years ago.

He puts his hand on my knee and squeezes. As he leans in, through the adult haze of cigar smoke that surrounds this grown man, this father, I breathe in that old familiar smell of a boy I once loved.

He kisses me. And the sky rumbles, a cosmic warning perhaps, and I wait for a moment before pulling away.

I'm gentle. Polite. I don't slap him, or yell, or reprimand.

And I don't say it, but it's loud and clear. *I'm taken.*
I'm all his.

"You don't want to?" he says.

"No," I say. "I don't."

"Ah. Not prudent to be rendezvousing with an old flame within hours of your vows?"

And I think we both know this, but this time, I'm not being coy, or fumbling with nascent sexuality. This has nothing to do with caution or practicality or the fact that it's my wedding day. No, this has more to do with beginnings and ends, and how sometimes in life they're not clearly demarcated but bleed into each other.

And, under snoring thunderclouds, swaddled in fresh air, I realize for the first time that endings don't have to be catastrophic like the murderous collapse of a landmark or dramatic like the loss of a heartbeat. Endings can be quiet and satisfying.

Even if they do sneak up on you.

"Phelps," I say.

"Yes?"

"I've always told myself I didn't know why. That it was one of life's many mysteries. But I think I know. I think I knew who I was going to become with you. I think I would have spent my days answering questions instead of asking them. I think I would have stopped dreaming."

And, at this, he nods. And I study his face, baby fat long gone, faint wrinkles of adulthood claiming territory. I look for hurt, for disappointment, for anger. But instead, I see something both new and old. Something I haven't seen for years: understanding.

"I spent so much time planning and plotting who I would become. Where I would go and how I would get there that I didn't realize that I was already becoming somebody."

I nodded. "A good somebody."

"Not good enough," he says, and tears sneak up. "Not good enough."

"There's no such thing as good enough," I say. "We are who we are. And we can't go back."

He nods, wipes tears. "I would go back," he says. "In a heartbeat."

"Impossible," I say.

"Exactly," he says, a tender mea culpa, too little too late. "There is something poetic about impossibility."

Just then as I am articulating the reasons for our end, putting that final period on our long and winding sentence, I realize that these are but shadows of reasons, shifting and gray. But as I utter them, the real reason becomes clear.

Because reasons are like grooms and wedding gowns. Sometimes, you don't find them when you are looking, but stumble upon them when you are living.

"Phelps," I say. "I left you because you weren't him."

I walk back to our cabin. And though it's the middle of the night, I'm more alert than I've been in a year. Back on our porch, as I step out of Dad's boots, a small spider sneaks down the screen door, and I think of little Charlotte.

Cigarette smoke. Mom waits for me, rocking slowly on the old porch swing.

"It's your wedding day, Prue," she says.

"You quit smoking twenty years ago," I say.

She looks at me, worry and understanding plain in tired eyes. It's been years since she's had to wait up for me.

"Pajamas and wading boots?"

"Beats all black," I say.

And so we dance.

We can escape the city, but we can't escape this—the profound understanding that only genes and genuine love and time can fashion. The ability to speak in a code of jabs and gestures and pregnant silences.

Outside, it begins to rain.

I watch as Mom stands up and goes inside. Through the window, I see the light in the kitchen snap on and off again.

She returns with two big glasses of white wine and hands me one.

"Seems like you could use one of these," she says.

Wind comes through the screen. Mom's face glows in the moonlight. The wrinkles are multiplying, a map of wisdom on alabaster skin.

Wrinkles should merely indicate where smiles have been.

"He's married, Prudence," Mom says. "And now he's somebody's father."

"So was Dad," I say, and look down.

And when I look up again, and meet her eyes, through the rumble of rain, I hear her say it: "I know."

"It's over," I assure her.

She pauses, sips wine. "I believe you," she says. But her eyes say something else: *Is it ever really over?*

"You know something?" she asks.

I look at her eagerly, hungry for one last morsel of motherly wisdom before I must grow up.

"It's never too late to become a good person," she says.

We sip wine without talking. The moon hangs there, witness to it all. After two decades of diatribes on the evils of tobacco, Mom offers me a drag of her cigarette and I take it. I inhale slowly, with purpose, and blow smoke into the November air, damp with possibility.

Chapter 32

I shave my legs the morning of my wedding day.

Here I sit, holed up in the tiny bathroom Dad never finished, naked, at the bottom of the bathtub, dragging cheap pink plastic over white legs. Hot water sprays from the old showerhead, pelting my back. Dad's Head & Shoulders is now gone, and now only Mom's shampoo rests on the edge of the basin.

As the room steams up, and the mirror above the sink fogs, something becomes clear to me. This isn't how I pictured the beginning.

And it strikes me that beginnings aren't always majestic, or trumpeted. Beginnings can be quiet and satisfying.

Even if they do sneak up on you.

The hours pass steadily. And the rain falls furiously. Everyone keeps telling me this is good luck.

Mom emerges from the kitchen carrying a mug. She hands

it to me and I see that it's a latte and she's swirled my initials in the foam—QOM.

I smile. "Thanks, Mom."

In the bedroom, Michael steams wrinkles from my wedding dress. Avery and I are on the porch. She hovers over my feet and fixes my chipped toenail polish.

She paints delicately and stands up, studies her work. "Perfect," she says.

Mom hands us each a flute of champagne, and we sip slowly and watch the rain come down. We go inside and find Michael hopping around my dress, getting closer and squinting, pulling away.

He turns the steamer off. "Perfect," he says.

I look at the dress, bright and innocent, white with promise.

Mom stands behind me and puts a delicate chain with a tarnished old key around my neck. "Something old. This represents continuity with our family and the past," she says. "Forgive me, I'm a professor. I like to know the history behind things."

Michael pulls my dress off the quilted hanger and holds it open, so I can step in. I do so gingerly, careful not to rip it or stain it. Avery zips it up. "Something new. To represent hope and optimism for your life ahead."

"I feel like it's Halloween," I say, glimpsing myself in the mirror.

"You know what I always said on Halloween," Mom says.

And in unison, Michael and I say, "All you need is one."

Mom smiles. Pulls her wedding ring and hands it to me. "Wear it," she says. "Something borrowed. So Dad's and my good fortune in marriage will carry over to you and Sage."

And Michael and Avery leave the room, to give Mom and

me a moment. And I take her ring and I slip it on my hand, the dull band that Dad slipped on her finger long ago. And Mom whispers in my ear: "Despite everything, despite the struggle—*because* of it maybe—we were happy."

And I think I believe her.

"And now," Michael says, his voice carrying loudly from the next room. "We have for you something blue . . ."

And Michael and Avery walk back into the room. And between them, with tears in her eyes, is Kayla.

"I'm sorry," she mumbles.

And then she reaches into her bag and pulls out the highest, most imprudent pair of stilettos I've ever seen in the brightest of blues. "Something blue," she says softly, her words laced at once with shame and hopefulness, "to symbolize love, modesty, and fidelity."

I take the shoes from her, and look at the five-inch spike of a heel.

"Let the heeling begin," she says.

And in this moment that's meant to be serious, where fibers of what might be forgiveness float about uncertainly, I can't help but laugh.

It's a start.

I look at her. "What happened to being disinvited?"

"I've spent my life doing things that I'm not supposed to do," she says. "I wasn't about to stop now."

Kayla hugs me. And I let her. Before she pulls away, she whispers something in my ear. "The second part of your gift is in your suitcase."

And I know what it is, this gift, but I go and look anyway. Sitting there atop my honeymoon clothes is a pair of handcuffs. White ones. Just like the ones in my dream. I pick them up and fiddle with them and smile. And then toss them back into my bag.

When I walk down the aisle this time, Mom's there. Not Dad. She grips my arm strongly, protectively.

This time there's no judge or jury.

No little flower girl waiting to erupt.

Under that vast oak tree by the water, Sage stands there, waiting for me. His tux is wrinkled and his fingers are shaking.

"Repeat after me."

And so I do. I like being told what to do. Like a child. It's easier that way.

But I go off script. Add one word.

"I, Prudence Quinn, take you, Sage, to be my husband."

Without looking, I can see Mom's smile. And feel Dad's.

And Sage kisses me.

Sometimes a kiss isn't just a kiss.

And there are no screams or burning petals. Nothing turns to black.

Instead, for the first time all day, the sun smiles coyly. And things are brighter.

We laugh and drink. And eat blackberry pie. Henry's pie. The berries are out of season. Bittersweet. And delicious.

Mom stands. After years of giving lectures, of captivating students and colleagues, her confidence flickers. This is her chance to say something about her little girl.

" 'Great Oaks from Little Acorns Grow.' That was her solo in the kindergarten play. Every night for months she'd stand next to me while I cooked dinner, practicing, her young voice unselfconsciously confident and loaded with uncertainty. She was only five. And the words were simple, beautiful, but repetitive. She stood up there all alone on that painted wooden stage. She remembered those words and belted them out so we could all hear. When we clapped, her eyes lit up and she smiled big. And then she clapped for herself too.

"Today, as we stand under the oak where her father and I baptized her twenty-seven years ago, I'm full of pride and nostalgia and most importantly, love." She wipes her eyes, lifts her glass. "To my little acorn. Today, you've decided to grow up. And you are a little like me, a little like Dad. But mostly, thankfully, just like you."

When everyone claps, Mom's eyes light up like a little girl and she smiles big. And then she claps for herself too.

She takes a large celebratory sip of wine, but doesn't sit. Pulls out paper this time.

"As you all know, Prudence's father was a planner. He liked to take care of things ahead of time. So, last June after Sage asked us for Prue's hand in marriage, my husband began scribbling away," she says, looking at me. "The man had delivered thousands of babies, was cool under pressure, but the thought of giving his only daughter away rattled him and he wanted to get it right. I found his notes, the beginning of what he planned to say.

"In this modern world, brimming with technology, I'm so happy we still have fishing. Good old-fashioned fishing. Rowboats, bamboo rods, flies made of nature's bounty, mayfly hatches, no-see-ums, fading quiet, and lily pads.

"Prue, I'm not convinced you really like fishing. Sure, you like to be out in the boat, to talk, to observe. But you never wanted to pry that fly from the lips of a fish. I told you this was a big

part of it all, but you were always scared. The slightest delay, the slightest wrong move, and the creature could die. But isn't it always this way?

"But one doesn't have to love fishing to have the soul of a fisherwoman. And that you do. My Prudence, you have eyes as deep as the deepest pond and as full of life. Sometimes, it's hard to tell what's going on under the surface, but if you have the patience and bravery to look and cast yourself in—and, Sage, I hope and trust you do—you will find there the beautiful chaos of life.

"My Prudence: You have a heart as healthy and fragile as life itself—forever pumping, energetic, but vulnerable to forces bigger than yourself—love being one of them. Love is one of those great mysteries like prudence and forgiveness, a beast more inscrutable than Faulkner's bear or Melville's whale. But we all understand enough of these things, each our own part, to feel their force, to be pulled this way or that, to make grand decisions, in their universal and commingling wake.

"When I first met Sage, like any good father, I wanted to hate him. I wanted a grave flaw to appear in him that would confirm for me that she was still mine, that I wouldn't have to give her away yet. I hoped that my daughter was still up to her old game of catch and release, that this was just another slimy beast she'd hooked but one whom she'd release into the waters of the world. But that first time I met Sage, I realized that like my dear daughter, this one was a keeper, one of those catches you can't bear to part with. Not a twenty-five-incher that you want to wax and mount and show off to all your friends, but a creature that's stunning and imperfect, so unique and yet so universal, so weighty and yet so transient, that as time elapses you have no choice but to hold on."

* * *

Under our table, the Jitterbug table, I clutch Sage's hand as we both cry.

I stand and hug Mom. Little acorn and big oak. A moment that's both an end and a beginning.

"I love you," I whisper as if this is a secret. "And he did too."

And now Sage takes my hand and leads me to a patch of grass, our makeshift dance floor. He leaves my side only for a moment to press play on Dad's old boom box.

Dear Prudence won't you come out to play?
Dear Prudence greet the brand new day
The sun is up the sky is blue
It's beautiful and so are you
Dear Prudence won't you come out to play?

Dear Prudence open up your eyes
Dear Prudence see the sunny skies
The wind is low the birds will sing
That you are part of everything
Dear Prudence won't you open up your eyes?

Look around round
Look around round round
Look around

Dear Prudence let me see you smile
Dear Prudence like a little child
The clouds will be a daisy chain
So let me see you smile again
Dear Prudence won't you let me see you smile

Dear Prudence won't you come out to play?
Dear Prudence greet the brand new day
The sun is up the sky is blue
It's beautiful and so are you
Dear Prudence won't you come out to play?

And we dance. My blue heels sink into the ground, and that beautiful white dress, once pristine and perfect, is soon covered in mud and grass, and a tiny speckle of blackberry juice. But none of this matters. What matters is that we are here, alive, together, dancing. What matters is that for the first time in a long time, I'm smiling. Really smiling.

Chapter 33

When I wake up the next morning, it's still dark outside.

Today, Sage's snoring is a familiar and lovely melody. It fills the quiet, in fits and starts, until the moon's shift is over.

And then the sun is up. A brand-new day. Light snakes through the cabin window and highlights a fallen white cloud, my wedding dress, badly stained and beautifully crumpled in the corner.

I pick it up. Sniff it. Study it. From the back, I pull out that little fishing fly.

In the bathroom, I study my face.

This morning, the wrinkles are welcome, proud reminders of where I've been. Mere indicators of where smiles have been. And will be.

Under a small box of Cheerios, I leave a note for my husband: "Gone fishing."

I kiss him on the forehead before sneaking out.

On the porch, I step into Dad's boots once more and walk

toward the Clubhouse. I pull the key from the chain around my neck.

This locker room has no naked bodies, no smooth jazz. Just sturdy chairs and mounted trout.

When I get to Dad's locker, I pause before trying the key, wondering if I want to do this. But I turn, and the gray locker swings open. The smell of sweat and fish and tobacco floats toward me. And I see his things. The rods he collected over the years, his old fishing vest, a tin of cigars. A handle of Irish whiskey, half full. A box of flies.

On a shelf at the top of the locker is a small stack of books.

The old maroon leather dictionary.

A first edition of *Charlotte's Web*.

I grab Dad's fishing creel and start filling it with these things.

I step into a boat, heft the anchor in, and start rowing. In the middle of the lake, under daisy chains of clouds in a periwinkle sky, I stop. Press pause. Look around.

The sun, the center stone of it all, shines bright.

I pull out Dad's old dictionary and flip to the P's. *Prudence. n.) exercise of sound judgment in practical affairs; wisdom in the way of caution and provision; discretion; carefulness.*

And I flip open *Charlotte's Web*. Charlotte, awaiting death, speaks beautifully: *We're born, we live a little, we die.*

And when she dies, she leaves her babies behind. And I think this part's from the movie version (sorry, Dad), but Wilbur asks Charlotte's daughters, *Are you writers?*

And they say, *No, but we will be when we grow up.*

And Wilbur says, *Then write this in your webs, when you learn: This hallowed doorway was once the home of Charlotte. She was brilliant, beautiful, and loyal to the end. Her memory will be treasured forever.*

And Charlotte's daughters say, *Ooh, that would take a lifetime.*

A lifetime, Wilbur says. *That's what we have.*

And out here on the water, under sunny skies, there's a chorus of singing birds. Out here, I'm Quinn and Prudence. And neither. I'm a lawyer and a thinker. A daughter and a wife. A flower girl, rightfully scared of growing up, and a sated bride for whom fear is foolish. A Berry Baby. His blackberry girl.

Out here, I'm untethered. And the moments and days and years are plentiful and stretch before me. Moments and days and years full of big love and big doubt, of grief and loss and hope and fear. Of victories and mistakes. Of dreams and realities and stories. Of Cheerios and snow angels and Halloweens.

And memories.

A lifetime, I think. *That's what we have.*

I take a large swig of Irish whiskey as the sun beats down on me.

I fight tears. And I take little fly from my pocket. That fly that's been through it all. Our Parachute Adams. I tie it on.

I cast and drink.

And cry.

And smile.

Soon there's a tug on the line.

She's a fighter, but I pull her in. A young rainbow. Frightened, but strong. Quaking, yet defiant. I hold tight to her small body, throbbing for life, slippery like truth. Bravely, I pry the fly from quivering lips and look into her eyes, keen and searching. I give her a kiss and throw her back into waters brimming with life and death and everything in between.

And, prudently, she swims away, disappearing into the murky depths of a future wonderfully uncertain.

Acknowledgments

Truth be told, I have never been very good at writing thank-you notes. And here I sit, penning perhaps my most important thank-you note yet, utterly, unequivocally confident that I will somehow screw this up. Quinn, my beloved protagonist of my first novel, would tell me that life is all about screwing up, to get over myself, and to plow forward. And so I will.

First, a no-brainer. Thank you to my wonderful agent, Jean Naggar, a seasoned and spirited literary soul, for believing in me—and in Quinn—and for shepherding me through this exciting process with wise words and true grace. Without Jean and her fine colleagues at JVNLA, I would still be puttering away at Starbucks. Wait, I am still puttering away at Starbucks, but now I can (and will) tell the barista that I have published a novel.

A big thank you to my talented and enthusiastic editor, Lucia Macro, for taking a chance on this eager, but unknown entity, for sharing my belief in the power of reality and less-than-perfect fairy tales, and for making my dream come true even in an abysmal economy. Thank you to the many others at HarperCollins for making this all come together—in particular, Esi Sogah, Meredith Rusu, Stephanie Selah, Robin Bilardello, Jennifer Hart and your marketing team, Mike Brennan, Brian Grogan, and the Morrow/Avon sales group.

Thank you, Sarah Burningham, for your tireless support, your magical publicity mojo, and your fast friendship.

Thank you to all the fellow lawyers who have glided in and out of my life over the past several years. To my friends and colleagues at Willkie Farr & Gallagher LLP—thank you for letting me make a brief cameo in your high-wattage world, for being kind, for giving me stories, and for teaching me, above all else, what I want and what I don't. Thank you to my attorney Jonathan F. Horn for helping me secure permissions for the Beatles lyrics I foolishly built this entire novel around.

Thanks to those who have encouraged, and helped me realize, my dream to write. First, a debt of gratitude to my many excellent teachers at my beloved alma maters—Dalton, Yale, and Columbia—who helped me hone my skills and find my voice. Thanks to Russell Rowland, my Montana mentor, a fine writer and devoted teacher, who read every line of this book more than once and held my virtual and shaky hand, chapter by chapter, to the end. Thank you Pete Putzel for putting me in touch with the fabulous Susan Isaacs and thank you, Susan, for pointing me in the direction of my incomparable and lovely literary agent.

Thank you to my brothers-in-law and to my bridesmaids. Thank you to my best friends and to my blog readers. And thanks to the best nanny ever. You all know who you are. And how important you are.

Thank you to the Rowley family for embracing me and accepting me and loving me like one of your own.

Thank you to my four sisters, the fabulous Donnelley girls: Inanna, Naomi, Ceara, and Tegan. You guys (and your little guys) continue to be my world.

Thank you, Dad. For your complex wildness, tough love, and contagious philosophy. For reading this story when yours was almost over. You are now fly-fishing in distant waters, but I feel your support and hear your deep laugh to this very day. Thank you for imploring us girls to seek genuine passion and to revere the rusty lunch pail. I love you always and miss you deeply.

Thank you, Mom. You have always been there, a strong force, a brilliant example—on the sidelines of my games, next to me at the dinner table, reading over my school papers. You were my very first and very best writing teacher. In many ways, in important ways, the words on these pages came from you as much as I did. I love you to pieces.

Last but not least, thank you to the loves of my life. To Bryan, my gorgeous groom, my favorite boy, my forever man. Simply stated, you are it for me. You understand me, you support me, you tolerate me. You knew I'd publish this story long before I did. You have made my life after yes endlessly rich and imperfectly exquisite. And, finally, thank you to my sweet little girls. I see everything good in your bottomless blues. Day after day, your love and silly laughter sustain me.

A+

AUTHOR
INSIGHTS,
EXTRAS &
MORE...

FROM

**AIDAN
DONNELLEY
ROWLEY**

AND

AVON A

May 18, 2010

Dear Mr. BigLaw,

How are you these days? We haven't seen each other or spoken in a while, but I do hear about you from time to time. From friends and newspapers. Despite the recession and everything else, it sounds like you are surviving.

I know this letter is foolish. It will likely be lost in a big pile of paper on your polished marble desk. It is likely that you do not even remember me. That I was just one of the fungible young girls who flitted through your golden revolving door, a girl who never quite got your attention.

Truth be told, I think of you sometimes. In particular, about that day I left you. It was a Friday in late January and I really didn't give you much warning. No, in many ways I blindsided you, spewing that clichéd excuse-upon-exit: *it's not you, it's me*. But I assure you this was true. Not that you care.

You were plenty good to me. You shrouded me with things: money and benefits and contacts. I basked in the glow of your impersonal warmth. But, in time, in a short time, I realized that in your corporate company, I felt stifled and sluggish and even a bit sad. I decided that I didn't want to spend many years in a relationship that was good and secure, but far less than thrilling.

It didn't take long to find your replacement. Writing. And he's a dodgy fellow, not always easy to live with, but he inspires me each and every day. He has taught me what love is. What laughter is. What learning is. Our romance is not stuffed with Town Cars and four-star lunches, but with words and ideas and most importantly, questions.

But sometimes, in this new relationship, I feel moments of loneliness. And, in these quiet moments, I long for our conference room banter and catered buffets. For more predictable things. For pinstripes and power and prestige. For the brainstorming and business trips we used to enjoy. Or pretend to. And sometimes I miss being able to say that I am with you because I know that some people, too many people, were so impressed with that.

Maybe we didn't have enough closure. Maybe I ran away too quickly because I could. Because I didn't need you to support me. Maybe I fled fast because I was a bit scared. That I was being hasty. That I was making a profound mistake. Or maybe I escaped with little explanation because I knew even then the power you had over me. I knew that after everything, after all those years of courting and commitment, it wouldn't be easy to quit you. And it wasn't.

I sometimes wonder who replaced me. Is she good and honest? Does she work hard? Too hard? Does she treat you well? Does she treat herself well? Will she stick with you through thick and thin? Will she wait out the tough times and see if you will ask her to commit? And, someday, if you ask her that very important question, if you ask her to be your partner, will she say *I do?*

Sometimes I wonder what things would be like if I never left. Would we still be together? Or would I have found another reason to walk away? Or would you, faced with the grim reality of a rabid recession, have let me go? If I had stayed and you had let me, would we be happy? Or, would things be the same as they were back then when I put on a good face with my good suit and we floated through long days together, graceful pretenders?

This is tough to admit, but sometimes, late at night, I lie in bed and think of you and wonder whether you would take me back. If I begged and pleaded and tried harder this time? But then I wake up in the morning and I'm relieved and pleased with the way things are. I am exactly where I should be. But that doesn't mean that I don't miss you sometimes and think about you and talk about our time together. Even though our relationship was relatively brief, a mere blip on that résumé radar, for me it was very real. In some small, but significant way, you made me who I am.

So, try as I might, I will not forget you. The things you showed me about myself and life and the enigma of happiness. About real risk and real reward.

Maybe we will meet again one day. Or maybe we won't. Only time will tell.

Insecurely yours,
Aidan

Q & A with Aidan Donnelley Rowley

What inspired this particular story? Is it autobiographical?

Life After Yes was inspired by my admittedly short stint as a litigation associate at a big Manhattan law firm and by my experience as a young New Yorker in the aftermath of 9/11. My experience at the firm was perfectly pleasant. Contrary to conventional wisdom, life as a BigLaw attorney was (for me) not miserable. But it wasn't happy either. I realized, and quickly, that I was far more interested in the life around me, the stories of colleagues and clients, than I was in the formal practice of law at a corporate firm. I would steal moments here and there and scribble essays. I would spend long stretches of time at my desk staring out the skyscraper window at the stunning views of the city in which I was born and raised. The Friday afternoon after returning from my honeymoon, I looked out that window and decided to jump. To take my very first risk. In that moment, I chose life over law.

Everyone implored me to be prudent and wait, to complete a full two years at the firm. But I didn't listen. I left, hungry to write a story exploring the virtue (and vice) of prudence in modern society, blissfully ignorant of just what this entailed, full of foolish confidence. I left my firm on a Friday and started *Life After Yes* the following Monday.

The story is fictional. Is it laced with some more superficial autobiographical elements? Absolutely. For instance, it takes place on the Upper West Side of Manhattan where I grew up and where I still live today. There are undoubtedly pieces of me and my life scattered throughout the story. I would say that I am present in each and every one of the major characters. But no individual character is based on me or on any person I know. Translation:

I am not Quinn. Quinn is not me. And I hate to break it to you, whoever you are, but you are not a character in my book!

You acknowledge that starting a novel with a dream is cliché and yet you start your novel with a dream. Why? What is the meaning of clichés in Quinn's story?

I felt strongly about starting my novel with Quinn's dream. In many ways, all of Quinn's hopes and fears and doubts about love and life and commitment are wrapped up in that one dream. Most of the story's significant events and questions are foreshadowed in the dream. I think dreams—actual and metaphorical— are hugely important in life. Our dreams say so much about who we are and what we want.

As a society and as a literary subculture, I think we are far too obsessed with originality. As people, we seek and strive to be different, to be unique. We act up, we rebel, we do *anything* so as not to be predictable. And yet, in our very predictable rebellions, we are utterly predictable. Quinn, the prototypical educated and privileged and disillusioned YUPPIE, is a cliché. We are all clichés. As writers, we are also preoccupied with standing out and apart, with being seen and celebrated as original. We are told to avoid clichés like the plague; that they have no place in literature and compelling stories. I don't agree. I think that clichés exist for a reason. I think they are part of who we are. Not every word or sentence or idea is fresh. That is okay. That is real.

You started writing *Life After Yes* shortly after you left your job at the law firm, but Quinn doesn't leave. Or does she?

The final scene of the book is intentionally gray, purposefully ambiguous. Quinn is alone in a fishing boat away from it all—her childhood, her hometown, her profession, her man. Out there on the lake she loves, she is free to ask questions and let them echo. She is free to embrace the contradictions and doubts within. She basks in the glow of autumn sun and a bright, but uncertain, future.

There are numerous BlackBerry references throughout *Life After Yes*. Do you think our society has become technology obsessed? Do you think technology is getting in the way of "real communication"?

The multilayered theme of blackberries—the man-made technology and the natural fruit—is significant in the book. I do think our society is growing more and more obsessed with, and dependent upon, tools of technology, and I wanted to capture this complex and evolving preoccupation in the pages of *Life After Yes*. More specifically, I wanted to highlight the role of the BlackBerry in the life of young professionals. In corporate contexts, BlackBerrys often become virtual leashes and impediments on freedom. I also find it fascinating that so many of the preeminent devices in our contemporary society are presumably named to conjure natural goodies—Apple, Mac, BlackBerry, iPod, Twitter. For me, this raises interesting philosophical and practical questions about what "natural" ultimately means.

In my humble estimation, technology is a blessing and a curse. Taken too far (and what's too far? I don't pretend to know.) technology can problematically threaten more traditional human communication. Screens should never replace smiles and spoken words. A tweet will never hold a candle to a hug or a handshake. But I do believe, and deeply, that technology will continue to have some genuinely positive effects on our culture and society. We have already seen the myriad ways in which technology can transcend geographical and interpersonal distance and enhance communication and learning. Ultimately, I think the concept of "real communication" is shifting as we speak.

The question of technology is also present in *Life After Yes* as a means to explore and evince the generational divide between Quinn and her parents. Quinn's parents, and particularly her late father, did not see the appeal of emerging technologies, but technology is a meaningful part of the identity of the BlackBerry generation of which Quinn is part.

Why did you give your protagonist two very different names? Why did you make her angst over her name such a significant thread of the story?

First, Prudence. *Life After Yes* is, among other things, a commentary on the virtue (and vice) of prudence in our modern world, on how it is often overvalued at the expense of happiness and love and passion. As such, Prudence was the perfect name for my protagonist. Also, I loved the idea of Quinn's parents being rabid Beatles' fans. The lyrics of "Dear Prudence" are exceptionally meaningful to Quinn's story and character. This song, which was once her lullaby in many ways, becomes her theme song.

And Quinn. First of all, I adore the name. Plain and simple. I would have saved it for a child of mine, but decided that an Aidan having a baby Quinn would be like Brad having a baby Pitt. I purposefully picked a name that was traditionally male, and contemporarily unisex, because Quinn is a tough woman in what is still in many ways a man's world. The name Quinn is also important because it is Quinn's mother's maiden name and Quinn and her mother argue throughout the story about feminist expectations.

I am a deep believer in the importance and power of names. Names are not just what people call us. They are how we see ourselves, realize ourselves, and interact with the world. I went back and forth about what name I would publish under. For me, this was a hugely important question. Ultimately, I decided to publish under Aidan Donnelley Rowley. Given name. Maiden name. Married name. This name is long and unwieldy and not the book editor's dream, but it is my name. It is who I am.

Speaking of names, why is the novel entitled *Life After Yes*?

The novel is named *Life After Yes* because it is the story of the time in a woman's life after she says yes to that infinitely important and culturally heralded question. In many ways, I think our society is unduly focused on the fanfare of the fairy tale: the utterance of that question, on the sparkling diamond, on the yes, at the expense of other important things. I set out to write a more realistic tale about the revealing emotional and existential tumult that can, and frequently does, ensue after engagement. I think couples, and very loving couples, can weather many things between engagement and wedding and I think this topic, this time, is underexplored. Additionally, I think the title is fitting because there are many jokes about how life is over after engagement, or after getting married. Ultimately, I think and hope this story shows that there can be life, a different and rich life, an exquisitely imperfect life, after yes.

Quinn seems particularly insecure in her romantic relationships although she is obviously thriving at work. Do you think this is common among successful women today?

I don't pretend to know what is common among successful women today. I don't pretend to know what exactly it means to be a "successful woman" today. What I do know is that many of the women whom I have encountered professionally or personally are riddled with confidence *and* insecurity just as Quinn is. I think it is a fallacy to think that these two qualities cannot coexist and commingle. Recently, I started a blog called Ivy League Insecurities to explore this idea, namely that insecurity is part of what it means to be human and that in exploring our own insecurity, we learn more about ourselves. The blog has resonated with many women (and some loyal men!) who embrace the idea that life is not black and white, but made up of glorious grays. Many of these women are extremely well-educated and have demanding jobs as professionals or mothers or both. Many of them "have it all" by society's standards, and yet are disillusioned and plagued by doubts.

A prime example of the insecure Ivy Leaguer, Quinn appears shakier in her romantic relationships than she does in her work life. This could be because she allows herself to be insecure in her personal relationships, she allows herself to embrace the thicket of doubts and regrets and fears. At the law firm, Quinn puts up a good front, an impeccable facade, because she feels she has to. I think this happens a lot. I think many of us present a certain side of ourselves, a more polished side of ourselves, in the professional or public arena because we feel like we must. I also think that *Life After Yes* illuminates the perennial difficulty of balancing work and life that women, and many men, face. It is hard, if not impossible, to commit wholly to a profession and a person at the same time.

At bottom, I think *Life After Yes* is a tribute to the complex beauty of insecurity and doubt and realistic love. Life does not need to be a fairy tale to glitter or to be authentically good.

We never actually meet Quinn's father and yet he plays an important role in the book. Why was it important to you to have him as a character, if only through flashbacks?

The loss of Quinn's father is pivotal to her story and who she is as a person. The suddenness of this loss, coupled with the broader national trauma of 9/11, affects Quinn and affects her deeply. Quinn's father played a significant role in her life and continues to do so even after he's gone. In the wake of his death, Quinn finds herself on shaky existential earth; she is forced to ask questions she has never asked before. In important ways, she is forced to grow up. Learning about Quinn's father through flashbacks helps reveal who Quinn is and is becoming.

Personally, I knew nothing about losing a parent when I wrote *Life After Yes*. Several years after completing this story, my own father was diagnosed with terminal cancer. At the time, I was sitting on a relatively polished draft. It haunted me and humbled me to realize that I had written an entire novel about a daughter's life in the wake of her father's death and now my own father was dying. I had serious reservations about seeking publication because I worried that people would think this book is a veiled account of my own recent family tragedy. I feared (and still do) that readers would assume this story is about me and my father and my life, which it simply isn't. Ultimately, I concluded that contemplating the loss of parents is part and parcel of adulthood

A+ AUTHOR INSIGHTS, EXTRAS & MORE...

and I wasn't going to relegate my story to a desk drawer out of personal fear. My father finished reading the manuscript of *Life After Yes* just a few weeks before he died. I found my wonderful literary agent a mere two weeks after he died. I think—no, I know—that he would be proud that I am pursuing my passion.

Life After Yes takes place in Manhattan in the immediate wake of the 9/11 attacks. Why did you make this setting choice?

I was born and raised in Manhattan. This is my hometown. This is what I know. I was here on that day. I was in the Towers three days before they fell. I was there, on an impossibly high floor, the portrait of professional perfection in my pinstripes and pumps, for an interview at a law firm. I remember sitting in a partner's office while he interviewed me. I don't remember a word he said, but I do remember looking past him and out the vast and spotless window. I remember the expanse of powder blue sky and the helicopters flying by.

And then, days later, just like that, that window, those towers, maybe that man, and our national innocence were gone.

Thankfully, I didn't lose anyone in the attacks. I do not pretend to know what it was like to lose someone in the attacks. But as a New Yorker and an American and a *person,* I was very much affected by that day. It changed me. It woke me up. It made me realize that life can be brutal and short and uncertain and that we should try to do things we love and surround ourselves with people we love. It taught me, and maybe us all, that we should never assume the existence of tomorrow. In many ways, I think that day, that terrible day, inspired me to become a writer. On that day and in its impossible aftermath, I started taking inventory of what matters and what doesn't.

Life After Yes is not about 9/11, but is a love letter to Manhattan and to post-9/11 Manhattan in particular. I hope that the story offers a small, but viable window into this incomparable city, a city that has bounced back and yet will never be the same.

Questions for Discussion

1. *Life After Yes* begins with a dream (or nightmare) that comes back to Quinn throughout the book. What is the significance of that dream? Ultimately, what is it that Quinn is so afraid of?

2. Quinn (a.k.a. Prudence) struggles with her name from a young age and is called different things by different people: Sage calls her Quinn but Phelps, her first true love, teases her as Prudence. The law firm knows her as Quinn but her family calls her Prue. What do these two names represent for her?

3. Do you think our society is overly concerned with the virtue (or vice) of prudence?

4. Quinn seems like a typical lawyer when she's talking and reasoning with other people—confident and rational—but her interior monologue is much more insecure. Do you think this is common, namely that our exterior selves are more polished than our interior selves?

5. In the book, the word "blackberry" refers to both the technological gadget and the fruit. How do these different meanings come together to define Quinn?

6. Do you know anyone who is a "Berry Baby?" Are you? Why do you think people feel the need to check their Black-Berrys at all times?

7. Quinn's best friends, Kayla and Avery, are very different people and seem to represent the contradictory parts of Quinn herself. As Quinn changes, so do they. How do their lives mirror Quinn's?

8. The loss of Quinn's father is prevalent throughout the book. How does Quinn deal with this loss? How does her father influence her decisions even after he is gone?

9. Both Quinn and Sage have lost a family member, but they deal with their respective losses in very different ways. How have these losses impacted their relationship? How have these losses changed their families?

10. Alcohol plays a conspicuous role throughout Quinn's story. Do you think that Quinn—and others—rely too much on alcohol to cope with existential unrest? Do you think *Life After Yes* paints an accurate portrait of the ubiquity of alcohol in modern culture, or do you think the portrait offered is exaggerated?

11. Do you agree that *Life After Yes* is not a fairy tale?

12. Do you agree that there is usually one nurturer in a relationship?

13. Quinn's mother says that growing up is not a fact, but a decision. Do you agree? When do you think childhood traditionally expires? When one marries? When one's parent dies? Or does childhood expire over and over?

14. Fishing is an important theme throughout Quinn's story. Discuss the significance of this particular theme to Quinn's character and to questions of life and love.

15. Late in the novel, Quinn realizes that her parents' marriage wasn't quite as perfect as it seemed. How does this affect her feelings about Sage and her impending wedding?

16. Quinn isn't exactly faithful to Sage and yet they seem to understand each other better after they both face infidelity. Why does this bring them closer?

17. Do you agree with the theory that it is never too late to become a good person?

18. If you were Quinn, would you have chosen Sage or Phelps? Why? Do you think most women have a Sage and a Phelps in their life?

19. As Quinn evolves, she comes to realize that we often don't find the best things in life when looking, but stumble upon them while living. Do you agree?

20. Shortly before the end of the book, Quinn realizes that sometimes beginnings and ends "bleed into each other." Why is this important for her? Do you agree that life is a series of overlapping beginnings and ends?

21. *Life After Yes* ends with a good deal of uncertainty. We do not know where exactly Quinn is headed professionally and personally. This is hardly the typical Hollywood ending, but it is also more real. As a reader, are you frustrated by the ending's murkiness or do you find it satisfying in that it reflects reality?

22. If there were a movie based on *Life After Yes,* whom would you choose to play the main characters?

Courtesy of the author

AIDAN DONNELLEY ROWLEY is a graduate of Yale University and Columbia Law School. The middle of five sisters, she was born and raised in New York City where she currently lives with her husband and two young daughters. Aidan writes daily about life as a mother and writer on her blog Ivy League Insecurities (www.ivyleagueinsecurities.com). *Life After Yes* is her first novel.

Aidan Donnelley Rowley